The Remarkable Adventures of
TOM SCATTERHORN
THE MUSEUM'S SECRET

The Remarkable Adventures of TOM SCATTERHORN

THE MUSEUM'S SECRET

Henry Chancellor

DOUBLEDAY CANADA

Trade paperback edition 2010

Library and Archives of Canada Cataloguing in Publication has been applied for.

ISBN: 978-0-385-66523-0

This book is a work of fiction. Names, characters, places and incidents are products of the author's imagination or are used fictitiously. Any resemblance to actual events or locales or persons, living or dead, is entirely coincidental.

Printed and bound in the USA

Published in Canada by Doubleday Canada, a division of Random House of Canada Limited

Visit Random House of Canada Limited's website: www.randomhouse.ca

10 9 8 7 6 5 4 3 2 1

For Louis, Inigo and Esme

CONTENTS

Prologue

Right Now, on the Edge of the World

Night came up suddenly in the Tosontsengel Valley. All day the jeep had bounced across an endless series of hills, straining to the top of one only to find yet another beyond it. And another beyond that. By late afternoon the road had dropped down into a wide valley floor heading due west and as the sun began to set, the smooth sides of the mountains glowed orange and the dark pine forests below them turned to purple.

'There, over there. That looks good.'

The jeep jerked to a halt. The tall blond man with a scruffy beard shaded his eyes and pointed up to a crest of flame-coloured trees on the edge of the forest, picked out by the last rays of the sun.

'You see something?' came a voice from the back seat.

The gaunt man did not reply, but raising his binoculars he picked out row upon row of collapsed pines above the bright crest, toppling over to form a long grey gash in the forest. It was a perfect spot.

'That's it.'

He pointed, and the driver, a thick-set Mongol in a tatty grey fleece, grunted an acknowledgement. The jeep swung off the dusty road and bounced up towards the ridge.

By the time they reached the edge of the trees the sun had gone. The westerner got out painfully and stretched, and moments later the back door slammed and he was joined by a small, shifty-looking Chinese man in dark glasses. The Chinese man looked up at the forest behind them and smiled approvingly.

'A landslide. Well spotted, Mr Scatterhorn.'

'Thank you.'

'Tonight I think we will be lucky.'

'You said that last night.'

The Chinese man smiled again, but this time Sam Scatterhorn did not acknowledge it. He had spent all day being thrown about inside that infernal jeep, breathing in the stale sweat of the driver, his head banging against the cushions nailed to the roof. He was exhausted, stiff, and the unfailing politeness of Mr Wong was starting to grate. There was something unpleasant behind that smile . . .

'To work then,' he muttered wearily, and reached into the jeep for a small bag and a thin metal stick. 'I may be some time.'

'Don't worry, Mr Scatterhorn,' smiled Wong, 'we won't be leaving without you.'

Sam Scatterhorn grunted. 'I thought as much.' Ignoring Wong's smile he stomped up over the rocks and into the forest.

'Idiot foreigner,' hissed Wong to himself as he lit a cigarette and inhaled deeply. This guy should count himself lucky. There were plenty who would give anything to be out in this remote stretch of Mongolia right now. Sam Scatterhorn was a nobody.

Wong had found him in a cheap hotel, living like a beggar. He had only just come out of jail, and he had no money, no clothes, just a microscope. Probably an illegal, thought Wong, running away, looking to make a quick buck and then disappear—Wong had met these types before. Many times before. But this 'Mr Scatterhorn'—whoever he was—just happened to be the best there was. Clearing his throat, Wong spat harshly into the dirt and smiled to himself. Wong had the patience of an elephant: Wong could wait as long as it takes. Scatterhorn would find what they were looking for, eventually. He *had* to. And if he decided to make trouble, well, it was very easy to disappear out here in the wilderness. Accidents happened frequently. No one would miss *him*, would they?

Barking out an order to the sullen driver who was already rolling out an old military mess tent, Wong returned to the jeep and pulled out his satellite phone. Setting up the aerial on the bonnet, he stubbed out his cigarette and waited for a connection.

By now the sun had disappeared, and the valley floor was an expanse of purple shadow. Up in the cool, dark forest, Sam Scatterhorn reached a clearing and paused, catching his breath against a tree. Closing his eyes he breathed deeply, drinking in the heavy, pine-scented air. At last he was starting to feel like himself again. The crickets zinged all around him, and far off he heard the distant tocking of a woodpecker. Between the wolf and the moon, he smiled to himself; the magic hour. This was his favourite time of day.

Then he remembered why he had come here. Casting an expert eye into the fallen trees around him, he began prodding about in the rotting wood with his stick, scraping back the leaves and turning them over. It was not long before he spotted what he was looking for. Kneeling down before a fallen trunk, he found a small hole in the soft white wood. Taking out his penknife he gouged out the hole, and then carefully withdrew his blade. There, balanced on the tip of his knife was a plump white grub, about four centimetres long.

'*Lamprima adolphinae*,' he whispered to himself. This was a good sign. The creature did not appreciate being removed from its cosy hole and began to wriggle blindly.

'OK, OK,' whispered Sam Scatterhorn softly, and returned it to its soft pulpy home.

Dropping to his knees, he carefully turned over the red earth around his feet and a moment later he saw a glint of gold and black. There he was. Gingerly lifting back a leaf he found the adult male. It was a Papua golden stag beetle, standing braced and motionless on its six black legs. Its body was a polished golden plate reflecting the inky blue sky above the forest canopy, and on either side of its head two pink barbed mandibles curved up towards the treetops, poised to snap. He was magnificent, like a creature from another world. For a moment Sam Scatterhorn felt the same sense of wonder as he had many years ago, as a boy, finding his first beetle in the woods above his house.

'You're a big fella, aren't you?' he said quietly, stroking the hard golden shell of the beetle's back, and he slowly took another box from his bag. With a practised hand he coaxed the creature on to the end of his metal stick, and in one movement slipped his box over the top of it and folded back the lid.

'You're coming with me,' he smiled, tapping the box with his finger, before placing it carefully in his bag. 'Now, do you have any friends for Mr Wong?'

By the time Sam Scatterhorn returned to the camp it was dark. Mr Wong was sitting beside the fire and as soon as he saw the tall westerner emerging from the trees he jumped up, eager for good news. But Sam Scatterhorn's sullen expression suggested otherwise and, checking himself, Wong sat down again, watching as Sam gently set down his bag and took a long, long swig from his water bottle. Finally Wong could not contain himself any longer.

'How many?' he asked. Sam Scatterhorn ignored him. 'One? Two? Four? How many, Mr Scatterhorn?'

Sam Scatterhorn splashed some water into his palm and slowly rubbed his tired eyes.

The driver, who was squatting over a pot of steaming rice, watched Wong out of the corner of his eye. The foreigner had found something, and Wong was attempting to control his temper. This was good.

'None then?' spat Wong.

'Twelve,' replied Sam Scatterhorn casually.

'Twelve!'

Wong scurried over to the bag to look for himself. There inside were twelve long paper boxes, all stacked and neatly labelled. He opened one up and carefully shook out the golden stag beetle into the palm of his hand. Wong gasped. It was larger than any stag beetle he had ever seen. With a book-keeper's eye he measured up the width of its mandibles, barbed and glinting in the firelight.

'This could be a champion fighter,' he said softly. 'Are they all this size?'

'Some are even bigger. The conditions up there are perfect.'

Wong made some rapid mental calculations. In Tokyo, beetle wrestling was big business and champion beetles from around the world commanded huge prices. Every millimetre of their length added hundreds of dollars to their value. And here were twelve fighting beetles! This bag could be worth fifty, even a hundred thousand dollars. He stifled a laugh: this was the jack-pot, but he mustn't show too much emotion in front of the foreigner, just in case he realized what a bad deal he was getting.

'I think a small celebration is in order,' said Wong carefully, putting the beetle back in its box. 'How about the last bottle of sake?'

It was all Sam Scatterhorn could do to force a smile.

'That's better,' grinned Wong. 'You know, you should smile more often. It's good for you.'

Later, after the inevitable mutton and rice washed down with Wong's cheap sake, Sam Scatterhorn lay beside the fire in his sleeping bag and stewed. Wong needn't have worried, he already knew what a bad deal he was on. But he had no choice but to accompany these pirates out into the wastes of Mongolia in search of rare stag beetles. Even if he saw only a tenth of what

Wong must be getting, it was still worth it. The money from tonight's find would last him a few more months, and he was getting closer to what he was looking for, he could feel it. Every day he was getting closer . . . Sam Scatterhorn lay back and stared up into the Milky Way, blazing brightly in the vast dome above the pine trees. Mr Wong could have his beetle fights in the backstreet bars of Tokyo for all he cared, he was out here in the wilderness for a higher purpose. But that was his secret . . .

The wind, which had died at sunset, was now picking up again and racing across the valley. It was cold. Though he was facing the fire, Sam Scatterhorn could feel the icy air creeping through his sleeping bag and over his back. Wong was in the tent, snoring, and the driver was there too, sprawled on the floor, dead drunk. As long as he got his fare and his daily bottle of vodka he didn't care whether they found any beetles or not. Sam Scatterhorn was in no mood to join them, so he pulled his hat right down over his head and burrowed deeper into his sleeping bag. Like a grub.

It must have been around midnight when he woke up. The wind was blisteringly cold now, far too cold to sleep outside. He had no option but to join Wong in the tent. Cursing softly, Sam Scatterhorn struggled out of his sleeping bag and slid on his boots without bothering to do up the laces. Stumbling out into the darkness, he had only gone a short distance when he realized that he was not walking on scrub any more. The ground snapped and crunched beneath his boots, like ice. How strange. Switching on his headtorch he bent down to see that he was standing in the middle of a long column of beetles that stretched right down into the valley. There must have been tens of thousands of them.

'Ha,' exclaimed Sam Scatterhorn, scratching his head. This was extraordinary. Excited now, he tiptoed across the column to the far side where he knelt down and carefully picked one beetle out of the mass. Holding the wriggling creature up to the light he couldn't contain his surprise—it was quite unlike anything he had seen before. The beetle was very large, about twenty centimetres long, and its body was the shape of a pebble encased in a dark bluish armour. Instead of mandibles it had sharp little pincers like a scorpion, a large black scorpion: *Pandinus imperator*, the imperial scorpion . . . Sam Scatterhorn's mind began to whirr . . . that lived in Africa, and anyway, scorpions are members of the arachnid family—they have eight legs like spiders, unlike insects with only six. Carefully he watched the struggling creature, snapping hungrily in the moonlight. This was definitely some kind of hybrid: *a new species*—perhaps . . . was this, could it be—Sam Scatterhorn's heart began to beat faster . . . wait, no, he must wait. Take it back to his hotel first, study it, test it, maybe he could even name it.

'*Lamprima Scatterhornus*,' he chuckled. Yes, that had a certain ring to it. And those pincers looked vicious, good for killing. He must show it to Wong. Wong would love this.

Shining his torch around him Sam Scatterhorn could see that the column he was standing in had now swollen into a river, and all the beetles were marching towards the forest. It was almost as if they were migrating—but why? What was up there in the forest? Just then Sam Scatterhorn felt the first nip. It was inside his boot. And then another, on his leg. Pointing the torch at his trousers, he discovered that the beetles were crawling all over him. At first he smiled: here he was, the beetle guy covered in beetles; Wong should take a photograph. But then he realized that this was serious. These little beasts were vicious, and they were biting him everywhere. Their sharp little legs clambering over his collar and falling down his back, and those pincers were as sharp as tiny shards of glass. He tried pulling one off his shoulder, but its black barbed feet clung on so hard he almost had to rip its legs off to get free. Whatever they were, these beetles possessed extraordinary strength. And there were millions of them. Now, for the first time in his life, Sam Scatterhorn realized that being here, right now, was asking for trouble. In fact they were all in big trouble already.

Stamping a path back to the camp Sam Scatterhorn found small black bodies swarming over everything. The water, the food, even the tent was covered in them. He was about to shout for Wong, but then he was distracted by a sight so extraordinary that it made him forget everything else. Columns of beetles were marching around the fire, whose embers were still white hot and flaming. Then one beetle, forced either by the sheer volume of insects behind him or being of a more intrepid character than the rest, suddenly struck out across the white hot ashes. Sam Scatterhorn fully expected the creature to shrivel and die immediately.

But the beetle didn't.

It just kept going.

Slowly, its six spiky legs turned from black to pink in the heat, and as it scrambled through the flames its body began to glow like molten steel. And still it carried on marching, as if performing some crazy circus trick. Once it had reached the other side of the fire the beetle merged back into the stream, its body rapidly cooling from pink, to amber, to brown and finally black once more, and soon it was lost in the crowd. Sam Scatterhorn swallowed hard and tried to think clearly. This was *impossible*; no insect on earth behaved like this.

He glanced back to the fire to find others now setting off across the white hot embers, clambering and struggling, until the fire was a living carpet of pink and gold. Each beetle glowed like a jewel in a furnace, entirely oblivious to the heat. Sam Scatterhorn was dumbstruck. These creatures, whatever they were, were the strangest he had ever encountered in his life. How could they possibly *do* that? Suddenly the pain of a thousand nagging bites all over his body blazed across his train of thought. These migrating beetles were crawling all over him too. He must get out of their way, right now. But what about Wong, and the driver?

Sam Scatterhorn stamped his way through the black tide to the tent and flashed his torch inside to find two shapes lying motionless on the ground.

'Wong? Wong, wake up!'

There was no answer. The sleeping men had become hidden beneath a living, moving swarm that covered every scrap of their bodies.

'Wong?'

Sam Scatterhorn shone his torch into Wong's face, and gasped as one large beetle crawled up his neck and forced Wong's lips open with its pincers.

'Oh my God,' he whispered, and the next moment the beetle had disappeared inside. It appeared to be *eating* him.

Suddenly Sam Scatterhorn felt his head begin to spin. Grabbing at the tentpole, he closed his eyes and tried to hold back a violent urge to be sick.

Breathe deeply, he told himself, *keep calm*.

But his heart was drumming a wild rhythm in his ears and he couldn't think. Are these beetles carnivorous? This can't be happening . . . it's a bad dream . . . and then he felt a pair of sharp pincers close on his own forehead.

'No!' he shouted; ripping the beetle out of his hair he stumbled across to the jeep, pulling frantically at the door. It was locked. Of course it was, the driver had the keys! They were in his pocket, but Sam Scatterhorn was not going back to that tent, not now. No way. Staring at the dark stain all around him he realized it would not be long before he too was overpowered. There were just too many of them. The sound of millions of scraping legs drummed in his ears. Pincers cut through his trousers and clamped themselves onto his flesh. It couldn't end like this.

It must not.

There was only one thing he could do. Frantically Sam Scatterhorn brushed thousands of beetles off the bonnet, and kicked his way up onto the roof of the jeep. The tide of beetles scrabbled up the windscreen after him, skidding back down the glass until the sheer volume of one on top of another reached the level of the roof. The creatures began to swarm up his boots and onto his trousers.

'Help!' he screamed. 'Please! Help! Someone! Please!'

Sam Scatterhorn's cries echoed down the empty valley, into the wind, up to the stars, to anyone out there in the wilderness.

And as it happened Sam Scatterhorn was heard. Just below the tree line on the other side of the valley, a man emerged from behind a sturdy wall of rock and stone into the moonlight. He wore traditional Mongolian dress with a cap raked at an angle, and even in the moonlight his proud, eagle-like features were unmistakably European. He raised a pair of night-vision goggles to his eyes, and peered across at the tiny figure standing on the roof of the jeep, frantically beating back the dark river of beetles that flowed all around him.

'Not another of those damn fool collectors?' came a voice from inside the cave behind him.

'Good Lord,' muttered the tall man, squinting into the lense. Sam Scatterhorn was on his knees now, and he was almost done. There were beetles crawling all over his face. The tall man cast away a thin cigar, and reached for an ancient rifle leaning against the wall, slinging its tasselled strap over his shoulder.

'In a bit of a pickle, by the look of it. Better go and give him a hand.'

Grabbing a cartridge belt and a small jerrycan he vaulted out into the darkness. Moments later his long, loping shape had disappeared . . .

CHAPTER 1

A Strange Reception

'What do you have in here; rocks, I suppose?'

It was three o'clock on a cold winter's afternoon, and a small round man struggled around the back of a taxi with a battered blue duffel bag and heaved it onto the pavement.

'Not exactly,' replied the skinny blond boy, standing shivering in the wind in a thin coat.

'Don't tell me, there's a few bricks in there too?' wheezed the man, raising his eyebrows as he reached into his pocket for some notes. The boy smiled politely and braced himself against the buffeting wind. Even though it was only mid afternoon, the streetlights had already come on up and down the grey street, and the minicab driver unrolled the top of his steamed-up window just wide enough to slip out his hand for the money. He wasn't going out in that; that was far too cold. That wind came straight from Siberia.

'Cheers, mate,' he said, taking the wad of notes and blowing noisily on his fingers, 'have a good Christmas yourself.' And away he sped through the puddles.

'Right Tom, let's get inside before we both freeze to death,' wheezed the round man, and grabbing the duffel bag in both arms he tottered up the wide steps of the large, crumbling brick building behind him and disappeared through a small side door. Huge hailstones had started to fall, cracking hard against the stone steps, and Tom was just about to follow him inside when he caught the eye of two angry-looking stone dragons above the entrance. Between them they were holding a crumbling stone plaque that read:

THE SCATTERHORN MUSEUM
FOUNDED 1906 BY SIR HENRY SCATTERHORN
BEQUEATHED TO THE PEOPLE OF DRAGONPORT
GOD SAVE THE KING

Despite the hailstones and the icy wind whipping his face, Tom found himself smiling. Maybe it wasn't going to be that bad after all. There couldn't be many children who were about to spend their Christmas holidays in a museum that was named . . .

'Tom Scatterhorn, get yourself in here right now before you turn to ice, boy!'

The voice boomed above the cracking hailstones and Tom suddenly remembered that his teeth were chattering. He scampered up the steps two at a time and ran inside.

'So Mum's taken off to Mongolia or some such place, has she?'

Tom nodded. He was now sitting in a small yellow kitchen at the back of the museum, with his fingers pressed onto the radiator. Slowly he could feel himself thawing out.

'Good old Sam. Full of surprises.'

'Well, let's hope to goodness she finds him; it's an awfully big place.'

'She will find him,' said Tom politely but firmly, 'I know she will.'

Ever since his father had disappeared six months ago, and his mother had gone to look for him, this is what Tom had wanted more than anything else in the world.

'Hmm.' Aunt Melba poured the tea thoughtfully. 'Well, let's stay optimistic, shall we?'

Tom nodded, though his teeth were still chattering. He *had* to stay optimistic—he had no choice. Just as he had had no choice but to spend Christmas with his only other living relatives, Uncle Jos and Aunt Melba, on the other side of the country. They were the proud owners of the Scatterhorn Museum, and he had never met them before in his life.

'Biscuit, Tom?'

'Oh yes please,' interrupted Uncle Jos, taking two.

'Now just you wait, you great heffalump,' snapped Melba, snatching one back and passing it to Tom.

'This boy's bound to be hungry; just look at the state of him.'

Jos crunched the biscuit noisily and peered over his spectacles at the skinny boy shivering on the other side of the table. Tom was eleven years old, tall for his age, but thin, with strikingly dark, piercing eyes. His hair was a wiry blond tangle that tumbled down over his forehead. He looked both young and strangely grown-up at the same time.

'Just like his old dad,' said Jos with a shrug. 'He's the spitting image of Sam.'

'But thin as a whippet,' added Melba with some concern. 'Don't your parents ever feed you, Tom?'

Tom looked across the table at the two strange looking people and all he could think about were his mother's words as she had kissed him goodbye at the station that morning.

'Just remember that Uncle Jos and Aunt Melba are a little bit different.'

'What do you mean?'

'Well, they are older, and they've not had children of their own. They're just a bit . . . different.'

'Like . . . eccentric?'

'No, not exactly,' replied his mother, weighing her words carefully so as not to put Tom off, 'just *unusual,* that's all. They've spent a long time in that funny old place.'

Tom had wondered what 'unusual' meant as he watched the raindrops racing down the train windows. It could be unusual like his own parents—they scarcely counted as normal. But now that he had arrived he was beginning to see what his mother had meant.

'Paste sandwich, Tom?' wheezed Uncle Jos, holding a tiny plate of bread triangles out to him. 'Go on, they're the best: sardine.'

Uncle Jos was a round ball of a man, with red cheeks and a bald head that sprouted small clumps of hair in all directions. His most prominent feature were his eyebrows, which were as thick as hedges and met in the middle, hiding a pair of dark beady eyes that were constantly on the move. At the moment he was wearing two cardigans, one on top of the other, and his head was cocked slightly to one side like a dog listening to a public announcement.

'Er . . . no thanks.'

'No idea what you are missing, lad,' said Uncle Jos, cramming another sandwich into his own mouth.

'I think he might, Jos,' clucked Melba disapprovingly. 'Tom dear, do have some more tea. One can never have enough tea.'

If Uncle Jos was one extreme, Aunt Melba was quite the other. Instead of being short and round and rather jolly she was pale and slim and, with her hair cut in a pudding bowl like a medieval king, she looked rather severe. At this moment she was picking the crumbs off her plate with quick birdlike movements and placing them on the tip of her knee, where a long white rat with red eyes sat nibbling. This was Plankton, and he was having his tea too.

'Plankton is the best mouser in town,' cooed Melba, gently stroking his back.

'Mouser?' repeated Tom, who was sure that mousers were cats and definitely not rats.

'Ah yes,' winked Uncle Jos. 'Didn't you know mice are terrified of rats? Particularly white ones with red eyes. They meet Plankton in the dark holes in the skirting board and they think they've died and gone to hell.'

Jos picked up two jam tarts and wedged them beneath his huge black eyebrows. 'He is the devil, you see, with big, red eyes! And he has come to punish them for all those naughty things they have done in their lives! Roah! Roah!'

Jos waved his stocky arms madly in the air like a weird little monster, and Tom stifled a laugh. The next moment Jos popped the jam tarts out of his eye sockets and winked.

'So them naughty little critters turn tail and skedaddle. They never come back!'

'Don't you listen to it, Tom,' said Melba with a smile. 'But devil or no devil he's a very fine rat, wouldn't you like to hold him?'

And before Tom knew it Plankton was scrabbling about on his lap.

'Er . . . thanks. I . . . er . . . ' Tom had never been sure about rats, and Plankton, who smelled slightly of straw, did not change his mind.

'I think he likes you,' cooed Melba.

'So . . . er . . . is this a . . . er . . . busy time of year for the museum?' said Tom, trying hard to ignore Plankton's scabby white claws investigating the pocket that happened to contain his last sherbet lemon.

'Oh yes lad, it's all go all the time,' Jos replied breezily, 'it never stops here, ever. Melba and I run this ship entirely on our own. Why, only last week we had . . . erm . . . who *did* we have, Melba?'

'The school party from St Denis's cancelled on Monday,' she said, feeding Plankton a crumb.

'Yes, ah, it's a wee bit cold for the little ones this time of year,' explained Jos. 'But those old folks from the Dragonport Historical Society came on Tuesday and they *definitely* enjoyed it—'

'Except for the two who swore blind they would never come again.'

'Why was that?' asked Tom.

'Scared,' replied Uncle Jos quickly. 'We have to keep it very dark in there, you see. Some of the old dears' hearts aren't up to it.'

'Three people on Wednesday.'

Jos harrumphed loudly.

'You see, my dear, I just don't think you're counting properly. It was definitely more than that—'

'Well, there was one old fellow who slipped in and out without paying at all.'

'Leaky Logan?' exclaimed Jos. 'Not him again!'

'He refused to pay because he says you owe him so much money for fixing the boiler that he deserves a free ticket in here for the rest of his life,' said Melba pointedly.

'Hagfish!' muttered Uncle Jos.

'Thursday, Friday, no one at all,' Melba went on, and with a smile she relieved Tom of the troublesome rat.

'Maybe so Melba, maybe so, but Saturday is always the biggest day of the week for the Scatterhorn Museum,' Jos replied, refusing to be put down. 'Why, in our heyday we've had thousands through here on a Saturday, crowds stretching right down the street. Like a cup final.'

'But last Saturday it was just two. And both were from the Council, with more demands for money.'

'All right,' said Jos holding up his hands, 'I know, it's not exactly profitable. But, Tom, the point is,' Jos cleared his throat, 'the point is—'

'What was it your father used to say?' prompted Melba quietly.

'As long as we're here,' boomed Jos, and standing up he suddenly grabbed Tom by the shirt, 'then boy, we're *here*.'

'As long as we're here, we're here, we're here, as long as we're here, we're here, we're here,' sang Melba in a thin reedy voice, and Jos's shoulders began to shake violently.

'As long as—'

'Stop it!' wheezed Jos, his eyes screwed up like tiny dots and his face turning such a deep shade of purple that Tom thought he might explode. Melba tittered. Tom looked from one to the other and smiled helplessly. He was beginning to wonder if Jos and Melba were completely mad.

'Dear oh dear, never could work that one out,' said Jos finally, wiping his eye. 'But I took it to mean keep the place open, come hell or high water.'

And being an ex-navy man, this was a phrase that Jos could understand.

After tea Uncle Jos led Tom up the rickety back stairs to a small attic room at the top of the narrow slice of building behind the museum that was Jos and Melba's home. The roof was so low and the door so thin that Jos struggled to get through it.

'Sorry about the mess,' he said, kicking some very old-looking packing cases out of the way and hefting Tom's bag onto the bed. 'Lord, that's heavy.'

Jos sank down beside it, puffing so hard that his breath turned to steam like a kettle.

'So, Tom,' he said, glancing up with his head cocked to one side, 'what do you think of your quarters?'

Tom looked around at the tiny room. It was dark and damp

and cold, and every wall sloped inwards under the eaves. At the far end was a small desk before a window with a view out over the wet rooftops of the town and the wide grey river beyond. On the far side, Tom could just make out the yellow lights from the docks and the shadows of huge cranes, looming up out of the gloom like dinosaurs.

'It's great,' he said, shivering slightly. 'Maybe a bit cold but I—'

'That can be sorted, lad,' interrupted Jos. 'Don't you worry. It may be cold in here but you can bet your life it's warmer than Mongolia!'

With a chuckle he heaved himself off the bed and navigated back through the boxes to the door.

'I'm sure you want to get your stuff shipshape now, so I'll leave you to get on. Tomorrow we'll have a good look around the old place and you can tell me what you think of her. And I'll want to know,' he winked, 'after all, you're a Scatterhorn. One day you may end up taking the helm yourself.' And with a wave he was gone.

Tom looked around the cold dark room once more, with its piles of musty books and old newspapers that smelt slightly sweet. Suddenly he felt very alone. Walking through the boxes to the window, Tom watched the moon racing through the silver clouds and listened to the howling wind. In his mind he imagined that same moon shining down on the other side of the world. There, on the edge of a vast forest, was a little tent with a fire crackling beside it. And there were two shadows beside the tent, always two shadows—

Tom turned away from the window, biting his lip. Right now he missed his parents more than he could possibly say.

'Be brave my darling,' Tom's mother had said as the train pulled out of the station. 'I'll find him. I promise.'

Tom flopped down on the low creaking bed and stared up at the peeling wallpaper above his head. Angrily, he wiped away the tears with his sleeve. This was not how it was supposed to be.

Where had his father gone?

Some strange, empty country, full of forests and rivers. Tom rolled over and tried to ignore the truth that haunted him. After all, it might have been so very different . . .

CHAPTER 2

The Divine Spark

That night Tom had a dream. It was the first of July, his birthday. It was a warm, sunny morning and as he was too excited to sleep he crept downstairs before his parents got up to look at the presents waiting for him on the kitchen table. There was a large pile at one end—his—and at the other end a much smaller pile for his father. Coincidentally, Tom and his father shared the same birthday, and even though he was dreaming Tom knew this to be true. Carefully, Tom picked up each present in turn, squeezing it gently and trying to imagine what was inside. Just then Tom heard the letterbox click shut and running out into the hall he found a small pile of letters scattered across the floor. 'Tom Scatterhorn, Tom Scatterhorn, Tom Scatterhorn.' . . . That last one felt promisingly heavy; money, hoped Tom as he carried the letters into the kitchen and spread them triumphantly on the table. It was only then that he saw, half-hidden behind all the other letters, a small, dirty envelope marked 'airmail'.

Tom picked up the letter and stared at it. The paper was yellowing and smudged, and it looked as if it had survived shipwreck, fire, and possibly an earthquake as well. It was addressed to *'Sam Scatterhorn Esq.'*, and despite its battered appearance there was something vaguely official about it. Tom was puzzled: his father never received letters on his birthday. One of the stamps was long and thin and had a colourful picture of a horseman with an eagle on it, surrounded by words in a language he had never seen before. Without knowing quite why, Tom carried the letter into the kitchen, lit the gas stove and held the yellowing smudged envelope over the blue flame. He watched as the paper slowly turned from yellow to brown and the orange flame licked down towards his fingers, closer, closer, closer—

Ah!!

Suddenly Tom sat bolt upright in bed, clutching his fingers. Glancing down he was relieved to find there were no burns, no marks, nothing. It was just a dream, nothing more.

A dream.

Wasn't it?

With a heavy sigh, Tom flopped back down on the bed, knowing that this wasn't a dream. It was a memory of his seventh birthday, and it was all true except for one thing. He never burned that letter, and he should have done. And he clearly remembered what happened next.

At breakfast Tom's father opened the letter and scratched his head. It was certainly very odd. Then he read it again.

'Who's it from, love?' asked Tom's mother.

'The International Movement for the Protection and Advancement of Insects,' he said slowly, turning it over. Tom could see the words 'Private and Confidential' written in heavy black type across the top.

'What do they want, Dad?'

'It seems they want to make me a member. Apparently it's very prestigious.'

'You?' said Tom's mother smiling. 'Why have they asked you?'

'Do you remember I used to collect beetles as a kid?'

'No.'

'Well I did. I used to be rather good at it in fact. Got a prize once.'

'And that's why they've written to you?' said Tom's mother, not quite sure that this wasn't a joke. 'Because you used to collect beetles?'

'So it seems,' replied Tom's father, utterly mystified. 'Well, there's a turn up for the books.'

Sam Scatterhorn was a tall man who worked for the local council as an accountant. He did not smile much, but his eyes were laughing all the time, and this was one of those phrases that he always used. If an elephant had sat on his car, or a dog had scored the winning goal in the Cup Final, or an alien spaceship had landed in the next-door garden, they would have all been greeted with, 'Well, there's a turn up for the books.'

So Sam Scatterhorn put on his jacket as he always did, failed to notice he was wearing odd socks, as he always did, and went out of the door of 27 Middlesuch Close. Tooting the horn of his car, he reversed out of the drive and drove to work. As he always did.

That evening Tom caught his father reading the letter again, and again the day after that. Then a week later, another letter from the mysterious International Movement came. It also had 'Private and Confidential' written on it. Sam Scatterhorn studied its contents, and that evening he came home with a large book on insects that he had borrowed from the library.

'I'd forgotten that one in four animals on this planet is a beetle,' he said, squinting at the pages over his cornflakes. 'Did you know that some of them have been here for two hundred million years—they're almost living fossils.'

'Is that so,' said Tom's mother as she hurried through the kitchen on her way to work, 'how totally fascinating. Let us know if anything changes by this afternoon, won't you?'

'I might if you're lucky,' replied Sam Scatterhorn, his eyes smiling as they always did. But Tom noticed that behind his smile his father was becoming more serious now, as if he was always thinking about something else. Every week more and more correspondence from the Movement dropped through the letterbox, all marked with the distinctive IMPAI symbol and covered with interesting foreign stamps which Tom wouldn't have minded collecting had his father not gathered them all up and squirrelled them away in his study. Then one night Tom woke up to hear his parents having an argument downstairs.

'But tell me how we are going to live!' shouted his mother. Tom could tell she had been crying.

'Well, you're a teacher, you have a job. Dearest, I have just *got* to do this. Please let me do it.'

Then his mother burst into tears.

This was the start of it, because the very next day Sam

Scatterhorn gave up his job with the council and bought a microscope. At first he began collecting insects in the garden, killing them, dissecting them, and then examining them for hours under his microscope. But after a few months of this work Sam Scatterhorn became restless, and he began to look further afield.

'Now *there's* a turn up for the books,' said Donald Duke who lived next door. He was staring dubiously at the old and rusty camper van now parked in the Scatterhorn's drive.

'Is that thing going to stay there?' chirped a bird-like voice from behind the hedge. That was Dina, his wife.

'Unfortunately it is, dear,' replied Donald.

'Well, you'll have to do something about it,' she whispered loudly, and jabbed him in the ribs with her trowel. 'What do they think this is, a scrapyard?'

But Dina Duke needn't have worried; the rusty old camper van didn't stay there—in fact it was hardly there at all. The moment every school holiday began, Sam Scatterhorn loaded up supplies and blankets into the van and they were off, heading for some distant river or mountain in pursuit of the only thing that interested him now. In France they collected weevil larvae. In Germany it was click beetles. In Hungary it was mayflies. In Italy it was small black scorpions. At first Tom discovered he was quite good at finding them; he would set off at dawn with a stick and a specimen box, and by lunchtime he had collected all sorts of creatures for his father to look at under the microscope. It was exciting for a while, and Tom was always thrilled when he managed to prise a particularly vicious little scorpion from under its rock, but as he grew older he realized that he didn't want to spend all day searching under stones and chasing through the woods with a net. And he also began to realize that his father's obsession was no longer about collecting. Sam Scatterhorn was chasing something elusive, a secret truth that he might never find.

'So,' asked Tom impatiently, 'what is it?'

They were sitting in a moonlit pine forest in Spain, watching fireflies dancing through the trees. For a long time his father stared at the campfire, watching the embers glow.

'In the old days it used to be called the divine spark,' he said slowly. 'It's the lightning bolt that kick-starts the motor. Makes everything breathe, move, be. The spirit of life, I suppose. Scientists can make things grow in their laboratories, copy animals and even graft one living thing onto another, but they all have to be *alive* in the first place, don't they? So what *makes* them alive in the first place?'

Tom thought he understood what his father was saying, but still it did not quite make sense.

'But . . . why insects, Dad? Surely everything that is alive has a divine spark?'

'Hmm.'

Tom's father stared at him intently across the fire. He seemed more serious than Tom had ever seen him in his life.

'I wish,' he began, 'I wish I could tell you. And Mum too. But we're not really allowed to say anything. It's like a big secret and once you knew . . . you'd never—'

But he never finished his sentence. Tom waited, burning with curiosity. The hiss of the crickets was deafening.

'Dad?'

'Hmm?'

What exactly *is* the International Movement for the . . . the . . . you know?'

'Protection and Advancement of Insects?'

Tom nodded. It was a question he had wanted to ask for a very long time, but still his father did not reply.

'It's just that, well, I can't see why they asked *you* to look for it,' Tom continued, feeling the frustration beginning to well up inside him. 'I mean, you're not a scientist. Why don't they get someone else, like a professor or something, to go and find it?'

Tom's father smiled and shook his head.

'Because Tom . . . they'd never understand. This is not science, it's more like . . . a quest, I suppose,' he said at last. 'Once you take up the challenge you can't stop. And what's more, they haven't really given me much choice.'

Tom poked the fire roughly, sending sparks floating up into the night.

'But what happens if you never find the divine spark? I mean, that's possible, isn't it?'

Sam Scatterhorn stared silently into the flickering embers. There was a deeply troubled expression on his face.

After that trip matters really did take a turn for the worse. Sam Scatterhorn rarely left the house now, and Tom could barely get up the stairs to his bedroom as boxes of insects and beetles crowded every step. Then Sam Scatterhorn noticed a car that was often parked at the corner of Middlesuch Close at odd hours of the day and night with two men inside it.

'There's double-o-seven and double-o-eight outside,' called

Tom as he came back home from school. 'They're watching you, Dad.'

But Sam Scatterhorn's eyes were not laughing any more. He peered nervously through the curtains at the car at the end of the road, and a week later he screwed the front door shut, forcing Tom and his mother to enter the house only through the back garden. He was convinced the men were about to break into the house and steal his specimens. Something was going very, very wrong, and both Tom and his mother knew it: Sam Scatterhorn was fast descending into a paranoid, crazy world of insects and scientific formulas where no one could reach him. At mealtimes nobody spoke and Tom dared not catch his father's eye for fear of starting an argument. He just could not find what he was looking for, and he was becoming desperate. Then one morning in June, the worst thing that could have happened did happen. Sam Scatterhorn went outside for the first time in months to find the camper van had been ransacked.

'Oh dear me,' smirked Donald Duke from the other side of the hedge, eyeing the smashed windows and ripped seats scattered across the oil-spattered drive. 'Now why would anyone want to do a thing like that?'

Sam Scatterhorn did not reply, he just stood blinking in the sunlight, staring at the chaos. Turning round, he squinted down the road to where the car was parked on the corner. The two men were still there. Somehow the destruction of his precious van seemed to have finally stunned him to his senses. He seemed almost pleased.

Later that night, a soft 'clink' interrupted Tom's troubled dreams. Tom rolled over to see that it was five past two in the morning, and pulling back the curtain a fraction he could just make out his father quietly closing the garden gate. On his back was a large rucksack, and in one hand he held his long butterfly net. Tom watched as his father peered cautiously around the hedge into the road. Apart from a tabby cat making its rounds beneath the streetlights, everything was quiet. The inhabitants of Middlesuch Close were all asleep. Sam Scatterhorn glanced up at the window and Tom saw that he was smiling, really smiling, for the first time in a long, long time. Tom wanted to shout out, say something, but already his father was striding purposefully out into the centre of the road. A minute later he turned the corner and disappeared.

For a few weeks Tom's mother pretended she knew where her husband had gone.

'Switzerland, Tom. We'll get a postcard soon I expect,' she would say as she busied about getting ready for school, and Tom half believed her. They started using the front door again, and Tom noticed that the car with the two men was no longer parked at the end of the road. But the weeks turned to months and there was still no word. Every morning Tom's mother would run downstairs to pick up the post and walk back into the kitchen trying to hide her disappointment, and every night she would quietly open the door of Sam Scatterhorn's study and start looking for clues. But it was all a sea of chaos, and Tom would often wake up to hear his mother crying softly. How Tom wanted to help his mother in those moments, but what could he say?

He knew that if his father had gone off to find the 'divine spark', whatever that was, then he might be anywhere on the planet. And somehow Tom didn't want to think of his father as a tall rangy man driven half-crazy by his obsession with insects any more. In his daydreams Sam Scatterhorn became the granite-jawed explorer of a comic book, one moment wading heroically through a mangrove swamp, ripping the leeches off his chest, the next battling up an ice face in a blizzard, ice axe in hand. His father was a man on a quest that was so secret he couldn't tell anyone about it, not even his own son. But one day he would come back a hero, having found the divine spark. And in Tom's dreams he would follow in his footsteps.

Then one morning a postcard did drop through the letter-box, but it was not from Sam Scatterhorn. The black and white photograph on the front was very curious: it showed an elegantly dressed man with white hair and a moustache lounging on a sofa. Sitting next to him was a large cheetah, and both the man and the cheetah looked rather bored. '*Sir Henry Scatterhorn and Friend: 1935*', it read at the bottom. The card was from Uncle Jos, hoping that all was well 'at your end', and 'wondering if we could have a wee chat about funds for HMS Scatterhorn, the family flagship, in the not *too* distant future.'

'As if we could give him anything,' snorted Tom's mother. 'He's as mean as mustard himself.'

The card was stuck on the fridge door, and Tom thought nothing more about it until some weeks later, when he came home from school to find his mother standing in the hall with tears streaming down her face.

'Mum? . . . Mum, what's happened?'

A knot of fear tightened in Tom's stomach: they'd found his father, hanging frozen to death on some glacier, or burnt to a crisp in the desert . . .

'He's OK.'

She held up a letter and waved it like a flag.

'He's in Mongolia.'

Tom felt his heart was ready to burst and he ran to her, hugging her as tightly as he could. There would be no pretending any more. He was OK, everything was OK. Mum smiled as she choked back the tears.

'He couldn't say where exactly, but he needs my help,' she whispered as she held him close. 'I must go and find him.'

Tom did not understand.

'But why—'

'I know. But I'll be back, Tom, I promise. I'll bring him back home.'

Tom felt as if the walls of his world were starting to cave in. He had lost his father, and now his mother was about to leave him as well. He felt a lump begin to rise in his throat.

'Can't I come with you?' he pleaded.

Tom's mother knelt down before him, and he could see her eyes were bright with tears. It seemed to Tom she so wanted to say yes.

'Please, my darling,' she murmured, 'don't make it more difficult than it already is. I just—'

'What?'

Tom's dark, questioning eyes searched her face. At last she looked at him, and for a moment they sat together in silence.

'You're a very brave boy, Tom,' she said, brushing a lock of thick blond hair away from his eyes, 'but I just can't afford to lose you both,' and leaning forward she hugged him tighter than ever. 'You will be safe with Uncle Jos.'

'Uncle Jos?'

'Yes,' said his mother drying her eyes, 'I've just spoken to him. He'll happily look after you for Christmas.'

'Uncle Jos . . . this Christmas?'

'That's right, my darling.'

Tom looked blankly at his mother, trying to take it all in. Suddenly everything seemed to have been worked out. One minute his father had gone, and they were just carrying on, pretending that everything was fine and he was just on holiday somewhere. Now that he had made contact, it was OK to admit that they had both been so worried about him they thought he might even be dead. And now his mother was going to rescue him. And that was that.

'So . . . so you really are going?'

'I'm afraid so, darling. I have to. You remember the state he was in.'

Tom stared at the floor angrily; he knew that there would be no changing her mind.

'When?'

'On Monday. After school.'

Tom stared up at the low attic ceiling and shivered. Monday was this morning.

CHAPTER 3

The Pride of the Scatterhorns

The next morning was bright and icy. Tom took off all the clothes he'd been wearing the previous night and put them on again in a different order to try to make himself feel warmer, and when he came down to the kitchen he found Melba already bustling about the cooker.

'Morning Tom,' she smiled as she set a thick bacon sandwich down in front of him, 'did you pass a good night?'

'Yes thanks . . . a bit cold but—'

'Damn pipe's cracked,' muttered Jos from behind his newspaper.

'Well, *are* you going to fix it, Jos?' asked Melba as she dried the plates and put them away. 'He can't stay up there without heating in this weather. It's cold enough down here, let alone . . . '

Jos put down his paper and gave Melba a hard stare over the top of his half-moon glasses, one end of which was held together with Sellotape. Tufts of hair were standing up like weeds on the dome of his bald head.

'I'll pop out to Stannards later and get him one of those little electric blowers,' he said shortly, 'they're not expensive.'

'You'd do better to fix that pipe,' retorted Melba with a sneeze, 'those things guzzle electricity as you well know.'

Jos hid behind his newspaper once more. Tom kept quiet, munching steadily through his bacon sandwich; the last thing he wanted to do was be the centre of an argument. He hated arguments. Glancing at the back of Jos's paper, his eye was drawn to a photograph of a strange looking man standing before a grand white house. The man had strikingly large eyes, a thin pointed nose, and his black hair was slicked back with a streak of silver running through it.

'CATCHERS SET TO RETURN TO CATCHER HALL' ran the headline, 'BUT THEY DON'T LIKE OUR WEATHER.' Tom leant forward and read on:

Catcher Hall, ancestral home of the Catcher family, is to be occupied once more. For many years the grand house at the top of Catcher Hill has stood empty, but now Don Gervase Askary, a Catcher relative from Peru, has decided to relocate to the property after thirty years working in the cocoa trade. Don Gervase will certainly need deep pockets to restore the house to its former glory, but as he told the *Dragonport Mercury* yesterday, 'This is my family home and I am prepared to spend whatever it takes. Millions, if necessary. The only thing that frightens me is your English rain!'

'Who are the Catchers?' asked Tom innocently. The moment the words came out he felt the temperature in the room drop by ten degrees. Jos put down his paper and peered at him.

'And why do you ask, Tom?'

'Well . . . it's just that there's a picture in the paper of one of them standing in front of Catcher Hall, that's all.'

Jos folded over his newspaper and studied the photograph closely.

'Don Gervase Askary—a chocolate millionaire from Peru, eh?' Jos snorted loudly. 'More money than sense, no doubt.'

'He's odd looking, certainly,' added Melba, craning over Jos's shoulder to take a closer look, 'but then of course, he's a Catcher, and one can't expect too much in that department.' And with a little sigh she returned to the sink. 'But just think of all that chocolate! I bet he's got cellars full of it . . . Mmm . . . I think I could have made an exception for that,' she teased. 'What say you, Jos?'

'I say you're barking mad,' snorted Jos, standing up briskly. 'Come on Tom, let's get out of here.'

Uncle Jos strode out of the door in his slippers, and pulling a large key from his dressing gown pocket he unlocked the heavy door before him.

'So who are the Catchers then?' asked Tom again. Jos cocked his head and frowned.

'Tom lad, you're in need of a little history lesson,' he wheezed, and with that, pushed open the heavy door and set off down a gloomy narrow passage decorated with faded engravings of lizards and snakes.

'You see,' began Jos, 'it's like this. Dragonport is a very small town, and for many, *many* years there were only two big families here, the Catchers and the Scatterhorns. The Catchers lived up on the hill over that side,' and he waved in the general direction of the river, 'and we Scatterhorns lived on this side. But ever since anyone can remember, Catchers and Scatterhorns have always hated each other. Loathed the very sight of one another.'

'Why?' asked Tom, trying to keep up as they turned a corner that led into another gloomy corridor, this time hung with grey engravings of parrots.

'Why? Why? It's the tradition, lad,' continued Jos. 'Name any war, sport, egg and spoon race, whatever you fancy, and you can be sure that Scatterhorns have taken one side, and the Catchers the other.'

Tom looked at Jos blankly.

'Nobody knows why—I certainly don't. It's just how it's always been, and probably always will be.'

'But . . . isn't that like picking a fight and then forgetting why you've picked it?'

'Maybe it is,' replied Jos arching his eyebrows. 'I'm not arguing with you, boy. But that's traditions for you. Things just start and no one can remember the hell why. Anyway,' Jos was moving at speed now and Tom struggled to hear what he was saying, 'there was one exception to this long-running feud. About a hundred and twenty years ago the unheard of happened, and a Catcher became best friends with a Scatterhorn. Fancy that! And there was zilch all either of their families could do to stop it,' Jos paused to admire a picture of a parrot chasing a spider, 'though I dare say they tried.' Then he peered down at Tom and whispered noisily. 'Their names were August and Henry.'

'Sir Henry Scatterhorn; you mean the man who founded this museum?' asked Tom excitedly.

'Correct,' winked Jos. 'Who happened to be your great-great-grandfather's brother, in fact. Now back then Sir Henry was one of the greatest hunters in the world, and his best friend, August Catcher, was one of the greatest taxidermists in the world—if not *the* greatest. So they decided to create this museum together. Sir Henry provided the specimens, and August stuffed them. And though I am biased, of course, I still think that it is one of the most impressive collections of taxidermy anywhere on earth.' They had reached the end of the corridor and stood before a high mahogany door.

'And here it is.'

With a flourish Uncle Jos flung open the doors to reveal a high square room hidden in semi-darkness. At that very moment there was a distant tinkling sound, and Tom saw something bright flash through the air.

CRASH!

The sound of smashing glass echoed around the room.

'Hagfish in a houseboat!' wheezed Jos, squinting up to the skylight now missing a small pane of glass. 'That was them hailstones, I expect. The size of blinking golf balls.'

Jos shuffled off to clear up the mess, and as Tom's eyes became accustomed to the gloom he found himself in a large, musty hall crammed with stuffed animals of all shapes and sizes. Some were standing in large glass cases against the walls, some were mounted on podiums dotted across the floor. Slowly Tom began to weave his way through the collection, peering into each dark case in turn. Against the back wall was a large cabinet labelled '*AFRICA*', in which a family of lions perched on a high rock surveying the plain where a collection of gazelles and antelopes were grazing. They seemed rather disapproving of the riot of warthogs and meerkats chasing between their legs.

Next to this was a huge rainforest scene, where frogs, snakes, and lemurs jostled through the branches and a tapir peeped shyly from behind the leaves. There was a large gorilla sitting on its own in the crook of a tree, opposite a wolf standing in the snow hungrily eyeing an arctic rabbit. Along one whole wall were lines of grim looking sturgeon beneath shelves crammed with puffer fish and sharks. Above them bats flew around the head of a screaming hairy armadillo, while beside the door a family of pangolins nuzzled around the base of a termite hill. In the case labelled '*SMALL MAMMALS*' an otter wombat stood grinning crazily at a wallaby, and on the shelf below, a proboscis monkey appeared to be explaining something to a ring-tailed coatimundi. In one corner there was a wide domed case containing a flower bush buzzing with hundreds of tiny jewel-like hummingbirds, and standing opposite a huge looming beast seemed to occupy the entire wall. It was only when Tom noticed the two vast curving tusks that he realized it was a mammoth. Everything was faded and dirty but Tom was truly amazed by it all. He had never seen so many different animals in his life, either stuffed or alive.

'This old gent was not, of course, found in the wild,' announced Jos cheerfully, looking up at the great shaggy mountain. 'August invented him. And I've always liked this one.' Jos ambled over to a large grey bird standing on a podium in the centre of the room. 'Do you know what this is?'

'It's a dodo,' replied Tom, peering down at the funny turkey-sized creature. 'I thought they were extinct.'

'They are,' winked Jos, 'but August bought some drawings made by a sailor who had actually seen the dodo and he decided to create one himself. It's a chicken mostly. Clever, don't you think?'

Tom looked at the stumpy bird with its curved beak and sad yellow eye. It was so real he imagined it might move at any moment.

'So did August make all these animals up?'

'Lord no. They are real, on the outside anyway. Once he had preserved their fur or feathers he would attach their skulls to a wire frame, or a plaster cast for the bigger ones, and then he'd stuff them. Sometimes he used their original skeletons, but mostly he didn't. It's a forgotten art-form really. Just a shame they're all getting a bit long in the tooth.'

Jos was right. Almost every one of them was a dull brownish colour, and some even had bits of stuffing falling out of their bodies. They reminded him of his old brown bear that had been washed so many times that eventually all the colour had run out of it. The mammoth even seemed to have large patches of hair around his middle missing, and other parts of him seemed to have been patched up with a slightly different colour. Nevertheless, Tom couldn't help thinking that these creatures looked alive somehow; maybe it was the poses August had set them in or the expressions in their eyes.

'They certainly *seem* pretty lively, don't they?'

Tom glanced up at Uncle Jos and saw his eyes twinkle mischievously beneath his enormous bushy eyebrows.

'I used to think that. I used to look at them just the way you are now and think: wouldn't it be great if they were alive!' He grinned. 'Well, let me tell you Tom, one of them was—well, *nearly* was. We had an elephant shrew in the small mammals' cabinet over there.' Jos pointed across to the long dark case beyond the mammoth. 'August Catcher's idea of a joke, I think.

It was clockwork. Used to hop occasionally, and wink. Gave the visitors the fright of their lives. Then one Christmas there was a carol service in here and it winked at the Salvation Army band and did a little somersault. They nearly swallowed their trumpets!'

Jos's shoulders began to shake at the memory.

'Dear oh dear,' he said, wiping a tear from his beady eye. 'Now Tom, come and look at this.'

Jos led the way across the hall to a low wide case that almost stretched the length of the wall. He flicked on the lights and, looking down, Tom saw a large model of Dragonport as it had been a hundred years ago. On a hill set clearly above the town Tom recognized Catcher Hall, and on the opposite side of the river stood the Scatterhorn Museum. It was winter, and the busy snowbound streets teamed with people and horse-drawn sledges jostling their way down to the river. Out in the estuary Tom could see the busy dockyards, where fishing boats were unloading their catches and a paddle steamer had just come in. Upstream of the town the river opened out into a wide crescent that had completely frozen over, and the ice was busy with skaters, thronging around stalls and entertainments. Pressing his face close up to the glass Tom could see that the detail was minute—even the feathers on the ladies' hats had been painted. It was like looking down on a complete miniature world.

'Watch carefully,' announced Jos, and he flicked another switch.

'Wow!' Tom gasped.

Suddenly the scene had transformed to night. In every street tiny electric lightbulbs lit up the gas lamps, and Tom could see that there were people inside the houses; families were eating in their kitchens, old men sat reading in front of their fires, there were dogs running up back stairs and babies in their cots. And as he looked closer Tom noticed more sinister scenes here too: in the back room of a pub two men were brawling, their faces smashed and covered in blood. There was a beggar freezing in a warehouse, a burglar climbing into an attic window, a thief stabbing a man in a doorway. It was as if the switch from day to night had revealed a completely different world, far more dangerous and strange.

'Do you like it?' whispered Jos. 'I used to spend hours staring at this when I was your age. It's another of August's creations.'

They stood in silence just admiring it for a while, and Uncle Jos seemed lost in his own thoughts. The only sound was the plop, plip, plop, plip of raindrops falling through the broken window onto the stone floor.

'Imagine what this place must have been like in those days,' he said at last.

'I can help you fix it if you like,' said Tom.

'Hmm?' said Jos, his mind still far away.

'The leaks in the roof. Clean everything up, if you want.'

Jos turned off the lights. Suddenly he looked much older than before.

'Well, that's nice of you. But Tom, take a look around. Do you really think there's any point?'

'What do you mean?'

Jos was avoiding his eyes and fidgeting with his broken glasses.

'I'll tell it straight, Tom. You have arrived at a bad time. The heating, the lights, and now the roof, it's all going belly up in here. I just don't have the money to fix it.'

'But don't the visitors pay to come in?'

'No one pays to come in here any more,' he said waving his arm around the gloom. 'No one's interested. There are no computers; it isn't interactive. It's just a load of knackered old animals, and they are knackered—I know they are. Relics from another age. They don't impress people any more, they just frighten them.' Jos stared vacantly at the dark cases all around. Rows of eyes and teeth loomed back at him. 'I can't even afford to fix *them* either.'

'What about the Catchers?' asked Tom suddenly. 'Couldn't they help out; I mean, August was one of them, they must be related?'

Jos shook his head grimly.

'I'm sorry to say that can't ever happen,' he growled. 'I know we Scatterhorns have never been any good with money and I know they have. Believe me, I don't enjoy huddling up in the back of this place while they are lording it up there on the hill, but that's just the dice, isn't it?'

By now Jos was feeling thoroughly sorry for himself. Tom couldn't think of anything to say.

'I dunno,' wheezed Jos, scratching his head, 'I reckon at the end of this year it's just about time to open the seacocks and wave goodbye to it all.'

Jos shambled away down the corridor and he was just about to open the large mahogany door when a loud bell rang out across the hall. Jos cocked his head and listened. Then the bell rang again, two bursts this time.

'What's that?' asked Tom.

Jos was very puzzled.

'Someone's at the door. Go to the window Tom, quick, and see who it is.'

Tom did as he was told and looked out. There on the pavement below him was an enormous brown Bentley the colour of dark chocolate, glinting in the pale sun. Tom could just make out a large man sitting heavily behind the wheel and, craning his neck round further, he saw another man in a cream cap and a long grey woollen coat waiting outside the door. There was a girl about his age standing beside him. The man at the door pressed the button again impatiently.

'Well?' huffed Jos, as the bell echoed through the empty hall.

'It's . . . it's some visitors—tourists maybe.' Tom had no idea who it was.

'But can't they read the sign? We're closed!'

Marching up to where Tom was standing, Jos flung open the window.

'*Ferme!*' he thundered. '*Chiuso! Geschlossen!* Fumbleclop!'

The man in the long woollen coat stopped ringing and inclined his head up to the window.

'Good morning sir,' he said, taking off his hat and bowing slightly, 'I don't believe we have met.'

It was Don Gervase Askary. Jos looked shocked. He raised his arm to wave them away but rubbed his nose instead.

'I am a distant relation of August Catcher. I wondered if I might come in?'

CHAPTER 4

The Visitors

Everything was thrown into a commotion.

'I suppose I'll *have* to let them in,' growled Jos, pacing up and down before the great entrance door, 'though I've a good mind not to.'

'I think maybe you should,' suggested Tom, eyeing Don Gervase rubbing his hands impatiently on the doorstep.

'Hagfish,' muttered Jos, frantically rummaging in the deep pockets of his dressing gown. 'My father would turn in his grave if he knew.' Tom watched as a cascade of pencils, small bits of wire, and toast crusts tumbled out onto the floor.

'Can I help?'

'The key, lad! The one and only confounded door key.'

Tom glanced at the door to see an old steel key with an ornate ring standing in the lock. It looked as if it hadn't been removed for a very long time.

'Is that it?'

Jos peered up over his spectacles.

'That's the one!' he cried, brushing away the dust. 'Now where the devil was it?'

'In the door.'

Jos looked at him wildly.

'Well of course it was!' And he began to force the lock.

'Wait. WAIT!'

Jos turned to see Aunt Melba standing in the shadows of the corridor.

'What?' he shouted back. 'WHAT?'

Melba stared at Jos in his slippers and cardigans, his hair sprouting in all directions and his broken glasses perched drunkenly on the end of his nose. He looked half crazy.

'The dressing gown dear, perhaps . . . '

And only then did Jos realize the state he was in.

'Of course, yes. Absolutely and entirely,' he snorted, taking off the old stripy gown and thrusting it at Tom, who caught it with both hands. 'A Scatterhorn must always be on his mettle when confronted by a Catcher.'

'That's my Tusker,' said Aunt Melba, smiling proudly.

'Now, Tom,' growled Jos as he turned the handle, 'just because I'm letting them in doesn't mean we like them. They're *Catchers*, remember?'

The great door groaned and creaked on its hinges, and out of the pale winter sunlight stepped two of the strangest looking people Tom had ever seen.

'Good morning,' said Don Gervase in a deep voice, clasping Jos warmly by the hand and bowing low. 'I cannot begin to tell you how pleased I am to meet the Scatterhorns at last.'

Don Gervase Askary was a strikingly tall man. He had high, narrow shoulders and a curiously bulbous head, and even bent double he still hovered well above Uncle Jos, who looked like a little garden gnome beside him. He was impeccably dressed in a long wiry woollen coat, black moleskin trousers, and a highly polished pair of chelsea boots. Tom could not help noticing that his feet were extremely small, and that despite his height he seemed to be making himself taller still by standing on tiptoes.

'I have heard so very much about you,' he smiled winningly, 'allow me to introduce my daughter—Lotus.'

And with a curl of his long fingers the dark-haired girl in a white snakeskin coat came forward. She moved gracefully, like a cat, and with a low bow took Jos's hand in her white glove.

'How do you do, Mr Scatterhorn sir,' she said softly.

Uncle Jos was completely dumbstruck. Such formality! Here was rare breeding indeed, even in a Catcher.

'How do . . . How do . . . di—' He tried to speak but all that came out was a little sigh. There was an awkward silence as everyone waited politely for Uncle Jos to recover the power of speech.

'Well, well,' said Don Gervase clasping his hands together, 'a chance to see the museum for myself. This *is* a treat.'

Turning around he spotted Tom standing behind the door, still holding the dressing gown.

'Ah-ha,' he said imperiously, 'and who pray are you?'

'Tom Scatterhorn.'

'Tom *Scatterhorn*, eh?' echoed the tall man, and his eyes narrowed to slits. He bent down to examine him more closely and Tom noticed that Don Gervase's great domed forehead was divided by a deep furrow that stretched from the centre of his eyebrows into his scalp.

'And what do you do?'

Even through the gloom Don Gervase's light green eyes held his like a magnet.

'I'm . . . I'm staying here,' mumbled Tom, 'with Uncle Jos.'

'So he's your uncle, is he?'

'No, he's . . . he's not my uncle exactly but I . . . we—my parents that is . . . erm . . . call him uncle. Jos.'

'Oh I see,' purred Don Gervase, moving his head a little closer. 'But you *are* a Scatterhorn then?'

Tom could see that Don Gervase had very small teeth, and they were almost black. Instinctively he leant back against the wall.

'Oh yes,' he admitted uneasily, 'yes, I'm—I'm a Scatterhorn all right.'

'Well, young Tom,' said Don Gervase quietly, taking Tom's hand in his long powerful fingers, 'I very much look forward to becoming friends with you,' and he gave Tom's hand a polite squeeze. 'Perhaps later you would be good enough to show my daughter around. She finds my conversation . . . somewhat boring.'

Lotus shot him a sulky smile.

'So you are August's . . . grandson?'

By now Uncle Jos had recovered enough to get a sentence out.

'Not quite,' replied Don Gervase. 'His brother married my great-aunt, I think. No, perhaps they were cousins. Yes, something like that. By marriage, you see, it was a up mix—mix up. Large family. Peruvian. A lot of people. Never really sure who was who.'

Don Gervase tried to cover his obvious confusion with a smile and Uncle Jos looked at him quizzically. He was quickly remembering that this Don Gervase Askary was a Catcher, and you could *never* trust a Catcher.

'What a great to do do,' added Don Gervase, 'but we all knew about August Catcher and his famous museum.'

'The Scatterhorn Museum,' said a cold voice from the corridor, 'it's the Scatterhorn Museum actually.'

Aunt Melba emerged from the shadows like a ghost.

'Mrs Scatterhorn, I presume?' enquired Don Gervase, offering his hand which Melba chose to ignore.

'So you have come to live at Catcher Hall?' she asked frostily.

'Indeed. And what a remarkable old place it is.'

Melba gave the faintest of nods and Don Gervase smiled graciously.

'Someone in the family had to take it in hand,' he continued. 'I had always dreamed that one day it might be me, but I never truly thought I would have that opportunity, until last year, when—' he paused and shot a glance at Lotus who dutifully hung her head, 'when my dear wife passed away.'

'Oh dear,' said Melba, suddenly beginning to thaw. 'I'm so sorry.'

'Such a terrible, terrible thing,' said Don Gervase with feeling. 'Madame, ever since the accident, it has been difficult for Lotus and me to find any meaning in our life.'

And with that he looked sadly at the floor. Lotus sniffed in sympathy.

'Indeedy deed,' rasped Jos, who was terrified Don Gervase might start crying at any moment. 'Well, how about—'

'We thought,' the tall man pressed on, 'we thought we could

come over here and make a new start,' he said, pulling a neatly pressed white handkerchief from his breast pocket and dabbing his eyes, 'away from all the memories.'

'Tea?' asked Aunt Melba in a fluster.

'Coffee, if you don't mind,' replied Don Gervase swiftly.

'Right-ho.'

Melba dived back into the kitchen, relieved to find any excuse to escape. By now Don Gervase looked thoroughly miserable. It was a very convincing performance indeed.

'Well, Mr Askary—'

'Don Gervase, please—'

'Don . . . er . . . Gervase,' blustered Jos clasping his hands together and trying to get matters back on an even keel, 'seeing that you have come such a long way I'm sure a squint at old August Catcher's work will cheer you up.'

'I'd rather hoped you'd say that,' sniffed Don Gervase, 'I have always been so interested in taxidermy, particularly August's. He was a genius, I think.' Don Gervase folded up his handkerchief and carefully tucked it away.

'How I envy you English, Mr Scatterhorn, and your upper stiff lips.'

'Stiff upper lip, dear chap,' said a relieved Jos. 'There we go. Can't be helped. Now Tom, why don't you take Lotus upstairs to the bird gallery?'

And so they separated. Tom led the way up the stairs and into a long gloomy room lined either side with every kind of bird set in different tableaux. They walked together in silence for a while, Lotus looking intently at the bitterns in their nest and the large river scene that was alive with shellducks and kingfishers.

She stopped in front of a large, mournful looking harpy eagle perched in a dead tree.

'I know this bird,' she said softly, 'it's from the rainforest.'

'Oh?' replied Tom politely, looking down at the label. 'It says here it eats snakes.'

'Yes it does,' replied Lotus confidently, 'but mainly sloths, and macaws too, like that one over there.'

Lotus swept across the room and came to rest before a small, dusty-blue macaw sitting on a perch.

'Spix's macaw,' she said without even looking at the label. 'None of those in the jungle.'

'No?'

'No. It's extinct in the wild,' she replied confidently, and bending forward Lotus studied the bird intensely. 'Collected to extinction. Odd isn't it, how some things survive and others . . . don't.'

'How do you mean?'

Lotus fixed him with her gaze. Tom noticed that she had the same wide, milky green eyes as her father, and he immediately felt rather uncomfortable.

'You want to know what happened, don't you? Shall I tell you?'

Tom did not understand, he was expecting her to give him a lecture about the macaw. Then a flicker of a smile crossed her lips.

'My mother, of course. '

'Oh. Yes,' said Tom, dropping his gaze, 'I'm sorry—'

'Don't be,' she replied coolly, 'we should all be dead really.'

Tom said nothing; he was very curious now. Lotus walked on and stopped before a case of long-eared owls.

'About a year ago,' she began, 'we all went up to visit my

uncle's cocoa plantation in the north of Peru. My father is a pilot, you see, and he was flying our plane with me in the front, and my mother and my aunt and my little brother and sister all in the back. As we were flying over the rainforest we hit a tropical storm. The sky turned black and we could see nothing. Then I remember a great flash and BANG!'

She glanced at Tom through the case and was pleased to see she had his full attention.

'So what happened? Did you—'

'We had been hit by lightning,' she said in a matter-of-fact voice, 'so the engine caught fire. Then it stopped completely. We fell out of the sky from three thousand metres, straight into the rainforest.' She ran her finger along the edge of the case and bent forward to examine the hinges. 'Of course the plane smashed into a thousand pieces when it hit the tree canopy.'

Tom was staring hard at Lotus now, and he could just see a hint of triumph in her pale green eyes.

'They were all killed, gone,' she added, clicking her fingers loudly. 'All dead except my father and me.'

Tom was astonished: he had never met anyone who had been in an air crash, let alone survived it. And then he realized he should say something sympathetic.

'Wow, that's . . . er . . . that's really terrible. So . . . what did you do then?'

'Oh, there's plenty to eat in a rainforest, you know,' said Lotus, moving on to a small case of kookaburras, 'all sorts of creatures, living in the jungle floor.'

'What, like—'

'Frogs, giant centipedes, tarantulas, that sort of thing.'

Tom shivered at the thought.

'And there's always a way out of the rainforest, if you know how.'

'With a map?'

'We didn't have a map,' replied Lotus confidently, 'didn't need one. We followed the raindrops.'

'The raindrops?'

'If you follow the raindrops you find that they trickle down into little streams. The little streams turn into big streams, and the big streams flow into small rivers. Then the small rivers flow into big rivers, and that's how, eventually, you find people, and they rescue you.'

She glanced up at Tom and could see that he was very impressed. She was rather pleased with the explanation herself.

'So . . . so that's how you got out?' he said at last.

She nodded. 'It took two months. Then some pygmies found us in their canoe, and when we got home we sold everything and came here.'

Tom whistled under his breath. That was some story; but there was something about the way she told it that he did not quite believe . . . Or maybe he was being too suspicious.

'I think I've seen enough now,' she said, casting one more exacting look around the gallery and noticing the broken skylight. 'Shall we go down?' And with a smile Lotus strode purposefully out of the room.

When Tom opened the door to the small yellow kitchen he was surprised to find a tea party going on.

'Hark, the next generation,' boomed Don Gervase, his long thin body looming over the table opposite Jos and Melba.

'Did anything particularly strike you, my dear?'

'Oh yes Papa,' replied Lotus sweetly, 'the birds are really fascinating. Quite a lot of extinct ones too.'

'Good. I am so glad. You see Jos, yet another Catcher has fallen under the spell of your museum. Now,' he said in a low silky voice, 'don't you think that it's about time the Scatterhorns and the Catchers buried the pratchet?'

'Hatchet.'

'*Exacto*. Made friends! How long have we been fighting?'

Uncle Jos whistled through his teeth as he made a rapid mental calculation.

'Four hundred years, give or take.'

'Four hundred years! *Surely* we should break with the past now. After all, the Scatterhorn museum, your life's work, is a monument to *both* our families—is it not?'

'Indeed,' snorted Jos folding his arms across his chest. That he could not deny.

'Well then, seeing that we shall be neighbours from now on, I for one see no point in continuing the quarrel. And apart from visiting the collection—which has been most illuminating for me—that is what I came here to say.'

Smiling to reveal his small, blackened teeth, Don Gervase rose to leave, his head almost touching the ceiling.

'Madame,' he purred, 'your coffee was quite excellent.'

'Thank you,' simpered Melba, who by now had been completely won over.

Don Gervase stooped down and made his way out into the

corridor followed by Lotus. On reaching the door of the museum he stopped as if he had just remembered something.

'Mrs Scatterhorn?'

'Melba, please.'

'Melba? Hmm . . . what a pretty name. Rather . . . peachy. Melba, it is a custom where I come from to repay one kindness with another, and now I should very much like to bring you a small gift of my own. I don't suppose you like real chocolate cake?'

'She's addicted to it,' Jos called out.

'Then I have a surprise for you, young lady,' declared Don Gervase, sweeping round to face her. Melba blushed; it had been twenty-five years since anyone had called her 'young lady'.

'Tomorrow I shall bring you a present. Gloria, my Peruvian housekeeper, makes chocolate cake using an old Indian recipe. Oranges, cinnamon, lime blossom and . . . the merest hint of chilli.'

'Gosh!' Melba clasped her hands in anticipation.

'It may smell rather strong,' added Gervase, 'or so I have been told as I must confess I have very little sense of smell. But don't let that put you off. It is quite spectacular.'

'Until tomorrow then,' said Jos opening the door.

'Indeed. Come, Lotus!'

Don Gervase clicked his fingers, and skipped down the steps towards the shining brown Bentley, where a heavy man was holding open the door.

'Thank you Humphrey,' boomed Don Gervase as he slipped inside.

Humphrey, who looked like an Inca god and was obviously very uncomfortable in his dog-tooth tweed suit, nodded shortly.

'Goodbye, Mr and Mrs Scatterhorn,' smiled Lotus, offering her hand, 'I did so much enjoy my visit.'

'Lovely to meet you, dear,' Melba cooed. Lotus turned to Tom and held out her hand to shake his. He took it with no enthusiasm.

'Bye, Tom. Come and see me sometime. You know you're my only friend in Dragonport.'

Tom smiled nervously and stared hard at the steps.

'You were all so kind.'

Tom, Uncle Jos and Aunt Melba stood together in the doorway and watched as Humphrey shut the heavy door behind Lotus.

'Never trust a Catcher,' hissed Jos between his teeth as the Bentley started up with a growl. Don Gervase grinned and waved.

'Well, I thought he was charming,' smiled Melba as she waved back. 'Odd looking, certainly, but charming.'

For his part, Tom did not know what to think. He could not forget those milky green eyes that had seemed to look right through his skull into his brain.

'He's after something, make no mistake about it,' wheezed Jos as he shuffled back into the museum and sat down heavily on the stairs. 'I just wonder what the devil it could be,' he said, pondering the dark cases all around. And he left it at that.

The questions thrown up by Don Gervase's visit refused to go away. After tea Jos decided to draw up a list. On one side he found seventeen reasons why the centuries-old quarrel between the Scatterhorns and the Catchers should never end, against the one and only reason why it should, and even that was suggested by Melba.

'Don Gervase has got the *money*,' she said as she sat knitting a pair of mittens. That was the truth of it. Money, it seemed, was the key to everything. Without it, the museum could not open, the roof could not be fixed, the heating could not be turned on and, most importantly of all, the animals could not be restored to their former glory. Uncle Jos thrust his hands deep into his pockets and stared hard at the long list of ancient grudges before him.

'I'm not fussy. Any old benefactor will do. So long as they're vastly rich and taxidermy-minded, like—'

'Don Gervase,' repeated Melba, her fingers skipping over the stitches.

'But he's a blinking CATCHER!'

Jos exhaled loudly.

'And a rare smelling one at that. No, he's *up* to something, they always are. I don't suppose you have any pocket money squirrelled away, Tom?'

Tom smiled and shook his head.

'What *nothing at all*? Bloody hell. No food, no pocket money; what *do* they give kids these days, eh?'

'Now get up to bed with you,' smiled Melba, putting down her knitting and handing Tom a hot water bottle, 'and take that as you'll need it.'

'Thanks,' replied Tom gratefully.

'I should think you've heard just enough nonsense for one night.'

'Allow me to escort you to your quarters, lad,' offered Jos, getting up and shuffling into the corridor, 'and let's give that confounded radiator one last try.'

Leading the way, Jos heaved himself up the rickety back stairs to Tom's tiny bedroom. Throwing open the door he found the small attic windows banging wide open in the wind. It was as cold as a morgue.

'Doesn't help, does it?' he muttered, shuffling through the obstacle course of boxes and slamming them hard shut. Tom shivered: it was so cold he could barely speak.

'Now then.' Jos bent down and, cocking his head, pressed his ear to the radiator which was making distant knocking noises. 'Let's see if we can coax this little lady into life.' He tapped it with his finger twice and listened.

'There's water there all right,' he wheezed, 'it's just not coming round this way. Here, what does that say?'

'I'm not really sure,' said Tom, squinting at the tiny rusted writing around the dial. 'Looks like another language.'

'Dutch most like, Tom, salvaged from a minesweeper. This is one my father put in. Stand by on the bilges,' he rasped, and slowly began to undo the nut. There was a distant hissing sound that seemed to get louder and louder until—pop! Suddenly a small fountain cascaded out of the radiator, and Jos immediately wedged his finger into the pipe.

'Well there's water all right. That's a start. Now,' Jos patted his pockets with his free hand, 'glasses—'

'In the kitchen?' suggested Tom.

'No no, before that. Must be in the museum somewhere.'

Tom thought for moment.

'On the stairs perhaps, where you were sitting down?'

'That's it, lad. Would you mind? Just go through the door, left into the corridor and follow it along to the main hall.'

'OK.'

'And don't be too long or else you may be needing a snorkel.'

'I won't,' called Tom as he scurried down the dark stairs and along the corridor towards the large mahogany door at the end. Turning the heavy brass latch he found it open, and the museum crouched in blackness beyond. The light switch was nowhere to be seen. Should he go back and ask Jos where it was? No—it's not far, he told himself. He knew where to go. Gingerly Tom stepped out into the corridor and holding on to the wall he started to edge forward. After a few steps he wished he'd brought his torch: it was so dark in there he could barely see his own hands and his feet seemed to have disappeared completely. He might have been walking along the rim of a volcano and not known it. Suddenly it seemed a very long way to the stairs. Still, best go on, before there's a flood.

Tom groped his way blindly along the wall until his fingers bumped against cold glass. He must have reached the first case. Fumbling his way around it he reached out and touched something round and smooth. That must be the round case containing the hummingbird tree, he thought, and squinting inside he could just make out tiny dark shapes against a spiky mass of foliage. Good, that meant he was close to the main hall. Feeling braver, he left the safety of the wall and held his arms outstretched. One step. Two steps. Three steps. How much further was it? Four—

'Ahh!'

Tom instantly recoiled. What was *that*?

Breathing hard he tentatively held out his hand again and very lightly traced along the edge of something hairy until he felt what might have been a finger. Or a toe. There was another scaly one next to it. Looking up, Tom thought he could see a long silvery tooth. It must be the gorilla, sitting in his tree.

Phew! Tom took a deep breath. It's only stuffed—long dead. Still, he didn't want to bump into any more. Dropping down to his hands and knees, Tom crawled across the hall to the corner of the stairs and felt along the carpet to the third step, where his hand brushed over something plastic. There they were, Jos's glasses . . . mission accomplished. Turning round, Tom peered out into the museum where he could just make out the shadows of the animals. But in the darkness if he hadn't known they were animals they might have been anything: a jumble of furniture—or rocks perhaps. It was better that way, thought Tom. Let's pretend they're rocks and get out of here.

Dropping down to his hands and knees again Tom crawled back across the hall until at last he reached the base of the corridor wall. Standing up, he groped his way back until he could just make out the large dark shape of the door at the end. He was nearly home now, only a few more steps.

Pud-pad, pud-pad pud-pad . . .

Tom froze. He listened. Peering out into the blackness he could see nothing.

Pud-pad pud-pad pud-pad . . .

A rhythmic unhurried sound, coming from the far end of the corridor. Then the sound seemed to turn a corner and as it did so Tom heard a click of something tapping on the stone floor.

Pud-pad, pud-pad pud-pad pud . . .

It was getting closer.

'Hello?'

His voice sounded tiny as it echoed out into the museum. Suddenly the sound stopped. There was silence. Tom felt the hairs begin to stand up on the back of his neck. He could see nothing, but he had the distinct sensation that he was being watched. By what? Perhaps it was that rat! That rat with its horrible red eyes.

'Plankton?' said Tom as loudly and bravely as he could. His heart was hammering against his chest.

'Hello?' he said again, this time more forcefully. The eyes were still on him. There was a shuffle just a few feet in front, then Tom had the distinct sensation of a shape moving past him in the corridor. If he had put his hand out he might have touched it, whatever it was. But he was too terrified.

Pud-pad, pud-pad pud-pad pud . . .

Listening hard, Tom followed the sound of the footsteps down the corridor towards the main hall of the museum.

Click!

The scrape of claws on stone again. And at that moment Tom saw, or thought he saw, the long grey outline of a wolf trot around the corner.

By the time Tom reached the safety of his bedroom he was shaking. Uncle Jos was sitting on the bed, wiping his hands with a rag and suddenly Tom remembered the flooding radiator.

'Looks like you won't be needing that snorkel after all, lad,' he said brightly. 'It's fixed. Left-hand thread.'

'Oh. G-g-great.'

Taking the glasses Jos looked up and saw that Tom was paler than ever.

'Are you all right, boy?'

'Yes . . . I'm . . . I'm fine,' stammered Tom, 'just a bit dark down there.'

'Indeedy,' said Jos with a twinkle. 'It tends to be at night time.'

Tom could barely manage a smile.

'And darkness plays all manner of tricks on the mind, don't you think?'

Tom felt the colour begin to rise to his cheeks. Suddenly he was beginning to feel rather foolish.

'Well, I *know* it does with mine,' said Jos patting the radiator. 'Anyway, she's up and running now so I'll be off. Thanks for the specs.'

And he was gone.

That night Tom lay in bed, his mind racing with questions. Should he *believe* what he could not see? And what *did* he see anyway? *Was* that wolf only in his imagination? Tom pulled all the covers over his head and before he had found the answers he drifted into a restless sleep, teeming with animals and ghosts. And somewhere near the centre of that kaleidoscope of dreams was the shadow of a large bird, sitting quietly on Tom's windowsill, watching him.

CHAPTER 5

To Catcher Hall

The next day dawned bright and cold and the wind had died completely. Such things happened, even in Dragonport. By the time Tom came downstairs he found Uncle Jos out in the backyard splitting logs with a heavy axe.

'Ah, there you are,' he said, looking up at Tom through his fogged glasses. 'Sleep OK?'

'Fine thanks.'

Tom had already decided to keep his adventure of the previous night a secret, but he had plenty of questions that Jos might be able to answer. He watched as Jos placed another log upright on the chopping block and slowly raised the axe, staggering backwards under its weight.

'Don't you want a hand?' asked Tom, as Jos wobbled this way and that, 'I could—'

'No,' interrupted Jos through his teeth, 'if it's too heavy for me, it's far too heavy for you,' and he brought the axe head flying down with a dull thonk!, sending shards of wood spinning in all directions.

'I tell you something, lad,' gasped Jos, leaning forward on the axe to catch his breath. 'As you get older you certainly don't get any younger.' His breath steamed out of his mouth like a dragon.

'Jos?'

'Hmm?' He spat loudly.

'You know the story about the little clockwork shrew that August had made?'

Jos thought for a moment.

'Indeedy. The winking shrew.'

'Have you still got it?'

'Have I still got it?' he repeated. 'I might. Why, I suppose you want to see it?'

Tom smiled. This was a good start.

'Only if it's not too much trouble. Whenever you—'

'Whenever, eh? Well,' he blew, 'I can't pretend I'm exactly enjoying myself so why not now. *If* I can find it, that is,' and with that he wedged the axe into the chopping block and grabbed his jacket. 'Follow me, lad.'

Jos set off towards the end of the garden where an enormous creeper covered the entire wall. Hidden underneath it Tom could just make out the shape of a small wooden shed flecked with cracked green paint.

'Your aunt calls this "the go down",' he puffed, pulling hard on a door that was so rotten it looked as if it might come away in his hand, 'because you have to "go down" the garden to get to it. Though I prefer its official title, "museum annex". Here lad, lend us a hand.'

Tom grabbed the bottom, Jos took the top, and after much heaving and panting they managed to force an entrance wide enough to squeeze through.

Inside the tiny shed were piles of boxes that almost filled the floor, and a shelf at the back on which rested stacks of old black and white photographs.

'Now then,' muttered Jos to himself as he began to rummage about in the junk. 'Most of this gubbins used to be in the museum, but my father had a clear out, God knows when, and—aha,' he said, bending down deep into a tea chest. '*This* might be what you're after.'

Wiping a thick layer of dust off the bench, he sat down and held up a very old and very dirty rodent with long yellow teeth. Blowing away the grime Jos set it down on its flat metal feet.

'Now, with any luck,' he said, placing his thumb in the centre of the shrew's back. A small compartment flipped open to reveal a thin black winder. 'The key's still in it.'

Jos turned the winder a few times, then closed the compartment and waited. The shrew began to whirr, and then suddenly it sprang up, turning a full somersault in mid-air before landing back on the bench.

'Not bad, eh?' rasped Jos appreciatively. 'But hold your horses, there's more. Here, get a little closer.'

Tom crouched down beside Jos and peered at the scruffy little creature. There was another whirring of springs, and then the shrew suddenly swivelled its head towards Tom—and winked.

'Ha ha!' shouted Jos with delight. 'The winking shrew! It works!'

Then the shrew gave one last leap and hopped right back into the tea chest.

'I should think that's the first time anyone's winked in here in about thirty years,' wheezed Jos, his small black eyes twinkling beneath his enormous eyebrows. Tom stared down at the small metal feet paddling in mid-air; it just looked like a toy that had been left in a bin. Was it really something like this that he had seen in the museum?

'Jos?'

'Mmm?'

Jos had retrieved the shrew from the chest and he was fiddling with the winder.

'Do you think August ever made an animal that moved in a better way?'

'How do you mean?'

'Not like a clockwork toy. More . . . sort of naturally,' suggested Tom. 'More like—'

'More like the real thing, you mean?' said Jos, squinting over his spectacles. 'I think not, lad. Everything in there's over a hundred years old and stuffed solid. They're all full of sawdust, cotton rags, even newspaper.'

'Newspaper?'

'Oh yes,' replied Jos. 'Once August had made the mould and stretched the skin over it, he often used newspaper to pack them out. Here.'

Jos picked up the shrew and inspected its neck. On one side just below the ear was a small hole.

'There you go,' he said passing it to Tom, 'you've got small fingers, see if you can grab a bit.'

Carefully Tom pinched a piece of paper showing through the hole and pulled at it. Out came a long crumbled slice of newspaper.

'See?' said Jos. 'What does it say there?'

Tom squinted down at the closely set print.

'*Burning of a Smack at Sea,*' he read, '*14th September 1899.*'

'That's a boat. Must have been the headlines of the day. And on the back?'

Tom turned it over and peered hard at the tiny text. He could barely read the sentences.

'Something about cricket,' he said.

'August used lots of that stuff. Particularly the brain cavities, I seem to remember.'

'The brain cavities?'

'Yep. My father had to sew up that arctic rabbit once; its head was full of it. I think it was from the Bible. Proverbs, if I remember correctly.'

Tom stared down at the long-legged shrew spilling paper out of its neck and remembered those paws scratching on the stone and that long low shape trotting away into the darkness. This was not right at all.

'Jos?'

Uncle Jos cocked his head and peered bewilderedly over at Tom. Was this thin blond boy *ever* going to stop asking questions? Something in those dark insistent eyes told him not.

'Do you think the museum might be haunted?'

'By what, lad?'

'I don't know. Ghosts of animals perhaps?'

Jos folded his arms across his chest and pushed his spectacles back up his nose.

'So, *that's* what spooked you in the museum last night, is it?'

Tom smiled sheepishly and he felt the colour flood to his cheeks. He had intended to keep his adventure to himself but Jos had guessed it.

'And that's why you wanted to have a squint at this old toy,' Jos continued, his eyes twinkling, 'just to see how realistic it is, in case there's another one in there. I get the picture.'

'I just, wondered—' Tom began, feeling very foolish, 'whether . . . if any of them did move—not to say that they do—but, say, *if* they did; then, maybe, they might be more special than they look.'

He glanced up, fully expecting Uncle Jos to burst out laughing, but he didn't. Jos just sat there scratching his chin, considering this idea very carefully.

'Well Tom, maybe you're right about that,' he said at last. 'There's always been a lot of talk about what's in this museum, one way or another. Old August Catcher was quite a character, you know, Sir Henry too,' added Jos mysteriously, staring at the piles of dusty photos on the shelves. 'I tell you what,' said Jos, suddenly turning to him, 'I wonder if you could do me a favour.'

Tom could not imagine what it might be.

'Why don't *you* go up to Catcher Hall?'

'Me?'

'That's right. By way of returning the compliment, so to speak. After all, the Catchers have paid the Scatterhorns a visit, and it's a good forty years since *that* last happened. These things don't occur by accident.'

Tom could see that Uncle Jos was serious.

'But . . . but I thought we didn't like them.'

'We don't. Necessarily. At all. We just need to see the cut of their jib.'

'The cut of their jib?'

'Size them up. See if they really is who they says they is.' Jos leant forward and raised one huge hairy eyebrow. 'Chocolate millionaire, recently widowed, escaped from the jungle and all that jazz. Quite a tale, don't you think?'

Tom thought back to Lotus in the bird gallery the previous afternoon. There certainly was something strange in the way she had told her story. It was almost as if she was *pleased* that it had happened.

'But—how?'

'Well, you could always try walking up the hill and knocking on the door. That's not illegal, now is it?'

Tom thought for a moment. He really wasn't at all sure about getting involved in Uncle Jos's ancient quarrel with the Catchers.

'Don't you want to come?'

'Me? Absolutely not,' snorted Jos, 'I wouldn't be seen dead anywhere near the place. Never have and never will. But you, Tom, you are the new boy. You can break the rules. And anyway,' he added, 'you've the perfect excuse or have you forgotten?'

Tom looked at Jos blankly.

'Little Miss Fancypants asked you over. You're her only friend in Dragonport, remember?'

Jos was right, Lotus *had* asked him. But even so, Tom shivered at the thought of meeting the weird Don Gervase again, and even Lotus . . . it felt as if he had been asked to enter the web of a vast spider.

'OK,' he said at last, 'I'll go.'

'Good lad.' Jos smiled cheerily, pleased that he had got what he wanted. 'Just act normal. Be polite. And check it out. I'll see you later.'

It was a short distance down the street to the river. At the bottom Tom reached a narrow bridge that he recognized from the model in the museum, as it had small triangular passing places which must once have been used by pedestrians to avoid being run over by carts. The bridge was busy with Christmas shoppers and Tom was careful not to catch anyone's eye. He was already beginning to regret his promise, and part of him was more than inclined to go and sit in a café for an hour or two and invent some story about how he had been up to Catcher Hall and what he had found there. But Tom couldn't help feeling a little curious too, despite himself, and maybe he could have a look around without actually having to *meet* either Lotus or Don Gervase in person . . .

By the time Tom had reached the top of the steep hill on the other side of the river he was panting hard, and pausing a moment he looked back at Dragonport spread out beneath him, glinting in the pale winter sun. The view must have been almost the same as it was a hundred years ago; for there were the crumbling towers of the Scatterhorn museum, still standing high above the rooftops, and beyond it the river, curling out into the estuary like a silver snake. Out on the horizon he could just make out the pencil skeleton of a radio mast, and beyond it the long grey shapes of tankers, barely moving in the mist.

As Tom stood there his attention was caught by a gang of angry seagulls below him. They were wheeling and circling around the silhouette of another, far larger bird, that was flying right through the heart of them, ignoring the commotion all around. Tom watched as the bird's vast wings beat out a slow, lazy rhythm and he was sure he had never seen any bird as big as this in his life. Perhaps it was an albatross blown off course by a storm, or an eagle escaped from a zoo. And as the great bird disappeared behind some trees below him, Tom reluctantly turned back to the task in hand: Catcher Hall.

On the other side of the road there was a small gravel drive that led up between two large laurel bushes. Tom walked across and he could find no number or name anywhere, except a small discarded sign in the undergrowth that read 'Beware of the Dog'. By the look of it that dog was long dead and seeing that this was the only house at the very top of the hill, Tom decided to explore a little further. Ten metres further up, the drive narrowed and bent round to the left, and Tom had just set off around the corner when he heard the low roar of a car accelerating towards him. Barely did he have time to fling himself into the dense laurel bushes before a large brown shape sped round the bend, and as it flew past he could make out the silhouette of Humphrey, the large Inca, behind the wheel, and next to him Don Gervase, his eyes set hard on the road. In the back seat sat a little old lady the colour of a nut, clutching a large white box to her chest. In a moment they had disappeared around the corner and the narrow drive was empty once more.

OK, thought Tom, this *was* Catcher Hall all right, and without Don Gervase around, the prospect of going on suddenly seemed a little more appealing. But Lotus might still be at home . . . Disentangling himself from the bushes Tom decided to walk just a little further, and soon he found himself standing on the edge of a long wide lawn dotted with trees. Beyond was a large white house with battlements, framed by three ancient cedars. The sun was so bright that he had to shield his eyes to look at it, but even so, he noticed that there were large cracks in the plaster and several of the windows on the ground floor were completely overgrown with ivy. It looked old, and once must have been very grand. As he drew closer Tom heard the sound of a piano playing somewhere in the house. It seemed to be coming from three tall windows that stretched down to the ground. Just then Tom spotted something glittering halfway up the window. It was a wire flashing in the sunlight. The next moment the wire wobbled slightly and Lotus suddenly appeared—apparently stepping through the air—halfway up the room.

Tom gasped; there was no net, no pole to help her balance, she was walking on the wire. Lotus stopped and seemed to compose herself. What's she going to do next? thought Tom, and as if in reply, Lotus suddenly leapt up into the air in a backwards flip. The wire bounced and rippled as she landed, but Lotus stayed completely poised, her head bobbing slightly and her arms held out, holding a perfect balance. Tom stood transfixed: that was some trick. Then she did it again, this time with a forward somersault, and again the landing was perfect. Lotus paused and then walked along the wire out of Tom's view. He expected her to come back and she did, moments later—doing cartwheels.

Tom could hardly believe what he was seeing now; how is that possible on a wire? He racked his brains, trying to remember watching the Olympics on TV with his father and wondering if he had ever seen gymnasts performing cartwheels on a high wire. He decided he hadn't. Lotus was extraordinary; there was no doubt about it.

With this in mind, Tom decided that he could quite happily

investigate the rest of Catcher Hall on his own. Creeping further around the house Tom found himself opposite a study. One of the french windows was open, and through it he could just make out the flickering blue lights of a computer screen. On the wall there was a large map, which had various small flags dotted about all over it. There was something inviting about this study, and for a moment Tom could not think what it was. Then he realized: it was the smell that was wafting through the window; the most delicious, mouthwatering smell of chocolate. It was intoxicating, and Tom closed his eyes for a moment, drinking it in . . .

'Ruuuuff!'

A bark as loud as a cymbal crashed in his ear. Tom whipped round, but instead of the large slathering Dobermann he expected, he looked down to see a small squash-nosed pug with enormous bug eyes staring up at him angrily.

'Ruffuffuffuff-uf!'

The noise was deafening.

'Shshhhh!' Tom whispered. 'Go away.'

The pug backed away slightly, flattened its stumpy little ears, then barked even louder.

'Ruffuffuffuff-RRR!'

This dog may have been small, but it was very, very noisy. Just then a window opened and Lotus leant out.

'Zeus?' she shouted. 'Zeusy!'

'RRR ruffruffruff-rrrrRUFF!' barked Zeus, louder than ever.

It was definitely time to go. With Zeus buzzing like an angry wasp behind him, Tom darted back between the yew trees, carefully trying to avoid being seen from the windows of the house.

'Zeus!'

'RRRRRrrrRRR!' Zeus the angry dog was not going to give up.

Tom sprinted even faster, and just as he raced out across the last stretch of lawn before the laurel bushes a large shadow appeared on the grass in front of him. At first Tom thought it was an aeroplane, but quite suddenly there was a loud rushing sound and Zeus's growling turned into a high-pitched squeal. It all happened so fast that Tom dared not turn round, and only when he tumbled into the safety of the bushes did he glance back to see Zeus racing towards the house, yelping in terror. What had happened? The dog must have been spooked by something—what? Tom was panting so hard he couldn't think, but there was a word drumming in his brain that sounded like 'theyellartowvit'. 'The—yell—ar—tow—vit'? Tom was convinced that someone had whispered it just now, someone very close . . . who . . . ? what . . . ?

Tom didn't want to hang around to find out. Instead of returning the way he had come, he tore into the thicket of laurel bushes and shrubs and forced his way through to the perimeter wall. Scrambling up the trunk of a magnolia tree he shimmied out as far as he dared onto the lowest branch and looked down. He was still a good three metres off the ground. He just needed to get a little further out to lower himself down . . . suddenly Tom heard the low growl of a car accelerating up the hill towards him. Could that be . . .

Crack! Glancing up, Tom saw the branch start to bend alarmingly. He barely had time to let go before there was a loud snap and Tom dropped to the pavement like a stone with the branch clattering noisily beside him.

Picking himself up off the ground Tom thrust his dirty hands into his pockets and began to walk away fast up the hill, tucking his chin into his jacket. The car behind him slowed. Don't turn round: it was Don Gervase, it must be. Lotus must have spotted him and the game was up. Tom focused on the cracks in the cement in the wall ahead of him and quickened his pace. Don't turn round. He heard the sound of an electric window winding down. *Don't turn round—*

'You all right, son?'

Across the road were two police officers sitting in a squad car watching him suspiciously. Tom smiled as innocently as he could.

'Yes. I'm . . . I'm just going . . . erm . . . home,' he said, trying hard to ignore his heart thumping against his ribcage. The older officer, who had a thin moustache, looked down at Tom's filthy jumper and muddy trousers.

'That was a bit of a tumble.'

'Yeah. I . . . er . . . it's my friends' house. We were playing a game,' explained Tom breathlessly.

'A game?' repeated the Moustache.

'Yeah,' Tom lied.

The Moustache raised his eyebrows and Tom shifted uneasily from one foot to the other.

'Catcher Hall's empty isn't it?' said the other officer, who had a babyface.

'No, no it's not,' replied Tom, 'there's—'

Just then a large shadow passed over the car, and both policemen leaned forward into the sun to see an object the size of a hang glider disappear over the tops of the trees.

'Might be our bird, sir,' said Babyface.

The Moustache grimaced.

'Indeed, Moon,' he said, and gave Tom one last long stare. 'It doesn't do to go monkeying about in other people's gardens, you know.'

Slowly the police car pulled away and Tom stood still and waited till it was out of sight. He felt as if he had been let off with a caution—for what, he was not sure.

By the time Tom reached the Scatterhorn Museum it was dark. He had deliberately taken his time returning, hoping that he would not have to join in Don Gervase's tea party, and as Tom let himself in the side door he was relieved to find the chocolate coloured Bentley no longer parked outside. All he had to do now was to try to think of something convincing to report to Uncle Jos. After all, his mission had not been a success; he hadn't even got inside Catcher Hall, and he could hardly admit that he had been chased off the premises by a very small and very angry dog. Still, there was Lotus and her acrobatics, that was something . . . Taking a deep breath Tom opened the door of the kitchen to find Uncle Jos and Aunt Melba smiling broadly, apparently at nothing at all.

'Hi,' he said, taking off his jumper.

Jos and Melba just giggled: maybe they were drunk. On the table before them were the remains of an enormous chocolate cake.

'Tom boy, you have just missed a real treat,' said Jos and he held up his hand. 'Your aunt and I must plead guilty to making complete pigs of ourselves.'

'Without a doubt,' added Melba, swaying slightly, 'that has to be the best chocolate cake I have ever eaten in my life.'

She leant forward and picked some crumbs off the large plate where Plankton was busy polishing up the remains. Tom noticed that even he looked a little unsteady.

'Have a smackerel, lad, before that greedy rat scrounges it all,' rasped Jos, and skewering a small piece on the end of his knife he offered it up to Tom. Tom took the slither between his fingers and put it in his mouth. Immediately the cake dissolved into the most wonderful series of tastes. It was like oranges, limes, cinnamon, ice-cream, and above all, chocolate. Rich, sweet, dark, mouthwatering chocolate, unlike anything he had ever tasted.

'Well lad?'

'It's amazing.'

'Don Gervase was very insistent that you should try some,' said Jos, 'but I am afraid Melba has gobbled more than half of it up on her own.'

'She's an artist and a magician that Gloria,' slurred Melba, 'and to think that Don Gervase can't even smell it—let alone taste it.'

'He has no idea what he is missing.'

Perhaps he does, thought Tom; perhaps he knows very well the effects of Gloria's cake. And Tom recognized that intoxicating smell: it was the same as that wafting through the window of Catcher Hall; a smell so good that you wanted to eat it. No wonder they both looked drunk.

Jos yawned loudly.

'Lordy Lordy,' he said, 'time for bed I think. Melba—what say you?'

Melba did not answer; her eyes were already closed.

'MELBETINA!' roared Jos.

Melba's head jerked up with a start, and she opened her eyes dreamily.

'Yes dear?'

'Bedtime, my peach!'

'Goodness me, is that the time already?' she said, dragging herself to her feet. Tom glanced up at the clock; it wasn't even seven o'clock.

'Right,' mumbled Jos as he shuffled towards the door, 'Tom, you can take the first watch tonight.'

'Uncle Jos,' said Tom quietly as Jos steadied himself on the door handle, 'I had an *interesting* time at Catcher Hall.'

Jos stared at Tom woozily. He had obviously forgotten all about Tom's little errand.

'Good lad. Well done. Now make sure you tell me all about it—' and he yawned loudly, 'tomorrow.'

Whatever was in that cake must have been strong, thought Tom. Even though he had only eaten a small slither he could feel his own eyelids closing too. Slowly he clambered up the narrow backstairs to the attic, hanging on to the banisters to stay on his feet. At each step the temperature seemed to drop several degrees, and the creeping cold sharpened his senses so that by the time he reached the low door he was wide awake once more. Opening the door Tom was hit by a blast of air that almost knocked his breath away. Moonlight streamed in through the open window and the curtains billowed wildly—it was like walking into an icebox. Cursing loudly, Tom picked his way over to the window and forced the latch shut. Why was it that whenever he came up to his room the window was always open?

Feeling angry now, Tom turned to look at the narrow sagging bed with its thin blankets and wondered how he was ever going to stay warm tonight. Jos would never understand, how could he? He had ample supplies of what he called 'natural insulation'; in other words he was as well padded as a walrus. He did not feel the cold, and neither did Melba apparently. But Tom did, he couldn't help it. He was born wiry and whippety, just like his parents, and he had no natural insulation whatsoever. Rummaging about in his bag, Tom pulled on another pair of trousers and two more pairs of socks, then searched about for his thick black fleece and a brown skiing hat his mother had given him. Then he grabbed all the blankets and wound himself up inside them like a cocoon. That was better. Lying on his back, Tom breathed out slowly and watched his own breath float up as steam in the moonlight.

For ten long minutes Tom tried hard to go to sleep. But the cold kept him awake and his mind was racing. Perhaps Jos and Melba had been drugged by the cake. Perhaps Don Gervase was planning something tonight . . . supposing there *was* something alive in the museum that Jos did not know about . . . shouldn't he go and find out? Tom didn't know. He closed his eyes and tried to think of something else. Slowly another picture began to form in his mind: his father camping on the edge of an immense forest and his mother battling through the icy wind towards him. They were there, both of them, and Tom half wondered if he would ever see them again. Would he? Tom didn't know the answer to that question either.

Half an hour later the cold had crept under Tom's bedclothes and his teeth were chattering uncontrollably. This room was probably the coldest place he had ever been in his life. Tom sat up and looked across at the window—it was open, again! Moonlight was streaking in and the curtains were flapping. Tom jumped up, and with all his blankets wrapped around him he hopped across the floor and forced the window shut once more. Lying back down on his bed he saw there was no point trying to get to sleep; he was too cold. What was it his mother used to say?

'If you're wide awake,' he whispered to himself out loud, 'it's much better to get up and—'

'Do something.'

Tom blinked. He had been about to say 'do something', but he hadn't. Someone else had. Tom stared at the wall, his eyes wide open. Someone had said 'Do something', here in this room; he was sure of it. Tom's eyes widened and he listened hard. Nothing. Then, very slowly he rolled over and looked across the room. The boxes of books and piles of newspapers were all there, shadows in the half-light. That was fine. The window was shut. Good. In the corner at the end of his bed was a large umbrella hanging on the wall. Fine. Wait a moment.

Wait a moment.

Tom's heart leapt in his throat. Large umbrella? There was no large umbrella in this room! Tom stared at the end of his bed again and saw that it wasn't an umbrella at all. It was the unmistakable shape of a bird, and a large bird at that. An eagle. And the eagle was watching him with its angry yellow eyes.

'Do something.'

The bird shuffled on its perch slightly. Did it say . . . ? No, it couldn't have. Tom wondered whether he was dreaming—maybe he was. Very slowly Tom slipped out of his bed and edged backwards towards the door.

'Do something.'

The voice sounded Australian . . . how? The huge eagle hopped off its perch and clattered down to a patch of moonlight in the centre of the room. It stood taller than Tom and began walking towards him threateningly.

'Downstairs, kiddo.'

In a moment Tom lifted the latch and fled as fast as he could down the rickety back stairs. Bursting into the kitchen he slammed the door hard behind him. Tom closed his eyes and struggled to breathe.

Control yourself. It's a nightmare. It's only a nightmare.

'We meet again.'

Tom looked up. Perched on a kitchen chair beside the open window was the eagle.

'Wrong room.'

Tom felt his skin begin to crawl and he had a strong urge to be sick. What was going on? Wrenching open the kitchen door he ran down the corridor to the large oak door at the end. With one jerk he pulled the heavy brass lever down and pushed hard against it, and the great door swung open silently as if of its own accord. Beyond it was the museum, pitch dark and silent. Should he go any further?

Tom stood on the threshold, his heart hammering in his temples. He certainly didn't want to meet that wolf again—or whatever it was. But what on earth was that huge talking eagle doing in his room—and in the kitchen? If he did not know better, he would have guessed that it was chasing him.

'Now that's more like it.'

Tom glanced back down the corridor and froze. The eagle had stepped out of the kitchen and was glowering at him.

'Much, much better.'

Stretching out its vast wings so that they brushed the walls the eagle began to march down the corridor. It *was* chasing him.

'N-n-no—' whispered Tom, 'please—'

'Rattle your dags!' growled the eagle, quickening its pace to a run.

Rattle your dags? Tom panicked. Scrambling out into the darkness he leant as hard as he could on the heavy door. Slowly it began to swing back until—thump! The brass lever clicked home and the door shut. Any second Tom expected the great door to burst open again and the eagle to appear, but nothing happened. There was a scratching sound, then a low clunk as the hasp rammed home. Tom gasped: the eagle had locked him in!

What was he supposed to do now? Shout for Jos? He'd never hear him. Try to phone the police? There probably wasn't a phone, and anyway, what would he say? 'Excuse me, sir, but I've been locked in the museum by a giant talking bird.' Tom cursed softly. No, that wouldn't work either. He would just have to wait. Wait until morning when Jos would let him out. He must spend the night in the museum. There was no choice. No choice at all. Taking a deep breath, Tom felt for the wall with his fingertips, and fumbled his way blindly into the darkness.

CHAPTER 6

Midnight in the Museum

At first they were all just black blobs. Tom did not know the museum well enough to recognize each animal in its case, but he guessed which shape belonged to which animal. There was a giant pair of sharp black scissors at the back of the African diorama—that must be the antelope. At the base of the rainforest there was a rolled up sleeping bag with a pipe attached to one end that was the anteater. Over to the left a long line of luminous loaves of bread stood on a shelf, which Tom knew to be sturgeon and dogfish, and at their centre was a pale spiky balloon with a pair of lips. The puffer fish. Everything was silent in the moonlight. Nothing moved. That's good. Tom drew up his knees on the velvet bench below the stairs and pressed himself deeper into the panelled wall. He might have been locked in, but maybe this wasn't going to be so bad after all.

Tom had no idea how long he had sat there, but he woke from his shallow sleep with a start. Suddenly he felt very stiff and very cold. He looked at his watch, it was five minutes to midnight. He tried to stretch out his legs but they wouldn't move, his knees had gone completely numb. Glancing around he noticed that the museum had become brighter now: the moon had risen and shone directly down through the skylight, picking out the head of the dodo, which was almost luminous. It was very, very quiet. Tom rubbed his eyes and wondered how much longer it would stay that way. Would that wolf reappear in the corridor? He had no idea. He still could not be certain if it had really been a wolf at all. Perhaps it hadn't, but he was certain that the eagle had herded him into the museum on purpose; after all, it had even locked him in. For whatever reason, he was supposed to be in here. Something was going to happen: but what?

Tom was just on the point of closing his eyes again when he was half aware that it had become darker. At first he thought it must be a cloud passing in front of the moon. Then, out of the corner of his eye Tom saw the reflection of something brown moving very slowly above him.

What was that?

There was a branch as thick as his leg floating in the air, stretching out until it had almost reached the far wall. Tom's eyes followed the branch to its bulbous end where the small but unmistakable shape of a small black tongue flicked out. A snake! Tom shrank back deeper into his shadow. *Was* it a snake? It certainly looked like a snake. Its skin was olive green and yellow, and as it stretched, Tom could clearly see dark markings all over its back. Suddenly Tom's heart began to thump louder in his throat. He recognized this snake, he had a picture of it on his bedroom wall. It was an anaconda, the largest snake in the world, powerful enough to squeeze the life out of a horse. And here it was, floating in the darkness just above his head! Tom was wide awake now, and he was terrified.

The anaconda's head disappeared around the corner into the foyer. Then from behind him there was a cough. It was loud and unmistakable, definitely someone clearing their throat. Tom turned round, half expecting to see Uncle Jos standing there, but instead he saw what looked like a giant climb out of a tree. The gorilla! The gorilla took a few paces forward and yawned loudly, revealing a set of sharp teeth that glittered in the moonlight.

'Another long day at the coalface.'

Tom almost jumped off his bench. The gorilla had just spoken! Was he dreaming? Tom was not sure. The gorilla flopped down onto the floor and stretched his legs in the air. Tom pinched himself hard, and then he sensed something moving down the stairs behind him. Hardly daring to turn round he saw a scaly anteater laboriously making its way down sideways, taking one step at a time. When it reached the bottom it nodded to the gorilla and trotted away.

'Nothing more than a chicken!' shrieked a high-pitched Welsh voice. 'Nothing more than a chicken, he said. Did you hear that?'

Suddenly there was a Welsh woman only a few steps from Tom's hiding place, only it wasn't: it was the dodo, who had stepped down from her podium and was preening herself in the pool of silver moonlight.

'I've never heard such nonsense in all my life,' she continued. 'Chicken indeed.'

Tom watched open-mouthed as the strange looking bird paced around in a circle, admiring her shadow on the floor.

'Now does that look like a chicken to you?' she said, looking up in the air expectantly. There was a very low rumbling grunt, that sounded far off in the distance but in fact was very close indeed.

'Ma'am, a chicken you are not,' said a voice, sounding as if it had been spoken down a long pipe. Then one whole side of the museum appeared to move forward and shake its front leg. It was the mammoth, whose great shining tusks swung gently to the floor.

'You are without question the finest looking dodo I have ever seen,' he said, uncoiling his trunk. The dodo cocked her head, slightly puzzled.

'I should hope that I am the *only* dodo you have ever seen.'

'Indeed, ma'am. First among dodos.'

'Well you, sir, are the finest looking mammoth I have ever seen,' she replied. The mammoth bowed low, pleased with the compliment.

'I have always thought that being extinct puts one at a tremendous advantage,' he boomed. 'When there's only one of one one cannot be compared with anyone else.'

'Unlike all this riff-raff,' said the dodo, casting her large yellow eye around the room. 'It's like Noah's ark in here.'

By now there was a steady hum of chatter all around. In each case animals climbed down from their perches and stretched and gossiped with one another. Some of the larger animals had opened their cases by themselves and were wandering about the hall, but the rodents and the birds waited patiently for the proboscis monkey—who seemed to be the appointed doorman—to slide open the back of each case in turn and let them out.

'Good evening, good evening, a very good evening to you,' he said politely to each and every one, as if welcoming them to a party. It was all done so casually it might have been an everyday occurrence. Perhaps, thought Tom with a shiver, it was.

Pad-pud pad-pud pad-pud . . .

Tom whipped round just as a large grey wolf with milky eyes trotted past his hiding place and up the stairs, touching its nose against a pillar before running down again. That was it! The wolf: it wasn't a ghost, it was real and he hadn't imagined it but . . . how could it be? It was dead, stuffed, and yet quite clearly it wasn't. It was a wild animal, running around inches away from him.

'I say,' boomed the mammoth as he shuffled forward, 'we really must take that dip in the baths one evening.'

'I can think of nothing more delightful,' replied the dodo, wiggling her tail feathers appreciatively.

'And then perhaps I could show you my new stroke. I've been practising, you know.'

'You have?'

'Oh yes. It's all in the arm. It actually goes over one's head. Like so.' And with that the mammoth attempted to demonstrate what might have been the front crawl with one front leg.

'No. Almost. Once again. Yes. Yes . . . erm . . . '

The mammoth lost his balance and began hopping sideways towards the case of small mammals.

'Hmm,' he boomed, just about recovering his feet, 'quite an extraordinary idea really. But they do say one goes twice as fast.'

'Well, you *are* the defending champion,' replied the dodo pointedly, 'I suppose you'll have to get used to it.'

'Yes, one really must adapt,' sniffed the great beast. 'Jolly hard though—if you're a mammoth.'

Tom sat listening in the shadows and wondered if he really had gone mad. First there was the bird—that was strange enough. Now he was hiding in the darkest corner of a museum full of tatty stuffed animals who, on the stroke of midnight, had all started moving about and talking to one another in English about swimming! It was frightening and yet, at the same time, it wasn't. It was funny and it was weird. He had wanted to find out if the animals moved or not; well, here was the answer, and the answer was unbelievable. Tom was no longer in a museum, he was in a zoo: a zoo full of talking animals.

The more he watched them the more impossible it seemed that the animals were moving by clockwork. They must have brains as well, how else could they hold a conversation with each other? Perhaps August Catcher *was* a genius after all, perhaps he had created a museum of incredible Victorian robots whose faded skins hid some kind of advanced mechanical engines that nobody knew about. Or maybe, *one* person knew about them: Don Gervase Askary.

That's it! thought Tom, his eyes widening at this sudden revelation. That's what he's after, that's why Uncle Jos is so suspicious. Don Gervase must know that all the animals move, which is why he is being so friendly. Don Gervase wants to have them for himself.

As Tom was thinking about the implications of all this he became aware of something cold and hard hovering just behind his neck. The cold hard thing nuzzled around his fleece as if searching for something. Instinctively Tom closed his eyes, and the next moment he felt a jerk and he was lifted clean off the ground by the scruff of his neck. Tom struggled, but whatever was behind him held his shirt with an iron grip and he was carried out of the shadows as if he weighed nothing at all. As he emerged the entire museum fell silent, and a hundred eyes peered at him through the darkness. Tom was set down roughly in the empty patch of moonlight.

'We have a guest,' said a gruff voice. Looking up Tom saw a large brown bear standing on its hind legs above him, pointing down with its black steel claw.

Somewhere out in the gloom came a low growl. Tom felt the hairs on the back of his neck stand on end. What were they going to do? Eat him? They couldn't . . . could they? Tom was now so frightened he could barely breathe. At last the dodo hobbled forward and looked him up and down with her large yellow eye.

'Come closer, boyo,' she said.

Tom bent down obediently and looked straight into the eyes of the turkey-sized bird.

'No, no, right up close.'

Tom bent even lower, and felt the dodo inspect every inch of his face. He closed his eyes, fully expecting to be pecked by that great bone-crushing beak at any moment.

'I thought as much,' she sniffed. The dodo waddled away and then turned to face him triumphantly. 'If it isn't young Tom Scatterhorn!'

An excited whisper went round the animals.

'Tom Scatterhorn, *Tom Scatterhorn* . . . It's Tom Scatterhorn . . . he's back . . . '

Tom glanced up to see the gallery above him was lined with birds all twittering to each other.

'Welcome back, Tom,' said a low booming voice and the mammoth stretched out its long hairy trunk and curled itself around Tom's hand. 'It has been a very long time.'

Tom looked up at the mountainous shape of the mammoth to see two bright black eyes twinkling. What did it mean welcome back; he had never been here before! Then the trunk let go of his hand and began to explore around him. As it brushed past his face Tom noticed that the inside of the mammoth's trunk smelt very peculiar and it reminded him of something, but he was not sure what.

By now Tom was bursting with so many questions that his curiosity got the better of him.

'So,' he said very quietly, looking up at the great hairy mountain, 'you're . . . kind of . . . alive?'

'Do I look like I'm anything else?' boomed the great beast.

'But you're stuffed . . . I mean, how can you talk? And move?'

'Well,' sighed the dodo, drawing herself up as if she was about to deliver a long and complicated answer, 'let's just say that you should know all about that. After all Tom, *you*—'

'SSSHHHH!'

A deafening hiss silenced the chatter in a moment. The anaconda, who had coiled around a pillar that stretched right up to the roof, was looking intently at the broken skylight. There was no sound except for the wind blowing softly through the broken pane of glass.

Crunch.

The sound of a footstep on the roof. It was unmistakably a footstep.

Crunch.

There was another.

Cerrrrlick.

'Arsenic!' hissed the anaconda.

Suddenly every animal and bird and fish in the museum noiselessly returned to the exact positions in which they had stood for a hundred years. It was like watching a film running backwards, and the proboscis monkey slid each case shut behind them so fast that he was almost a blur. Seconds later Tom found himself alone in the empty museum once more. The transformation was so sudden that it was as if he had just woken up from a dream. Had he?

Cerrrlick!

The sound was directly above him now. *That* sounded real enough. Quickly Tom tiptoed around the side of the stairs to the velvet bench and hid himself in its shadow. Everything was dark and silent. Then he peered up and saw a black-gloved hand extend through the broken window pane and pull the catch on the skylight. The window protested, then creaked open noisily. A burglar! Tom squeezed himself deeper into the shadow and watched, wide-eyed. Then a figure, dressed entirely in black, slid down through the open window on a wire until it had reached the level of the balcony. There it stopped and, stretching its legs, it swung forward gracefully, then back, then forward again and this time hooked a leg over the balcony. A moment later the figure had disappeared from Tom's view, and all he could see was the slack wire hanging above him. The burglar must have detached himself and crept into the bird gallery on the upper level. Tom glanced back at the dodo and the gorilla, hoping that they would be able to see what he couldn't, but the two animals weren't even looking in the right direction. Somehow their poses were entirely still, like shop dummies. Of course they would be—they were *stuffed animals* remember? What was he *thinking*?

Slowly Tom raised his head out of the darkness as high as he dared. Craning his neck through the banisters he could see nothing, hear nothing. What was the burglar doing up there? Feeling braver now, Tom slid off his bench and began to crawl up the stairs like a cat. At the top he raised his head up to floor level, and peered off to the right into the bird gallery.

There, in the far corner, the burglar was hard at work with a small diamond wheel, cutting a hole in the glass of the kookaburra case. His movements were fast and precise, and moments later there was a muffled tinkle—the hole had been made. Stretching a slim black arm inside, the burglar deftly extracted the smaller of the two kookaburras, shoving the bird into a pouch on his back. Zipping the diamond cutter into a pocket the burglar turned and sprinted on tiptoes back towards the stairs. Towards Tom—

Tom barely had time to duck down and press himself hard against the top step before the black shadow flew right over him—leaping down the stairs two at a time. Phew! Tom could feel his heart throbbing in his temples . . . that was close. He had not been spotted—yet.

Once on the ground floor the burglar made straight for the small mammal case and unzipped the diamond wheel. With great speed and economy he began grinding a circle in the glass. Tom watched on, fascinated, ideas tumbling through his mind. This must be a professional . . . he seems to know exactly what he wants, as if he has planned it all beforehand . . . could he be working for

Don Gervase? Maybe . . . and had Don Gervase prepared the way with that cake, knowing that tonight he would not be disturbed?

Tom pressed himself hard against the top step of the stairs racking his brains. Surely they *must* be connected . . . but what to do next? Should he tackle him? He didn't look that big. What then? Perhaps he is armed . . . if he had a diamond cutter then he probably had a knife too . . . no . . . getting into a fight was not the answer. But he's a thief and he's going to get away with it! Tom *must* stop him somehow. If only the animals would come alive again . . .

Cerrlunck!

A low, heavy sound echoed down the corridor. Tom froze. Glancing down he saw that the burglar had frozen too, his arm motionless inside the glass case around the pangolin's neck. What was that noise? Was it Uncle Jos? No, he was fast asleep surely. Then it must be that enormous bird, banging around in the corridor outside . . . that was the sound, Tom felt sure of it.

But the burglar did not know that. Very carefully his hand slithered out of the case and he moved silently towards the stairs. This time it was impossible for Tom not to be seen, there was no escape. Tom's breathing quickened, he knew he must be brave, he must *do* something . . . what? The burglar began to creep up the stairs towards him and suddenly, without quite knowing why, Tom stood up. The black figure stopped dead before him, frozen still. There was silence. What now?

The black figure tensed like a cat, waiting for Tom to make his move, but Tom did nothing. He had no idea what he should do except stand there, barring the burglar's path. Somehow the burglar sensed this, as the next second he leapt up onto the handrail and flung himself out into the darkness towards the balcony, catching hold of the banisters with both hands.

'Stop!' shouted Tom and sprinted up the stairs after him but already he had swung over and hurriedly reattached himself to the wire. Just as Tom reached the balcony the black figure kicked off into the air and began scurrying up the wire like a spider.

'Hey, come back!'

The burglar was already crawling up out of the skylight and the wire swung tantalizingly in front of Tom, just out of reach. The wire . . . maybe . . . without a second thought Tom clambered up onto the handrail and balancing precariously, waited for the steel hook to swing back in his direction. Lunging at it desperately his fingers closed around the cold steel, but at that very moment Tom felt a jerk from above. The momentum began to pull him out into the darkness . . . no—

For a second Tom teetered along dangerously on the handrail . . . should he let go? What if it wasn't secured? Too late . . .

Before he knew it Tom tipped forward and swung out over the heads of the animals, suspended beneath the skylight. Wriggling frantically, Tom took all his weight with one arm and grabbed at the wire above, but his fingers slithered straight back down again. How had the burglar climbed up? It had looked so easy. Again and again Tom flung his arm up at the wire but he just couldn't raise himself. There was nothing to grip on to. He was stuck. Panting hard, he looked down to see the floor swinging a long way below him. If he let go now, he would break his leg at the very least—probably his back—and he could not hold on much longer. His fingers were beginning to chafe on the steel hook, and the muscles in his shoulders were screaming . . .

'Please . . . ' he whispered breathlessly to the silent animals all around him, 'help me . . . someone.'

At that moment there was a heavy rap on the door outside. Tom tried to ignore the burning pain in his arms and glanced towards the foyer, where the beam of a torch flashed in through the window. The beam hunted around the museum in the darkness, searching for something, before coming to rest directly below . . .

Oh no . . .

Looking down, Tom was horrified to see his socks picked out by the torch beam. Slowly the light travelled up his body till it shone directly in his face, blinding him. Tom squirmed violently, trying to twist his head away. The police, he knew it must be; they must have heard the footsteps on the roof, maybe even spotted the burglar climbing up and now they have him inside. *He's* the thief . . .

The banging on the door began again, more insistently this time, followed by a loud blast on the bell.

'Just a minute . . . Lordy Lordy.'

Tom gasped. The shadow of Uncle Jos shuffled beneath him towards the door. In a moment the police would be inside and the lights would come on. What could he do? How could he explain himself? Tom glanced about him wildly and saw the mammoth's back a few metres away. From where he was hanging the dark brown shape seemed inviting, like a deep hairy blanket. Maybe he could hide himself in it.

'Key, key, key,' muttered Jos to himself, and Tom heard the lock scrape in the front door. There were only seconds left now. Stretching his legs out as far in front of him as he could, Tom forced himself to swing slowly forward. Below him the door was already half open and there was a burst of crackle from a police radio.

'Good evening, Mr Scatterhorn.'

Tom tried to blank it from his mind. He was swinging back. Concentrate, one more swing and the momentum would carry him there . . .

'Burglary?' he heard Jos say. 'Hang on a minute . . . '

Jos shuffled towards the light switch and it was now or never. Tom swung forward as far as he could and let go . . . the dark carpet of the mammoth's back rushed towards him—Bang! Tom hit it so hard that it knocked the breath out of his lungs but he clung fast, burying his fingers in the long hair. At that moment the lights flashed on.

'Good Lord,' blinked Jos, staring up at the wire swinging aimlessly in the centre of the room.

'Missed the little tyke,' grunted another voice that sounded familiar.

Tom raised his head an inch and saw two police officers staring up at the roof. One had a moustache, the other was baby-faced.

Now he was for it.

What if *they* found him here? Tom tried to think of a single reason to explain what he was doing—but he couldn't.

'Ah-ha,' said the Moustache, walking over to examine the case with the pangolin inside it. Bending down he picked up the neat circle of glass that had been cut out of the side of it.

'Diamond job, by the look of it.'

Jos shuffled over and peered in through the hole.

'Well now that *is* strange.'

'What is?' asked the Moustache.

'There's nothing missing.'

'Are you sure?' replied the Moustache, watching Jos very carefully.

'Absolutely. Definitely. It's all there.'

The Moustache raised an eyebrow. 'Then why did he bother to cut his way in?'

Jos shrugged his shoulders. His hair was flying in all directions and he looked crazier than ever.

'Could it be . . . that the thief was . . . erm . . . disturbed?' he suggested sleepily. The Moustache narrowed his eyes and stared suspiciously around him. The old man might look half-mad but he did have a point. And if the thief had been disturbed then there was every chance that he might still be in the museum.

'You stay right here,' he said to Jos. 'Don't go anywhere as I shall need to talk to you later. Moon!' he shouted.

'Sir?' squeaked Moon, who had an unusually high voice for one so large.

'Upstairs, Moon, search high and low. Our man might still be on the premises.'

'Right sir.' And Moon galloped up the stairs like a hippopotamus.

'Now, where's that little reprobate got to,' whispered the Moustache as he laboriously began to investigate each case. At first Uncle Jos thought about joining in, then decided against it. Instead, he shuffled wearily over to a chair beside the hummingbird case and sat down to watch the proceedings. He wore the resigned expression of someone who had been in this position many times before.

From his vantage point high up on the mammoth's back, Tom considered his options. Things could hardly be worse. It was only a matter of time before the policemen looked over the balcony and spotted him spread-eagled in the fur. The only reason that they hadn't seen him already was probably because his dark fleece was almost the same colour as the mammoth itself. Perhaps he could slide down the mammoth's leg and escape. But how was he going to do that under the glare of the lights?

'Sir!'

Moon came thundering out of the bird gallery and the Moustache poked his head out from behind the bear.

'What is it, Moon?'

'Sir,' he squeaked, 'there's another one up here gone. A kookaburra if I'm not mistaken. How about that?'

The Moustache looked very serious. He crawled out, straightened his hat, and walked very purposefully up the stairs.

'Kookaburra, eh?' he repeated, as if that was some kind of clue.

'Yes, sir, laughing kookaburra. Funny looking.'

'Right, Moon.'

Together the two policemen disappeared upstairs into the bird gallery. Once they had gone, Tom glanced up to where Uncle Jos sat next to the hummingbird tree, and saw that his head was nodding against the case. He had fallen asleep again. It's now or never, thought Tom, *go now*.

Pushing himself backwards with his hands Tom slithered down the mammoth until he was clinging to the top of its left leg, and half-falling half-sliding he dropped to the ground. Now what? Should he risk crossing the hall and running back to his bedroom? Yes, he must escape. Run for it—

But Tom had only taken a few steps out of the shadow of the mammoth when he heard the policemen coming back.

'An antiquity theft, Moon, just my luck,' grumbled the Moustache.

'Sir?'

'Paperwork, Moon. Oodles of it. Age, value, description, you name it—'

Tom tiptoed as fast as he could back behind the mammoth, his heart thumping against his ribcage. Where now? Behind him there was a triangular cupboard door under the stairs—that was the place. In one movement Tom darted across to it and reached down for the handle. It was open! Quickly he slipped inside and closed the door softly behind him. It was pitch black. Tom could feel beads of sweat breaking out on his forehead.

This was madness.

Why was he playing a game of cat and mouse with two policemen when he was innocent! What was he doing? But there was too much to explain. They'd seen him in the street looking suspicious; they'd probably recognized him on the wire as well. Whatever he told them they'd never believe him. He had started a chain of events that had spun out of control. He had decided to hide now, and hide he must.

Peering into the shadows Tom could just make out the shape of a white wicker trunk in the corner. *That* was the place; if he could just get inside that trunk no one would find him, and he could sleep there until tomorrow. Yes, that was the best plan. Now all he had to do was get there.

Tom reached out his arms and took one cautious step towards the trunk. That was fine. Then he took another; that was fine too. Halfway. Ahead of him Tom had a vague impression of mops and brushes but he couldn't really see any of them. Tom was just in the middle of his third step when instinctively he knew that it was a mistake. His foot hit something hard, like a steel bucket, and as he leant forward it seemed to get wedged inside. Before he could stop himself he was toppling forwards, sideways, crashing blindly into brushes and mops and bottles as he fell. The noise was terrible. Tom lay in the middle of the mess, his heart pounding.

You idiot!

Surely they would come for him now; he was cornered. There was silence . . . maybe they hadn't heard—

Suddenly the scuff of footsteps echoed heavily on the stone floor outside. Tom twisted his foot hard, kicking it violently out of the bucket and then dived into the large wicker trunk in the corner. Just as the lid fell onto his back the cupboard door flew open and the silhouette of Moon peered inside. Tom tried not to breathe. What next? He was lying on a deep pile of rags and horsehair that lined the bottom of the trunk.

'A rat probably, sir,' squeaked Moon. There was a hint of relief in his voice.

'Are you sure there's nothing there, man?' barked the Moustache outside.

'Well . . . there's a trunk in the corner, sir,' added Moon uncertainly. 'But—'

'Go on then Moon, open it. He might be hiding inside.'

Moon let out a high-pitched whistle.

'Right you are, sir.'

Officer Moon began to thread his way noisily through the chaos.

'Now don't you try anything fancy, laddie,' he whispered nervously as he hovered directly above the trunk, 'no tricks, you hear?'

Moon was panting heavily as he bent down to lift the latch; he was so close Tom could hear his every breath. In desperation Tom squirmed deeper under the rags, trying to hide beneath them. As his fingers felt further down he realized that the bottom of the trunk was not where he expected it to be, and soon he had managed to burrow further and further under the rags until he was now completely hidden. Good. Somewhere above him Tom heard the squeak of the wicker lid opening. The policeman must be peering inside. Could he go just a little deeper? Tom felt for the sides of the trunk to force himself lower but there seemed to be nothing there . . . this trunk must be truly enormous, thought Tom, much wider than it had appeared and deeper too. Perhaps it had a false bottom, or it was sitting on top of a mountain of rags, or it led down to a cellar . . .

Suddenly Tom felt himself drop as if he had been thrown off a diving board. Grabbing wildly at the rags around him, he tried to hold on, but there was nothing at all to grab on to. He was falling down, down, as if in a dream, through empty, dark space . . .

CHAPTER 7

The Other Place

Bump.

It was a soft kind of landing, and not exactly like a landing at all, as Tom felt he hadn't so much arrived somewhere as stopped moving. Opening his eyes he saw nothing but darkness. Maybe he had fallen down some disused lift shaft under the museum. Maybe he was dead. No. Wait a minute . . .

As his eyes became accustomed to the light he could just make out the shadows of horsemen in the distance, riding towards a sand dune. Where was this place? A desert . . . at night . . . how . . . Tom raised his hand to rub his eyes and directly in front of his face his fingers brushed against something familiar. Paper. Looking around he saw more horses galloping towards more sand dunes. They were all exactly the same. It was a pattern. Wallpaper. Pushing the surface above him Tom felt it give and open outwards. The wallpaper was stuck on the lid of a trunk, and he was lying inside it.

Sitting up, Tom found himself in a small, square room, panelled on all sides in dark wood. It was like being inside a nut. Looking up at the ceiling, Tom half expected to see a hole which he had fallen through, but that was made of solid wood too. This must be some sort of cellar, under the museum, that Jos hadn't told him about. How did he get in here? Don't worry about that, Tom, he told himself; think about how you are going to get out of here. Well, that was simple. There in the corner was a low wooden door.

Climbing out of the trunk, Tom walked over to the door and listened. There was no sound, so he tentatively tried the handle. The door creaked alarmingly, but instead of revealing a dark staircase that would lead him back up to the museum, the door opened on to a long corridor. At the end was a small moonlit window and Tom could just make out white shapes drifting past. Were those snowflakes? It seemed unlikely. If he was under the museum then surely he must be underground. Why did Jos never tell him about this place before? This museum really was a labyrinth. The police would never think to look down here.

Gingerly, he stepped out of the doorway and tiptoed up to the window. Instead of looking up at the street, Tom found himself looking down across a moonlit scene. Below him was a terrace blanketed with snow, that gave on to a formal lawn dotted with yew trees, and at the bottom of the hill he could see streetlights and small houses, jostling together around a silvery river that snaked away out to sea. Somehow this was all familiar, and for a moment Tom couldn't think where it was; then he recognized it. This was Dragonport, it must be, he recognized the view from yesterday. There was the town, spread out before him, and the river was just the same. And if he was looking down on that garden then, this must be . . . could it be . . . Catcher Hall? But how did he get here, had he fallen down some underground tunnel? What about the trunk—

Suddenly there was a loud throbbing sound close by, and Tom flinched away from the window just as a small airship hovered right past the glass and away towards the river. Hanging beneath the balloon was an engine belching black smoke, and behind it sat a man in a cradle wearing goggles and wrapped in furs. He waved cheerily. What was *that*?

'There he is!'

'Lord, wis bin wondrin' if you'd got lost or summat!'

Tom spun round to see two people in the corridor smiling at him. There was a red-faced woman in a long dress and apron, holding a tray with a half-eaten cake on it. Beside her stood an equally red-faced boy in a cap and britches.

'We bin lookin' for ya, Tom,' said the boy. 'We thought you's gon' down the fair already.' The boy had a strong accent and an easy smile, and he seemed to know him.

'N-n-n-no,' stammered Tom, 'I—'

'Wull yous be goin' wi' Mister August then?' said the woman kindly. She too spoke in a kind of singsong way that turned everything into a question. 'Cos I jus' seen him in his workshop and I know he's expectin' ya.'

'Yes . . . I . . . I think I might. Er . . .' Tom felt himself flush with embarrassment. Who were these people? Why were they wearing strange clothes? And how did they know his name?

'All righty. See-yers there then,' smiled the boy. 'Do-wint figet them skates now.' With a laugh they left him standing in the corridor and continued downstairs. Tom looked after them, utterly dumbfounded. He was definitely sure that he had never seen either of them before in his life. Perhaps he should go back to the trunk right now and find a way out of this place. But something stopped him: the woman had said August was expecting him, could that be . . . *August Catcher*? He looked up the narrow staircase and saw a small light on at the top. Was that the workshop? There was only one way to find out.

At the top of the stairs Tom arrived on a small landing that seemed to be up in the attic. Peeking in through a small door he saw a long narrow room that must have run the length of the roof, at the end of which was an enormous round window. On either side the walls were lined with shelves, full to bursting with jars of different coloured liquids and trays. And animals: all around were models of birds and animals, some stuffed, some just pelts, neatly organized in rows along the workbenches. At the far end, a man in a black fur-lined jacket and hat was bent over a table, stitching something. Then he held the object up and examined it before the light and Tom saw that it was a bright blue kingfisher, holding a small silver fish it its mouth. Tom swallowed hard. This must be August Catcher. 'But that's not possible,' insisted a voice in his head. 'August Catcher's dead. He lived over a hundred years ago.' Just carry on, Tom told himself. Be normal. Everyone else is.

At that moment August turned round, and Tom could see that he was wearing some kind of mechanical lens over one eye. He flipped it up and smiled.

'Ah-ha. If it isn't my new assistant Tom. I'd been wondering when you'd arrive. Well, what do you think?' he said brightly, holding up the kingfisher. Tom shifted from foot to foot and smiled nervously. 'That fish was caught this morning.'

Tom hovered uneasily in the shadows.

'I—I think . . . erm . . . I think there's been—'

'Come come, Tom!' August beckoned him to come closer. 'You'll never see it from there.'

Tom took a deep breath and walked carefully into the workshop. He noticed that the room was filled with confusing smells that were both sweet and nauseating at the same time and everywhere there was an unmistakable aroma of animal. Ignoring it as best he could, Tom went forward and stared at the bird. He had seen it before, somewhere in the museum. Then he remembered where: it was the kingfisher that perched on the sluice gate in the large river scene in the bird gallery.

'Like it?'

August held it up for Tom to see and turned it in his hands. 'I think it's turned out rather well, though I say it myself.'

The kingfisher was indeed extraordinarily lifelike. August had even given the bird's head a slight twist as if it were still struggling to hold on to the wriggling fish.

'But it's a devil of a job to think of a setting,' he went on. 'It's either up in a tree in a case on its own, or as a father coming back to the nest to feed his young. What do you think?'

Tom wondered whether he should reveal what he already knew.

'Maybe,' mumbled Tom, 'it would look good . . . er . . . in a large . . . erm . . . river scene?' he said, trying to sound as natural as possible. 'Perhaps . . . erm . . . above a weir?' August looked up at him quizzically. He had sharp features and restless eyes whose corners turned upwards as if he were permanently smiling.

'Well now Tom, I do believe you are reading my mind,' he replied cheerfully. 'I think I'm inclined to agree with you.' August carefully set down the bird on the bench, and then leapt up and grabbed a long package from the top shelf. 'Now I've been waiting to show you this.' Taking a small knife from his pocket he slit the paper in two, revealing a long brown leather case. 'It's a ten-by-thirty,' he said excitedly, opening one end and pulling out a slim brass telescope, 'the very latest.'

Extending the telescope to one eye, August looked out through the large round window before him.

'There is so much that one can almost see, but not quite,' he paused, focusing the lens, 'until now. There! The packet's in from Holland. Oh, and so are the passengers. Madam, you are about to lose your scarf!' August chuckled to himself.

'Here,' he said, handing it to Tom, 'why don't you try it? The magnification is remarkable.'

Tom pressed the telescope up to his eye. Even though it was night-time the docks below him were bustling with life. All along the quayside foremen were directing stevedores as they unloaded the steamer that had just docked. Heavy dray horses stood about in pairs, steam puffing from their muzzles and their backs almost entirely covered in snow, while men rolled large wooden barrels up onto the carts behind them. Further along, a crew of burly fishermen in large yellow sou'westers poured their slippery silver catch into a great pile on the quay. The flapping fish splashed out in all directions and children scurried about collecting up the loose ones, throwing them into wicker baskets on their backs. Through all this confusion Tom could just make out the looming shadow of a large grey ferry tied up on the far side of the dock.

'Can you see them?' asked August. 'Winter tourists mostly. They've come for the fair.'

Tom watched as one by one the passengers emerged from the ship, bracing themselves against the icy wind. He followed the procession of fat women and small men, swaddled in all manner of furs and scarves, down the gangplank to the quayside, to where . . . Tom felt as if his heart had turned to ice.

'What is it?' asked August, glancing up from his kingfisher.

Tom could not reply. In fact, he could barely breathe. There, just beyond a group of ragged boys huddling around a brazier, stood a very tall man in a black sealskin coat carrying a small leather bag. He was giving instructions to a porter, waving his arms about so wildly that the porter cowered like a whipped dog beneath him. Next to the tall man was a dark-haired girl, wrapped in white furs, who stood like a ballet dancer. They both had their backs towards him, sheltering from the wind, but Tom instinctively recognized them; he would recognize those silhouettes anywhere. It was Don Gervase Askary and Lotus. Definitely. Then, as if he sensed that he had been seen, Don Gervase turned and looked up in Tom's direction. Through the powerful telescope it was as if Don Gervase's huge head was right there in front of him, staring Tom in the face. His skin had turned yellow and blotchy in the cold, and his large green eyes looked bored. Tom shrank back from the window and shivered. What were *they* doing here?

'I say old chap, you've gone white as a sheet. Are you sure you're all right?' August was staring up at Tom with some concern.

'Fine,' he spluttered, 'just . . . just . . . a little cold, that's all.'

'Yes, it's beastly up here. And they say it's going to get even colder. Why don't you go down to the kitchen and warm up a bit.'

'Thanks. I think I will,' said Tom, who was glad of any excuse to go. There was so much to think about, almost too much.

'Good,' replied August, who had returned to his workbench and was busy stitching the kingfisher once more, 'and I like the idea about the river scene, I really do. We definitely need something massive for the bird gallery. I can just see this little fellow perching on a sluice gate.'

'Right,' mumbled Tom as he quietly made his way through the jars of chemicals to the door.

A minute later Tom was relieved to find himself back in the small wooden room. The trunk was still there in the corner, just as he had left it. Was that the way back to the present? Maybe. He had to find out. He had to return to his own time. He must tell Uncle Jos everything and see what he had to say the moment he got back. But supposing, just *supposing*, there *was* no way back? Tom kicked that nasty little thought firmly to the darker recesses of his mind and tried not to think about it. The prospect was too terrifying; there will be a way back. There *must* be.

Lifting the heavy lid, Tom climbed into the trunk and looked around him. Just like the wicker basket, the bottom was also lined with old rags. What should he do, bury himself in them? Probably. He couldn't remember whether he had been covered or uncovered when he had arrived. Closing the lid gently, Tom lay down in the darkness and began to worm around, gradually twisting himself down beneath the surface of the rags until at last he was completely submerged. There. He had done it. Now what? Should he wait for something to happen? Or should he keep going down and hope that somehow he would just fall out of the bottom as he had done before? It must be the same going both ways, mustn't it?

Tom was just beginning to burrow deeper into the rags when suddenly another thought occurred to him. Supposing that he did return, but somehow time had not moved on at all. What had been happening the moment he left? Officer Moon had opened the wicker basket. Perhaps he was rummaging around . . .

But before this terrifying idea had even finished forming, the bottom of the trunk caved in and Tom was falling down through the darkness. Moments later he felt himself slowing and rags began to wind themselves around him, covering him completely, until he bounced gently to a stop. Tom lay completely still, breathing hard. Was he back?

Somewhere up above him he heard the squeak of a lid being shut very quickly.

'Nothing in there, sir,' said a squeaky voice, 'nothing at all.'

Then a cupboard door closed.

Very slowly Tom emerged from the rags and looked up. He was inside the wicker basket once more, he was in his own time. Tom felt a great wave of relief surge over him, and suddenly he felt very tired indeed. Creeping out of the basket, he inched across the dark cupboard and pressed his ear to the door.

'Will that be all?' Uncle Jos asked in a sleepy voice.

'For the moment,' replied the Moustache. 'Obviously we'll need a formal ID, dot all the Is, cross all the Ts, etcetera, etcetera.'

'Obviously.'

'I don't suppose you would be able to put a value on that kookaburra, Mr Scatterhorn?'

Jos cocked his head and rubbed his nose thoughtfully.

'One old kookaburra . . . erm . . . well—'

'Shall we say one hundred pounds?'

'If you say so.'

'I do sir,' replied the Moustache. 'I like a round number at this time of night. Moon?'

'Sir?' squeaked Moon, who was standing with his nose pressed against a case.

'Keen on small mammals are we, Moon?'

'Very very keen, sir. Take photographs of them. Actually I'm a member of the Grunting Bandicoot Club. Every month we—'

'Indeed, Moon.'

The Moustache fixed him with a withering stare. He was not in the mood for Moon's grunting bandicoots, or anything else for that matter.

'Sir.'

With a very serious expression Moon put his hat back on his head.

'Goodnight Mr Scatterhorn,' said the Moustache as he opened the door, 'and *if* you don't mind me saying so, you'd be doing us all a favour if you got that roof of yours fixed.'

'Right you are,' muttered Jos as he pushed the heavy door hard behind them.

'Not that we don't *enjoy* looking for stuffed kookaburras at this time of night.'

'A very goodnight to you too,' huffed Jos, and turning the heavy lock he shuffled off to bed.

Tom waited until Jos had gone, then he let himself out of the cupboard. Everything was quiet, as it should be. But Tom's mind was burning with questions in which one loomed larger than all the rest. Walking over to the low case containing the model of the town as it had been a hundred years ago, he bent down and peered at Catcher Hall. At once he recognized the large round window tucked in just under the roof. Then his eye moved across to the busy docks below where the steamer was tied up at the end of the quay. This was where he had been only minutes earlier, he was sure of it. Miniature figures stood motionless on the quayside, but there was no one who looked like either Don Gervase or Lotus. But they *were* there, Tom told himself, he had seen them; and he had seen August Catcher too. Was it possible that he had somehow shrunk inside this scene, and it had somehow come to life? Or was this a route *into* the past? And then there were the animals, standing silently in their cases all around him. How had *they* come alive?

There were so many questions that Tom had no answers to, but he made himself a promise: he was going to find out.

CHAPTER 8

A Good Story

But somehow, Tom's promise to himself did not go quite as planned. A week passed by and still he had not told Uncle Jos about his adventure into the other place. Somehow asking a question about a time hole that led from the cupboard under the stairs into Dragonport a hundred years ago just seemed too silly. Tom was not at all certain about it himself. Had he dreamt it all up? He wasn't sure any more. He had spent two whole days searching for any signs of a cellar, or a trapdoor leading underground that Jos did not know about, and found nothing. He had examined the mammoth, the dodo, and all the other animals that had spoken to him that night, searching for signs of electric wires or cogs poking through their faded pelts, but he had found nothing there either. They all appeared to be exactly what they were; stuffed animals, in urgent need of restoration.

When he hadn't been searching for cellars or wires Tom spent many hours staring down at that model of the town in the snow, losing himself in its detail. How *could* he have been there? Such things only existed in fairy tales, not in real life. And on top of everything else there was the question that bothered him most of all—Don Gervase and Lotus. They had been there too.

The only place Tom did not return to was the cupboard under the stairs. Somehow he did not want to look at that wicker basket again. He just wanted everything to be normal.

And in a way, everything was normal. Almost *too* normal. Every morning Jos opened the doors of the museum and Melba settled herself behind the till with a blanket, waiting for the swarms of visitors who never arrived. By lunchtime the only person to have come in was the postman, with his piles of bills, and more often than not there seemed to be some sallow-faced government inspector loitering in the foyer too. Tom had no idea where these people came from, probably some vast grey ministry somewhere, for they were all sickly young men and women dressed in pale leather overcoats, brandishing very large clipboards that bristled with pointless questionnaires about everything from the size of the door handles to the condition of the stuffed fish. The only remarkable thing about these strangely suspicious visitors was that they seemed more than ready to swallow any old answer Melba chose to give them.

'So you said you *wash* the stuffed animals then?'

A thin young woman stared at Melba through her thick green glasses. She had a large badge proclaiming she was from 'The National Museums Inspection Team' pinned to her lapel.

'We do need to know, you know.'

'Only on . . . Thursdays.'

'Only on . . . Thursdays,' she repeated, 'what with?'

Melba glanced up from her boiler manual at the insistent young lady scribbling hard on her questionnaire.

'Well, it depends. You see we prefer lavender soap for the birds, turpentine for the antelopes and gazelles, and for the echidnas and pangolins we use a walnut.'

'Lavender . . . turpentine . . . wal . . . nut?' The young woman frowned, copying down every word as if it contained some hidden meaning. Melba stifled a little smile.

'And *how* did you say you cleaned the floor?'

'Erm . . . that will be with the girls.'

'I'm sorry, I need details. The girls?'

'Germaine and Gertrude. Wombats both. Strapped to the feet they make fabulous little polishers. We glide this way and that, through the cases. Now you see me . . . phusssh!' Melba flung out her arm as if she was skidding the length of the hall, 'now, you don't.'

'Wombats . . . strapped . . . to . . . feet . . . polishers . . .' repeated the young woman slowly to herself, filling in the form.

'Got the picture now?'

These little interrogations happened so regularly that Melba hardly noticed them, and they lasted just as long as it took the inspector to fill in all the boxes on their forms before glancing suspiciously into the gloom and making a hasty exit. Melba's madness could be very convincing.

Only a few brave families of tourists, lured to the Scatterhorn Museum by an unreliable yellowing guide book, ever dared venture out beyond the foyer.

'Oh wow, Mom, look!' the little ones would shout, spying the mammoth in the corner and taking his photograph. 'Isn't he just so cute?'

But when they peered into the darkness at the rest of the

faded, frightening looking creatures parents would clutch their children's hands just a little more tightly.

'But Mommy,' the smallest children would ask, 'why are all those animals staring at us?'

'Don't be silly, darlings. My, what nonsense you talk,' said Mommy, glancing nervously at the dusty cases and their faded inhabitants—all fangs and eyes and claws—and suddenly the little darlings would be ushered quickly out of the door, leaving with the worried expressions of people who had just visited another planet.

The only person determined to enjoy it was Leaky Logan, the plumber.

'You'll be taking nothing off me, Mrs Scatterhorn,' he said as he marched in past Melba. 'You owe me so much money I fancy I'll come in here just as much as I want. Every day if I want to, even if it is damp and dark and downright unpleasant. It's my right.'

Leaky walked quickly around the main hall, occasionally prodding the wolf or drumming his fingers on the sturgeon's nose before marching straight out again, very pleased to be making his point. But a daily visit soon became too much—even for Leaky. By Thursday he was complaining that 'Only a toad could enjoy these musty conditions,' and 'The air was making him ill.'

'Well, don't come back then,' said Melba, sneezing loudly.

'Don't think you can get rid of me that easily, Mrs Scatterhorn,' he replied.

That Friday Leaky was walking past the gorilla when he distinctly felt a kick up his backside.

'Ow! What the—'

Leaky turned round to find the gorilla motionless. But he could have sworn that the anteater was sniggering. And the wombat. And that proboscis monkey too.

'Right, that's it!' he declared and marched straight out of the door, complaining that a 'very aggressive poltergeist' had taken a shine to him. Leaky Logan did not return.

For his part, Uncle Jos did not seem to care if anyone visited the museum or not. The burglary had stung him into action and he spent the best part of each day pottering about in the gloom with his toolbox, determinedly patching this and fixing that, but even Tom could see that it was a losing battle. The whole place was like an old warship that had been kept afloat after many skirmishes on the high seas, and now it was finally starting to sink.

'My father's motto was: "if it ain't broke, don't fix it",' rasped Jos as he wrestled with an iron pipe at the top of the stairs. 'Now when your father says that you know you're in trouble,' he added grimly, 'because by the time he pops his clogs and you get your mits on it—odds are it's utterly shot.'

Despite all his 'running repairs' as Jos liked to call them, he seemed to deliberately ignore the hole in the roof, and he paid no attention to the broken glass in the cases either. In fact, Jos scarcely even mentioned the burglary.

'So is there any news from the police?' Tom would ask every morning after breakfast. 'Have they caught anyone yet?'

'No news, lad,' muttered Jos from behind his paper, 'not a sausage.'

'Not even any suspects?'

'No leads. No suspects. No one.'

Whereupon Jos would quickly change the subject. Tom could

not understand it at all, it was almost as if Jos had forgotten the burglary had ever happened. Either that, or he was making a good attempt at pretending he didn't care. So one morning Tom decided to change tack. Uncle Jos had just batted away Tom's daily question and was settling himself down to the sports page of the *Dragonport Mercury*.

'Uncle Jos?'

'Hmm?'

'Did you know that there is a tightrope at Catcher Hall?'

'Is there now?'

'Suspended *across* a room. I saw Lotus doing cartwheels across it last week.'

'That's nice,' mumbled Melba, her long nose deep in her knitting. 'I loved doing cartwheels when I was a girl.'

'But this is in *mid-air*. Don't you think that's a little . . . strange?'

Uncle Jos scratched his head.

'No. Not really,' he muttered, turning the page of his paper. Tom could feel the exasperation begin to simmer up inside him. He tried again.

'But . . . but don't you think that if Lotus is a *gymnast*, who can do incredible *tricks*, on a *wire*, then . . . well, I mean, isn't that just a massive coincidence?'

Tom wasn't sure how much clearer he could spell it out. Melba appeared not to have heard, but Jos sat with his head cocked across the kitchen table. He could hardly fail to notice Tom's disgruntled expression.

'I believe you and I, Tom, are in dire need of a change of scene,' he said at last. 'Melba, where's the key of *Sugarmouse*?'

'*Sugarmouse*?' repeated Melba. 'In it, if I'm not mistaken,' she said, looking at Jos over the top of her half-moon glasses. 'Thank goodness you are going to take him off to do something more exciting for a change. I must have spent years watching you fix things and I can tell you it's hardly entertainment.'

'Point taken,' admitted Jos, grinning at Tom. 'That's why this morning, lad, we're going to have a little chat. And more importantly, see if we can't catch ourselves a fish or two.'

'Isn't she magnificent?' roared Jos above the din of the tiny outboard motor. They were sitting on board a small plastic tender speeding towards a boat moored near the centre of the river. In the grey mist she looked to Tom like an old fishing boat from a black and white photograph, but as they drew closer he saw that in fact she had low round sides and was quite tubby in the middle—rather like a mouse. And curiously, she was painted bright pink.

'Sits on the mud most of the time of course,' shouted Jos. 'Perfect for all the creeks round here as she draws next to nothing.'

Tom nodded, but he had no idea what Uncle Jos was talking about.

'That means she's very shallow in the water,' grinned Jos, turning off the outboard and reaching out to grab the rail as they drew alongside. 'Good for creeping about. Very popular with fishermen once upon a time. Smugglers liked them too,' and he winked knowingly. 'Still do.'

Tying a swift knot round the rail, Jos heaved himself aboard, and extending one hand he hauled Tom up after him.

'Lord, what a mess,' he wheezed, staring down at the grubby decks spattered with seagull guano. 'I thought you were supposed to stop this lot,' he said, addressing a large plastic owl lashed to the mast. 'Twit.'

Chortling to himself, Jos untied the owl and carried it down below in search of a brush. Twenty minutes later *Sugarmouse*'s decks were clean and her diesel engine was thudding contentedly as they headed out into the grey estuary.

Tom could not help but notice that the moment Jos stepped aboard *Sugarmouse* he seemed to have become ten years younger. There was a spring in his step as he cheerfully barked out naval commands and then translated them.

'Now you take the tiller and aim for that patch of darker water out there,' he waved to a spot almost in the centre of the river, 'that's where we'll find 'em. If you need to change course, just think of it like reversing a car. To go left, steer right. To go right, steer left—do everything backwards. OK? I'll just see if I can locate those rods,' and with that he disappeared below.

Tom clasped the wooden handle and held on, feeling the heavy throbbing note of the engine beneath him. Like reversing a car? Tom had never reversed a car. Come to think of it, he had barely even been allowed to sit behind the wheel of the camper van. He had certainly never driven it.

Sugarmouse seemed quite content to carry on in the same direction, but very soon Tom realized he was going to have to make a turn. Push left to go right—OK. He eased the tiller over and waited. At first nothing happened, as if *Sugarmouse* was thinking about what he had asked her to do, then very slowly the bowsprit began edging across the horizon. It worked! Tom smiled, but then he realized she was still turning. He pulled the tiller back towards him and nothing happened, she was still turning. OK, he thought, let's just carry on and turn a full circle—Jos won't notice. Tom held the tiller over and *Sugarmouse* made a long leisurely circle out into the middle of the river.

'Aha,' said Jos, reappearing in the hatch with a rod in each hand to see the horizon slowly spinning past. 'Getting the hang of it then, eh?' he grinned.

'Just about.'

'Good.' Jos clambered up to the deck. 'Now, I'll cut the motor and let the tide carry us onto it.'

In the next half hour Jos taught Tom the basics of fishing with a spinner, how to tie the hooks, and how to cast out using the weight to carry the line as far as possible from the boat. It was not as hard as it looked, and was actually quite fun.

'That's good,' said Jos approvingly. 'See, there's not much skill to it really. It's not a battle of wits with some wily old salmon. We're just hoping some hungry bass is going to mistake your lure for lunch.'

Tom cast out again and reeled in slowly till eventually the silver lures were bouncing along the surface towards him empty. Somehow he had expected that he was going to catch a fish immediately.

'Nothing doing?' said Jos. 'Try again lad,' and Jos cast his own line out once more. 'That's the thing about fishing: you have to be patient. You could be here all day and not get so much as a tickle.'

After another twenty minutes of casting and reeling in, Tom felt his enthusiasm for fishing begin to wane. He was convinced that he must be doing something wrong.

'How do you know if they are hungry?'

'Well of course, they may not be,' replied Jos. Then he cocked his head and stared down into the murky river. 'In fact they may not be here at all.'

'How do you mean?'

'Bass eat little fish, Tom. Sprats, whitebait—that sort of thing—and seagulls are partial to little fish as well. So if you can see a flock of seagulls diving into the water and coming up with fish in their mouths, then odds on there's a shoal of bass down there feeding on them too.'

Tom looked out across the estuary. The only bird he could see was a solitary cormorant flying low across the glassy water.

'I know,' said Jos, catching his eye, 'no birds. Still, this is a good spot, and part of the fun is just being out here. If you always knew what you were going to catch then fishing would be boring, don't you think?'

Tom wasn't so sure about that. He cast out again and watched the oily pink reflections lapping against the side of the boat. Perhaps now was the time to tell Jos what had happened to him. Perhaps away from the museum it didn't sound so crazy after all. He looked across at Jos who was gazing out at the weak midwinter sun trying to break through the low cloud.

'Once I snagged an old carriage lantern out here,' said Jos absently, 'and a horseshoe. Funny things to find in the middle of a river, aren't they?'

Tom didn't reply. Sensing Tom's frustration Jos put down his rod and pulled out an old packet of toffees.

'Here,' he said, handing them over, 'I find these take your mind off the boredom.'

Reaching into his other pocket Jos pulled out a pipe and a tin of tobacco wrapped up in a plastic bag. Tom watched as he held the pipe bowl over the tobacco and expertly filled it with one finger.

'Melba thinks I've given up,' he said, his eyes twinkling underneath his bushy eyebrows, 'so you'll have to keep it a secret. Promise?'

Tom nodded, his teeth cracking on the ancient toffee.

'Good lad,' said Jos, cupping a hand over his pipe to light it, 'because . . . ' Jos took a few hard puffs then he coughed so violently that his shoulders shook. Tom wondered whether the pipe was really worth it, but eventually Jos recovered and wiped his eyes with a handkerchief.

'Never start smoking a pipe, Tom,' he wheezed. 'It's an anti-social habit at the best of times, but worse than that it ruins your conversation. Now, where was I? Ah yes. Seeing as you're going to keep my little secret, I shall let you into an even bigger one.' Pulling hard on his pipe, Jos stared down into the milky water. 'I know you've been wanting to ask me a certain question. Well, I can tell you the answer.'

'You can?'

Jos nodded.

'Yes I can.'

Tom's heart leapt. Maybe there was someone else who knew his secret. Maybe Jos knew about the animals, and he had been back through the wicker basket himself . . . Jos leant forward conspiratorially.

'I know what that burglar was looking for.'

'Oh.' Tom tried not to sound disappointed. 'Really?'

'Yep. Really. Used to be every ten years we'd get one. Now it's every five. Come to think of it, there was one only last year. Anyway, it's always exactly the same kind of job.'

Tom felt his curiosity returning. This was strange indeed.

'But—why don't you go to the police?'

'Why, Tom? Well I'll tell you why. Because *if* I told them what I thought, they would probably cart me off to the madhouse and throw away the key. So I never tell them, and,' he added forcefully, 'neither did my father. It's all to do—'

Jos paused to relight his pipe. Tom knew by now that this was how Jos always told his stories. He liked to pause at the crucial moment—just to make sure that everyone was listening.

'It's all to do,' he said, puffing violently on his pipe again, his eyes screwed up like dots, 'with a sapphire. The largest uncut sapphire ever found.'

Tom chuckled. He couldn't help himself.

'You see? You're laughing,' beamed Jos. 'Now why do you think I didn't tell that to the police?'

'A sapphire?' snorted Tom.

Jos raised his eyebrows, clearly enjoying every minute of the suspense. Tom smiled and shook his head, really not sure whether to believe Jos or not.

'OK,' he said slowly, 'go on then.'

'You know that great Bengal tiger at the top of the stairs?'

Tom nodded.

'Well, many years ago, that tiger had a big price on its head. When it was alive it was a man-eater, it had killed over four hundred people, including the Maharajah of Champawander's daughter. Now, the maharajah was so distraught at the death of his daughter that he offered his largest sapphire as a reward to anyone who could kill the beast. Not surprisingly, this great prize attracted all the big game hunters of the day. Captain Ernest Eagleburger, Boniface Quixote . . . ' Jos blew a thick cloud of smoke from his mouth, 'even the legendary Klaus von Grit . . . *none* of them were able to track it down. This tiger was clever, see, and it lived in a wild stretch of country criss-crossed with ravines and covered in dense jungle.'

'So how did—'

'It get into the museum?' interrupted Jos. 'Well Tom, you get no prizes for guessing that Sir Henry Scatterhorn was one of those hunters—he was. He travelled to India with August Catcher and a beautiful young adventuress named Mina Quilt. Of course he wanted it for his museum, but there was a big problem.' Jos leant closer and lowered his voice as if he didn't want to be overheard. 'The story goes—and Tom, remember, it is a *story*, there was no one who could claim with certainty that they saw what *really* happened.' Jos cleared his throat once more. 'The story goes that the tiger was possessed by an evil spirit. The locals called it a *shaitan*.' Jos raised his eyebrows for effect.

'*Shaitan*?'

'Means devil, disguised in a tiger's body. Firebreathing monster, all that jazz. Bullets just glanced right off it, see, so it can't be killed. Now, this *shaitan* realizes it's being hunted, so one night it comes up to their jungle camp. Scenting Mina first, it creeps into the tent where she lies sleeping. Mina manages to scream out, once, but—' Jos pulled hard on his pipe, 'that was the very last breath she ever took. So her cry wakes August, who comes running from his tent to see the *shaitan* making off with Mina's body. Grabbing a flaming torch he challenges it, but this great tiger—who's absolutely fearless, remember—drops Mina like a hot potato and springs at him. It swallows the burning torch whole and smashes him to the ground. He's out cold, and the tiger's just about to break *his* neck too, when Sir Henry appears and he challenges the beast. The *shaitan* steps forward. They circle, slowly, looking to land that first hammer blow,' Jos was growling like a cat now, ducking his shoulders like a boxer, 'when suddenly that tiger springs and—' Jos shot an arm out in front of him, 'Sir Henry parries with his silver dagger, stabbing the beast right through the heart! Killed. Stone dead. But—'

Jos took a long pull on his pipe and found that it had gone out. 'Not before it utters a terrible curse.'

'How do you mean?'

'The *shaitan* curses the sapphire, the reward for its death.'

Jos paused to refill his pipe, and Tom wondered whether any of what he had just heard could be true.

'So . . . so what has this to do with the burglaries?'

'The *sapphire*,' whispered Uncle Jos impatiently. 'Sir Henry was not a superstitious man but he found he couldn't do anything with the damn thing; he couldn't sell it—he couldn't even cut it up. It was bad luck, see. *Cursed*. So . . . ' and here Jos added another one of his long theatrical pauses, 'that is why some people think that he hid it.'

'Where?' asked Tom.

'In the museum. Buried *inside* the stuffing of one of the animals. What other reason can you think of for a thief to take all that trouble just to steal one tatty old kookaburra?'

Tom had to admit it did sound plausible. Was that really what

Don Gervase was after? He looked up and for the first time saw a twinkle in Uncle Jos's eyes.

'Have you looked for it?'

'A long time ago,' said Jos, leaning back, 'when I was about your age, I used to take a little screwdriver and nose about here and there. I looked for about ten years on and off and I found . . . ' Jos lowered his voice to barely a whisper, 'absolutely and precisely . . . *nothing*. Nothing whatsoever!' Jos's shoulders started to shake with laughter.

'It's a legend, Tom! *Shaitan*'s curse, indeed. It makes a good story though, and many sane people believed it. Including my *father*—of all people! He wasted years of his life looking for that blasted sapphire, and what did he find?' Jos paused to puff on his pipe, which had gone out yet again.

'The truth is Tom, I have no idea why the museum is burgled. But I very much doubt it's our new friends up at Catcher Hall. They know there's nothing here. Perhaps—now, *here's* a radical thought—' Jos screwed his eyes up so tight that they were no larger than bullets, 'perhaps it's just a few good old-fashioned criminals stealing a few tatty old animals to make a few quid. And if it is, well, good luck to them. I can't stop it.' He clapped Tom hard on the knee. 'But it would be one hell of a story if it *were* true. Don't you think?'

Tom sat there staring into the grey water, thinking long and hard. It certainly would be one hell of a story. But could it really explain everything that had happened so far?

CHAPTER 9

That Old Chestnut

'How old did you say you were?'

'Thirteen,' Tom lied.

'Hmm.' The large untidy man stood in the doorway staring at Tom, thin and shivering on the grey pavement. It had just started to rain.

'And your mum's coming to pick you up?'

'That's what she said. I told her I had missed the train and she said to wait in here,' replied Tom, smiling as innocently as he could. 'She said you wouldn't mind.'

'She did, did she?'

The man, who sounded as if he might be Russian, stood rubbing his unshaved chin.

'OK, OK,' he said wearily, 'come in zen.'

'Thanks.'

Tom walked into the fuggy little café and sat down on the nearest chair. The walls were lined with computer monitors and there was no one inside except a couple of backpackers in the corner, noisily tapping out an email. Tom had noticed this internet café outside the station when he had first arrived, and because Uncle Jos did not have a computer, and Tom had no idea where the library was, this seemed to be the best place to find out what he wanted. But he would have to be patient. The large Russian slumped down in the chair next to him and rubbed his eyes violently. He looked as if he hadn't slept for a week.

'I don't suppose I could look something up while I'm waiting?' asked Tom as innocently as he could.

'£5 an hour, which, my friend, you probably do not have because you left it at your home. Am I right?'

'No,' said Tom quickly. 'It's just that we don't have a computer and I need to look something up for a school project.'

At least part of that was true.

'Please?'

The Russian stared at him through glazed eyes.

'Ven did you say your mother was coming?'

'Fifteen minutes. I won't be long, I promise.'

The Russian shook his head, and then with a huge effort wheeled his chair up to the screen. He tapped the dirty keyboard a few times.

'Vat do you want to know?' he said, with no enthusiasm.

'I want to find out about the largest uncut sapphire in the world.'

'*Bozhe moi,*' the Russian swore to himself. He typed 'largest-uncut-sapphire-in-world', thumped his index finger down on the send key and waited. 'There,' he said nonchalantly, and swivelled his chair to face the window. The rain was pelting down on the glass. Tom watched as the screen flickered for a moment, then it came back.

Results: 94,800.

Tom clicked on the first match.

Until 1900, when the Star of India (563 carats) was presented to the American Museum of Natural History by Mr J. P. Morgan, ***the largest uncut sapphire star in the world*** *was the now lost 'Champawander Sapphire' (471 carats) found by Raski Swarminarthan, an illiterate miner excavating the Ulongapam riverbed in 1856. It was first owned by the Maharajah of Champawander, who had originally intended that his daughter should wear it at her wedding, but fate intervened when the girl was eaten by a tiger. Instead of giving the stone to his daughter, the Maharajah offered it as bounty to the man who killed the beast. In 1906 an English hunter and collector named Sir Henry Scatterhorn succeeded and claimed the Champawander sapphire as his reward. The stone has never been seen since that date and it is commonly believed to have been stolen. It remains one of the largest sapphires ever found.*

So part of the story *was* true. The sapphire did exist after all.

Tom noticed that the Russian was still transfixed by the drops of rain running down the window. Did he have time to try something else? Yes—it was worth the risk. Turning to the computer once more, Tom typed in the words '*time hole*' as fast as he could with three fingers. Send.

There were 57 *million* results! Maybe that meant that there were 57 million time holes in the world, but after looking at the first page Tom realized that the results had nothing to do with the time hole he meant. There were black holes and white holes and worm holes and Jackson Hole and people with holes in their heads.

OK then, try this. Tom typed '*shrinking back in time*', and pressed the send key. This time only 14 million results came back. That sounded better, but they were all about lasers and the Bible. Then he tried '*talking animals*' and found himself in a website for people who like to telephone their pets: '*Ever wondered what woof woof really means? Hello? Goodbye? I'm hungry? I love you? Wrong! Learn how to speak dog in five easy lessons! It's sooooo easy!*'

It was all useless. Maybe his dad was right after all—the modern world was rubbish.

'Is zat your mother?' said the Russian, pointing at a white car pulling up on the other side of the station.

'Yep, that's her,' replied Tom quickly. 'She . . . er . . . must have forgotten that I'd be in here.'

'Of course she did.'

The Russian was too tired to care.

'Well, thanks anyway,' said Tom, zipping up his coat and walking over to the door.

'You know, they really should get some computers in your school.'

'Sorry?'

Tom had momentarily forgotten his excuse for being in there.

'Yes, my friend. Yesterday someone else came in here doing that school project.'

'Oh?'

Tom was genuinely confused.

'She had no money either.'

'Really? Who was she?'

'A dark-haired girl. Slim. A little bit older than you. Looked like a dancer.' The Russian eyed him suspiciously. 'I'm surprised you don't know her.'

'No,' mumbled Tom. 'I . . . er . . . it's a big school. I don't think so.'

The Russian continued to stare at him and Tom felt the blood rushing to his cheeks. Could that be . . . ?

'OK my friend. Just go.' The Russian waved him away.

Tom stumbled out into the rain, his head buzzing. Was it Lotus? It sounded like her. Perhaps it was. Tom hurried away down the pavement trying to make sense of it all. He felt like a detective trying to catch up with a story and he didn't even know what the story was yet, it kept changing so fast. So was the sapphire what Don Gervase and Lotus really wanted? Then they were thieves after all. But Jos had looked for the sapphire for ten years and never found anything, and his father had looked for it all his life. Surely there was nothing there.

Unless . . . unless Don Gervase and Lotus *had* discovered something Jos did not know about. Some lost papers perhaps, some new clues somewhere in Catcher Hall. After all, Jos knew nothing about the hole in the wicker basket under the stairs, or the model. Don Gervase and Lotus did, didn't they?

Reaching the top of Museum Street Tom crossed the road and walked down towards the Scatterhorn Museum, where a group of children had gathered outside. They looked as if they were waiting for someone, a pop star perhaps; but when Tom drew closer he saw that they were all gathered around a large car parked at the foot of the steps. Tom recognized that rich mahogany colour instantly—it was Don Gervase's Bentley. He must be inside, talking to Jos. Tom hovered on the other side of the road, not sure whether he wanted to go in, and then he began to sense something delicious and familiar all around him. Chocolate, peppermint, orange blossom, banana cream . . . each flavour drifted towards him through the rain, so real that he almost felt he was eating them. Tom recognized this smell: it had wafted through the study window at Catcher Hall; it had filled the kitchen the day Don Gervase had brought the Peruvian cake. Now it was here again in the street, almost oozing out of the Bentley itself. This is what had brought the children out in the rain, just to stand around with no particular reason. That magical, mouthwatering smell.

Suddenly the museum door flung open, and out stepped Don Gervase in his long woollen coat, quickly followed by Lotus.

'Ah—children, how delightful!' boomed Don Gervase.

A little girl let out an involuntary squeak. Don Gervase bent down low and pinched her cheek.

'Thank you so much, my dear, for minding my car.'

The little girl was too terrified to speak.

''Ere, mister,' piped up a red-cheeked boy braver than the rest, 'is yous real famous?'

'I don't *believe* I am,' replied Don Gervase. 'Why, do I remind you of a famous person?'

The boy squinted up at the strange looking man with yellowy black teeth smiling down at him.

'I dunno,' he said cautiously, 'Count Dracula?'

Some of the children behind him sniggered.

'Hmm. Count Dracula,' repeated Don Gervase in all seriousness, 'I don't believe that I've ever heard of him. Does he like chocolate as much as I do?' And with that, Don Gervase opened the heavy door and reaching into the glove compartment, pulled out a large bar of homemade dark chocolate. The smell was almost overpowering. The children pressed forward, unable to help themselves.

'Now, as a reward, I'm sure you would like some of this,' he smiled. 'One at a time, if you please!' He placed a small dark square into each grabbing hand.

Tom watched intently as the children swarmed around the tall man, fighting and climbing on top of each other to grab more chocolate. A silky voice suddenly broke into his thoughts.

'Hello Tom.'

Tom jumped; he hadn't noticed that Lotus was standing right next to him.

'Oh . . . er . . . hi,' he said awkwardly.

'Jos said you'd gone to use the computer in the café.'

'Yep, that's right,' said Tom thinking fast. He had been taken completely off his guard. 'I just wanted to send an email . . . erm . . . to my parents.'

'Oh. And where are they?'

'Mongolia.'

'Mongolia?' repeated Lotus softly.

'Yeah . . . I dunno. Maybe. Somewhere like that.'

'Why Mongolia?'

'My dad's . . . they're on an expedition, looking for . . . caterpillars or centipedes, not sure exactly,' he said, forcing a smile, 'something wriggly.'

But Lotus did not smile; she did not even blink. Her green eyes burnt into him like lasers.

'How fascinating,' she purred, 'you never told me they were interested in insects.'

'No,' replied Tom uneasily, 'but then you didn't ask.'

'You know I *adore* insects, and so does my dad. We—'

'Lotus!'

There was Don Gervase sitting in the car impatiently, with the children still crowding around him.

'Come along, my dear.'

Seeing Tom, he raised his long bony hand and smiled thinly.

'Well, until the next time,' she said, and with a quiet smile she strode across the road to the car. The Bentley kicked into life with a quiet rumble.

'Bye bye, Tom,' she waved, and Tom waved back. They were gone.

Always more questions—never any answers. Tom was even more confused than ever; and opening the door to the museum he discovered he was not alone. There was Uncle Jos pacing up and down in the gloom in a state of high agitation. He tried sitting down on the stairs, but that didn't work, so he shambled over to the bench on the other side of the hall and found that that didn't work either.

'He *is* a Catcher, I suppose,' mumbled Jos to himself, pulling at the stray tufts of hair scattered across his head.

'And he has *oodles* of money, so he's ideal,' said a slurred voice from above. It was Melba, sitting at the top of the stairs, and Tom noticed that she was swaying a little.

'If he didn't come here with his oodles of chocolate you might think differently,' grumbled Jos as he peered up at her.

'Well it was very thoughtful of him to bring it,' she replied defiantly, 'and I enjoyed every crumb—so there.'

She's drunk, thought Tom.

'Hagfish on a houseboat,' growled Jos, jumping up and thrusting his hands deep in his pockets. Turning round he saw Tom standing there in the half-light.

'Bad news, lad,' he said carefully. 'The worst, I'm afraid.'

Tom wasn't sure what to say. Was it his parents, had they heard something? No, it couldn't be . . .

'What's happened?'

'Don Gervase wants to buy the museum. Lock, stock and barrel.'

Tom felt as if someone had just knocked the wind out of his chest. Of course Don Gervase did, the museum contained the sapphire. It all made sense now.

'But . . . but . . . when?' he spluttered. 'I mean . . . how?'

'He's just made me an offer, and he wants an answer by Christmas.'

'But he can't,' protested Tom. 'Don Gervase can't do that—can he?'

'I'm afraid he can, Tom. *If* I sell it to him.'

'But you *can't*. I mean . . . I mean you *wouldn't*.'

Jos was pacing up and down again, violently scratching his head.

'Would you?'

'He has limitless funds, apparently. He says he loves this old place and wants to restore it—'

'Plus he's a Catcher,' Melba chipped in from the top of the stairs.

'That too. Which in one sense, couldn't be worse, but then again, August had a lot to do with the Scatterhorn Museum, as we all know.'

'Of course he did,' added Melba.

Tom suddenly felt a wave of anger rising up in him. The museum wasn't even his, but still he felt angry. He wanted to punch something.

'So . . . so just because he's got the money you're going to let him buy it? It doesn't seem fair.'

'You're right there, lad—it's not fair. Life ain't fair neither.' Jos stopped pacing and stared at the puddle of rainwater on the floor. 'But what do you want me to do? Bury my head in the sand and just let it fall down all around me?'

Jos glared up at the broken skylight and the tatty animals all around him. Suddenly he looked as desperate as if he had just been marooned on a desert island.

'This museum deserves a whole lot better than what I've got to offer,' he said at last. 'I know that. Nothing's ever simple, is it?'

And away he shuffled, into the gloom. Tom swallowed hard; he was trying to pretend that he understood but he didn't.

'I'm sure if Don Gervase buys it the very first thing he will do is offer us a job,' said Melba brightly as she swayed down the stairs.

'What makes you think that?' replied Tom, doubting very much if Don Gervase would offer anyone a job. Surely all *he* wanted to do was to tear the place to pieces.

'Well, we know the ropes,' she said. 'Lord knows we have been here long enough. And we're *Scatterhorns,* after all. That's got to be worth something.'

'Has it?'

Being a Scatterhorn had never meant anything to Tom. Except that it rhymed with Matterhorn.

'Of course,' she smiled. 'Don't you worry about this old place, Tom. It can take care of itself. It always does.'

Melba seemed almost happy as she trotted unsteadily down the corridor and closed the heavy wooden door behind her. Tom sat down in the middle of the stairs feeling utterly deflated. At last the whole picture was becoming clear in his mind. Sapphires and talking animals, that's what this was all about, and the small matter of a model that seemed to be alive. Simple as that, really.

'So,' said Tom, his voice echoing around the empty museum, 'so I suppose you heard all that.'

There was no reply. A car alarm sounded in the distance. Might as well be talking to himself, thought Tom—there was no one listening. Why should there be? He was in a museum full of tatty stuffed animals. Tom was just about to get up when he heard a low, rumbling grunt from the bottom of the stairs. It sounded like someone trying to stifle a giggle. Tom listened and there it was again. Unmistakably, giggling. No doubt about it. Then some muffled words were clearly discernible.

'Dear oh dear.'

Tom could barely see anything at all, but he was aware that he was being laughed at.

'What?' he said out loud. 'What's so funny?'

Tom turned to see the mammoth shaking, trying to contain himself.

'It's a guinea a minute,' he said, stretching his vast hairy trunk up to wipe a tear from his eye.

'Well?' said Tom, who was becoming angrier by the second. 'What are you all laughing about? I wouldn't be if I were you.'

'Bless his cotton socks,' sighed the dodo, wriggling her tail feathers and stepping down from her podium. 'Oh Tom, your concern is very touching. Very touching indeed.'

'You must remember,' announced the gorilla, 'that most of us have been in far worse scrapes than this.'

'You have?'

'Well, *I* haven't,' said the dodo, 'not personally mind. But that's because I'm special you see, like my good friend the mammoth here. Extinction brings distinction. But the rest of this lot—'

'We've already been killed once, haven't we?' said the proboscis monkey, padding across the floor towards him.

'So what is there to worry about?' added the gorilla.

Tom could not argue with that. Of course, they were right. They *were* all dead—in a way.

'And, if I might add,' whispered the mammoth, raising his trunk close to Tom's ear, 'some of the smaller members of our club, particularly the mice, rabbits, shrews, that sort of thing, are *very* religious. Can't tell them anything.'

'What's that got to do with it?'

'You know, *life after death* and all that,' said the mammoth, his eyes twinkling. 'Heaven. See for yourself.'

The mammoth lumbered over to the small mammals cabinet and pulled open a drawer with his trunk.

'Jerusalem the gol-den with milk and honey flow-ow-ow-ow-ing,' came a choir of squeaky voices. Tom looked in and saw twenty mice lying on their backs all singing together.

'Bravo,' whispered the mammoth.

'Thank you, brother mammoth,' said a mouse, 'and a very good day in paradise to you.'

'Indeed.' The mammoth nodded and carefully closed the drawer. Reaching up he pulled open another, to reveal a congregation of pygmy shrews listening to a preacher standing on a thimble.

'And what have we found, brothers and sisters, on the other side? Yes, the lion *does* sit down with the lamb!'

'Hallelujah!' shouted all the shrews together.

'Yes! The mouse he *does* feast with the mammoth!'

'Hallelujah!' they all shouted again.

'Hallelujah! Brothers and sisters,' squeaked the preacher shrew, 'you are saved!'

'We're saved! We're saved!' they squealed.

'You see?' whispered the mammoth. 'These little fellows were dead, and now they're alive. And what's more, they find themselves in a place full of terrifying chaps whom they have spent a lifetime avoiding at all costs,' the mammoth lowered its vast shaggy head right next to Tom's ear, 'but, quite extraordinarily, in here *no one wants to eat them*. They feel safe. And so, it follows,' twinkled the mammoth, 'that this must be heaven.'

Tom thought back to that morning with Jos in the garden shed. What had he said about the brain cavity of the arctic rabbit? It was full of shavings from the Bible.

'And is that what you think, too?' asked Tom uncertainly.

'Me? Well, religion has never been my tipple. Sport's the thing. Play up, play the game! Oh yes. But as my lady friend the dodo explained, extinction does indeed bring distinction.

One is . . . more of a construction if technically one has never been *alive* in the first place. But anyway,' the mammoth continued, 'eating each other would be *extremely* uncivilized, don't you think? I mean—this is hardly the stone age. This is the twentieth century, old boy.'

'Twenty-first century, if you must know, my dear,' corrected the dodo.

'Quite.'

'So, does that mean that none of you is worried about what happens next? Supposing the sapphire—'

'The sapphire!' interrupted the ring-tailed lemur. 'Oh yes, the *sapphire*. What a hoot.'

'It's not here, Tom, never has been,' said the dodo categorically, 'and Lord knows they've all looked for it.'

'In the most embarrassing places, I can assure you,' added the aardvark, with feeling.

'But . . . are you *sure* it's not here? I mean, how do you know?'

'Well, no one's found it, so it can't be, can it?' replied the proboscis monkey, cleaning its nails. 'People generally know where to look for these things.'

Tom wasn't so sure about that. 'Have you ever asked the tiger about it?'

There was a pause and Tom noticed that all the animals fell silent. He sensed that he had just asked a very difficult question.

'Well, actually no, since you ask,' whispered the gorilla.

'Why not?' said Tom innocently. 'Wasn't the sapphire the prize on his head?' The awkward silence continued and the gorilla stared uneasily at the floor.

'The fact is,' whispered the dodo, shooting a glance up to the top of the stairs, 'the fact is that the tiger has never spoken. To any of us. Ever.'

'Man-eater, you see,' whispered the mammoth. 'Bad business,' he added, shaking his vast head. 'We don't really like to talk about it.'

'So . . . are you saying you're *scared* of the tiger?'

Tom looked around and saw that it was true, though none of them cared to admit it. Even the great brown bear avoided his eye.

'It's eaten over four hundred people,' hissed the anaconda. 'Four hundred . . . '

Tom could not understand it. Here was a collection of the most dangerous wild animals in the world, who between them could have killed thousands of people. Yet they were terrified of a single tiger. Why? And then Tom had another thought. If they *were* still alive in some way, and he accepted that now, then it was remarkable that these animals hadn't killed each other already. What was stopping them? Perhaps what the mammoth had said about the mice was true for them all. Perhaps all the papers stuffed inside their heads, old newspapers full of stories of right and wrong, sermons, morals, bits of the Bible—whatever—had prevented them. They didn't think it was right to kill each other any more. And because they weren't hungry, they didn't need to. But *maybe* the tiger was different. Maybe it was all animal on the outside *and* the inside—and that's why it had never spoken: it couldn't. Maybe the tiger was the only creature in the entire museum whose head was *not* stuffed with Edwardian newspaper, but, if it wasn't, it might also be the only creature in the museum that really knew where the sapphire was. And at that moment, Tom knew instinctively that was what he must do. He must find out. Turning round, Tom began to slowly walk up the stairs.

'What the devil are you doing?' hissed the dodo.

'Come back, Tom!' whispered the proboscis monkey anxiously. 'Don't be so foolish.'

But Tom did not reply. Before him he could just make out a vague stripy shape on the landing where he knew the tiger to be. The museum had fallen completely silent and Tom felt the eyes of all the animals on his back as he climbed higher and higher. At last he reached the top, and there before him lay the great animal, its pelt faded to the colour of old paper, stretched right out as if sunbathing on a rock. Tom walked a couple of paces forward and then stopped abruptly when he saw its ears flatten and the white end of its tail flicker quickly. No closer, the big cat seemed to be saying. The tiger turned its huge head towards him and its flame-coloured eyes met his: half-bored, half-curious. There was nothing friendly about this animal at all.

'Excuse me . . . erm . . . sir,' he heard himself say, his voice small and echoing, 'I don't suppose . . . er . . . you happen to know . . . where the . . . the . . . sapphire is?'

There was no reply. The great man-eater watched him curiously, as if recognizing him, but it said nothing. An uneasy silence hung heavily all around the museum. Not an animal moved. Tom peered into the gloom and saw that those flaming eyes were no longer fixed on him, they were watching something scuttling across the floor. A small black beetle. Idly the tiger stretched out one heavy paw and placed it on top of the tiny creature. Holding it there for a moment, the cat then lifted up its paw, whereupon the beetle struggled to its feet and continued with its journey. The tiger waited, then repeated the game.

'I admire the humble beetle,' it growled, watching the small black creature get up once more, never altering its course, 'an example to us all, don't you think?'

Tom said nothing. He was wondering how many seconds the beetle had left to live. Somewhere down below he heard frightened gasps.

'It speaks,' whispered a voice, 'it's a talking tiger!'

'You're a talking anteater!'

'You're a talking pangolin.'

'Shh!' said another voice.

The tiger ignored the murmuring and turned its eyes back to Tom. 'A beetle is not afraid of anything—or anyone,' it said, 'even me.'

Suddenly the tiger slammed its paw down with a heavy whump! crushing the beetle flat. Then the big cat stood up and stretched lazily, before stepping down from the podium and padding silently along the gallery. Reaching the far end, the man-eater turned around to survey the entire museum.

'Hmmm,' it growled, 'just as I suspected.'

There was complete silence. The tiger inspected them all with its flame-coloured eyes. Every animal was waiting for something, but they were not sure what.

'Nothing but a collection of ridiculous creatures,' the tiger sniffed. 'So *civilized*, and so utterly *useless*. To think I could have eaten any one of you lot.'

The tiger's eyes came to rest on the huge shaggy mammoth. He glanced up uneasily.

'Especially you.'

The mammoth gulped.

'One day I might just do that.'

'Lord,' whispered the proboscis monkey, 'it's a speaking, man-eating, woman-tiger-thingamajig.'

'That's correct,' growled the tiger. 'I'm female. And how completely typical of you all to assume that because I am superior in every way, I must be male. I'm not. Though you may call me "sir" if you like. I rather like it.' The tiger grinned to herself, and there was a murmur of frightened voices all around.

'Perhaps she's one of those suffragettes—'

'An anarchist, more like.'

'She'll want a vote—'

'Society will collapse—'

'There'll be a revolution—'

'Madam!' squeaked a high rasping voice from the shadows. 'Madam!' A porcupine trotted out to the centre of the hall.

'I feel I must protest. On no occasion could you have eaten me.'

There was a piercing silence. The tiger stared curiously at the black and white animal.

'And what, pray, are you?'

The porcupine rattled its quills violently.

'Precisely. You are but quills and air—nothing more. Why would I ever want to eat a quill?'

'It is a question that vexed me too,' replied the porcupine boldly, 'on the occasion when you attacked me.'

The tiger's eyes narrowed; she was not sure whether she had just been insulted or not. With one heavy paw she reached up to scratch her mouth, as if she was trying to remember something.

'Take care, little porcupine,' she said with menace, 'accidents can happen. Even in here, amongst "civilized society".' She drew back her black gums to reveal a set of huge front teeth, shining like daggers in the gloom. 'Hsssssss!'

The porcupine squealed and scrambled back to the safety of his cabinet as muffled cries echoed around the hall. The tiger smiled to herself, then turned and glowered at Tom, still standing at the top of the stairs.

'You asked me about the sapphire,' she sniffed. 'That *is* an old chestnut. However, I do believe the "chicken thing" at the bottom of the stairs may be correct. It's not here, and who knows, perhaps even the curious Don Gervase Askary realizes that. *I* have a little theory of my own, but—' she turned to address the entire museum, as if they were all her subjects and she was their queen, 'why on earth should I share it with you lot? I think you will all find out soon enough.'

Her flaming eyes came to rest on Tom, and he felt his skin crawl.

'Particularly you: Tom *Scatterhorn,*' she hissed, spitting out the word.

Instinctively Tom took a step back, groping for the handrail behind him. Was she going to attack? She couldn't—not here. But she might. The tiger padded lazily towards him. This animal spoke but Tom sensed it was unpredictable; it was real. It might do anything at all. On she came, like a cat stalking a mouse.

'Stay there as long as you dare, little boy . . . '

Suddenly Tom turned and dashed down the stairs.

'Hmmm.'

The tiger seemed more interested now, and she peered curiously down into the hall. All the other animals had retreated to their cases and Tom stood completely alone; alone—with a man-eater. Tom glanced to his left and saw the small cupboard door under the stairs. How quickly could he get there? Three seconds? Two seconds? She would be on him by then. Looking up at the top of the stairs he saw the long brown shape of the tiger slide out of the gloom towards him. His heart was thumping against his ribcage, and he was trying hard to control his urge to run. Don't panic . . . don't even move . . . that's what she wants you to do . . . it's a game.

But it was already too late, the tiger had smelt his fear. She stopped dead on the stairs, her ears pricked up and her muscles quivering, alert. She was no longer some strange talking relic, she was now a man-eating cat out hunting. And Tom was her prey. She could kill him now if she wanted to—he knew that. But he also knew that he could not control his instinct, and that was to hide, hide somewhere she could never follow.

Suddenly he ran. In five paces he reached the cupboard door and flung it open, just as steel claws scratched on the stone and something brown flashed behind him. She had missed! But only just; the mouse was safe. Then a large brown paw pushed the door open and the tiger's huge head peered inside.

'Ah-ha,' she said slowly. 'So this is your little hidey-hole.'

The tiger let out a growl so low that it seemed to pass right through one side of Tom and out the other. Tom tried to breathe but he couldn't, he had never felt more terrified in his life. Without thinking about the consequences he scrambled over to the wicker basket and dived inside. It was exactly as he had left it, and pushing rags out of the way he began thrashing around wildly, trying to dig himself deeper. Last time he was here he had disappeared by accident—this time it was a matter of life and death.

'Let me in, please, let me in,' he gasped, and then he felt it, a small gap in the rags below him. It was starting to open. Tom wriggled and burrowed like a mole and before he knew it, he had fallen headlong off a precipice, plummeting down into the darkness.

Tom did not try to cling on. He let himself go limp and waited, until at last the feathery softness enveloped him like a blanket and he landed. At first he saw nothing. Then, as his eyes became accustomed to the darkness, Tom could just make out the grey shapes of cavalrymen riding towards a distant sand dune. He had made it. Tom lay completely still for a moment, taking long deep breaths and trying to calm his galloping heart. It was OK. He was back. Back in time, back to the other place, inside Catcher Hall, a hundred years ago. And he was safe—for now. That was good enough.

CHAPTER 10

The Power of Life and Death

Tom stepped out into the empty corridor and listened. There were sounds of voices somewhere else in the house below him, and this time Tom felt a lot braver about being back in Catcher Hall. He knew now that this was not a prison; there was a way back, should he choose to take it. And he also knew that however long he spent here, back in the museum, in his own time, time was standing still. Jos and Melba would not miss him. So—what next? Tom didn't want to meet anyone else, not yet at any rate. But he did want to find out more about how he got here. Maybe it would give him a clue as to how Gervase and Lotus had found their way into the past too.

Without really knowing why, Tom climbed up the narrow winding stairs that led to August's large workshop at the top of the house. He knocked on the door and, hearing no answer, he opened it gently to find the long high room much as he had left it. A pale winter light filtered in through the large round window at the end and there was a fire blazing in the grate. August was not here. Tom walked up to the fire and gazed about him. In every corner, on every shelf, and even hanging from the high ceiling, were models of animals in various states of completion. Tom immediately recognized the dodo and the coatamundi, both half-stuffed. In one corner there was a large wooden mannequin with the skull of an antelope at one end on a wire, and hanging on the wall opposite it was a pair of vast wings, so much taller than Tom that he imagined they must belong to some kind of giant bird. Beneath them stood a large wooden construction that might eventually become their body. There was something oddly familiar about this, as there was about everything else in the workshop, and as Tom ventured on past piles of stoats and civets his attention was drawn towards a large wooden cabinet containing drawers of all different shapes and sizes.

'*Eyes—Big Cats,*' read one label. Tom gently pulled it open to find rows of blue velvet pillows bearing pairs of different coloured glass eyeballs. '*Leopard*', '*Puma*', '*Lion*', and at the very back, a large flame-coloured pair marked '*Tiger*'. In the drawer below labelled '*Quack*', slim plaster casts of bills were arranged in ascending order of size and lined up like silver spoons in a box. On every surface there were jars of chemicals and stacks of newspapers and every kind of tool, lying about in confused heaps. Tom marvelled at the strangeness of it all. The workshop was the lair of a strange toymaker, or a wizard, and the longer Tom spent there the more he felt that he was trespassing. He was just trying the lock on a cupboard marked '*Curiosities*' when there was a knock at the door.

Tom turned round to see two boys struggle in carrying a large heavy sack between them. Both were wearing fur hats and thick tweed jackets tied up with string.

'Where will he wan' put it?' said the taller of the two. 'Here?' He pointed at the only clear stretch of bench beside the door.

'Reckon,' mumbled the smaller boy, glancing across at the fire. 'Don' wan' it thawin' out' fore Mr August comes back though.'

Together the two boys lifted up the sack and carefully set it down on the bench. Whatever was inside stood about a metre high and was a very awkward shape. It was only when they turned round that Tom recognized the smaller boy from the landing the first time he was here. As soon as he saw Tom he grinned.

'All right, Tom? Din't see yous lurkin' there in the dark.'

Tom smiled nervously. He had forgotten that this boy knew his name.

'When's Mr August back, d'yer know?'

Tom shrugged. 'Sorry, I—'

'Jus' that my brother Abel here's found somethin' inneresting'.'

'Somethin' he'd pay us for, p'raps,' added Abel, blowing hard on his cold fingers. Abel was a head taller than his brother and rangy looking. He obviously felt awkward in these strange surroundings.

'Found it out on the Skeet marsh this mornin',' said the smaller boy excitedly, 'do yous wan' take a peek?'

'Cost yer, mind,' added Abel sullenly.

'Here,' said the younger boy, beckoning Tom forward. He undid the knot at the top of the sack and carefully slid it halfway down, revealing the icy feathers of a large grey bird.

'Heron,' announced the younger boy, 'frozen solid as a stoon it was. Had to chip it out of the mud with an axe.'

'No yous din't, Noah,' snarled Abel.

'So-s? I'm only tellin' him the story.'

'It's my bird,' said Abel, grimacing. He elbowed his younger brother hard in the ribs.

'All right! So it is,' winced Noah. 'Anyways, a heron ain't nothin' on its own. Here's the whole picture.'

Noah pulled down the rest of the sack to reveal the large grey bird standing upright on a plinth of frozen mud, with its head angled towards the ground. At first Tom thought that the heron had a long grey pipe wound round its neck, which was somehow attached to its beak. But peering closer, he saw that the pipe had glassy eyes and a toothy mouth, split in half by the heron's sharp yellow beak. The pipe was not a pipe at all. It was an eel.

'Battle to the death, I reckon,' sniffed Abel, as he admired the extraordinary sight.

'But what if the eel killed the heron at precisely the same moment as the heron killed the eel?' came a voice from above them.

The boys looked up to see August Catcher climbing down a small ladder from the skylight. His cheeks were flushed from the cold, and he wore a racoon hat raked at an angle on his head.

'Then an icy mist rolled in off the sea, freezing the mud on which the heron stood, locking both bird and eel together in frozen combat. For ever.' August bent down to look closer. 'What a truly remarkable find,' he said quietly. 'In the marshes, you say?'

'Y-yes Mr August,' stammered Abel, 'just about fifty yards up from the fish traps.'

'Nature never ceases to amaze me. Abel, you have done well.' August smiled and Abel looked embarrassed.

'And so have you, Noah, for making your brother bring it to me.'

The smaller boy beamed proudly.

'So as a reward,' August reached into his waistcoat pocket and pulled out two gold coins. He put one in Abel's hand, the other in Noah's. Tom had no idea what these coins were but the brothers' faces lit up when they saw them. This must be a lot of money.

'*Thank you*, sir,' said Noah quickly, glancing first at August and then his brother.

Abel could not stop staring at the shining coin in his palm.

'Mr August, sir,' he faltered, 'I wonnerd, it's just . . . because I found it, if—'

'If you could have something more than Noah?' suggested August, arching his eyebrows. Abel blushed and stared hard at his shoes. August pulled out another gold coin and slipped it into Abel's palm.

'Will this do, Abel?'

Abel's eyes widened and he let out a little gasp. Now there were two gold sovereigns in his hand. What could he buy with that—what *couldn't* he buy with that?

'You're very generous, Mr August, sir,' he stumbled, glancing up.

'Think nothing of it, Abel. This is indeed a rare find and you deserve it, both of you. But remember, boys,' added August, his voice becoming sterner, 'this is not an invitation to trap any common or garden bird, or steal any tail feathers, or filch any eggs for that matter. Do you understand?'

The two boys nodded and stared down at their boots.

'Yes, Mr August,' said Noah quietly.

'Right,' smiled August. 'Now get off, the pair of you.'

'Thank you, sir.'

Abel pulled on his heavy black cap and backed out of the door, followed by his younger brother. Tom heard a muffled cheer as their heavy boots echoed away down the rickety stairs.

'Really quite remarkable, don't you think, Tom?' said August, bending over the scene of frozen combat on the bench. 'Who do you think is the winner?'

Tom looked at the struggling animals. He wasn't sure. 'Neither?'

'Precisely. Nature has won.'

Tom smiled to himself, relieved. He seemed to have got the first question right.

'So—will you be able to preserve them like this? I mean, is it possible?'

'Now there's a question,' said August glancing up at him, 'and one which, as my new apprentice, you are absolutely entitled to ask.'

August furrowed his brow and studied the heron and the eel before him.

'The taxidermist must be many things. A naturalist, a carpenter, a chemist, a blacksmith, an anatomist, a painter, but above all, he must be able to look—to *observe*, to see the wildness in all wild things. That is the first and only golden rule in a profession without rules.'

Bending forward, August scrutinized the heron like a doctor inspecting a patient. His voice was cool and precise.

'You know, if I had invented this scene, I am quite sure that no one would have believed me. I would have been roundly lampooned as a fantasist. But this, Tom, this is real nature; the ice has captured it for us. And the devil is in the detail.'

August walked around the back, scrutinizing every line and contour.

'See how the heron's muscles are jerking its head back. Observe the flashing anger in its eyes. And here,' he pointed to the eel, 'look how the shape of its slippery grey body changes as it curls around the heron's neck, strangling the life from it.'

August stopped to examine the angle of the heron's wing.

'Do you know, Tom, I think this heron realized at the very last moment it was going to die. Here,' he pointed to the large grey wing just extending from the body. 'It's trying to take off, to escape. But it's too late.'

August looked up at Tom, his eyes sparkling with excitement.

'There's a story here, Tom. You must fix it in your mind like a three-dimensional photograph. That is vital, because after you have preserved it and made your model, that fleeting moment, frozen in time, is what you want to end up with. *If* you can get it right—and it is an "if", I'm afraid—you will have created something wild and true. If not, it will be nothing more than a toy, and a very dull toy at that. Come.' August picked up an oil lamp and, turning on his heel, he walked quickly down to the long table in front of the round window. There before him, rising up out of the chaos of scrapers and stitching needles, was a small tree in full flower, dotted with tiny, brilliantly coloured hummingbirds.

'Do you like it?' August asked. He could see that Tom did.

'We'll come back to that. But first, smell these and tell me what you think.' August reached across to the windowsill and picked up a small white jug with a bunch of violets in it.

'I hope they're still fresh as I picked them only this morning.'

Tom took the jug and lifted it to his nose. Try as hard as he might, Tom could smell nothing at all.

'No smell?'

Tom nodded blankly. It was just dust.

'Not even the faintest *whiff*? Are you sure?'

'I'm sure.'

August arched his eyebrows.

'Are you sure you're sure? How very odd. How very, very peculiar. That's exactly what Queen Victoria thought.'

Tom looked at him completely bewildered; and he suspected he was supposed to be.

'When she smelt that bunch of violets at the Dragonport International Fisheries exhibition, twenty-five years ago!' August's face broke into a wide smile.

'You see Tom, these were the first objects I ever made. With my sister; I was seven and she was eleven at the time. Now the opening of this exhibition was a terribly grand affair, and the whole town turned out to see it. Our instructions were very simple: as soon as Her Majesty stepped down from the royal train, my sister and I were to go forward, present her with a bunch of flowers and then bow very low. But,' August chuckled to himself, remembering the scene, 'I am afraid I was a very cheeky young boy, so instead of presenting Her Majesty with the bunch of violets my mother had given us, I decided to copy them, using paper and wax. Just to *see* if the queen would notice.'

'And did she?'

'Well,' admitted August, 'there was a *brief* moment of royal confusion when the queen raised the violets to her nose to inhale the perfume, only to discover—like you did just now—that there was nothing to smell! And I'm not sure that the mayor was very pleased.'

Tom looked down at the violets. They were incredible: even twenty-five years later they still looked as fresh and real as living plants. It was easy to imagine the royal confusion, but then he remembered that Queen Victoria always looked rather fat and grumpy.

'Wasn't she angry?'

'Angry?' exclaimed August. 'Goodness no! As soon as she realized they weren't real she started to laugh. And then of course the mayor laughed, and everyone else laughed too. And then, when I told her I had actually *made* the violets, she refused to take them. She handed them back and awarded me a gold medal for flower modelling on the spot.'

'A gold medal for flower modelling?'

'Indeed. One of the advantages of being queen of half the world is that you can hand out gold medals for pretty much anything you like. And that's how my sister and I became the first official flower modellers in the entire British Empire. Isn't that tremendous?'

'Wow.'

'You see Tom, taxidermy is not just about stuffing animals; it's making everything. *Everything*,' he exclaimed, waving his arms around the room. 'Look at this tree, these blades of grass. Here,' reaching out across the workbench August picked up a handful of long dead nettles and placed them before Tom, 'go on, pick one up.'

Tom held the longest stem gingerly between his thumb and forefinger, half expecting to be stung at any moment.

'Convincing, isn't it? In fact the dead nettle is one of the hardest plants to make, and a staging post in the career of any great taxidermist.'

August grinned. He was obviously still pleased with this work.

'I made those when I was about your age.'

Tom stared down at the dead nettle in wonder. He couldn't begin to imagine how August had done it.

'So what happened after you were given your gold medal?'

'Well, we carried on, naturally, my sister and I, until I was about twelve I think. Then I left school and went into business. I moved on from violets and nettles to orchids and aspidistras, then to mice and badgers, anteaters and snakes, crocodiles, and finally, a mammoth. My parents didn't mind me following this crazy career, as both my older brothers had serious jobs. Fighting wars in Africa, growing sugar in the West Indies, that sort of thing. In fact I think they rather liked it, particularly when my name appeared in the papers and all that.' August winked and stroked his beard. 'The only thing they really *did* mind was my best friend and patron Sir Henry Scatterhorn.'

'Why was that?'

'Well obviously, because he is a Scatterhorn and I am a Catcher. Haven't you heard the rhyme?

"'Tis an ancient grudge, born in the sludge,
And neither side ain't never gonna budge."'

Tom nodded, he had heard it; Uncle Jos used to mutter it at breakfast, but he never got beyond the first line. August carried on:

'"*Now God had decided, when Time first began*
That Catchers should fight the Scatterhorn clan.
So out of the swamps two ugly beasts came,
Scattersaur and Catcherdon were their names.
One had a spike, the other a club,
To bash and to wound, to flail, to flub.
'This marsh is myne!' roared the Saur. 'Nar it ain't!'
howled the Don.
And then they went at it—hammer and tongs,
For millions of years, without resolution,
They never bothered stoppin' for evolution,
Only changed their names, that's all—more's the pity!
And on that great stinkin' marsh now stands this city.
And do we care? Do we hell, do we heck!
Let 'em all break their bleedin' necks!
As it was in the beginning, so it shall be at the end,
Catchers'll never be a Scatterhorn's friend."'

August smiled broadly as the rhyme came to an end.

'You see Tom? An age-old tradition, and like all traditions insufferably boring, don't you think? I'm afraid *I* do. I have always been one of those people who likes to do the opposite of what I am told, and the fact is that that old dinosaur Henry Scatterhorn is not only my oldest and greatest friend, he also happens to be the best shot in England—possibly even the world. Which helps a good deal.'

'Why?'

August paused. He was still smiling, but for the first time Tom noticed a cloud pass over his eyes.

'The truth is,' he said, 'I am hopeless with guns. Always have been. Can't hit a thing, and I don't like it much either. Which, as you can imagine, is not helpful in this profession. So I have always relied on Sir Henry to provide the specimens, and enterprising young chaps like Abel and Noah to bring me what they find. And of course, there is the seemingly endless procession of farmers and their "oddities".'

'Oddities?'

'Oh yes.' He winked, taking a small key out of his breast pocket. 'Interestin' oddities.'

Unlocking the long cupboard labelled '*Curiosities*' August reached inside and picked out two small animals, setting them on the table before Tom.

'Nature is constantly baffling, don't you think?'

It took Tom a moment to see what was wrong with them. The duckling had four legs and the kitten had two heads.

'No, I didn't make them up,' smiled August, 'though I must admit I do, on occasion, indulge in a bit of "creating" myself. Keeps the boredom at bay. But these extraordinary little creatures are precisely as they were born and hatched. Of course they couldn't live for long, so I . . . hastened their journey, shall we say.'

'With what?'

'With chemicals,' replied August flatly. 'I am a killer, Tom, there is no denying it. I have to be, in order to preserve and immortalize. And when the time comes, so will you.'

August walked across to the other side of the room to where a row of long-eared owls stood, their feathers wrapped in wire.

Pushing the larger two aside, he drew back a black velvet curtain to reveal a narrow gunmetal cabinet.

'My box of delights,' he said reverentially, and with a silver key he unlocked the door revealing a collection of small clear bottles of different sizes.

'Come,' he said, indicating for Tom to climb up onto the chair next to him.

Tom did as he was asked and stared in at the racks of bottles and brown packets bearing mysterious labels.

'We have the power of life and death in here,' murmured August, 'so we must show them all the greatest respect. Now . . . where to begin . . . let me see, ah yes, chloroform, for the painless killing of vertebrates.'

'Chloroform. I've heard of that,' said Tom confidently.

'Well I'm glad to hear it, my boy, but have you heard of this?' August turned a clear bottle round so that Tom could read the label.

'Goatby's fluid?' read Tom.

'I thought not,' replied August, 'but you should remember that Dr Ezekiel Goatby is a maniac who would kill us all if he could. It contains strychnine, a poison far, far too dangerous to handle. Now this is a good one.'

'Cyanide of potassium,' read Tom, 'for frogs and mice?'

'That's right. They don't even notice it. Nice and quick.'

'Potassium bichromate, for dogfish and sturgeon, nicotin solution for narcotizing hermit crabs and sea anemones . . . Swainson's arsen—arseni—'

'Ar-sen-ical soap,' said August helpfully, handing Tom a fat paper packet of greenish white flakes, 'essential.'

'What's it for?'

'Read on and it will tell you.'

'To use,' continued Tom, 'moisten a camel-hair pencil with alcohol and with it make a lather from the soap. Then apply to the inner surface of all parts of the skin to prevent moth and beetle damage.'

'Keeps the pests at bay, but jolly dangerous to handle also,' added August. 'Those little flakes have a habit of finding their way into the smallest cut.'

Tom swallowed nervously; the idea of using arsenic soap was terrifying.

'Now,' said August, carefully turning each label round in turn, 'somewhere amongst all this poison is a little invention of my own.'

His fingers stopped on a small blue bottle almost hidden at the back.

'Ah yes—the *blue* bottle. I had quite forgotten.'

August carefully slipped the small phial into his top pocket and locked up the cabinet once more.

'This,' said August, drawing up a chair and clearing a space before him, 'is something quite remarkable. So remarkable, in fact, that it is, and has to remain, an absolute secret.' August turned to Tom with a look of excited anticipation on his face.

'Do you think you can keep such a secret?'

Tom had more than enough secrets of his own that August could never find out about. He nodded confidently.

'I know I can.'

August's eyes searched Tom's face for any sign of doubt, but he found none. The boy was telling the truth.

'Good,' he said at last, 'because you are about to witness something truly astonishing.'

August reached over and carefully picked out a tiny flame-headed hummingbird from the tree, laying it gently in the palm of his hand. It was barely larger than his thumb.

'This is the bee hummingbird, Tom, the smallest bird in the world.' August held it up admiringly. 'Remarkable, isn't it? Fully grown it is barely two inches long and its egg is smaller than a pea.'

Tom wondered how the miniature creature could really be a bird at all. It looked more like a feathered insect.

'Where's it from?' he asked.

'This one was living in a monkeyfiddle bush on the Isle of Pines off the coast of Cuba until six months ago, when a sailor found him. By the time he'd been brought back to Dragonport the poor little creature was dead, so I skinned him, preserved him as carefully as I could, and then stuffed his tiny body with wool. I managed to retain his skull, and for his eyes I used the smallest black glass beads I could find.'

August was concentrating on the tiny bird intently. 'Now,' he whispered, 'watch this.'

Very carefully, August drew the stopper from the small blue bottle and passed it around the head of the bird, before quickly replacing it. Tom had a fleeting sensation of a very strange smell coming from the bottle stop. It was a rich, heavy smell, like hyacinths, mixed with something else . . . something chemical, that reminded him of his long, miserable hours at school. School corridors perhaps. Floor polish! That was it—hyacinths and floor polish. But just as Tom's mind had begun to wander back to his other life, he glanced down at August's hand and his heart almost skipped a beat.

The bee hummingbird in August's palm twitched. It blinked. Then it flopped over onto its chest and stood up unsteadily. Tom's eyes widened as the tiny bird turned a drunken circle on August's hand.

'He's coming back,' whispered August excitedly, 'watch.'

A moment later the bee hummingbird was airborne, its wings ablur. It hovered right in front of Tom's nose, inspecting him like a flower.

'Stay very, very still.'

Tom tried not to breathe. All he could see was a thin black beak like a pencil, poking out in front of a fiery red head. He felt his cheeks tingle as the tiny wings buzzed the air around them. Tom closed his eyes, not sure whether he was about to be pecked or licked. But then the buzzing moved away, and Tom opened his eyes to see the bee hummingbird flit down towards August's jar of violets on the bench. Tentatively it dipped its beak inside, probing for nectar.

'Now that *is* a compliment,' murmured August, completely spellbound.

'It's incredible,' whispered Tom, 'how does it work?'

'The smell. It's the smell that reawakens them.'

'But how?'

By now the bee hummingbird had given up on the violets and was probing the small white flowers on August's tree. Soon it was lost amongst all the other brilliantly coloured birds.

'To tell you the truth I am more than a little mystified by it myself. In fact, I'm utterly flummoxed. It's a scientific impossibility.'

August continued to stare at the tiny bird buzzing through the tree, his eyes shining.

'But you have seen this much, Tom, so here are the facts. I always use a version of this liquid inside my specimens. Before I set the animal's pose, I paint a thin layer of it over the inside of the skin. Originally, I invented it to act like an extra preservative, to protect them against the ravages of time, but as time went on I realized that my preparation seemed to make the animals more alive somehow, more animated—though quite how it does that I'm not sure. Every taxidermist has their own little secret, I suppose, and this is mine.'

August paused to gather his thoughts.

'Last night I was experimenting with changing the ingredients slightly; a little more mercury, strychnine, alum, a little less boracic acid, beeswax—I won't bore you with precisely how and what—but I found that by making my preservative slightly differently, adding a few flowers, heating it a bit, cooling it down a few times, it suddenly became a lot more concentrated. And then, rather accidentally I might add, I found my little concoction was producing this quite remarkable vapour.'

August picked up the small blue bottle and pushed the stopper home.

'Those fumes are toxic, but also unbelievably powerful. As you can see for yourself.'

Tom watched the tiny flame-headed bird darting through the flowers.

'But . . . it's not really *alive* is it? I mean, it's full of cotton wool and wire and—'

'I know,' whispered August, 'I know, it doesn't make any sense.

It's supposed to be impossible. But Tom, *if* this creature is not alive in some way, then, what is it?' August glanced up at Tom, his eyes probing.

'Well, what do you think?'

Tom stared at the hummingbird. It *was* most definitely alive and his mind was flooding with so many questions that he did not know which to ask first.

Keep calm, try to think straight.

But he couldn't.

'Supposing,' said Tom, trying to speak as clearly as he could, 'just supposing that in a hundred year's time, when all your animals get moth-eaten and a bit tatty—'

'Moth-eaten and a bit "tatty"?' snorted August. 'I should certainly hope not.'

'No, of course they won't,' said Tom, swallowing nervously, 'but if the arsen—arsener—'

'Ar-sen-ical soap?'

'Yes. It wears off for some reason.'

August pressed his fingers together and stared at him quizzically.

'Indeed. It's a possibility, I grant you. Continue.'

'But *this* potion—your own secret invention—*doesn't* wear off at all. And it still keeps them . . . alive, in some way?'

August looked at Tom blankly.

'Well, maybe. Chemicals do deteriorate at different speeds. Why, what is it, Tom?'

Tom was smiling uncontrollably as he tried to contain his rising excitement. He wanted to shout out loud.

'Oh, it's . . . it's nothing.'

So it *was* real: he hadn't dreamt it all up! Floor polish and hyacinths, that was it . . . that *smell* . . . August had no idea that his concoction—whatever it was—was far stronger than any of his other chemical mixtures. It had outlasted them all. And could it be that this potion had also made the animals conscious? Had it given life to their brains, which were stuffed with old newspapers and cuttings from the Bible? Was this the reason why they could *think,* and even *speak*? Tom's eyes widened as he stared down at the small blue bottle on the workbench. If it was, August had accidentally discovered something so powerful it was almost too big to comprehend. And he didn't even know it.

'Do you think that the vapour might revive any animal?' asked Tom at last.

August picked up the blue bottle and turned it over in his hands.

'Hmm. Do you mean a real animal, a dead animal? Not one that I have already treated and stuffed?'

Tom nodded.

'Well, now what a question *that* is . . . .' August's voice trailed away and he stared out of the window at the winter sun that was just about to set. 'I'm not entirely sure I want to know the answer to that question. Or . . . do I?'

August drummed his fingers on the table with a vexed expression on his face. Tom could tell that he found the idea intriguing.

'I tell you what,' he said suddenly, 'can you skate?'

Tom looked at him blankly. 'Erm . . . '

'Never mind, you'll learn soon enough.'

August jumped to his feet and was already halfway to the door.

'Here, take my fur coat—and a hat; it really is most extraordinarily cold out there.'

'Where are we going?'

'Out, of course.'

August threw him a hat and wound a heavy scarf around his neck.

'Out to find the answer to your question,' he said excitedly, and with that August grabbed his coat and ran down the stairs.

CHAPTER 11

OUT ON THE ICE

By the time they reached the river it was twilight, and the full moon was already hanging low in the sky.

'Keep close,' said August, marching ahead and forcing a path through the noisy throng of street hawkers and carriages jostling and sliding about in the deep snow. 'There are people here from all over Europe and I don't want to lose you. This way.' August slipped down a gloomy side street to avoid the crowds descending on the river.

'What's going on?' asked Tom breathlessly, slithering to keep up.

'You mean you've never heard of the Dragonport Ice Fair? Where on earth have you been hiding yourself, Tom? Look at this.'

As they turned a corner an icy blast whipped off the river to greet them, and holding on to his cap tightly, Tom could see that the wide expanse of river before them was completely frozen over. All along the shore beside the waterside pubs and chandleries were fairground stalls lit by braziers. There were brightly painted coconut shies, barrel organs with dancing monkeys in top hats, hot-chestnut sellers, and at the far end, a Punch and Judy show, surrounded by laughing children. Out beyond the stalls the ice was dark with a mass of moving figures. It seemed as if the whole town was skating. There were couples linked arm in arm, old men in heavy cloaks taking long graceful strides, and large dogs pulling babies in toboggans. Men with rings of Chinese lanterns suspended around their hats skated slowly through the crowd.

''Ranges! Choclatee! Marzy-o!' they shouted, their trays loaded with steaming bowls of hot chocolate, sugared oranges, and buttons of marzipan. And at the centre of it all was a castle, complete with battlements and flags and turrets, carved entirely out of green ice. Tom had never seen anything like it. It was like a picture from a dream.

'Isn't it remarkable?' said August as he returned with two pairs of skates in his arms. 'Every five years or so the river freezes over completely. Well, almost completely—out in the middle is a little thin—and this is how we celebrate. People come here from all over the country to see it. Here, put these on.'

Tom laced up his skates and in no time he was sliding through the crowd, holding tight to August's arm. Skating was much harder than he'd thought it would be, and he looked across enviously at the group of boys tumbling and racing each other around the ice castle.

'Race yer, Tom,' said a familiar voice behind him, and suddenly Noah flashed to a halt in front of them.

'Hi.'

'Seen me new skates, Mr August? Next year's model they are—the best,' and he executed a perfect spin in front of them.

'Very impressive, Noah.'

'Hows 'bout it, Tom, fancy a race?'

Tom smiled back guiltily. 'I can hardly stand up I'm afraid, I've never skated before in my life.'

'Never mind,' said Noah brightly, 'I'll teach yer.'

'Later, Noah,' said August quietly, putting a hand on his shoulder, 'I'm afraid Tom and I have got some work to do first.'

Noah looked disappointed, and suddenly Tom felt a little disappointed too. Skating with Noah sounded fun.

'Now, what did your brother do with all that money I gave him?' smiled August, changing the subject.

'Oh, he's thinkin' 'bout buyin' hisself a share in an 'orse or somethin' sensible like that. Not like me,' grinned Noah. 'I see somethin', Mr August, an' I just gotta 'ave it—no matter.'

'Good for you,' said August approvingly.

'So I'll see yous later sir,' he said, tipping his hat to August, 'an' don't think I ain't comin' lookin' fer yer, Tom,' he winked. 'That race is on.' And with that Noah turned and sped away through the skaters.

'Right,' said August purposefully, 'now let's see what we can find.' Taking Tom's arm he led the way through the stalls towards the grey ice at the edge of the fair, and he was soon examining the snow-covered riverbank where a confused jumble of flotsam and jetsam was stuck fast in the frozen mud.

'What are we looking for?' asked Tom as he watched August prodding and poking about.

'Something quite large . . . like this perhaps.' August skated across to a small brown sack he had spotted sticking up on the edge of the ice. Stamping around the sack with the blades of his skates he tugged at it until eventually it broke off in his hands.

The sack was frozen as stiff as a piece of card, and Tom noticed that there was a small bulge at the bottom of it. What could August possibly want with an old sack someone had left on the riverbank? It made no sense.

'People can be very cruel, Tom,' said August grimly, 'which is why I know what is inside this sack.' Prising the two sides open, August forced his hand inside and pulled out a small black and white object.

'Here.' He set it down on Tom's lap. Tom brushed away the icicles and suddenly he recognized what it was.

'One unwanted bull terrier puppy,' said August, 'about two months old, I'd guess. Bred for fighting, so the weakest of the litter, like this little fellow, are surplus to requirements. Frozen to death. Absolutely frozen solid. Remarkable.'

The pathetic creature just looked as if it had fallen asleep and turned to ice. August brushed the ice off its nose thoughtfully.

'Now remember, Tom, whatever happens next has to be kept an absolute secret. Do you understand?'

'Of course.'

'Good. Well done. You know, I'm not absolutely sure it is right to do this . . . ' August's voice trailed away and Tom noticed the smallest flicker of doubt in his eyes. For a moment he seemed to be hesitating. 'Knowledge is a most powerful thing . . . but I suppose . . . well, anyway. Best get it over with.'

Glancing swiftly behind him to make sure that they were completely alone, August reached into his breast pocket and took out the small blue bottle. Quickly he shook a few drops of the liquid into a violet handkerchief and replaced the bottle inside his coat.

'Ready?'

Tom nodded, whereupon August bent down and gently pressed the violet handkerchief over the nose of the puppy. Holding it there they watched and waited in silence.

'Anything?'

Tom squeezed his fingers along the hard icy puppy, lying completely lifeless in his hands. It was like holding a stone.

'Nothing.'

'No reaction,' breathed August, visibly relieved. 'As I suspected. It has no effect on a real animal.'

Just then Tom felt the smallest movement. It was very weak, like a distant pulse, but it was there, unmistakably.

'Wait,' Tom whispered excitedly, 'wait, something's happening.'

The pulse was growing stronger and more insistent, and the puppy slowly began to change colour. What had been grey and frozen and dead was fast becoming soft and warm and alive. The pulse quickened to a heartbeat, throbbing in Tom's fingers, and moments later the puppy's legs began to move; slowly at first, then faster and faster as if it were chasing a fly in a dream. Suddenly it opened its eyes.

'Rrrf! Rrrr-rrrr!'

Tom gasped—he couldn't help himself. The small dog was alive! And it was angry. He struggled to hold on to it in his hands.

'See? You did it!' he said triumphantly. 'I knew it would work! I knew it!'

August smiled palely, but he was too shocked to speak. The vast implications of what he had witnessed were just beginning to dawn on him.

'Can we keep him?' asked Tom hopefully, beaming down at the angry little bundle of brown fur. 'Let's keep him, let's call him Phoenix, seeing as he's risen from the dead, and—'

'We will do no such thing!' snapped August suddenly, and snatching the puppy out of Tom's hands threw it down harshly onto the ice.

'Go on!' he shouted savagely. 'Get away with you!'

The bull terrier, who had every reason to be afraid, whimpered loudly, and scrabbling to its feet it bolted away towards the ice fair. Tom looked up at August in astonishment, stung by this strange reaction.

'I'm sorry Tom,' said August hoarsely, watching the puppy disappear amongst the crowds. 'That had to be an accident. Just . . . a fluke.'

'It looked pretty real to me!' replied Tom incredulously.

August just shook his head. He was struggling to understand.

'No, it wasn't. I was mistaken. It can't have been really dead at all, perhaps just comatosed . . . in some kind of deep sleep—'

'That puppy *was* dead, you *know* it was,' Tom interrupted angrily, 'but if you think it was an accident, fine, let's try it again on something else. Accidents don't happen twice, do they?'

August stared into the crowds, grimacing. It was quite clear to Tom that he did not want to believe what he had just seen.

'Go on,' Tom persisted, 'do it again. *Prove* it doesn't work.'

August muttered under his breath and glanced down at the boy beside him, his dark eyes staring fiercely beneath that tangled mop of blond hair. Why was he allowing himself to be bullied by his assistant? He was rude, obstinate, and there was something familiar about him. But worst of all, he was right.

'Very well,' replied August petulantly, 'for you, Tom, I *will* try again; and this time it will be something far deader than a frozen puppy. Then that will be the end of it. Come along.'

Taking Tom's arm, August skated swiftly back to the fair. Very soon they were amongst the crowds once more and Tom spotted a large lady with a beetroot complexion flustering about the fish stall. Strewn across it were heaps of mackerel, herrings and skate, piles of whelks and coils of eels suspended in shallow trays of grey jelly.

'How much?' she shrieked.

'Pound a tray.'

'Pound a tray! Pound a tray of boiled eels! Do you hear that, girls?'

The three young girls standing behind her did indeed hear it, but they were too embarrassed to say anything.

'You've some nerve, Ned Badger. Seeing as you didn't precisely *catch* them in the first place, did you? I didn't know you even *owned* a fish trap.'

Ned Badger looked about him uncomfortably.

'I've no idea what you's talkin' 'bout,' he hissed. 'One pound. That's me price an' I'm stickin' to it.'

'I'm not a tourist, y'know. Hows 'bout sixpence?'

'Cost me more 'an that to nab 'em.'

'Seven.'

'Keep talking.'

'Now don't you start that, Ned Badger. Nothing's fixed round 'ere.'

August stared across at the large lady making a scene.

'Mrs Spong is most *definitely* alive,' he said to himself

thoughtfully, 'but Ned Badger's boiled eels have been here almost since last Christmas.' A mischievous smile crossed August's lips. 'Follow me.'

And with that August skated towards Mrs Spong. She had finally haggled down the price, but she was still grumbling about it as she stuffed the tray of eels into her basket.

'Come along, my dears,' she clucked as she skated away, her daughters trailing in her wake like a line of ducklings. August followed along behind them, minding his own business, then accelerating forward he surreptitiously tucked his violet handkerchief into the basket, making sure it covered the eels' heads just breaking the jelly's surface.

'Good evening, Mrs Spong,' he said, drawing alongside.

'Oh Mr Catcher!' she squawked. 'You half frightened me to death. Cold out, innit?'

'Indeed it is; they say it's going to get even colder.'

'Rid'clous cold, I call it.'

''Ere, sir?' said one of the girls skating forward.

'Yes?'

'You've dropped yer 'andkerchief, sir,' and reaching in she pulled it out of the basket.

'Oh, so I have. What a stroke of luck. Thank you my girl.'

Bowing graciously, August took his violet handkerchief and slipped it back in his pocket. The girl smiled shyly.

'I 'spect you'll be needin' that in this weather,' laughed Mrs Spong. 'Me and my girls have been sneezin' and hawkin' all day, haven't we, girls? Like little barrels of snot we are!' and she tittered once more.

'Indeed. Well, a very good evening to you, Mrs Spong.'

'Ta-ra, Mr Catcher. Nice seein' yer.'

'Come, Tom,' whispered August, and together they skated a safe distance into the crowd. '*Now* we'll see if lightning strikes twice.'

But August had barely finished his sentence before there was an ear piercing shriek. Mrs Spong's basket began to shake, and she turned around just in time to see four long grey shapes drop off the back and slither away across the ice.

'Lawks a'mercy!' she shouted. 'Me eels! Me eels is gone! Grab 'em, somebody!'

There were screams of panic and shouts of laughter as the wriggling grey creatures darted this way and that through the crowd, tripping up skaters and upsetting stalls. The Spong girls and a few stray dogs set off in hot pursuit.

'Badger!' shrieked Mrs Spong, skating purposefully back to the stall. 'Them eels you nicked ain't cooked!'

Ned Badger's face fell. 'What you's talking about,' he protested, 'course they're cooked, I boiled 'em meself.'

'Well, how's it that they've just jumped out me basket, eh?' And with a well aimed swing she brought the basket crashing down on his head.

'Hey! Steady on!' he shouted, and a crowd gathered around the irate Mrs Spong as she laid into the unfortunate Badger, cursing loudly above the hoots of laughter. Tom could not help smiling at the confusion, but August Catcher said nothing. Instead he turned away, and watched the dogs and children chase the eels across the ice in stony silence. Tom was right: this could be no accident. What awful power had he invented?

'The divine spark,' he whispered to himself, barely able to

believe it. 'The elixir of life.' August's eyes widened at the thought. 'The divine spark.'

Tom had heard those words somewhere before, in some other place, long ago; but before he could remember where his eye was caught by a black figure skating past the irate Mrs Spong out towards the middle of the river. She was carving long looping arabesques with great speed and grace, and on reaching the empty ice she leapt and spun like a ballerina. It was Lotus—it had to be. Tom shivered a little and drew himself deeper into his coat. What could he do? Nothing. It was inevitable that she should be here, and that meant Don Gervase was here too. Perhaps standing right behind him, watching him; even at this very moment.

'Mr August Catcher? It's August Catcher, isn't it?'

Tom shuddered and spun round, but instead of Don Gervase he saw a tall, willowy young woman in a long white coat skate up through the glowing braziers. She had a wide smile and sparkling blue eyes, and even in the darkness Tom could see that she was very beautiful.

'I just *had* to come and say hello.' She smiled, holding out her hand. 'My name is Mina Quilt.'

In an instant August had quite forgotten about his great problem and was concentrating on the beautiful apparition before him. He took Mina's hand and bowed low.

'Do I know you?'

'Not yet,' she replied, 'but you will do shortly. I'm staying with Sir Henry for the grand opening of the museum. I'm his cousin, you see.'

August was quite enchanted.

'Well, that's marvellous, quite marvellous.'

Mina looked across at Tom and giggled.

'August, my dear fellow! Where *have* you been hiding?'

A tall man in a herringbone suit appeared at Mina's side. He was blond, powerfully built, and had the sharp, quick eyes of an eagle. Sir Henry Scatterhorn—it could be no one else.

'Well spotted, my dear. Where have you been, old boy? We've been searching for you.'

'Oh, you know,' breezed August, 'just experimenting, as ever.'

'Experimenting?' repeated Sir Henry, raising his eyebrow. 'Out here at the ice fair? You see Mina, August cannot help himself. Unlike other mortals his mind is never satisfied. Forever wrestling with some great problem or other. It comes from being one of the cleverest men in England.'

'So I have been told,' said Mina.

August blushed.

'And my oldest friend,' added Sir Henry, slapping him jovially on the back. His quick eyes came to rest on Tom, barely visible under August's fur coat.

'You must be Tom, I presume?'

Tom nodded. For some reason he didn't want to look too closely into the eyes of his great-great-great-uncle.

'Well I hope you're keeping Mr Catcher in order. He's a box of tricks, you know.'

'Oh he is, don't worry,' replied August pointedly. 'Tom has some very definite ideas.'

'I'm very glad to hear it,' said Sir Henry warmly, 'I like people with definite ideas. No point shilly-shallying about.'

'Indeed.'

'Good good. Now Mina, shall we see if we can find that chocolate fountain? I'm told it's in the shape of an ice dragon, and chocolate gushes from its mouth.'

'How exciting.'

'But we must get there before August does.'

'Why is that?'

'Well my dear, I'm sure the very moment he sees it he's bound to find some clever way to preserve it. Or worse still, turn it into a real dragon, breathing fire instead of chocolate. And then where would we be?'

For a moment Mina was not quite sure if Sir Henry was joking or not. Then he winked at Tom and August smiled.

'Don't worry,' he said, 'I'll wait until after you've gone.'

'Thanks old boy,' laughed Sir Henry, ringing August's hand, 'see you later.'

'So pleased to meet you at last,' beamed Mina. 'Bye, Tom.' And with a wave she took Sir Henry's arm and they skated away briskly towards the ice castle.

'She's quite a girl, don't you think?' said August, watching the elegant couple weave through the crowds. 'How curious that Sir Henry never mentioned her before.'

Tom did not reply. He was thinking how strange it was to be back in the past, meeting all these people whom he had only imagined from Jos's stories.

It was now quite dark and the ice fair was humming with people. Tom and August watched a conjuror for a while, then they took a tour of the ice castle where children were having skating races. Tom looked for Noah in the crowds around the chocolate fountain but he couldn't find him, though he did notice that Phoenix had found a home. Two small girls were sitting next to a brazier holding a bowlful of milk for the dog to drink.

'You were right, Tom,' said August, watching the puppy slurping greedily, 'it's very much alive; and happy to be so by the looks of things. Let's hope the little fellow has more luck this time around.'

Tom could not but agree. They skated on in silence for a while.

'So have you thought about what you are going to do with your potion now,' he asked, 'I mean, now that you know it works?'

August did not answer immediately. This was obviously a question that he had been turning over and over in his mind.

'I'm not *absolutely* sure it works,' he replied, avoiding Tom's eye. 'But it's certainly very powerful. And you can bet your life it'll be something that a lot of people may want.'

They had left the ice castle and were now standing looking back at the town where a large bonfire was blazing on the foreshore.

'And people who want something badly enough are usually prepared to do anything to get hold of it.'

Tom watched as the sparks from the fire flew high into the air like rockets, and he knew that August was right. After all, his father had sacrificed everything in search of some kind of elixir of life, some divine spark. Could it be that August had stumbled upon the same thing?

Just then there was a commotion around the bonfire. At first it sounded as if a fight had broken out, then there was a loud whinny, and a panicking horse reared up above the crowd, followed by a man struggling to catch its bridle.

'Steady, boy! Steady!' he shouted. 'STEADY!'

WHOOSH!

There was a great rushing sound and suddenly the crowds around the bonfire parted, and a horse-drawn sledge thundered down onto the ice, completely out of control. On board Tom just glimpsed a small boy standing up, frantically grappling with the reins.

'I can't hold him!' he screamed.

The horse was wild-eyed and terrified—for good reason, as the whole of the back of the sledge was on fire. A stray spark; a firework perhaps. The flaming sledge bolted right through the heart of the ice fair, overturning stalls and smashing into braziers and sending skaters screaming into the darkness. The faster the horse galloped the louder the flames roared, and soon the very seat on which the boy stood was ablaze.

'Jump, lad! Jump off!' cried stallholders and fishermen, standing bravely in the path of the oncoming sledge waving coats and lanterns, only to dive out of the way at the very last second as the flaming sledge swung past.

'Help!' screamed the boy desperately wrestling with the reins as the flames licked higher and higher. But the ice screamed and the fire blazed and the wild-eyed horse galloped on and on; faster now, desperate to escape the blaze roaring behind its ears, and there was nothing the boy or anyone else could do to stop it. Smashing through the Punch and Judy stall the horse bolted towards the dark centre of the river. Some men in the crowd immediately gave chase, but they could only watch as the flaming sledge careered out into the darkness, getting smaller and smaller as it raced on towards the thinner ice . . .

Seconds later a deep and resonating boom rolled out across

the river as the ice split. Suddenly a gaping zigzag mouth opened up, and the very next moment the horse, boy, and blazing sledge plunged headlong into the freezing water, which swallowed them up with a hiss. A party of men with torches raced out towards the hole, and soon they were joined by a breathless crowd, gathering around the jagged edge of ice and peering down into the murky waters.

'Where is he . . . please God he's safe!'

A distraught woman pushed her way through the crowd and when she reached the front, Tom recognized her instantly. She was the red-faced serving woman he had encountered in the corridor the first time he visited Catcher Hall. She stared wildly into the grey pool.

'Is he there? Is he in there? For God's sake get him out!' she shrieked.

The men carrying the torches bent down to the water level, trying desperately to see anything in the dark water.

'There he is!' someone shouted. 'Over there!'

A grey form nudged against the edge of the ice on the far side. Immediately a man flung himself onto his belly and crawling across stretched his arm down into the darkness.

'P-p-please God Abel's all right . . . please God he's not drowned,' she whimpered . . . 'Please God—'

The man got hold of the grey shape by the scruff of the neck.

'Mother!'

A boy's voice rang through the crowd.

'Mother, I'm here! I'm here—'

The woman spun round and uttered a little scream as Abel appeared at the water's edge, breathless and flushed.

'I'm here.'

'Oh thank God,' she cried, and running over she grabbed him and hugged him tight. 'When I saw that sledge with your new 'orse I thought . . . I thought . . .'

But Abel wasn't listening; he was looking on, terrified, as the men dragged the small grey body out of the water, and when it emerged he let out a cry and covered his face with his hands. Then his mother stopped sobbing and she too looked down at the small body lying there. It was Noah.

'No—'

The woman fainted dead away. Already a doctor was kneeling beside Noah, pummelling his chest, attempting to empty his lungs of water.

'Here, let me in there,' grunted another burly man, shoving the doctor aside. He began taking great lungfuls of air and blowing hard into the boy's mouth in a steady rhythm. But Noah didn't move. His face was ashen white and his lips had turned a blueish black.

'I just said try him out, I didn't know he'd bolt, swear to God I didn't,' blubbered Abel. He was shaking inconsolably.

The burly man crawled away and then the doctor tried thumping the little boy's chest once more, but after a minute or so he too sat down exhausted. There was silence as everyone stared down at the lifeless body of Noah. The doctor shook his head. Somewhere a woman started to cry.

Tom shot a glance across at August, who was standing on the far side of the hole. His brow was furrowed, and he was staring grimly at Noah's pale face lying there on the ice. Why won't he use his potion! Why? Tom had to use every scrap of self control to stop himself screaming; he wanted to *force* August to bring Noah back to life. But when August looked up he caught Tom's eye and with the merest shake of his head Tom knew all he needed to know. August wasn't prepared to use his power in public. It was too dangerous.

And there, standing in the shadows behind him stood Lotus Askary. She also gazed down at Noah's lifeless body, then her eyes travelled curiously around the crowd, many of whom were weeping openly now. She wore a puzzled expression, as if she had never seen people cry before and she plainly couldn't understand it; what on earth were they all crying about?

A rough blanket was thrown over Noah's body and slowly the crowd began to drift away, skating back across the ice in small, sad groups. The mood at the ice fair was sombre now, as stall-holders picked up the remains of their shops and mothers gathered up their children to take them home. Tom and August returned to Catcher Hall without saying a word. All the while Tom was trying to understand, trying to reason it out, but he couldn't. Frustration was just burning him up inside.

'Close the door, Tom,' said August quietly as they entered the study and August sat down heavily in a chair. Bringing his hand up to his eyes he rubbed them wearily and stared at the floor, his thoughts far away. Tom did as he was told, but he was much too angry to sit down. He could not contain himself any longer.

'You should have saved him!' he shouted. 'Why didn't you?'

'I couldn't save him, Tom.'

'That's NOT TRUE! You know it isn't.'

August shot him an angry look.

'Can you imagine what would happen if everyone knew about

it?' he snapped. 'Death, chance, fate, they are all part of life, we cannot change that. We cannot change the rules of nature.'

'But you use it on the specimens in the museum! How is that different?'

'That is for effect, for show! They are not really alive, as *themselves*, because I have created them. They are wire, wood and newspaper. Puppets, Tom! Not living, not real!'

'That puppy was REAL, those eels were real!'

'Yes, they were, *they were*,' replied August, who seemed to have momentarily forgotten what had happened earlier that evening, 'but, these are . . . small animals! They may be dead again for all I know!'

'They *are* still alive, I'm sure of it,' replied Tom indignantly. He knew very well how strong August's potion was, but even now, with his blood boiling in his veins, he still couldn't bring himself to tell him.

'Besides,' said August in a tired voice, 'I have my doubts whether it would work on a human being. Supposing something went wrong?'

'Well how will you ever know that, if you are not prepared to try?'

August stared out of the window at lights from the docks below him and shook his head. Somehow the events of this evening had changed everything. Suddenly this potion was like a heavy stone that had been hung on a rope around his neck.

'I do not *want* to have the power of life and death,' he said finally. 'I am a taxidermist, a chemist, an inventor even—yes I am. But I am *not* a judge. And I don't want that . . . responsibility. Would you?'

Tom wanted to say yes, but he wasn't sure. If this had been a fairy story then he would know what he should do. He should accept the power and use it as a force for good and change nature—change the world. But this was no fairy story, and Noah really was dead. Was it right to change fate? Was Noah supposed to die? Tom did not know; all he was certain of was that they could have saved him, and now, somehow, he felt that Noah's death was on his conscience. That was enough.

CHAPTER 12

Opening Night

The following morning the mood of gloom continued at Catcher Hall. Tom sat despondently at the table, playing with his breakfast. At the other end August drank his coffee in silence, his head deep inside a scientific journal. The clock struck nine. Tom was wondering whether it was now the moment to go back to his own world. Was there any point in him being here any more? Not much that he could see. Idly, he balanced a crust of toast on the end of his knife. A flick in the air would decide it: butter side up he would go; burnt side up he would stay. He raised his fist above the table and was just about to bring it thumping down on the knife when there was a loud rap at the front door. Footsteps clattered across the hall and the next moment Sir Henry burst into the dining room, his red cheeks blazing.

'August!' he bellowed. 'You must come with me this instant!'

August looked up absently, his head brimming with chemical calculations. It was as if a large ball of fire had suddenly appeared at the door.

'Do sit down and have some coffee.'

'I'm afraid that coffee will have to wait. I insist you come to the museum immediately.'

Sir Henry paced about, rubbing his hands impatiently.

'Immediately!'

'Has something happened?' asked August, suddenly concerned.

'Everything's happened! Everything, August! The museum is finally finished and it is *tremendous*. Tremendous! I insist that you see it before everyone else in the town—and you, Tom. Let's skedaddle chaps, the carriage is waiting.'

Tom could see that Sir Henry was a man of boundless enthusiasm and he was not used to being disobeyed. With a sigh August pushed back his chair and obediently went out into the hall.

'You do know I have seen it all before,' he said, patiently putting on his hat.

'Of course you have, dear chap! Of course—you *made* it. But now it's all complete! Finito! Well, almost.'

'Almost?' repeated August. 'But the opening's tonight?'

'I have one more idea; but more of that later. Come on, come on!'

Sir Henry bustled August and Tom down the steps and into the waiting cab. Slamming the door behind him he banged loudly on the roof with his cane, and the driver set off at breakneck speed down the hill. All the way Sir Henry talked incessantly about the museum and the grand opening ball to be held that evening, and Tom felt Sir Henry's exuberance begin to thaw his cold heart. It was like being close to the sun, and by the time they arrived at the gates of the museum Tom had almost forgotten the tragedy of last night and was bursting with expectation himself.

'Excited, chaps?' Sir Henry beamed. 'Lord knows I am.'

The cab came to a halt and, throwing open the door, Sir Henry jumped down onto the pavement. Tom looked up to see the familiar façade of the Scatterhorn Museum, but he wasn't prepared for how different it looked brand new. It was sharp and shining in the sparkling winter sun.

'God save the King?' said August, looking up at the workmen setting the stone plaque between the two griffons above the door.

'Of course! Why not?' snorted Sir Henry, galloping up the steps. 'Very important to get royal approval.'

'Have you?'

'No no no! But it's the idea that counts. Now do hurry up!'

Inside was a bustle of activity as preparations for the grand opening party were in full swing. Swags of material festooned the ceiling and pyramids of champagne glasses were being set up in the foyer. Sir Henry began directing activities while at the same time giving August and Tom a lightning guided tour.

'So the eye is drawn from the arctic wastes of Greenland, to the deep jungles of the Amazon and then out onto the endless African plains,' he enthused, sweeping his arm around the room, 'and over here . . .'

But Tom was not listening, he was just staring about him in amazement. He could not believe how rich and dazzling everything looked: the colours were extraordinary. The tropical rainforest really was a deep bottle green, the arctic fox was a brilliant, blinding white, almost lost in the snow. A humming-bird tree shimmered and sparkled with every colour of the rainbow and even the mammoth looked shiny and real. Tom looked at everything he knew well as if he was seeing it for the first time, just as August had intended. How powerful that potion must be, he thought.

'It's a triumph,' said August admiringly.

'A triumph for both of us,' corrected Sir Henry, 'and the scribblers of the press will love it, I'm sure.'

'Sir Henry Scatterhorn, the great explorer and collector,' announced August with a wry smile, writing imaginary letters in the air.

'*And* August Catcher, master taxidermist,' continued Sir Henry, 'have created what must surely be one of the greatest specimen collections in England.' Sir Henry gazed around at the cases in silent admiration. 'I really do not know how you have achieved such life, August. It's magical.'

He paused in front of the gorilla, sitting in his cleft in the tree.

'One day I hope this museum will be used like a treasure chest of rare things. For people to come and admire animals that might no longer exist in the wild.'

'Or those that have never actually been in the wild at all,' smiled August, giving the mammoth a friendly pat.

'Indeed,' grinned Sir Henry, 'but it looks near as dammit like the real thing, and who's to know anyway? Now, I want to show you both something.'

Sir Henry led the way up the stairs, through the bustle of cooks and waiters to a blank alcove on the landing. There stood a large display of flowers, but something was missing, and for a moment Tom could not remember what it was.

'Do you not think,' said Sir Henry, walking into the alcove, 'that this seems somewhat empty, compared to the dazzling displays down below?'

August shrugged his shoulders. On reflection it did seem a trifle bare.

'I think so too. So, what about a savage, terrifying, man-eating—'

'Tiger?' suggested Tom helpfully.

He had just remembered, and couldn't resist it. Sir Henry eyed the boy curiously: this lad really was very perceptive.

'*Precisely,* Tom, precisely,' he continued. 'Just imagine it August, a vast cat, glowering at the visitors as they walk up the stairs.'

August did not need convincing.

'A quite brilliant suggestion,' he grinned, 'but where on earth would you find—'

'Here.'

Sir Henry reached into his jacket excitedly and, producing a small folded scrap of newspaper, gave it to August to read.

'Four hundred villagers, including the Maharajah of Champawander's daughter?' he said incredulously. 'It certainly sounds savage enough.'

'Even better,' added Sir Henry, winking at Tom, 'and there's more.'

August's eyes skipped down to the bottom.

'The reward is an uncut sapphire—the largest in his collection?'

'Imagine that!' Sir Henry's eyes were shining. 'We shall go there, my friend, we shall go there. I shall shoot it, you will preserve it, and Mina shall write the story of the adventure.'

'Mina?'

'Of course; you remember Mina?'

'How could I forget?'

'Well she grew up in India. She knows all about tigers, snakes, elephants—you name it. She's a lot braver than you or me, you know.'

August didn't quite know what to say. He had never actually accompanied Sir Henry on any of his expeditions before. Here was an opportunity . . . and of course, there was the delightful Mina.

'Well?' said Sir Henry expectantly.

August felt the searchlight of Sir Henry's enthusiasm burning into him.

'When do we leave?'

'Tomorrow, of course!' beamed Sir Henry, clapping him on the back with glee. '*After* the ball, old boy. After the ball.'

As Tom strode up the steps of the Scatterhorn Museum that evening, he made a promise to himself to be as inconspicuous as possible. He had spent most of the afternoon hunting around in August's wardrobes for something to wear to the grand opening, eventually finding an itchy old suit August had worn at school. It had a waistcoat and a stiff white collar to match, which felt so uncomfortable and looked so ridiculous that Tom wondered if he would be able to last the entire evening without taking some part of it off; and to make matters worse, August had insisted that he oil his hair down flat. Tom felt as if he was going to some terrible fancy dress party. But he needn't have worried, as when he walked up into the foyer he saw that he was not alone. Inside there were people wearing costumes of every colour and description: there were merchants with pink sashes and walrus moustaches, ruddy-faced farmers with vast sideburns wearing tweed suits and lavender spats, soldiers in bright red tunics and tartan trousers, with ladies on their arms. In the centre of it all was Sir Henry, looking elegant and sleek as a lion as he gracefully accepted the congratulations of his guests. And there was August too, shouting into the ear trumpet of a very old man in a blue velvet coat.

Walking through the heavily scented air into the main hall Tom found it had been transformed into a ballroom. Couples whirled and spun around the mammoth, to the breathless rhythm of a small but very enthusiastic dance band. There was the dodo with a garland round her neck, and the gorilla in his tree with a straw boater on his head. Was he tapping his fingers in time to the beat? If he was, nobody noticed. Tom leant against a pillar and drank it all in. The past was a much more lively and colourful place than he had ever imagined: perhaps it was because all the old photographs were in black and white it seemed serious and melancholy—but it was turning out to be nothing of the kind. The past was dangerous certainly, and brutal too, but it was also colourful and crazy. In fact, he rather liked it.

'Burdo Yarker, quite a character he is.'

August had appeared at Tom's side.

'Who?'

'The old boy with the ear trumpet. Likes nothing better than to creep up trees at night and slip bird's eggs into his mouth.'

Tom stared across at the scrawny old gentleman peering down at the dodo. That was one of the most extraordinary things he had ever heard.

'Why does he want to do that?'

'Lord knows. The thrill of it, maybe. And then he puts the eggs back in the nest and the bird sits down on them again.' August chuckled to himself. 'Certainly taught me more about birds than anyone I know. Gave me the drawings of that dodo as a matter of fact.' He looked out across the whirling couples to where a tall young man was spinning around with a girl in a shimmering turquoise dress.

'Quite something, isn't she?'

Tom followed his gaze, and saw it was Mina Quilt. August waved and in a second Mina had darted over to them like a swallow.

'August Catcher, you are a genius!' she declared, and before he had time to reply she had pulled him out onto the dance floor.

'I really am so impressed.'

'I would be nothing without my patron.'

'Tush, you are too modest,' she teased, 'and you know it.'

August bowed, and placing his hand upon her shoulder they began to dance. Looking down at his sleeve he noticed that he had absent-mindedly tucked his small violet handkerchief into it. No matter.

'Sir Henry has told me all about our adventure. It's so exciting.'

'It is.'

'And he has already promised to give me the sapphire,' she laughed. 'Do you really think we shall get it?'

'Of course.'

'And if we do—would it suit me?' Mina spun around, a blur of brilliant blue. 'What do you think, August?'

August was dazzled. He was quite sure that he had never seen anyone so beautiful in his life.

'My dear, it would suit you more than anything else in the world,' he said. And at that moment, a new thought came into his mind. How would it be if he, and not Sir Henry, gave it to her? Mina looked up at him and smiled radiantly.

'You are very kind. Perhaps it will match this dress; it's a gift from Sir Henry, you know. Look closer: it's quite unusual.'

August peered down at Mina's shoulder. Under the fine lace were hundreds of small iridescent blue butterflies.

'Hewitson's blue hairstreak,' he whispered, marvelling at the creatures hiding there.

'From the South American rainforest, I know,' added Mina. 'Sir Henry has been telling me all about them.'

'How remarkable. Really, it's quite—'

Then suddenly August remembered his violet handkerchief. What if the smell . . . but already it was too late, as he felt the wings of one of the butterflies directly beneath his hand begin to move.

'Utterly charming,' said August with a nervous smile, trying to keep his hand discreetly over the tiny creature as it made its way towards the edge of Mina's dress. 'What a party this is.'

Mina smiled politely, and tried to ignore August's hand as it crept further and further towards her neck until suddenly the butterfly found a gap in the lace and took off, fluttering away through his fingers towards the chandeliers. August was thrown into confusion.

'Gosh! Erm . . .' he laughed awkwardly, 'your dress, Mina, it seems—'

He was about to apologize when the look of wonder in Mina's eyes stopped him. She was staring at the butterfly in amazement.

'It seems they weren't quite dead after all,' he murmured. 'Chemicals can be so unstable. I believe the heat has probably woken them up.'

Mina was simply too enchanted to reply. They danced on, watching as one by one the small brilliant creatures fluttered up and away like a stream of tiny blue lights. Nobody else seemed to notice. At last Mina turned to August and stared at him curiously.

'I'm not sure whether to believe you, you know.'

'What?'

'The heat waking them up,' she giggled. 'I think *you* had something to do with this, August Catcher.'

'Me?' replied August with a ready laugh. 'I preserve animals, Mina, I don't bring them back to life.'

Mina smiled to herself. 'Are you quite sure about that?'

'Of course not,' he blustered, 'how could I? How could anyone? It's scientifically impossible.'

But even as August denied it, another, darker thought came into his mind. Maybe his little invention might help him get what he wanted . . .

'Yes, I'm sorry,' blushed Mina. 'Of course, you would know that better than anyone. How silly I am.'

'Not silly at all, my dear,' bowed August graciously, 'merely imaginative. And there is nothing wrong in that.'

And away they spun into the crowd.

'Ah, Tom! There you are.'

Tom was just returning downstairs balancing a full glass of lemon sherbet when he saw Sir Henry wave cheerfully as he made his way through the dancers towards him.

'Helluva jamboree, don't you think?' He smiled, beckoning him forward, and Tom was just about to reply when a tall silhouette emerged from behind the gorilla.

'Why, if it isn't Sir Henry Scatterhorn himself,' said a familiar, rumbling voice. 'May I be so bold as to introduce myself?'

Tom shivered as he felt the air suddenly grow cold around him. He darted back behind a pillar. Could it be . . .

'My name is Don Gervase Askary.'

'Very pleased to meet you,' said Sir Henry politely, shaking the long bony hand of the strangest-looking man towering before him.

'I arrived from Holland merely days ago, and on hearing about your new museum and its extraordinary specimens, I felt it my duty to pay a visit.'

'Well I'm . . . err . . . flattered, sir.'

'Tell me, Scatterhorn,' Don Gervase went on, 'how *is* it that they are all so—forgive me, my English is not so good—like life? Is that what you say?'

'Lifelike, I think,' smiled Sir Henry. 'But if I may suggest, Sir, you are asking the wrong man.'

'I am?'

Don Gervase furrowed his brow and tried hard to look as confused as possible.

'But I thought this was the Scatterhorn Museum?'

'It is, my dear fellow,' corrected Sir Henry, 'it is. However I am merely the collector. August Catcher is the artist; and here he is.'

Tom peeked around the pillar to see August arrive breathless from the dance floor.

'August!' exclaimed Sir Henry, clapping him on the back. 'May I introduce Don Gervase Askary.'

Don Gervase bowed low and smiled, revealing all his blackened teeth.

'How do you do.'

'Mr Askary has just arrived from Holland,' explained Sir Henry, 'and he is so impressed with your creations that he wants to know all your trade secrets. What do you say to that—eh?'

August's attention was still focused upon Mina, whirling across the dance floor in the arms of a new partner.

'Yes, Catcher,' boomed Don Gervase, 'I dibble-dabble in chemistry myself. Your preparations must be very complex.'

'Oh, not really,' replied August airily, 'dash of this, dribble of that. The usual. It's mostly patience, luck, and skill.'

Mina caught his eye and waved, and August waved back.

'Just patience, luck, and skill.'

'Is that so?'

'Indeed. Trial and error, my friend.'

Don Gervase cocked his large head, clearly not believing a single word. He was not at all pleased at being so dismissed.

'Well then, you must be very patient and very lucky,' he went on, somewhat rattled, 'and perhaps a little bit skilful as well, when you shoot that man-eating tiger.'

At the mention of the tiger both August and Sir Henry turned and stared at Don Gervase in amazement.

'*What* did you say?' asked Sir Henry, clearly intrigued.

'I—'

'How could you possibly know about that?' added August curiously.

'Well, a little *oiseau*, my . . . er . . . daughter, actually,' stumbled Don Gervase, suddenly realizing he had just landed himself in a very awkward situation.

'Your *daughter*?'

'*Jawohl. Meine Tochter.*'

Don Gervase had just dug his own hole a little deeper. August and Sir Henry were utterly perplexed.

'What an imagination *she* has!' he declared. '*Magnifico!* She say, Papa, just think if they went to India, to shoot that man-eating tiger, how nice it might look at the top of the stairs, yes? No?' Don Gervase shrugged his shoulders and rumbled on wildly, 'I says *yes*, of course, *meine liebe*, but they *also* want to win sapphire—carramba, no! Yes! I mean yes! To win sapphire, yes! To make secret *cadeau* for the girl. But only *one* can give it. *Uno. Ein. Un*. And this will be *eine katastrophe*. *Disastro per tutti*. *Absoluto tragicissimo*. Yes? No?'

He smiled breezily and scratched his chest. Sir Henry and August stared open mouthed at the man with yellow-green eyes and large bulbous head.

'Forgive me you,' Don Gervase bowed low, 'but talking small in English is not my skill. Toodle-pip.'

Turning on his heel, he disappeared into the crowd.

There was a moment of silence as both August and Sir Henry

tried to make sense of Don Gervase's extraordinary performance. It was quite possible that he was a lunatic, and yet how could he possibly know about the tiger, the sapphire, and that each of them had secretly promised to give it to Mina?

'What a very curious fellow,' said Sir Henry, breaking the stunned silence at last. 'You don't think he's a mind-reader?'

'I have no idea,' replied August, equally baffled, 'but I have a feeling we haven't seen the last of him.'

No sooner had Don Gervase disappeared than a large lady dressed head to foot in purple taffeta came striding towards Sir Henry.

'Ah, Mrs Spong, always a delight.'

'Sir Henry!' she shrieked, loud as a cockatoo. 'This museum of yours is quite the business, but I have just one complaint.'

'And what is that, ma'am?'

'The dodo, sir; Lord, it's a dead ringer for my sister!' and she whooped with laughter once more.

'I'm afraid there may be some truth in that,' admitted August, hiding a wry smile. Slipping away around the other side of the pillar he almost tripped over Tom who had been listening to it all.

'Tom? What on earth are you doing hiding down there?'

'Erm . . . I'm . . . erm . . . I don't know really,' he mumbled, struggling to his feet. 'Sorry. I was just having a nap.'

'Having a *nap*, in all this fun and dancing? What's the matter with you, boy?'

Tom looked down awkwardly. He was not prepared to admit that he was hiding from Don Gervase, but having overheard their conversation, there was now something else pressing heavily on his mind.

'Mr August—'

'What is it, Tom?'

Tom hesitated: it was so difficult knowing what was going to happen next—*if* Uncle Jos had been right . . . supposing he hadn't?

'I've been thinking, and I think . . . err . . . maybe . . . it might be a bad idea for you and Mina and Sir Henry to go to India.'

There, he'd said it now. August looked down at him blankly.

'Now why on earth do you think that?'

Tom struggled to find the words. His tight fitting suit felt itchier than ever.

'I dunno . . . . I just—I just have a feeling that something bad is going to happen, that's all. Something you may all regret.'

August raised his eyebrows.

'Not you as well! Why is it that I am now surrounded by mind-readers? Only a moment ago, a very odd looking fellow whom I have never met before in my life seemed to know all about the tiger—and the sapphire.'

Tom had nothing to say. He simply shrugged his shoulders.

'Yes, he is a bit odd.'

August turned to Tom in astonishment.

'Do you mean to say you *know* him? Don Gervase something or other?'

'Oh, we've met before, a long time ago,' said Tom quickly, 'I . . . er . . . I don't know him very well.'

'Really.'

August stared hard at Tom. There was something very unusual about this boy, something he couldn't put his finger on. Tom avoided his eyes.

'Well, your premonition or not, I'm going,' said August firmly, looking up at the dancing couples once more, 'and besides,' he added, lowering his voice, 'I shall see to it that nothing bad does happen.'

Tom did not understand.

'What do you mean?'

'Exactly that, Tom. Exactly that.'

August looked away across the dancers, his eyes widening. There was a strange expression on his face that Tom had not seen before.

'Things have changed now, make no mistake about it.'

With a flicker of a smile he walked towards a group of farmers admiring the dodo.

Tom watched and wondered what August could have meant; how had everything changed? Perhaps it was to do with Mina and the sapphire—or something else. But before he could decide what it was Tom felt a prickly sensation running down the back of his neck.

'E-hem.'

Someone cleared his throat directly behind him, and whipping round Tom found himself face to face with Don Gervase. He was so surprised he let out an involuntary gasp and shrank back towards the pillar.

'Well, well, well.'

Don Gervase bent forward to inspect him, his enormous eyes the colour of yellow milk.

'Tom Scatterhorn, is it? We meet again. *What* an unexpected surprise.'

CHAPTER 13

Curiosity Kills the Cat

Tom shifted uneasily from one foot to the other. This was exactly what he had hoped would not happen.

'Hello,' he said quietly.

Don Gervase stooped down to take a closer look at the thin blond boy before him, and Tom pressed back against the pillar. Even though Don Gervase's large milky eyes were inspecting every inch of him, Tom sensed that he wasn't entirely sure of who he was looking at. Perhaps it was because Tom appeared so different in his suit and high collar; and then there was his hair, which instead of its usual unruly blond tangle was now at August's insistence slicked down and combed neatly.

'I believe we have met before have we not?' said Don Gervase, with a trace of uncertainty in his voice.

'I don't think so.'

'How very peculiar. Perhaps you are a different Tom Scatterhorn.'

'Perhaps I am.'

'Hmm. That would be a coincidence indeed. Two Tom Scatterhorns, how about that?'

Don Gervase drew himself up to his full height and considered what to do next; then he tried a different tack.

'You see, the Tom Scatterhorn that I know is a runty, opinionated little brat, whose parents have abandoned him with his mad old uncle. He is very worried about them, and so he should be.' Don Gervase paused for effect, and stared down at Tom imperiously. 'That's not *you* then?'

Tom felt the anger welling up inside him, but he knew that this was exactly what Don Gervase was looking for. With a huge effort he held himself back.

'No,' he said flatly, 'I don't have an uncle. I have no idea who you are talking about.'

'Well, that is good,' replied Don Gervase, lowering his voice to a whisper, 'because if you *were* him, I would advise you to be very careful indeed.'

'Why?'

'Because you might be meddling in matters you do not understand.'

'I would?'

'Indeed you would.'

Don Gervase's tongue darted out of his mouth and flickered over his thin dry lips.

'*If* you were him. And that would be a shame.'

He smiled menacingly, and Tom was just on the point of trying to bring this awkward conversation to an end when something very peculiar happened. A small butterfly with bright blue wings appeared directly above Don Gervase's head, and began to circle inquisitively around him. The tall man was momentarily speechless, and his enormous yellow eyes followed the small creature as it descended in ever decreasing circles until finally coming to rest on the very tip of his nose.

'What kind of magic is this?' he growled in a low voice.

August, thought Tom . . . a new trick.

'Ahhhrgh!'

There was a loud shriek from across the hall and turning round Tom saw Mrs Spong collapse to the floor like a felled tree. Immediately she was surrounded by anxious dancers, fanning her ample neck upon which at least a dozen more blue butterflies were crawling.

'The lady needs air!' shouted a voice in the crowd. 'Make way!'

Several burly men stepped forward and each grabbing a limb of the unfortunate Mrs Spong they carried her like an enormous pig towards the door. Even as they did so more and more butterflies began to descend from the rafters, searching for food amongst the ladies' bright dresses. Soon the small brilliant blue butterflies filled the hall like confetti, and the cries of panic gave way to shouts of 'Bravo!' and 'Hooray!' and 'Three cheers for Sir Henry!' as if it was all some kind of marvellous stunt.

Sir Henry smiled and waved politely, having no real idea what had happened himself. And then, as one brave butterfly came to rest on his waving hand, the crowd erupted into spontaneous applause. It was the perfect moment to escape; leaving Don Gervase still pondering the flickering blue butterfly probing at his nostril, Tom stole away through the crowd to the door. Grabbing his thick woollen coat and cap he scampered down the steps of the museum and out into the snowy streets.

Where now? Anywhere, it didn't matter. Turning up his collar

Tom bent towards the wind and tried to make sense of it all. There could be no doubt that Don Gervase was threatening him, of that he was sure, and his ridiculous performance wasn't fooling anyone. But what was he really interested in? Was it August's secrets, or the sapphire? Or both, in some way, and maybe they were all connected? Tom went back and forth with reasons but he could not decide, and before he knew it he found himself down on the edge of the ice once more. Had he not been thinking so hard he might have noticed that he was being followed by a slim figure in a white fur coat.

The scene before him was much the same as last night. The fairground stalls were doing a brisk trade and the ice palace was full of children, all racing and throwing snowballs at each other. The only difference was out in the centre of the river, where a long string of lanterns had been erected. Beneath them Tom could just make out the shadows of workmen, fencing off the huge hole in the ice that had swallowed up the horse and the sledge. And Noah: suddenly Tom's mind was jolted back to that grey pool and the rows of pale faces, staring down at the lifeless body lying there, cold on the ice. Noah must have been about his age. Tom shuddered and drew himself deeper into his coat; fate just seemed so cruel. They should have intervened, Tom knew it; August should have done something. Just as the frustration began to well up inside him once more Tom glanced across at the skaters and his eyes met those of a gaunt boy with hunched shoulders, holding the arm of a woman. It was Abel and his mother. Tom raised his hand and tried to smile, but Abel looked right through him, just as if he wasn't even there. They skated on past him in silence, staring blindly ahead, as if in a dream.

'It's strange, isn't it, how some people survive, and others . . . just don't.'

Tom recognized that voice: it was Lotus, standing quietly behind him. She was staring at him intently.

'You're August Catcher's boy, aren't you?'

'That's right,' mumbled Tom, pulling down his cap further over his eyes. 'Who wants to know?'

Surely she must recognize him.

But somehow Tom felt that she couldn't. It was as if Lotus, like Don Gervase before, was unable to see beyond what he was wearing. His shape was different.

'Oh, my name's Lotus Askary,' she said briskly, and held out her hand for Tom to shake. He took it briefly; it felt as cold as an icicle.

'I'm here for the fair with my father,' she went on, 'I saw what happened last night. It was awful. Did you know that boy?'

'Yeah,' muttered Tom, looking down at his feet, 'yeah I did.'

He noticed that Lotus was wearing white skates with polished steel blades. They seemed unusually long.

'That was his family, wasn't it, who you smiled at just now?'

'That's right.'

Tom could not stop staring at her skates. Those blades looked dangerous, their points were as sharp as knives.

'Of course, you *must* have known him,' Lotus continued, 'because didn't Noah work for Mr Catcher—like you?'

'Hmm.'

Those blades were definitely sharp enough to cut through ice, Tom felt sure of it. Then a chilling feeling crept up his back and his mind began to race. What if—supposing Noah's death had *not* been an accident of fate? Supposing that hole in the ice had been made deliberately? Don Gervase and Lotus, working together; one setting fire to the sledge, the other cutting a hole in the ice . . . hadn't he seen Lotus skating out there in the darkness before the accident? Hadn't he seen Don Gervase amongst the stalls? He wasn't sure. But why, why would they do that? Tom had no idea. Staring at those long black blades he suddenly felt numb to the core. Don't react, don't reveal anything, he told himself; she still doesn't know who you are.

'So what do you do up there at Catcher Hall?' Lotus continued. 'August Catcher's such a clever man. It must be fascinating.'

'Not really. I'm only just starting out. It's gobbledegook mostly.'

'Gobbledegook? *Gobbledegook*?'

Lotus seized on this unusual word as if it were some kind of clue.

'Yeah. I don't understand it.'

'Oh.' Lotus seemed a bit disappointed. 'And what did you do before you worked for Mr Catcher?'

Tom looked at her blankly.

'How do you mean?'

'Were you his chimney sweep or stable boy or what? I just wondered how you came to work for him, that's all,' she said, her milky eyes boring into him. 'After all, it's such a great job. I would love to be Mr Catcher's apprentice.'

Tom felt his cheeks redden. What could he say to that? Don't tell a complete lie, she'll never believe him. Just a half-lie, or a half-truth, as his father liked to say.

'My parents know him. They're map makers . . . err . . .

geographers, more like, and they left me in his care until they come back. That was a while ago now.'

'I see,' she said carefully, 'and your parents, have they fallen down a glacier or something?'

'I don't think so.'

'Are they dead?'

'No.'

'How can you be so sure?'

Lotus's eyes were still on him.

'I mean, if you haven't heard from them, and you don't know where they are, how do you know they are not dead?'

Tom felt the blood begin to pump in his temples.

'I just know they are not,' he replied in as matter-of-fact a voice as he could manage. This interrogation had gone on long enough.

'So August Catcher's going to keep you on—indefinitely?' persisted Lotus.

'Maybe. If he wants to.' Tom shrugged his shoulders as non-chalantly as he could. 'It's up to him, isn't it?'

'How fortunate for you.'

Lotus stood right in front of Tom blocking his path. If she had been a complete stranger he was sure he would have punched her by now and run off; but of course, it was Lotus, and he couldn't do that. And anyway, there was something about her manner that suggested she really did not recognize him; or at least, she could not be certain. Better to keep pretending, and find another way out. So Tom tried the oldest trick in the book.

'Would you like to meet Mr Catcher?'

Lotus's eyes lit up.

'Could I?'

'Yep. I'm sure he'd tell you all about how he stuffs things and preserves them—if you're interested.'

'Do you really think so?'

'Yeah. He tells me loads of stuff but I don't understand any of it. Why don't you ask him, he's just over there.' Tom pointed over Lotus's shoulder into the crowd. 'Mr August!'

The moment her back was turned Tom darted behind a coconut shy and scrambled out on to the ice, throwing himself onto a toboggan full of twigs that was being pulled by a wizened old man. The old man grumbled a little but kept going, and when Tom was far enough away from the shore he shot a glance back over his shoulder. There was Lotus, buzzing back and forth along the edge of the ice like an angry wasp, scowling into the crowds. She hadn't seen him. Then the tall figure of Don Gervase appeared at her side. Tom jumped off the sledge and slipped inside the ice palace amongst the other children, just in time to spot Lotus and Don Gervase skating past the window.

'You must be more careful,' scolded Don Gervase, his eyes searching the crowds.

'I'm not sure it's *him*,' hissed Lotus angrily, 'how am I supposed to tell? *You* can't.'

'Well we must *not* lose him again. Instruct Humphrey to keep a watch on the house.'

'He's there already. I'm not stupid, you know.'

They skated around the palace and out of sight. Tom's heart was beating faster now; he had escaped, but the thought that they were still looking for him was of no comfort at all. He pressed himself to the ice wall, waiting until they came round again.

'And if he *is* one of them, what are you going to do?' whispered Lotus as she reappeared at the window.

'What has to be done—of course,' rumbled Don Gervase, his voice dark with menace. 'Travellers are not tolerated, you know that. *Whoever* they are.'

And they disappeared out of earshot once more.

Tom had heard more than enough to be worried. *What* had to be done? Was he a traveller? He wasn't sure, but he was certain that he should not stay at the ice fair a moment longer; it would only be a matter of time before they found him. He must return to where it was safe. Flitting through the crowds of skaters like a ghost, Tom ducked into an unlit side street and set off up the snowbound hill towards Catcher Hall.

The house was completely quiet when he reached it. Tom was just about to go up the main drive to knock on the door when out of the corner of his eye he saw a thin shape hovering in the shadows of the yew trees. Who was that? Certainly not August; he was still at the ball. Stealing into the shadows himself, Tom waited and watched. The shape appeared once more, and this time Tom recognized it as the rim of a top hat, worn by a large man in a long black coat, rubbing his hands together in an effort to keep warm. Tom could not see his face, only his heavy, bulging neck and the cruel set of his jaw. He seemed to be very cold. Was that Humphrey, the Askary's Mexican driver?

Maybe it was; he was keeping watch, just as Lotus had told him to. Tom racked his brains, how could he get inside without being seen? Then he remembered that almost the first time he had met August he had appeared as if by magic, through a small window in the roof. Perhaps he had some secret entrance of his own.

Staying hidden in the deep shadows of the trees Tom tiptoed through the snow to the other side of the house, towards the study on the ground floor. On reaching it, Tom found the windows locked, but in the corner there was an old iron drainpipe that ran straight up to the battlements. Perhaps this was August's route; the pipe certainly looked sturdy enough.

Sure enough, as soon as Tom began to climb up he found well-used footrests and arm-holds in the slabs of stone: this was August's own private way up to his attic. Why the secrecy? Tom had no idea why he should need to break in and out of his own house, but it was useful now. Heaving himself over the battlements Tom found a small wooden ladder running up the roof to a skylight. Climbing up it carefully he reached the window and he knew that he had arrived at the right place. There below him was the workshop, and the catch on the skylight was already open.

A short while later Tom was sitting in August's armchair, warming his cold feet in front of the coals glowing in the grate. Here, at last, he was safe, and soon August would come back from the ball and they would surely never dare attack him then. Even so, Tom could not feel completely at ease; that conversation he had just overheard was haunting him.

'If he is one of them, what are you going to do?'

'What has to be done. Travellers are not tolerated . . . whoever they are.'

Tom turned the words over and over in his mind; if only he knew what they meant.

Walking over to the large round window he gazed out at the town spread before him in the moonlight. Somewhere down there were people who he felt sure were plotting against him. Maybe now was the time to escape, to leave this place and return to his own world. But Lotus and Don Gervase were there too; either way they would find him, if indeed it was him they were after, and Tom was not at all sure about that. After all, what on earth could *he* tell them?

Tom drummed his fingers idly on the workbench wondering what he should do next. Then, looking down at all the paraphernalia in front of him his eye was caught by a small movement. Looking closer, he saw that it was a small black beetle, making its way across the busy surface of wires and nails and needles, until it clambered up across a small, silver key. Tom recognized it immediately: this was the key to the gunmetal cupboard, August's box of delights. He must have dropped it. How strange, as August was always so careful to keep it in his pocket; but nevertheless there it lay, an unremarkable object carelessly placed on the workbench. Yet, somehow, it was inviting Tom to pick it up.

For a moment Tom hesitated; should he ignore it? No—how could he? This was August's inner sanctum, access was strictly forbidden. August would never let him open this on his own; which was *precisely* why he should open it now. After all he only wanted to have a look, and where was the harm in that? Just one little look, that's all he wanted. Letting his natural curiosity get the better of him, Tom walked over towards the shelf of long-eared owls, and lifting them aside he drew back the small black curtain. There it was, the narrow gunmetal cabinet on the wall.

Gingerly Tom placed the key in the lock and felt it turn sweetly to reveal the rows of glass bottles standing on the shelves. They looked so harmless, it was hard to believe that every single one of them was a deadly poison; all that is, except one, and that was the only one that Tom was really interested in. Reaching up to the top shelf he felt for the small hexagonal blue bottle that contained August's potion, and found it standing in the corner at the back. Cradling the bottle in both hands he peered through the blue glass at the colourless liquid. Was this really the elixir of life? Bottled lightning? The divine spark? Was this what his father had gone halfway across the world to find? Was this really what might have saved Noah?

Slowly Tom turned the bottle round and round in his fingers, watching the liquid slooping about inside. It was just a dash of this, a dribble of that; it all seemed so unlikely.

'Besides, I have my doubts whether it would work on a human being. Supposing something went wrong?'

'Well, how will you ever know that, if you are not prepared to try?'

Last night's argument with August came flooding back. But what if . . . suddenly Tom had a crazy idea. What if he did try—on *himself*. Then he would know, then he could stop feeling guilty about Noah.

No . . . Tom smiled and shook his head; that *was* a stupid idea and anyway, supposing it did work, what would that prove? Nothing could bring Noah back now.

But then it suddenly dawned on Tom that August's potion might bring someone else back: *his parents*. After all, wasn't this exactly what his father was looking for? Supposing he took it back with him through the travelling trunk into his own time, then somehow got word to them what he had found, they would be back in an instant. Imagine the look on his dad's face when he told him!

Tom stared down at the small blue bottle once more, watching the firelight dance off the glass. There was something so powerful about it, now that he knew what force was captured inside . . . he *must* take it, and he must leave immediately. But what if August missed it? He wouldn't mind, reasoned Tom, he could always make some more. And what if he missed *him*? Well . . . too bad.

'Hello mate.'

Tom froze: all the hairs stood up on the back of his neck: who said that? The voice was gravelly and seemed to be coming from the ceiling . . . Looking down the rafters of the long room, Tom saw that the skylight was still open, as he had left it, but on the central rafter at the far end was the shape of a very large bird.

Oh no . . .

Tom felt a knot of fear tighten in his stomach, and the next moment he bolted for the door, but even as he did so, the large shape lifted its wings and clattered down in front of him.

'You're in a bit of a hurry with that, aren't ya?'

It was the eagle, the large black eagle that had chased him into the museum, and it was now standing directly in front of the small attic door. Tom instinctively took a step back into the centre of the workshop, his nerves jangling. This really was the very last thing he was expecting.

'Who . . . who are you?' he stammered bravely. 'And why do you keep chasing me?'

'I ain't chasin' you, Tom. Quite the opposite.'

'Then—then how did you get here?'

The eagle fixed him with its yellow eye.

'This is where I come from, *remember*?'

Tom stared uncertainly at the enormous bird. Maybe it was right. After all, this *was* August's workshop, in the past, where all the animals had been created. But still, there was something very odd about this creature. Somehow it didn't look entirely real . . .

'OK, so why aren't you in the museum with the rest of them?' asked Tom defiantly. 'Shouldn't you be at the opening tonight?'

'Ooh,' hissed the bird, shaking its head angrily, 'you *do* like to ask 'em, don't ya? Listen, nobody's perfect, mate, are they? I mean look at yerself, wouldn't have taken *you* for a thief, Tom Scatterhorn!' The great bird began to clatter about, muttering strange curses to itself. Tom could see that this creature was very offended at not being included in the museum.

'All right then,' reasoned Tom as calmly as he could, 'I'm very sorry you're not in the Scatterhorn Museum, really I am, but—'

'I is what I is! I didn't ask for it!'

'No. Fine. But please get out of my way now. I'm going home.'

Tom took a step forward and immediately the eagle rounded on him menacingly.

'Not with that bottle, you ain't.'

Even as a shadow in the darkness Tom could see that the great raptor was far larger than he was, and there was no way he would make it to the door without a fight.

'You can't just go stealin' stuff like that!' it rasped, its angry eyes fixed on the bottle. 'Put it back son, it'll do your nut in. Doolally!'

Tom swallowed hard; what choice did he have? The eagle obviously meant it.

'But I don't understand, what's it got to do with you?' protested Tom angrily. 'What are you, some kind of—'

'Duck,' interrupted the eagle.

Tom blinked hard.

'Duck—?'

'DUCK!!'

The very next second something silver wanged past Tom's head and stood quivering in August's poison cabinet, sending the bottles tumbling noisily to the floor. A knife . . . ? Tom spun round in horror as glass shattered and a large black shape pushed the outside of the round window forwards and somersaulted into the room.

'Hey!' shouted the eagle. 'What the—'

But the eagle never finished its sentence, as at that moment the heavy figure slammed into Tom with the force of a rhinoceros, knocking him clean off his feet and hammering him back onto the floor. Tom felt a terrible pain in the back of his head and looked up, dazed, to see a grey steel mask with a grill for a mouth and two small black holes for eyes looming over him. A crushing weight squeezed all the air from his lungs and in the next instant two huge hands reached around his neck and began to squeeze. Tom tried desperately to cry out, but his throat was dry, nothing came.

'Not dead, my frien'?' grunted the mask. 'No, not yet?'

The two leather hands lifted Tom's neck off the floor and slammed his head back down again and again. A helpless sense of panic rose within him and the room began to swim. Tom felt a hot, chocolatey breath on his cheek.

'Oh yes, my frien', you soon will be.'

Tom felt another terrific crack on the back of the head. The room was growing darker every second. Dimly he saw the steel mask turn round and heard the sound of a knife being unsheathed.

'What the bloody hell do you think you're doin'!' came a shout from the background. 'Oh no you don't! OH NO YOU DON'T!'

Then a terrifying screech split the darkness.

Suddenly Tom felt the leather gloves loosen on his neck, and gulping for breath he glimpsed the mask's piggy eyes suddenly change from surprise to pure terror.

'GIT-THE-'ELL-ATOVIT!'

A black blur hit the man so hard that it lifted him clean off the ground and sent him flying back, spread-eagling him against the round window. The very next second the vast bird leapt up onto his shoulders and its talons tore into his face, ripping the steel mask away. The man screamed and fell backwards against the glass, forcing the window to revolve . . .

'Good Lord!'

August opened his carriage window just in time to see a heavy figure tumble backwards out of his workshop window, closely followed by a vast bird, flapping away into the night air.

'What in heaven's name is going on up there?'

The man's body hit the stone steps with a sickening thump, but Tom did not hear it. Panting for breath his head lolled limply sideways, and through his blurred vision he could just make out the shapes of smashed bottles, their liquid poisons creeping across the floorboards towards him. Somewhere beyond them lay a small blue thing, but even as his eyes saw it, the blue began to fade to black . . .

CHAPTER 14

The Lair of the Shaitan

'Is he still asleep?' said a woman's voice.

'Yes—still resting.'

'Good. Far too hot to do anything else at this hour.'

Tom opened his eyes, and the bright white light blinded them. He closed them again. For a moment he thought that he had gone home. It was early morning in summertime, and the sunlight was streaming in through the half-open curtains of his bedroom. The house was still quiet, and outside it sounded like a thousand birds were chattering and twittering . . . Tom yawned and tried to remember the dream he had been having. He was sitting wrapped in a blanket on the deck of a large ship that was slowly rolling back and forth in the big ocean swell. There were the sounds of seagulls and laughter, and a young man with dark hair was sitting next to him reading out the most amazing stories that seemed to go on and on for ever . . . Tom opened his eyes once more and saw that he had been mistaken. He was not on a ship, nor was he in his bedroom at home; he was lying in a trunk, the sides of which were lined with pictures of men on horseback riding towards a distant sand dune. This was the trunk from Catcher Hall, but it was no longer in the small wooden room. The lid was open, and above him curtains of thin white material swayed in the breeze. Then for the first time Tom heard a deep rhythmic throbbing somewhere below him. That sounded very much like an engine. Pulling himself up on an elbow, Tom found himself inside a cone of muslin sheets.

'Where am I?' he said out loud.

'Tom? Tom dear boy, we are almost there. Look!'

A woman in a wide-brimmed hat pulled back the curtains and smiled sweetly at him beneath her parasol. It was Mina Quilt.

'You've been asleep for days, darling. You must look at this, isn't it charming?'

Mina pointed at three brown figures and an elephant, standing on the riverbank. She waved and they waved back.

'Isn't India heaven?'

India . . . Suddenly the present came rushing in and hauled Tom out of his dreams. He was on a small boat in the jungle—*in India*. But what about . . . suddenly he panicked.

'Where's the tiger?'

'The tiger?' said another familiar voice. 'Well, we haven't found it yet.'

Tom looked up and saw a man in a neat white suit and hat come and sit down next to him. It was August.

'Now, how are you feeling, old boy. Any better?'

August was staring at him with some concern and Tom could not think what to say. Had he been ill?

'I think so. I . . . I don't know.'

'You haven't been very well, Tom,' said August softly. 'In fact, you have been extremely unwell.'

'I have?'

'Indeed you have. Quite delirious, old chap.' August bent forward and whispered in his ear. 'And spouting the most extraordinary stories.'

Tom thought hard about this; what had he done? He could remember nothing at all. He looked up at August and Mina blankly.

'Is our young adventurer awake?' bellowed yet another familiar voice. There was Sir Henry in a tatty old bush hat, standing at the bows with a thin, birdlike Indian in a turban. Seeing that Tom had woken up he strode down the deck towards him, smiling broadly.

'You are a very brave boy, Tom,' said Mina gently.

'Rather too brave perhaps,' added Sir Henry, sitting down beside her. 'I'm not sure I would have shown such gumption at your age. What a journey!'

Tom stared up into his handsome beaming face. He had no idea what Sir Henry was talking about.

'Journey? What journey was that?'

'You mean to say, you can't remember?' August looked down at him curiously.

'Remember what?'

All three of them stared at Tom in amazement, and all he could do was to smile back helplessly. What did they want to know about—his dreams?

'Confound it lad, only one of the greatest journeys ever undertaken by an eleven-year-old boy!' exploded Sir Henry.

'Perhaps he's still not well,' said Mina gently, taking Tom's hand.

'Yes, he still looks rather feverish,' added August, feeling his forehead.

'Well, seeing that you can't remember,' said Sir Henry briskly, 'I think we shall need to remind you, as it is a tale worthy of any Scatterhorn.'

'Or Catcher,' added August.

'Them too,' winked Sir Henry. 'You ran away to sea, Tom. Desperate to take part in the tiger hunt you were. Stowed yourself away at Dragonport in the lifeboat of a steamer bound for Bombay. Made friends with the cabin boy who brought you food, and that kept you alive. Endured a hurricane around the Cape of Good Hope, and when you reached India you jumped ship. Stained your skin with elderberry juice, put boot polish in your hair, and passing yourself off as a banana seller you rode on the roof of a train for a thousand miles to Delhi!'

'Where you joined a caravan of spice merchants travelling up to Champawander,' continued August. 'However the caravan never even reached the foothills as it was attacked by bandits. There was a fierce gun battle in the jungle, but you alone managed to escape. Lying low until nightfall, you then attempted to cross a dangerous river using a rope bridge—'

'Where you lost your footing and fell,' Sir Henry went on. 'Easy mistake in the dark. But rather unfortunate as the river was infested with crocodiles. You weren't to know that, of course. Still, you managed to swim over to a tree trunk and haul yourself up on it. And there you fell asleep.'

'You floated downstream for days and days, Tom,' said August, 'until you finally woke to find yourself snagged in a fishing net.'

'That's right,' continued Sir Henry, 'so you shouted for help, half scaring the fishermen who had caught you out of their wits.'

'So they jumped out of the boat, thinking you were some kind of river spirit,' smiled Mina. 'I do like that bit. And then, by quite *extraordinary* coincidence, at precisely that moment when you were standing on the log shouting for your life—'

'You were spotted by a party travelling upstream on their way to shoot a notorious man-eating tiger—'

'That happened to be—us.'

Tom lay looking at them in stunned silence.

'I did *that*?'

'If you say so,' said August with a wink, and Sir Henry was grinning too.

'Of course you did, my darling,' exclaimed Mina, handing Tom a scrap of newspaper. It was from *The Times of India* and the article read: '*Eleven-year-old Boy's Extraordinary Adventure. As told to Mungo Natterjee.*'

There it was, the whole story, written in print. It must be true.

'Who is . . . Mungo Natterjee?'

'He came to meet us last week, Tom. Journalist chap, nice young fellow,' said August, 'keen to get on. Rather impressionable.'

'Couldn't resist your wonderful story, Tom. Who could?'

Tom was still struggling to understand. A whole reel of jumbled pictures whirred through his mind.

'But . . . it's not . . . *true*, is it?'

'No, Tom darling,' giggled Mina. 'You've been very sick, and you've been with us all along.'

'Just so happened the moment you regained consciousness

you sat bolt upright in bed, quite delirious, and out it all came. Just like that. And lucky old Mungo Natterjee was there, pencil at ready, to jot it all down as God's own truth,' said August.

'So now the whole of India believes it,' added Sir Henry mischievously, 'and you're famous, old chap. Everyone's talking about it.'

'But . . . why?'

'You tell us,' replied August, arching his eyebrows, 'as I distinctly remember that you didn't entirely approve of our tiger-hunting expedition, did you?'

Tom said nothing. He stared up at the white curtains swaying gently in the breeze trying hard to remember. Slowly, painfully, it was all starting to come back. August was right, he *had* tried to warn him not to come to India, but August had ignored it, and now, somehow, he was here too. He must have passed out that night on the floor of the workshop. Perhaps those poisons had almost done for him, and somehow his head was full of incredible stories . . .

'I think that earnest young chap on the boat had more than a little to do with it,' smiled Sir Henry, 'all those tales of derring-do he used to read Tom on deck. What was his name?'

'Elias something. Welsh name. Jones, that's it. Elias Jones.'

'That's the one.'

Elias Jones . . . the name registered a complete blank in Tom's confused mind.

'The truth is, Tom, during the grand opening of the museum you just disappeared,' August continued. 'I half wondered if you might have taken off with that Don Gervase character, as you seemed to know him.'

'I was rather glad you hadn't,' added Sir Henry. 'A very odd fellow he was. But talk about bad luck, no sooner had you returned to Catcher Hall than you had a burglar to contend with. But I suppose you don't remember much about all that do you?'

'Erm no, not . . . not exactly.'

'Well I'm not surprised. Did they ever find out who it was?'

August frowned as if he had just been reminded of something rather unpleasant.

'Unfortunately not. Some lunatic. Lord knows what he wanted. We never did get to the bottom of it and I dare say never will.'

'No. But my goodness, you certainly gave as good as you got, Tom,' laughed Sir Henry. 'Why, I don't think even old August would have defended his own workshop like you did. Like a lion, you were. Did you know you threw a fully grown man straight out of the window?'

'A *very* curious affair indeed,' agreed August, remembering the enormous bird flapping away into the night sky. 'And what's more, you somehow managed to swallow as much poison as could kill a horse.'

'Well thank goodness you're all right now,' said Mina. 'You're not going to be allowed to leave us again, you know.'

Tom smiled at the three friendly faces beaming down at him as best he could.

'Don't worry. I won't.'

'Very glad to hear it,' said August.

'Anyway,' Sir Henry continued cheerily, 'given your appetite for adventures, Tom, you won't be surprised to find yourself at the beginning of another one. Pulany here is the best shikary in these parts and he has been giving us the gen.'

Sir Henry called out in a language Tom did not understand to the Indian standing on one leg like a heron at the bow. Turning round, Pulany fixed his wizened face on Tom and smiled, revealing only one tooth. Then he said something very fast to Sir Henry.

'Pulany says your waking up will bring us good luck,' Sir Henry translated, 'and we will certainly need it, as this,' Sir Henry waved at the steep hillsides tumbling down into the river, 'is where the tiger lives. Fifty square miles of it. It'll be like looking for a needle in a haystack.'

Tom looked at the squat heavy trees clinging on to the sides of the ravine. There were no paths or breaks in the vegetation of any sort: it was just a solid wall of green. He wondered whether the tiger was watching them, even now.

'The mountain people barricade themselves into their villages at night,' Sir Henry continued, 'they daren't go out any longer. Pulany says only last week it dragged off a poor woman washing dishes just outside her door. In broad daylight. It has no fear of humans, you see, it knows they're defenceless. They're not armed.'

'I'm glad we are,' whispered Mina, shuddering as she peered into the thick jungle. The river was becoming narrower now, and soon the great trees that lined the banks began to brush against the boat. Pulany turned round and shouted out a command to the Indian pilot at the wheel, and they began to slow down.

'He says the head of the river is around the next bend,' said Sir Henry. 'There the water runs out. That's where we shall make our camp tonight.'

Chugging around the tall rocks they saw ahead of them a small landing stage beside a narrow beach of white shingle. There, sitting at the water's edge, were two ragged children, a boy and a girl, watching them approach. By now the gorge was so narrow that it was almost as if they were at the bottom of a deep well, with only a small patch of sky visible above. As they approached the jetty the sounds of the jungle grew louder, and then from somewhere deep in the trees there came a low and terrifying roar.

'The monster's lair,' whispered August, staring nervously up at the towering hillsides and the ancient trees looming all around. Tom could not pretend he wasn't a little terrified by this sinister place himself. The two children ran out onto the landing stage to catch the bow-rope Pulany threw them and, tying it up to a stake, they pulled the boat alongside.

'Do they live here?' asked Mina.

'I very much doubt it,' replied August. 'They have probably been waiting here all day just to catch that rope because they know Pulany is going to tip them for it later.'

But August was wrong, for as soon as the boat was secure the children scampered over the guard-rail and crowded round Pulany speaking very fast and at the same time. Pulany tried to calm them down, and Tom heard them repeat the word '*shaitan*' over and over, and point back into the jungle. Soon Pulany's expression changed and he now seemed very concerned. Coming over towards Sir Henry he spoke a few words in his ear, and Sir Henry nodded severely. He went below and emerged with an ancient looking rifle and a belt of cartridges.

'It might be that we are in luck, if you can call it that.'

'What's the matter?' asked Mina anxiously.

'Their mother went up into the valley to gather some nuts for breakfast. She hasn't come back.'

'What does that mean?' asked Tom.

'It means that August should stay here with a gun at the ready, and you should make camp and wait till we get back,' he replied, stepping on to the small landing stage. 'Don't worry, we shan't be long.'

With a cheerful wave he set off into the jungle in long loping strides, with Pulany scurrying at his side.

An hour or so later, August, Tom and Mina had put the tents up on the narrow shingle beach, and the pilot had made a fire over which a large billycan was steaming away. Neither August nor Mina mentioned the tiger at all, preferring instead to talk merrily of jungle life and the excitement of camping in such a remote spot, but occasionally Tom caught them snatching anxious glances into the dense trees.

Meanwhile, the small Indian boy and his sister sat a little distance away, watching the white people. They were frightened, but also fascinated by all the paraphernalia of the camp that had been unpacked from the boat. Eventually Mina went over and offered them two small cups of tea and some biscuits, which they accepted and greedily gulped down as if it were the first food they had eaten all day. Nevertheless, they did not want to come any closer.

The small patch of sky had turned from blue to pale purple by the time Sir Henry and Pulany returned. Both men looked very troubled, and Sir Henry took a long draught of water from the bottle before wearily sitting down beside the fire. Producing a cheroot from his breast pocket he lit it and inhaled deeply, watching the pungent smoke drift up on the warm evening air. August, Mina and Tom sat in silence, watching him.

'So you found her?' asked August at last.

'Unfortunately we did. We followed the trail about half a mile up there into a narrow ravine.'

No one said a word; Sir Henry's dark expression told them all that they needed to know.

'Oh dear,' sighed Mina, biting her lip. 'What do you think happened?'

'I think she was surprised; from behind, probably, just as she was climbing a tree. So at least it was quick, her neck was clean broken. But the fact that we found her at all suggests the tiger was surprised too.'

'By us?' suggested August.

'Exactly so,' replied Sir Henry. 'Must have heard the engine of the boat coming up the river, and decided to leave the kill. Probably even watched us getting out of the boat.'

'Gosh,' said Mina quietly. She glanced up at the rapidly darkening trees all around. 'Do you think he is watching us now?'

'I doubt it,' Sir Henry went on, 'she will probably wait until we've gone before returning for the rest of her meal.'

'She?'

'So I believe. Pulany found a footprint. You can read an awful lot into a footprint. Age, weight, that sort of thing.'

'Where did you find it?' asked August, impressed with his old friend's jungle knowledge.

'Just by that tree,' replied Sir Henry nonchalantly, waving at a small stump not two metres away, 'fresh this morning, I'd say.'

Tom swallowed nervously, and he noticed that August looked worried too. Suddenly the jungle that hemmed them in on all sides seemed full of hundreds of eyes, watching them.

'Don't you think . . . don't you think we should go after it tonight?' asked August, trying hard to conceal his nerves.

'Unfortunately it doesn't do to go stumbling about in the jungle after dark, old boy,' said Sir Henry, pulling on his cheroot. 'Tigers can see seven times better than we can, so we're at a distinct disadvantage there. No; my bet is to wait for dawn, and then stake out the kill—if it is still there. She'll certainly be back for it.'

They all sat staring at the crackling fire for a while in silence. Tom was racking his brains, trying to remember what Jos had told him that wintry morning out on the boat. How was this drama about to unfold? Would it be as Jos had told him? Would the tiger really come up into their camp, and snatch Mina from her tent? Would it knock August unconscious, and would Sir Henry finally kill it with a silver dagger? Tom looked at the faces around the fire and he shuddered. It couldn't be true; it was just a good story—Jos was right. But even so, somehow the story had been handed down. Who was the witness, was it Pulany? The wizened shikary sat on his haunches, stirring the rice in the pot. It must be him: whatever happened, Pulany must have seen it all.

'Pulany,' Sir Henry called out, and he asked him a question in his own language. Tom heard the word *shaitan* again.

'*Shaitan* now killed four hundred thirteen people, *sahib*,' replied Pulany in English, 'it is devil. You fire gun—boof!' He slapped his chest hard as if the bullet had glanced away. 'Bullet no good. No kill devil. Some people are thinking that, yes, *sahib*.'

'Hmm.'

'Do you believe it?' asked Mina.

'Of course not,' snorted Sir Henry.

'But local superstitions can be very powerful,' added August.

Mina looked across at the two small children, who had gradually edged closer to be near the warmth of the fire.

'Poor little mites,' she said pityingly. 'Do they know about—'

'Not yet,' replied Sir Henry. 'Pulany's going to take them downstream to their uncle's village when this is over.'

'Why not back to their father?'

Sir Henry fired another question over to Pulany, who gave a brief answer. Sir Henry nodded once, and turned grimly back to the fire.

'I'm afraid, my dear, our tiger's had him too. Last year.'

Mina stared hard into the flames, biting her lip. Her beautiful face was flushed and her eyes were blazing with anger.

'Well I think that whoever kills that beast will do a noble, decent thing!' she exclaimed passionately. 'And if he saves more children from becoming orphans—so much the better!' Her eyes flashed across at Sir Henry and August. 'One of you *must* do it. Quickly. Tomorrow.'

Mina turned away towards the two small children lying sleeping on the shingle beach, her pale blue eyes filled with angry tears. Neither Sir Henry nor August said a word; they were both secretly weighing up their chances of being that St George, who would slay the dragon and win the damsel in distress for themselves.

'Well well well, August old chap,' muttered Sir Henry finally, 'sapphires, man-eating tigers, not to mention everything else. It's shaping up for one hell of a story.'

'Indeed it is,' replied August, grasping the size of the stakes ahead of him. He glanced across at his old friend, and saw there was a look of recognition in his eyes too. It was a competition, and Mina had thrown down the gauntlet. He smiled wryly.

'Whoever would have thought it would come to this?'

'Quite.'

Tom did not notice what was passing between Sir Henry and August at that moment. If he had, he might have come to think about the future quite differently. Instead he couldn't stop wondering what tomorrow might bring.

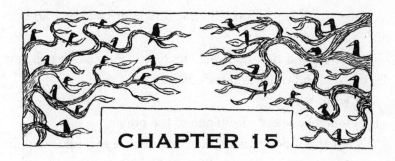

CHAPTER 15

The Hunt

Tom woke with a start at dawn the next day. It was barely light, but already the sound of the jungle was deafening. It seemed that every creature that could croak, squawk, rattle or hiss had decided to do so at precisely the same time. Pulling on his clothes as fast as he could, Tom poked his head outside his tent to find a thin layer of mist hanging over the camp.

'Ah, morning, Tom,' said Sir Henry, who was kneeling beside the billycan, filling his water bottle. Even in the pale light Tom could see that he was hardly thrilled to see him. Neither was August.

'You're up very early, aren't you?' said August, strapping a small revolver to his waist.

'Well, I knew it would be an early start,' said Tom brightly.

'For what, exactly?'

'The tiger hunt, of course.'

Tom had been thinking hard about it all night, and he had decided that the best plan would be to witness everything, however terrifying it might be.

'Yes,' murmured Sir Henry, screwing the top on to his bottle, 'you see, the thing is, Tom, I'm not sure your coming with us is such a good idea.'

Tom could see that both Sir Henry and August had already discussed it and come to this decision.

'But why? Why not?'

He looked hopelessly from one to the other.

'It's not that I don't trust you, Tom; believe me, I do,' said Sir Henry, slinging the rifle over his shoulder. 'But you must understand this is a man-eating tiger, an extremely cunning and dangerous animal. It's not like a game.'

'I *know* it's not a game,' replied Tom fiercely. 'I'm not playing a game.'

He could feel the disappointment turning to anger and simmering up inside him. Sir Henry took a deep breath and looked down at the slim blond boy. There was an intense glare in his eyes, which, had he been an adult, might have been almost frightening.

'Listen old chum,' said August, trying another tack, 'why don't you stay down here on the boat with the other children and the pilot where it's safe? We'll tell you all about it afterwards.'

Tom knew there was no chance of that.

'Well, if you want to leave me behind—fine. I'll just wait and then follow you into the jungle anyway. You can't exactly *stop* me, can you?'

Sir Henry shook his head. Dammit—the boy was obstinate. And that would be far more dangerous.

'Don't think you can just sneak off without me either,' said a voice behind him. Turning round Sir Henry saw Mina appear from her tent dressed in jodhpurs and boots and a dark corduroy jacket.

'I haven't come six thousand miles just to listen to your stories. I want to see it myself.'

Sir Henry looked from Mina to Tom, and saw from their expressions there would be no changing their minds. They were both as stubborn as mules.

'So we're all going then?'

'Yes,' replied Mina, 'all of us. Together.'

'All right,' he said, holding up his hands in defeat. 'But you'll have to promise to stay out of the way and do *exactly* as you are told.'

'And when don't we ever do that?' teased Mina, flashing a victorious smile at Tom.

'Frequently,' replied Sir Henry, slinging a cartridge belt over his shoulder. 'Come on then. Let's go.'

The jungle was dark when they entered it.

'Step where I step, and don't say a word,' instructed Sir Henry.

With Pulany bringing up the rear, the party formed a long line and began to pick their way up the gorge, sliding over large boulders and broken-down trees. Every so often Sir Henry held up his hand to stop, whereupon they all stood silent and still while Sir Henry and Pulany listened hard to the birds screeching and calling above them.

'The jungle folk will see her long before we do,' whispered Sir Henry, pointing up to the treetops, 'and when they do, they warn each other—and us.'

Tom stared up into the dark trees; it was comforting to know that all that strange hooting and buzzing of the jungle world was somehow on his side. Glancing back down the track he noticed that August was spellbound by the sheer variety of life around him. Whenever they stopped for any length of time he quietly took out his knife and took a cutting of some interesting looking plant, or coaxed some unsuspecting creepy-crawly into his specimen box. He just couldn't help himself.

After an hour of picking their way very slowly up the gorge they reached a pile of smooth boulders and Sir Henry called them all together.

'We are not far away now,' he whispered and, taking a small stick, he drew a long tapering V shape on the ground.

'This is the valley,' he said, and marked a small cross at the widest part. 'We are here, at the entrance. Now halfway up, beside a large bush,' he drew another cross halfway up the cone, 'is where our man-eater has left the poor unfortunate woman. The tiger is certain to return, and the plan is to ambush her when she does. So I suggest we split up. August, you should take Mina and make your way up that side of the valley,' Sir Henry pointed at the steep slope ahead of him, 'walk along the ridge until you reach a tall rock tower,' and he drew a series of small circles on the far side of the V, opposite the cross. 'Pulany will guide you and show you where it is.'

'And what will you do?' asked August.

'Tom and I,' continued Sir Henry, 'will climb up the hill behind me, and hide ourselves under another large rock on this side.' Sir Henry added this new rock to his map. 'The valley is very narrow at this point so we should be able to see each other easily.'

'What happens then?' asked Mina excitedly.

'We wait,' replied Sir Henry flatly, 'perhaps all day. But I'm sure she will show her face soon enough.'

August contemplated the map of the narrow valley that Sir Henry had sketched in the dirt, which now looked like this:

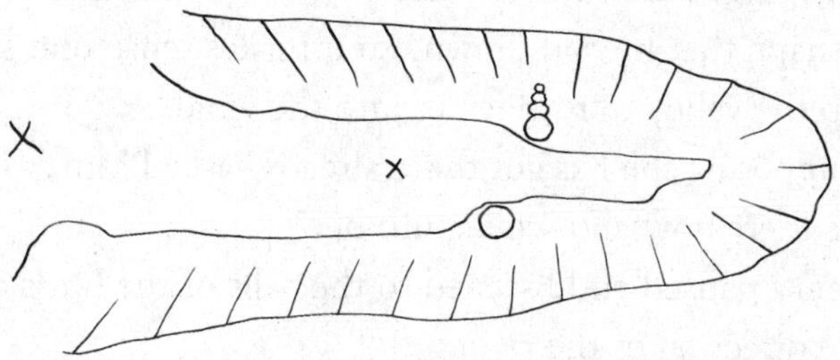

'I have just one question,' he said at last. 'How do we know that the tiger will walk up the valley floor towards us? Isn't it possible that she might come down here,' and he pointed to the head of the valley, 'or even worse, here,' he said, indicating the slopes just above Sir Henry's rock tower, 'and she decides to jump right down on top of us.'

'That is a possibility, I grant you,' admitted Sir Henry, studying his plan, 'but I don't think it's likely today.'

'Why not?' asked Mina, studying the lines in the dirt. 'Surely the tiger is far too cunning to take the most obvious route up the valley to retrieve her . . . her . . . ' Mina did not want to say the word.

'Breakfast?' volunteered Sir Henry. Mina gulped awkwardly. He stood up and sniffing the air he looked up into the trees.

'Tigers are hunters. And like all hunters they value surprise above all else. Which is why they always approach their prey into the wind. They don't want to be smelt before they can be seen. We wouldn't be able to smell her, of course, our noses are not nearly sensitive enough, but *she* doesn't know that. She thinks that we are cats just like her. Today the wind is blowing down the gorge and into the jungle,' he swept his stick down the long V shape that he had drawn, 'so it makes sense that she will come up the valley to retrieve it, into the wind.'

'But supposing she has got there already,' asked Mina, 'supposing she's there now and we disturb her?'

Sir Henry paused and listened to the calls of the birds coming from the direction of the river.

'I think not.'

'How can you be so sure?' asked August curiously.

Sir Henry listened again.

'Because she is right behind us.'

'Oh!' Mina gasped, covering her mouth.

Tom swallowed nervously; he shot a glance back down the path.

'The jungle folk have seen her,' said Sir Henry coolly, pointing up at the trees. He seemed so relaxed that Tom wondered for a moment if he was really telling the truth, but there was not the slightest doubt in his eyes. Pulany, who all this time had been studying the trees, nodded too.

'*Sahib* is correct,' he whispered, '*shaitan* coming up.'

'Gosh,' said Mina.

August fingered his rifle nervously. Tom thought of that huge snarling tiger at the top of the stairs in the museum, and shuddered to think what she must be like in the flesh. Suddenly he felt very relieved to be accompanying Sir Henry, the supreme hunter.

'August,' said Sir Henry quietly, 'I think it's time we took up our positions.'

August nodded grimly. 'Be careful old boy,' he smiled, 'and good luck.'

The two parties separated. Sir Henry set off up the steep escarpment like a mountain goat, leaping from rock to rock and barely pausing for an instant.

'Whatever happens, Tom,' he said, 'stick to me like a shadow, and I promise you'll not come to any harm. Got it?'

Tom hardly had time to reply before Sir Henry was off again, and twenty minutes later they had traversed the ridge and slid down behind the large rock that Sir Henry had drawn in the dirt.

'Isn't this exciting?' he whispered as they came to a halt at last. Tom was panting so hard he could barely nod in agreement.

'There they are.'

Sir Henry pointed across the gorge to the rock tower on the other side, where Pulany, Mina and August were just descending the rough scree at the top of the ridge.

'Beat them to it,' he grinned. 'Come on, let's see what we can see.'

Dropping to his hands and knees, Sir Henry crawled around the base of the rock, hugging its deep shadows until he slipped down under a large overhanging lip that gave onto a view of the narrow gorge.

'Not bad,' said Sir Henry softly, contemplating the valley floor spread out below them like a theatre stage. 'Not bad at all.'

Swinging his long-barrelled rifle off his shoulder he laid it down silently on the rock. Tom stared at the weapon; he had never seen anything so well used and ancient. It looked like something out of the Wild West.

'The Martini Henry Mark IV modified cordite rifle,' whispered Sir Henry proudly. 'Cumbersome, with a kick as vicious as a wild buffalo. But it'll knock the cork out of a bottle at two hundred yards, though I'm hoping our *shaitan*'s going to come a little closer than that.' He smiled, and flipping up the sights he adjusted the screws a couple of turns.

'Which direction will she come from?' asked Tom, who had got his breath back at last.

'I can't tell you precisely,' Sir Henry replied, 'but here, see her quarry for yourself.'

Undoing his breast pocket, Sir Henry produced a small leather telescope and handed it to Tom.

'There is a large grey boulder in the centre of the valley. At four o'clock down from that is a patch of sand, and to the left, a bush.'

Tom held the small telescope up to his eye and after turning the ring a few times he managed to find what he thought was the boulder. Then he moved down across the patch of sand to the bush.

'Have you got it?' asked Sir Henry.

'Yes,' replied Tom, not entirely sure that he had.

'What do you see at the other side of the bush?'

Tom tracked across, and there on the corner a wisp of something yellow flapped gently in the wind.

'Material?'

'You've got it. It's the hem of the poor woman's sari,' whispered Sir Henry, 'she's lying just below it. That's the tiger's destination.' Sir Henry leant forward and carefully lined up the sights on that boulder. 'But we must be very patient, as this particular tiger is more cautious than most. It may take rather a long time.'

Tom trained the telescope on the far end of the gorge and began to scan back and forth across the valley floor, searching for any signs of movement. After a while he found concentrating so hard on every bush and stone made him feel dizzy. This was a good position, but Tom could see that there were many more rocks and bushes on this side of the valley floor than on the other. Glancing across to the rock tower he saw a small brass telescope flashing in the sunlight. August was scanning the bushes too, with Mina and Pulany beside him.

Tom sat back, and taking a long swig from his water bottle, he wondered at the strange nature of this competition that Sir Henry had set up. Who was going to see it first? August had a far better opportunity, but then Tom remembered how August had told him, long ago, that he was hopeless with guns and disliked the whole business of hunting. Perhaps Sir Henry knew that, and perhaps that was why he had generously offered August the best spot, to give his friend a sporting chance. Even so, Tom wasn't sure why August had allowed himself to be drawn into this competition in the first place. How could he hope to succeed against Sir Henry? There must be something more than the sapphire at stake; something that had persuaded August to take part, against his better judgement . . .

Slowly the hours passed. By now the sun was high in the sky

and the heat in the valley was stifling. Tom was beginning to feel drowsy, and he was just on the point of closing his eyes when a squeak from the other side of the valley jolted him awake. It was Mina, pointing excitedly down the gorge.

'I think she's coming,' whispered Sir Henry, stealthily leaning forward until his eye was fixed down the barrel of the gun. Tom picked up the telescope and finding the yellow edge of the sari he drifted down, through the grey rocks and patches of white sand towards the deep shadows of the undergrowth at the far end. Nothing. Then he came back again, and everything was the same.

Wait . . .

No it wasn't. Something had changed.

Tom's hand was shaking with excitement, and breathing as deeply as he could he steadied the end of the telescope and drifted back down again. It seemed that one rock had shifted to the left slightly, though it wasn't a rock at all; it had a coat that was shining golden in the sun, and it was crawling on its belly, very, very, slowly towards him. Tom gulped.

'Any moment now she will stand up,' whispered Sir Henry, who had seen it too. Tom was mesmerized. He didn't want to watch but somehow he had to; was this great animal that had eaten over four hundred people about to breathe her last breath?

Crack!

The sound split the air from the other side of the valley and Tom just saw a puff of dust kick up from behind the tiger's head. There was a flash of white and the next second the tiger was racing back towards the green wall of undergrowth where it disappeared inside.

'He's missed!' cursed Sir Henry, and at that moment August vaulted over the rocks and dashed down to the valley floor with his pistol drawn.

'August! Come back you damn fool!' shouted Sir Henry. But August didn't hear him; he was already halfway to the undergrowth.

'I don't believe it—he's going in after it,' spluttered Sir Henry. 'He'll get himself killed . . . August! Come back!'

August had already disappeared into the thicket, and the next moment Sir Henry leapt down the rocks and was sprinting after him across the valley floor.

Tom had no idea what to do. For a split second he thought he would stay where he was, and then he remembered what Sir Henry had said: 'Follow me like a shadow'—and he had meant it. Sir Henry was a hunter, Sir Henry had a gun; he knew what he was doing. Don't stay in the jungle on your own, not with a man-eating tiger.

'Wait!' shouted Tom.

Sliding down the rocks he reached the ground just in time to see Sir Henry squeeze himself into the thick undergrowth on his hands and knees. Without a second thought Tom raced across to the small opening in the bushes and forced himself inside.

But as soon as he set foot in that place Tom sensed that he had made a big mistake. The thicket was an animal labyrinth; a web of dark tunnels no bigger than him snaked away through the tangled branches in every direction. Where had they gone? Tom strained every nerve to listen—but there was nothing. They couldn't be far away, could they? They had only just come in . . .

Tom took a deep breath and tiptoed a little way down the

widest tunnel, stopping every few paces to listen again. There seemed to be some movement up ahead of him, but before he followed it he glanced back quickly to check the direction he had come from. Already the web of animal tunnels looked exactly the same; forwards, backwards it was identical; there seemed to be no entrance or exit. If he met the tiger now there would be nothing he could do, he was just one more defenceless human, with not much flesh on him at that.

'Sssh!'

What was that? A voice? A growl?

Tom felt his heart begin to race; it sounded like a voice, just to the left of him. Tom peered into the dense undergrowth in the side of the tunnel, and through the tangle of branches and leaves he could just make out the crouching figure of a man. It was August.

'August,' Tom hissed.

But August did not turn round. He seemed to be rooted to the floor, staring dead ahead, motionless as a statue. August must be in some parallel tunnel, thought Tom; but why couldn't he hear him?

'August!' Tom hissed again, louder this time.

Again there was no response.

This is ridiculous, thought Tom, and seeing a small opening up ahead he ran up to the corner and turned immediately into a side tunnel . . .

'Rrrrrrrrrrr.'

Tom froze.

'Don't move an inch,' whispered a voice in the shadows.

Tom remained absolutely still, his heart hammering in his

temples. He was in some kind of chamber, made entirely of small twisted branches. There was no light except for a narrow shaft of sunlight that pierced the centre of the roof like a silver blade. As his eyes adjusted to the gloom, Tom saw August a few paces in front of him, half crouched as if he was playing grandmother's footsteps. His revolver was shaking in his hand. Sweat glistened on his temples, and he seemed transfixed by something white moving in the dark space in front of him. It was the tiger's tail, flickering back and forth. There, five metres in front of him, was the great red shape of the cat, coiled and ready to spring. On the far side of the chamber stood Sir Henry, also crouched as if in suspended motion, holding his rifle in one hand with the barrel pointed at the ground.

'No one move,' whispered Sir Henry once more.

Tom tried to keep calm, but his heart was beating so fast he could hardly breathe. Any second now the tiger was going to spring, he was sure of it. Why didn't August run! But he couldn't, he was too terrified. Then, out of the corner of his eye, Tom noticed something dull and grey moving in front of Sir Henry. It was almost imperceptible, but it was slowly arcing across the chamber. The muzzle of the Martini Henry rifle; with one hand Sir Henry was very, very carefully raising the barrel, and swinging it around to face the dark space where the tiger crouched. The rest of him remained as still as a statue. The seconds passed and the tiger kept on flicking its tail . . . Come on! shouted Tom inside himself; he could hardly bear to watch. Any moment now surely the tiger will spring and August will die. But the barrel kept on coming, up and around, up and around, slowly, slowly, slowly . . . only a quarter turn left now . . . and all the while Sir Henry's sharp eyes were fixed dead ahead. Ten more endless seconds went by, and at last the barrel was there.

Not a moment too soon.

Suddenly there was a flash of orange and yellow as the huge tiger leapt through the air. In the very same instant a deafening boom reverberated through the thicket. And then silence once more. A strong smell of cordite filled the chamber. There was the great man-eating tiger of Champawander lying spreadeagled on the floor. Sir Henry ran forward to check the beast's pulse; there was none. He had shot it clean through the heart.

'Dead,' he said definitely. 'Absolutely dead.'

With a great sigh August leant back against the wall of the chamber. He was still trembling like a leaf.

'Th-th-thank you,' he breathed, 'I think you might have just saved my life.'

'Think nothing of it, old fellow,' said Sir Henry calmly. 'I'm sure you would have done the same thing.'

August smiled wryly and shook his head.

'I'm quite sure I will never, *ever* be able to do that. You fired that rifle with one hand.'

'Hmm. Yes, that was rather lucky, I admit,' replied Sir Henry modestly. 'Sometimes one needs a bit of luck.'

The coolness of Sir Henry was quite breathtaking; it was almost as if he had just swatted a fly. Turning round to put down his rifle, he saw Tom lurking in the shadows.

'So Tom, glad you made it in time?'

Tom nodded, utterly unable to speak. The noise of the gun was still ricocheting through his brain. He was quite sure that this was one of the most frightening scenes he had ever seen in his life.

Having recovered himself, August came forward to examine the tiger. Even though it was dead, the great cat looked absolutely terrifying. It was a full four metres long from nose to tail, and its paws were the size of shovels. Sir Henry knelt down beside the great head to admire the huge front teeth that glittered like knives in the dust.

'Now that's very odd,' he said, peering into the great tiger's mouth, 'it seems to be missing a few teeth.'

Tom came forward and saw that Sir Henry was right: on one side of the tiger's jaw, where a line of large chewing teeth should be, there was nothing but empty gum.

'I just wonder,' whispered August to himself, examining the gum.

Taking out a small pair of pliers from his pocket he poked around inside the tiger's mouth until he grasped something small stuck into the jaw. Then, pulling as hard as he could, he extracted a small black object that looked rather like the end of a nail.

'What's that?' asked Tom.

'If I'm not mistaken, that is the end of a porcupine quill,' replied August. 'This tiger has had a fight with a porcupine.'

'And lost, by the looks of it,' added Sir Henry. 'Probably tried to kill it, then lost its temper.'

'But somehow this quill got stuck in the gum, and infected it. Which is probably why those teeth fell out.' August paused a moment, holding the small stubby object up to the light. 'You don't think, by any chance, that—'

'I do,' said Sir Henry, staring at it. 'In fact, I'm sure of it. This little quill has a lot to answer for.'

Tom did not understand what they were talking about.

'This little quill is responsible for what?'

'Man-eating,' replied Sir Henry darkly. 'Humans are not a tiger's natural prey, Tom, they don't like us and would rather stay as far away from us as possible. But sometimes they have no choice. Once this tiger lost those back teeth I'll bet she couldn't eat half what she killed. So eventually, in desperation I imagine as she was so hungry, she turned on something outside her normal diet. Something soft and defenceless and easy to kill.'

'Do you mean . . . people?' said Tom, not wanting to believe it.

'I'm afraid so. Four hundred and thirteen men, women, and children, to be precise.'

Tom stared down at the magnificent animal lying stretched out on the floor. He almost felt sorry for it, despite the misery and terror it had caused. But even as he did so, a spark of doubt flickered at the back of his mind. What was it that Uncle Jos had said, about the tiger and the camp at night? Could that really be just some superstitious old folktale about a *shaitan* that had been repeated and repeated until it was finally accepted as the truth? Perhaps it was; it *must* be, he told himself. Here was the great tiger laid out before him, dead. This was what had really happened and he had been proved wrong. That was good. The great man-eating tiger of Champawander had claimed its final victim. Hadn't it?

CHAPTER 16

The Devil Comes Out at Night

'Hold very still,' said August. 'Three, two, one . . . '

Mina, Sir Henry, August and Pulany stood in stony silence, mournfully looking straight at the camera with the great tiger laid out at their feet. Only Tom, standing at the edge of the group next to the boat pilot and the two small Indian children smiled broadly.

Cllll-ick!

There was a wild burst of applause and a crowd of villagers came forward to congratulate the party. The news that the tiger had been killed had travelled fast, and even in this remote country there were now a number of dugout canoes drawn up on the shingle beach beside the camp, with more arriving. Everyone wanted to see for themselves the great animal that had terrorized them for three long years. Sir Henry was immediately surrounded by a crowd of ancient-looking headmen from the villages all talking at the same time.

'What do they want?' asked Mina.

'The tiger; everyone wants a piece of it to bring them luck.'

'Which piece of it?'

'Any piece of it,' he grinned. 'A *shaitan* is very special. Hang a little square of bone around your neck and it will keep the jungle spirits at bay.'

And with that Sir Henry calmly sat down and motioned to everyone else to do the same. Carefully he explained that he intended to keep the skin, but they were welcome to the rest of it. Further down the beach, Tom and August busied themselves taking every measurement of the man-eater's body.

'How are you going to set it?' asked Tom when they had finished.

At first August didn't seem to hear him. He stared vacantly over to where Sir Henry was patiently listening to the villagers with Mina by his side. He couldn't hide his disappointment.

'Sorry, Tom, what was that?'

'The tiger; how are you going to set it?'

'Oh. Yes.'

August contemplated the great cat lying there in the dust.

'There was a moment when I was standing there in the thicket, waiting for it to spring. It was crouching, tensed, ready, and I was just . . . transfixed by it. I couldn't move. I felt like a mouse quivering before a cat.'

Tom knew exactly how August felt. He had quivered like a mouse before that tiger too, but he couldn't tell him so.

'I suppose I'm just not much good at killing things really,' he murmured to himself with a wry smile. 'Ironic, don't you think?' August sat stroking the tiger's back, lost in his own thoughts. 'But perhaps,' he went on, 'perhaps there might be another way.'

'How do you mean?'

August was now staring down at the tiger with a peculiarly determined expression on his face, and Tom had no idea what he was talking about.

'Another . . . opportunity,' he said finally.

Just then the long, low hoot of a foghorn echoed up the valley, followed by a great shout. Tom stood up and there, emerging from behind the rocks, was a small flotilla of boats all decked out in flags and bunting. At its heart was a tiny paddle steamer, its engine thudding vigorously, and as the flotilla drew closer Tom heard the tinny sounds of a gramophone. The ragged crowd of villagers began to chatter to each other excitedly and point to a small fat man in a bright green turban sitting on the deck.

'Who's that?' whispered Tom to August.

'I have no idea,' he replied, equally intrigued, 'but he looks rather important.'

'Maharajah of Champawander, *sahib,*' rasped Pulany, anxiously brushing the dirt off his filthy bush shirt. 'Maharajah coming to see if *shaitan* really dead.'

The small paddle steamer crunched up onto the beach, whereupon three servants splashed down into the water and ran out a narrow gangway up onto the shingle, followed by a red carpet. This was done so quickly that barely a minute later the maharajah stood up, tapping his cane impatiently, and Tom could see that he was very small indeed. The maharajah looked very grave beneath his large walrus moustache, and he was wearing a strangely tight-fitting blue and white striped suit, tucked into a pair of high brown riding boots. With some ceremony he marched down the gangplank onto the beach, where the small crowd of villagers bowed their heads before him.

'Where is it?' he asked.

No one dared to speak, but the crowd parted to reveal the enormous tiger lying in the dust. At once the maharajah's expression turned to wonder. Walking up through the crowd he stood contemplating the great animal for a full minute in royal silence. Nobody moved. Then, quite suddenly, his wonder gave way to fury, and raising his bamboo walking stick above his head he brought it crashing down on the tiger's belly.

Thwack! thwack! thwack! thwack!

Again and again he pummelled it, and tears began to roll freely down his cheeks. Then, quite as suddenly as he had started, the maharajah stopped. Taking a small white handkerchief out of his pocket he solemnly dabbed his eyes.

'That was for my dear little Parvati,' he said, his voice breaking, 'and all the others you have gobbled up too.'

Having recovered his composure, the maharajah turned around to face the ragged crowd on the shore.

'Where is the man who shot this brute?'

'Here, Your Highness,' said Sir Henry, who had been standing at the back all this time, watching the proceedings. He walked forward, whereupon the maharajah held out his small fat hand for Sir Henry to shake.

'Sir Henry Scatterhorn at your service,' said Sir Henry, bowing low before the brightly dressed little man before him.

'Sir Henry Scatterhorn, ah yes. I have heard all about you and your museum in the newspapers. It's quite something, I am told.'

Sir Henry nodded graciously.

'No doubt you want to take this tiger away with you to add to your collection?'

'If possible, Your Highness; that is, if it is not too much trouble.'

'You are most welcome to it. I never want to see this creature again as long as I live.'

'Thank you.'

'Tell me, has the intrepid young boy I read so much about joined your party?'

'Indeed he has, sir. Tom!'

Tom felt all eyes turn on him and he swallowed nervously. Carefully he made his way forward through the villagers until he stood beside Sir Henry.

'Riding on the roof of a train, battling with bandits, escaping from crocodiles, eh? A story worthy of Phileas Fogg himself!' The little maharajah eyed him up and down curiously. 'Well young man, you certainly came a long way for your tiger hunt. I hope you enjoyed it.'

'Oh yes, sir. I mean, Your Royal Highness, sir. Very much so.'

'Good good,' smiled the maharajah. 'It's just a shame you didn't all come a little sooner. And then perhaps my little Parvati—' He broke off, sniffing a little. 'Never mind. What's done is done and one can't change that.' He blew his nose loudly once more. 'Biren!' he shouted.

'*Sahib!*'

A fierce-looking man with a beard and a rifle ran forward and bowed low before him.

'Give Sir Henry what he has come for, no doubt.'

Biren reached into his cloak and produced a small velvet bag tied up with string. He nodded at the maharajah, who signalled impatiently for him to pass it over.

'Open it,' he commanded.

Sir Henry reached into the bag, and gingerly pulled out what looked like a large egg. It was a strange dull colour, of the deepest blue, and it seemed to be almost glowing from within. A wave of excited murmuring rippled through the crowd.

'That was the largest sapphire in the world until last week,' said the maharajah with some embarrassment. 'Unfortunately some railway millionaire in America has just discovered a larger one. My sincere apologies.'

Sir Henry smiled politely at this little joke.

'But it is yours now, and you must do with it what you will,' the maharajah went on, 'though I must warn you that some of my people believe that such a reward is unlucky. You have no doubt heard talk of the *shaitan*?'

'I have, sir.'

'Take absolutely no notice of it,' said the maharajah, coming closer, 'it is an old Indian superstition. That tiger is a tiger, nothing more; and the sapphire is just a sapphire—nothing more. Take it home and have some fun. Give it to a girl perhaps; I can see a very pretty one over there.' The maharajah looked admiringly at Mina. 'But don't believe what these jungle wallahs tell you,' he said, lowering his voice to a whisper, 'they really are a very wild and woolly lot up here. I want to bring them motorcars and electricity—the modern world—but they couldn't give a hoot. All they are interested in is *shaitans* and curses; in this day and age, I ask you?'

And with that the maharajah gave a little chuckle and held out his hand for Sir Henry to shake once more, which he did. The formalities over, the fat little man turned to face the ragged assortment of villagers and smiled briefly in their direction.

They bowed low once more, whereupon the maharajah led a dignified procession back up the gangplank of the paddle steamer, followed by his entourage. Just before he left he whispered to Biren, who barked a command to the headmen.

'I have told them they must all buzz off now and leave you people alone,' shouted the maharajah, 'so now you may enjoy my marvellous jungle—in peace!' and he waved triumphantly at the great green slopes all around him. Biren translated and immediately all the villagers cheered and clapped. The maharajah smiled, and settled himself back down into his cushion with a look of great satisfaction on his face. A servant rapidly wound up the gramophone, but soon the sounds of the music were drowned out by the dull thudding engine as the pocket-sized paddle steamer made a stately turn and set off downriver once more. As soon as the maharajah was under way all the villagers hurried down to their canoes, gleefully splashing and shouting as they raced each other trying to keep up. One by one they rounded the bend in the river, until at last, as if by magic, the final canoe disappeared from sight behind the rocks and they were alone in the deep jungle gorge once more. Tom looked up at the small purple patch of sky above the trees and saw that it would soon be dark, but somehow the jungle seemed completely different now that the tiger was dead; there were no longer eyes watching him at every moment. The great tangled walls of green were just trees, nothing more. The reign of terror was over.

'So August, why didn't you shoot the tiger? After all, you found it first.'

'I wanted to, believe me,' August said briskly, 'and I was just on the point of doing so when I found that—a certain small boy had played a dastardly trick.'

'A dastardly trick!' exclaimed Mina, her eyes sparkling. 'Tom you are a brute. What did you do?'

Tom smiled politely, going along with August's joke.

'I was just about to fire when he whispered, "Which came first, Mr August, the chicken or the egg?" Well, what could I do? It's the eternal question!'

Sir Henry grinned and Mina giggled loudly.

'What a question for dear old August,' she said, 'just at his great moment of triumph too!'

'Indeed it was,' said August, smiling painfully.

It was evening, and they were sitting around the campfire telling Mina what had happened inside the labyrinth.

'It really was very odd in there,' Sir Henry went on, 'rather like being inside a giant bird's nest. Frankly, August old boy, I can't think what possessed you to go inside it at all.'

'I thought maybe I'd winged it,' August replied. He was still smiling, but he was obviously embarrassed about what had happened. 'I suppose I just wanted to make sure.'

'A very brave decision, and perhaps, a little foolish—seeing that you'd missed it completely,' said Sir Henry with a hint of reproach. 'Very nearly got yourself killed, old chap.'

'Maybe,' considered August, shrugging his shoulders. 'However, that was a risk I was prepared to take.'

There was a moment of uneasy silence as both men stared into the embers, avoiding each other's eye.

'But if you *hadn't* pursued the tiger back to its lair,' Mina pressed on, 'Sir Henry *wouldn't* have followed in after you, and shot the man-eater that has caused such misery and pain.'

'Indeed,' admitted Sir Henry.

'So, bravo to that.'

There was silence. Tom could see that August felt very uncomfortable about being reminded of what had happened in the labyrinth. He sat hunched in his chair, lost in his own thoughts. But Mina could not have been more cheerful, and in the firelight her eyes were bright with anticipation. She looked more dazzling than ever.

'So Sir Henry,' she said sweetly, 'what are you going to do with that beautiful sapphire now that you have won it?'

'Well, I think I'll have it cut first of all,' he replied nonchalantly, 'and then, who knows? It might serve some purpose.'

'And what purpose might that be?'

Sir Henry laughed. 'Well, y'know, perhaps I have promised it to someone.'

'Oh?' she said innocently, knowing full well that it was her.

'Perhaps I will honour that promise.'

'Perhaps?' replied Mina smiling. 'Only perhaps?'

'We shall see,' he said, refusing to be drawn further.

Mina's eyes gleamed hungrily. 'I think promises, once made, should be kept. And the gift of a such a sapphire would melt anyone's heart.'

'It would?'

'I'm sure of it.'

Mina stared at the fire, the flames dancing in her eyes.

'Quite sure, in fact.'

August could stand this talk no longer.

'I must say I'm suddenly feeling extraordinarily tired,' he announced, standing up so sharply that his chair fell over behind him. 'I'm afraid I really must say goodnight.'

'Goodnight, old chap,' said Sir Henry smiling up at his old friend.

'G-g-goodnight all,' he stammered, and with the briefest of nods August stomped off to his tent. It was quite obvious that he was very angry indeed.

'Er . . . I think I'll turn in too,' added Tom quickly. He always avoided arguments if he could.

'Goodnight, darling Tom,' Mina called out sweetly.

'Goodnight.'

Tom let down the flap of his tent and flopping down on his camp bed he realized what a very strange situation this was. What he had thought of as a friendly competition between two friends was not turning out to be very friendly at all, and it wasn't just about the tiger; now it was quite obviously about Mina too. They must have both promised themselves that they would be the one to give it to her. That was why August had allowed himself to be drawn into the competition, but it was plain that he could not stand being beaten—even by Sir Henry, his best and oldest friend. The sapphire had divided them.

Tom listened to the laughter of Mina and Sir Henry around the fire, and suddenly he felt much less certain about the future. Perhaps he had been too quick to dismiss Jos's story, perhaps it wasn't over yet after all. *The tiger was a shaitan who could not be killed . . . it came up into their camp one night* . . . the words tumbled over and over in his mind. But how? The tiger was dead. Dead. Dead. Dead. He had *seen* it with his own eyes. Rolling himself up into a ball, Tom buried his head in his chest and eventually fell into a restless sleep, filled with dreams and ghosts.

A little while later, Tom woke up. The jungle was much quieter now; the only sound was the tinkling of the river and the low hiss of the crickets, broken by the occasional lonely call of a bird in the treetops. All was well; so why did he feel so uneasy? Jos's story was still haunting him, smouldering like a match at the back of his brain. He just couldn't shake it off.

In an effort to get back to sleep Tom turned over and thought about Sam Scatterhorn, his father. Was he at this very moment also lying in a tent, somewhere in a distant forest? Had he found that divine spark, or whatever it was that he was looking for, and had Mum found him? Tom longed for it to be true. Suddenly he found himself missing his parents terribly; he just wanted to know that they were safe, he wanted to know that more than anything else in the world. His home, his school, all those other parts of his normal life had never seemed so far away as at this moment, and Tom wondered if he would ever return to them. But even as these thoughts began to flood into his mind Tom was distracted by a shuffling sound close by. Someone was getting out of their tent.

At first Tom tried to ignore it, but he couldn't stop himself listening to the footsteps crunching away up the shingle towards the edge of the jungle, where they stopped. There was silence, and Tom strained his ears to hear more, but no sound came.

Who was that?

Tom was wide awake now; sleep was impossible. Kneeling down beside the flap of his tent, Tom carefully raised the corner and peeked outside. The narrow beach was glistening brilliant white in the moonlight, and as his eyes became accustomed to it he noticed a dark figure standing over the body of the tiger on the far side of the camp. It was August, and he seemed to be muttering to himself. Tom could not hear what he was saying, but he kept glancing back towards the tents furtively, as if he was making some sort of calculation. There was something about his manner that told Tom he should remain hidden. Whatever August was doing was a secret, and he did not want to be disturbed.

Then August knelt down beside the tiger's head and examined it. He was still talking to himself, but more quickly now, almost babbling as he reached inside his jacket pocket and brought out a small dark bottle and a white handkerchief. Opening out the handkerchief into the palm of his hand August removed the cork with his teeth and carefully shook out some colourless liquid onto the handkerchief. That looked familiar . . . suddenly a knot of fear began to tighten in Tom's stomach; he could hardly believe what he was seeing. What was August about to do—revive the tiger? But why, why on earth would August want to do that? To send it out into the jungle again? Did he really want to win the sapphire that much? He must have gone mad . . . .

Replacing the cork in the bottle, August jumped to his feet and it did indeed look as if he had gone mad. His hair was wet with sweat, and there was a feverish look in his eye as he glanced back towards the camp. With a wild movement he flung the bottle out towards the river where it landed with a small silver splash, and then he turned to face the tiger once more.

Tom's heart was thumping wildly in his temples. What should he do? August doesn't know what he's doing . . . he'd gone crazy . . . he had to be stopped before . . . before—

But it was already too late. August leant forward and pressed the open handkerchief over the tiger's nose.

'No!' shouted Tom, bursting out of his tent.

At that moment there was a low grunt, and the whole of the tiger's body jolted as if it had been given an electric shock. August raced back towards the fire, hurling the handkerchief into the embers and grabbing at a smoking stick. In his other hand he nervously drew his pistol. There was another grunt, louder this time, and the tiger raised its huge head and sat up. It looked confused and groggy, but not for long, as every second it was gradually coming back to life: the fire was returning to its flame-red coat, the angry sparks were beginning to dance in its yellow eyes. Climbing unsteadily to its feet, the great man-eater surveyed the jungle behind it, and then turned to face August.

'Go on, get away!' shouted August, brandishing his stick. 'Go on now! Go back to the jungle!'

But the tiger ignored his shouts and began to advance towards him.

'Get away!' shouted August again, louder now, jabbing the stick at it as if he was trying to shoo a dog.

The tiger paid no heed; it just padded towards him, its ears flattening and its lips beginning to curl. August stood his ground for as long as he dared before turning and running back to his tent. The tiger pricked up its ears and began to trot after him, but as soon as it saw Tom it stopped. Those yellow eyes glowered at him uncertainly, almost as if it was frightened of him.

Tom felt he should do something, but his body was paralysed. He was too scared to even speak.

Suddenly there was a scream to Tom's right. Mina was standing at the entrance of her tent, staring at the tiger in horror.

'Go back to the jungle you beast, shoo!' shouted August desperately, but the tiger was no longer interested in either August or Tom. Mina screamed again and disappeared into her tent, whereupon the tiger bounded in after her.

'NO!' shouted August. 'N-n-no! That was not supposed to happen at all! STOP IT!' And at that moment August closed his eyes and fired the pistol into the air.

CRACK!

'What the devil's going on?'

Sir Henry suddenly appeared from his tent in his vest. 'August, what *are* you doing with that gun?'

August looked terrified and helpless. 'I . . . I . . . '

There was another scream from Mina's tent followed by a sickening grunt.

'What on earth—'

Before Sir Henry could finish his sentence the enormous tiger reappeared carrying Mina in its jaws as easily as a rag doll.

'Mina!' shouted Sir Henry in horror.

But Mina did not reply—she couldn't. Sir Henry leapt forward to grab a long machete and raced out onto the beach before the tiger, barring its path.

'Come on you brute!' he roared at the tiger. 'Put her down!'

The tiger growled, but it would not put Mina down. Shaking its head angrily, it bounded out into the shallows attempting to go around him.

'Oh no you don't!' shouted Sir Henry, splashing down into the water himself. 'You put her down THIS INSTANT!'

The tiger hissed.

'RRRRR!' Sir Henry growled back. With a loud roar he began to advance through the water towards it, whirling the machete around his head. The tiger flattened its ears and spat again, clearly confused by this aggressive behaviour. It retreated first one way, and then the other.

'Sir Henry!' shouted Tom. 'Don't!'

But nothing could stop Sir Henry now. He was marching through the water like a man possessed, whirling the long knife above his head.

'COME ON!' he screamed. 'COME ON!'

The tiger was enraged. Suddenly it snarled and Mina dropped from its jaws into the water. Sir Henry lunged forward to grab her and at that very moment the tiger sprang up, flying through the air with its great paws outstretched. Sir Henry just had time to hold the long knife out in front of him before the tiger slammed into his shoulders, knocking him backwards. Both man and cat tumbled back into the river with a colossal splash. For a second, time stood still. Tom half expected to see the tiger break the surface and bound off into the jungle, but the silvery water swirled and settled into an eerie silence.

'*Sahib!*' shouted Pulany, breaking the spell and hurling himself into the river. 'Sir Henry, *sahib*!'

Moments later August and Tom had joined him, half-wading, half-running to where Sir Henry had fallen.

'He'll drown, quick!' shouted August, and together they heaved Sir Henry out from under the body of the great tiger lying motionless in the water with the machete through its heart. Dragging him up on to the beach, they could see Sir Henry's face looked deathly pale in the moonlight. A small trickle of blood ran from the back of his head.

'Henry! Henry wake up, for God's sake!' mumbled August, desperately pounding his chest. Sir Henry spluttered a few times and coughed loudly, but his eyes remained closed.

'He's alive,' whispered August feverishly, 'thank God for that . . . I never—'

'Mr August, *sahib*, come quick!'

August looked up and saw Pulany kneeling beside Mina in the shallows. August scrambled over and found her lying face up in the water with her eyes open. There was a strange angelic look on her face, as if she was staring up at the stars above them in wonder. Was she? Gently Pulany put his hand in the water and felt the long livid mark on her neck where the tiger had snatched her, then he looked up at August and shook his head. Mina was dead.

'N-no no,' stammered August, 'no she isn't, SHE ISN'T! I can save her! I can . . . ' and he began frantically searching about in the river on his hands and knees.

Tom stared down at Mina's beautiful face and felt the tears begin to well up in his eyes. He had known all along that Mina would die, even before they had set foot in India, but somehow with August's potion, the power of life, he had hoped that history could be changed, reversed in some way. He had never believed that August's potion would be responsible for it.

'I've got it!' shouted August triumphantly as he emerged from the water with a small blue bottle in his hand.

'It's going to be all right, it's—' and then his face fell as he saw that the small cork from the top of the bottle was missing; there was nothing inside but river water. Throwing the bottle away helplessly, he dragged himself back up the shore. Tom could do nothing more than stare at August in disgust; he felt angry, sad, but most of all very, very confused. It just didn't make any sense.

'*Why* did you do it?' he blurted out. 'Why? Did you not even think what might happen?'

August shrank at the fierce expression in Tom's eyes; the boy must have seen it all, and there was no point pretending any more. Sweat was pouring down his cheeks.

'I . . . I . . . I just wanted to change things; with my potion I could have another go,' he mumbled uncertainly, 'and prove I could do better . . . because I *could* have done! I could have, but—'

August cast a wild look down at Mina and Sir Henry, lying motionless on the beach. He was utterly distraught.

'Believe me Tom, I NEVER intended this!'

'I thought you didn't want the power of life and death?'

'I didn't!' replied August vehemently. 'I didn't. But . . . but something got in the way, and . . . and . . . now look what I have done. I seem to have destroyed everything.' August sat down heavily on a rock, more wretched than ever.

'I'm sorry Tom,' he said, 'truly I am.' And holding his head in his hands he began to weep.

Tom stared at the tragic scene all around him and wondered at the madness of it all. It was one thing to bring hummingbirds and puppies back to life, but man-eating tigers? August was right when he had said that fate could not be controlled; you could not expect it to do what you wanted. Yet somehow, in one moment of pure madness he had forgotten that, and this was the result. Tom stared angrily at the shoreline to where Mina lay lifeless in the shallows. Beside her, a small black shape rolled gently on the edge of the water. There it was, the blue bottle . . . empty. The glass glinted mysteriously in the moonlight. August's potion was just so powerful—too powerful perhaps for anyone to be trusted with it, even him. Tom's eyes met Pulany's, and he saw a flicker of recognition in the wizened old Indian's face. This was also what the *shaitan* had wanted. This was meant to be.

At dawn the following day Sir Henry had opened his eyes, but he still lay motionless, as if in some kind of trance. Pulany and the boat pilot had gone into the jungle at first light and returned with a small tree, half of which they would use to make a litter for Sir Henry to lie on, and the rest for a small makeshift coffin for Mina.

Meanwhile August set about skinning the tiger. It was a long, arduous job that he seemed to relish, and when he had removed the skin and head he stretched out the huge pelt on the shingle and rubbed every inch of it with a mixture of arsenical soap and salt. Occasionally he stopped to take a long drink from his water bottle, but otherwise he said nothing, preferring to work alone and in silence. Perhaps it was easier that way, thought Tom, as he sat in the shade with Sir Henry, mopping his brow and every now and again passing him small sips of water. There was no point thinking about last night now, that was the past; much better to concentrate on the journey ahead.

Only Pulany seemed uncomfortable with the silence. All day he bent his arm to his axe, muttering to himself and occasionally glancing about with a mixture of fear and disgust.

'What's the matter Pulany?' asked Tom, as the old Indian leant on his axe and stared at the high jungle walls all around.

'*Shaitan* still here, *sahib*,' rasped Pulany, screwing up his eyes and spitting into the dirt.

'The *shaitan*'s dead, Pulany,' said August irritably, 'there's your *shaitan*.' He pointed at the large canvas sack now lying on the boat.

'No, *sahib*. *Shaitan* spirit still here in the trees.'

'Oh what nonsense you talk,' blustered August, but there was a trace of uncertainty in his voice. He couldn't deny it, there was something terrifying about this jungle prison.

'Sir Henry kill *shaitan* two times,' Pulany went on, cutting the air twice with his bony fingers, 'two times! She *still* not dead.'

'The tiger's absolutely dead, Pulany. I guarantee it.'

Pulany shook his head, unsure whether to believe him or not.

'Maybe you are thinking it is so, *sahib*,' he muttered darkly, 'but *shaitan* curse on sapphire, *sahib*, and sapphire on boat. Maybe we're all drowning.'

'I can assure you that is not going to happen,' replied August definitely, 'believe me, Pulany.'

'As you say, *sahib*,' muttered Pulany, nodding his head, 'as you say.'

'Come on. Let's get out of here.'

'Let's just go *home*,' sighed Tom, and he really meant it.

'Yes, Tom *sahib*, that is the very best idea. Let's go home.'

By evening time the last of the unhappy cargo was stowed safely aboard and they were finally ready to depart. The small diesel engine clattered to life, and Tom felt a huge surge of relief as he cast off the bow-rope and in one great leap jumped from the small landing stage onto the boat. Slowly they turned out into the centre of the river, and began to chug downstream once more.

'Thank God for that,' said August, rubbing a weary hand across his face. For the first time that day a ghost of a smile flickered across his face, and suddenly he looked very tired indeed.

'Feels good to be leaving, doesn't it?'

Tom said nothing, he merely stared back up at the high jungle walls to the narrow shingle beach, still glowing under a pale pink sky. Despite the wild beauty of this mysterious place, he was quite sure that he never wanted to see it again in his life. And he knew that he would never be able to forget it, either.

CHAPTER 17

An Unexpected Exit

Six weeks later there was a knock at the door of Catcher Hall.

'Tom, be a good fellow and see if that's the doctor.'

Tom ran across the hall and opening the door an inch he found the postman, his face flushed with cold, cradling a large pile of letters and packages in his arms.

'Mr Catcher's daily dose,' he muttered grumpily.

Struggling forwards the postman thrust the whole pile into Tom's waiting arms before grabbing his sack and slithering away down the snowbound drive. Slamming the door shut with his back, Tom teetered across to the study with his load. August looked up from the mountains of letters that already swamped his desk.

'Not *more*—surely?'

'So it seems,' panted Tom, adding one more mountain to the range. 'The price of fame.'

'Indeed.'

August impatiently opened the envelope at the top of the pile.

'Dear Mr Catcher', he read,
'Please excuse my presumption as I have never written a letter of this kind before. But I visited your extraordinary exhibits at the Scatterhorn Museum last week, and I have to say it was the greatest experience of my life. The mammoth, the gorilla, the antelope, the humming birds, and the—'

August tossed it aside and picked up another official looking envelope.

'From Colonel Flowerdew Bone, secretary to the Cavalry Club of India. What on earth can he want?' snorted August, ripping it open.

'Catcher,
I have been reliably informed that you are now the greatest taxidermist in the British Empire. For that reason I am taking the liberty of sending you the skins of two small pachyderms, shot by myself, for the express purpose of turning into porters' chairs for our lobby. I hope this will not be too much trouble?'

'Porters' chairs indeed!' exclaimed August. 'Look, Tom, he's even sent a diagram.'

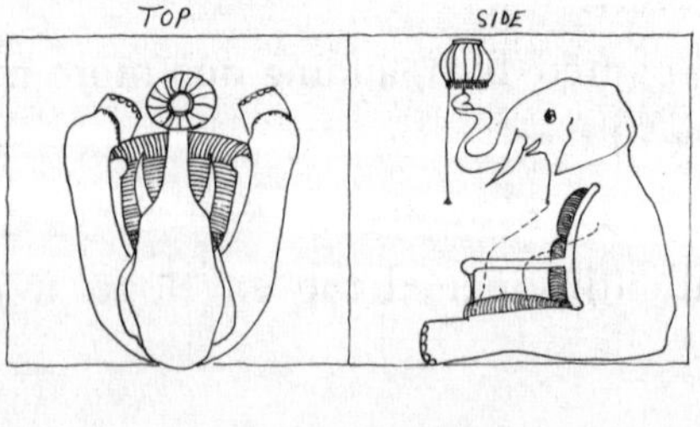

'And what the devil's that?' demanded August, glancing across at the newspaper headline in the *Dragonport Mercury*.

'TIGER SENSATION IN SCATTERHORN MUSEUM', read Tom, 'MAYOR'S WIFE ALARMED.'

'Oh Lord, the inestimable Ursula Spong,' chuckled August to himself, 'go on.'

'Last night the latest addition to the Scatterhorn Museum was unveiled before a large crowd by Mr August Catcher. The Bengal tiger, a man-eater that had claimed over four hundred lives, is set in the most dynamic pose, on the point of leaping forward with claws outstretched, at the top of the stairs. The beast is so terrifying that Mrs Ursula Spong, wife of Mayor Spong, fainted at the very sight of it, and would have certainly tumbled the length of the staircase were it not for the quick thinking of Mr Ned Badger, who, without a thought for his own safety, threw himself into her path and mercifully broke her fall. The lady bears no malice towards the tiger, or to Mr Catcher, or indeed to the brave Mr Badger, but wishes that such excitements should contain warnings to the weak hearted in future.'

'Well well.' August put down his spectacles and smiled. 'Poor old Ned Badger. That's twice she's nailed him.'

Tom leafed through the rest of the pile until his eye stopped on a large yellow envelope with a brightly coloured stamp, postmarked India.

'If it's another request to turn a crocodile into a humidor or a lizard into a cigarette holder you have my permission to throw it in the fire,' said August briskly, settling back to his own pile.

Opening the letter Tom saw from the great gold flurry at the bottom that it was from the maharajah.

'My dear Catcher,

My heartfelt greetings to you. I am pleased to report that at long last Miss Mina Quilt's headstone has been completed to my satisfaction and it looks very well in the corner of the English cemetery, close to the banyan tree. I chose the spot myself; it enjoys the afternoon shade and faces a large bougainvillea that is now in full bloom. I enclose a small sketch by my court artist, Monsieur Hanratty, that quite captures the scene.'

Wedged inside the letter was a small watercolour sketch of the graveyard, showing the large grey banyan tree and a handsome headstone carved with flowers beneath it.

The letter went on:

'Please convey my greatest good wishes to Sir Henry Scatterhorn. If he should ever recover from his monumental bash on the head, tell him I would be flattered to receive him once more.

Yours ever, etc. etc.,

Maharajah of Champawander

P.S. I trust that the sapphire remains in your most capable hands until his terrible affliction is over. For his sake I hope it will not be long.'

Tom handed the letter to August, who read it in silence. When he had finished, he got up and stood at the window, watching the snowflakes drifting down across the town. His thoughts seemed to be far away.

'Sometimes I do wonder if old Pulany was right, you know.'

'How do you mean?'

'The *shaitan*'s curse; all that mumbo-jumbo about the sapphire. Hasn't precisely brought us any luck has it? First Mina, dear Mina, and now Sir Henry, whose condition is scarcely improving.'

August turned to Tom with a pained expression on his face.

'I just can't understand it. It's almost as if there is something *preventing* him getting any better.'

Tom stared at the fire in the grate and he knew that it was true. Throughout their return journey Sir Henry had remained in a kind of trance, and now they had arrived at last he lay upstairs with his eyes wide open, eating and drinking small amounts but unable to speak or even raise his hand. It was as if Sir Henry was in a deep, deep sleep, and nothing could wake him.

'Maybe,' Tom began, 'I mean, if that's really what you think, then perhaps you should get rid of it.'

'What, the sapphire?'

'Well, yes,' suggested Tom, who had never seen it since that fateful afternoon, 'if you think it's bad luck.'

August turned to face the window once more.

'I couldn't do that,' he replied, 'even if I wanted to I couldn't. The sapphire is not mine to give away, Tom, it belongs to Sir Henry. But I have hidden it, for safekeeping. The maharajah needn't worry about that.'

Tom continued to sort out the letters into piles, gathering his thoughts. He was searching for the right words for what he wanted to say.

'So then, *if* you can't get rid of it,' he went on, 'isn't there . . . another way you can help him?'

He looked up cautiously and August immediately understood what he meant.

'No Tom,' replied August firmly, raising his hand, 'absolutely not. I am never, *never* going to use that again. I can't, and I won't—it's just not worth it. Medicine will have to find the answer. And I believe it will. It must.'

'But what if . . . what if it doesn't and Sir Henry stays asleep for ever?'

Tom was fidgeting nervously. August looked out of the window in silence and a shadow passed across his face; it was a thought too dreadful to contemplate.

There was a knock at the door.

'Mr Catcher, sir?'

'Who is it?'

'Doctor Shadrack and another gentleman are here to see you, sir.'

'Ahh,' said August, spinning round, 'the new man. An expert at last. Let's hope he can cheer us all up.' And with a determined smile he marched out into the hall.

Waiting there for him were two small, thin, and rather strange looking gentlemen. They appeared at first sight to be almost identical, for they both had narrow bony faces and tiny hooked noses, and they were dressed in long black coats.

'Dr . . . Shadrack?' said August, staring bewilderedly from one to the other.

'I am he,' announced the man on the left in a thin nasal voice, 'and this is my colleague from Belgium, Dr Skink.'

The man on the right nodded curtly.

'Skink at your service,' he barked, and clicked his heels loudly.

'Dr Skink has some valuable experience in these cases. I have asked him to give a second opinion.'

'Good,' smiled August, looking down at the strange pair. 'Two opinions must be better than one.'

'Absolutely,' sniffed Dr Skink.

'Indubitably,' chimed Shadrack.

The two men stared up at August in anticipation, and for a moment he had the curious sensation that he was seeing double.

'Well then gentlemen, if . . . er . . . you'd like to follow me.'

August led the way up the stairs to the first floor bedroom, and opening the door, he walked over to the curtains and flung them open, flooding the room with pale winter light. There before them lay the sorry figure of Sir Henry, propped up against the white pillows. His eyes and his lips were open just a fraction, and his breathing was slow and rasping. He looked as grey as a statue on a tomb.

'May we?' enquired Dr Shadrack.

'Please, go ahead,' said August as he sat down next to Tom on the sofa.

The two doctors then descended upon Sir Henry like a pair of insects, carefully inspecting him up and down. First Dr Shadrack picked up Sir Henry's limp hand and felt his pulse; the beat was very weak.

'Slow slow, quick quick slow,' he muttered, then he nodded to Dr Skink, who leant forward and peered into Sir Henry's mouth.

'No,' he said, 'no, no, no,' and he clicked his fingers sharply. 'Zer *allumette*, if you please.'

Dr Shadrack produced a box of matches from his pocket and, striking one, he held it up to Sir Henry's eye while Dr Skink lifted the eyelid. There was not a flicker of a response.

'Hmm,' grunted Dr Skink, clearly confused. 'Zen maybe zer tip-tap.'

Delving into his black leather bag he pulled out a stethoscope and listened to Sir Henry's chest.

'Tip-tap!' he barked.

Dr Shadrack tapped Sir Henry's knee twice with a small hammer, and Dr Skink listened hard to Sir Henry's chest.

'Again. Zis time try zer tap-tip!'

Shadrack used the hammer once more.

'Tip-tap.'

And again.

'Tap-tip.'

And again.

'Tip-tap, tap-tip, tip-tap.'

'Well?'

Dr Skink listened again.

'Ja. Zer tip-tap is there for sure; but vere is zer tap-tip?'

Tom watched the hammer go up and down on Sir Henry's knee and wondered whether either doctor had any idea what they were doing; it was certainly unlike any medical examination he had ever seen.

'Anything good to report?' asked August hopefully. He too was rather bewildered by this strange routine.

Dr Shadrack peered down his long nose over his half moon spectacles at Sir Henry's pallid face.

'Thin. He's definitely getting very thin.'

'And veek,' added Dr Skink, 'very veek. And zomeone must please clean his teeth. Zay are oranj!'

'But other than that he is fine.'

'Fine?' repeated August, folding his arms across his chest and looking very glum. 'He's fine, you say?'

'Ja, for now surely. Alive. Breezing. He's not dead, you know.'

'Dr Skink,' said August, trying hard to control his temper, 'you've seen this sort of condition before, tell me honestly, how long could it—'

'Go on?' interrupted the doctor, scribbling something in his notebook. 'He vas a fit and healthy man before zer accident, yes?'

August nodded.

'Zen he vill most probably last longer zan most. Maybe months, maybe even years before he finally zuccumbs.'

'Succumbs?'

'Mr Catcher,' Dr Shadrack cut in sharply, 'you must be aware that Sir Henry's condition is at the very frontier of medical science. His body is wasted, his brain is kaput, his senses zero. At this moment he is almost more dead than alive, and there are all manner of diseases in this town. Why, only this very morning Dr Skink and I have found diphtheria, typhus, and cholera, right here in Dragonport. Eventually the weak will all succumb to one, or two, or all three, together. Excuse me,' he said, and sneezed loudly.

'Disease affects both zer poor and zer rich, Mr Catcher,' nodded Dr Skink gravely, 'it spares no one.'

'So, what do you suggest we do?' asked Tom. He did not like the doctors' tone one little bit.

Dr Shadrack stared at him angrily.

'There is no miracle cure for this kind of condition, young man.'

'None zat I can zink of either,' added Dr Skink, twining his thin fingers up into a knot, 'unless . . . *you* can zink of something, Mr Catcher.'

The two doctors turned their thin pointed faces towards him and stared hard. Neither of them appeared to blink.

'Me?' snapped August incredulously. 'I'm just a taxidermist. What could *I* do?'

'Vat in-deed,' repeated Dr Skink, glancing across at Dr Shadrack. 'Vel in zat case, seeing as *nobody* has ze answer, my advice to you is to pray zat zer end is svift.'

With some ceremony Dr Skink opened his black bag and handed a small leatherbound book to August.

'*Sermons for the Day of Judgement*?' exclaimed August, reading the small gold letters on the cover.

'Read them to Sir Henry aloud,' ordered Dr Shadrack. 'Canon Mumble is a great comfort. He will be of more use to Sir Henry on his final journey than Dr Skink or myself.'

The two small men stood up together and snapping their bags shut they marched over to the door.

'Until next time,' said Dr Shadrack forcing a smile, 'good day to you both.'

Dr Skink bowed slightly and clicked his heels. 'Goodbye,' he trilled, 'and very good luck. I zink zat you vill need it.'

Tom and August sat in stunned silence after the doctors had gone. What was there to say? Skink and Shadrack, the experts, if indeed that's what they were—and Tom had his doubts—

could not have made it any clearer. Slowly but surely, Sir Henry was going to die.

Soon the nurse came in with a bowl of watery soup. Patiently she began to pour teaspoon after teaspoon into Sir Henry's mouth, wiping his chin each time he coughed. Tom thought back to the first time he had met Sir Henry, how he had burned so brightly with life and energy and fun. Now, in less time than had scarcely seemed possible, that great furnace had been reduced to a single, spluttering flame, and Sir Henry was nothing more than a sick baby. It was pitiful to watch.

'You *have* to use it,' whispered Tom forcefully. He shot a glance across at August who appeared to be staring blankly at the wall, as if in a dream. 'You just can't leave him like this.'

August said nothing; but he was thinking hard about his elixir too, only this time he was trying to weigh up the consequences of using it. The new doctors merely confirmed what he had long suspected but had tried so hard to ignore: that medicine had no answers to Sir Henry's condition. Canon Mumble indeed! Was that *really* the best they could do? Only *he* had the power to make Sir Henry better, he knew that now. But if he did use it, what would happen then? Sir Henry would almost certainly recover his memory of what had happened that night in the jungle. He would inevitably ask himself time and time again how the tiger had come back to life, and what would be the answer? Eventually Sir Henry would surely suspect that August had meddled in some way, and that was how it killed Mina. Sir Henry might never forgive him for that. Their friendship would be over surely; but what was the alternative? There was a weak cough, and a teaspoon of soup dribbled down Sir Henry's chin.

'There there,' said the nurse, quietly dabbing his mouth.

August gazed up at his oldest friend lying stricken in the bed. Could he bear to watch as Sir Henry grew paler and paler, until one day he just faded away like a ghost? August knew that he could not.

'You're right, Tom,' he said finally, 'once again. I think we *have* just about reached the end of the line.'

August Catcher spent the rest of the day up in his workshop alone, with express orders that he should not be disturbed by anyone, even Tom. To make sure Tom was kept occupied, he decided to set him the considerable challenge of making a bunch of dead nettles by nightfall.

'This is the first great staging post in the career of any taxidermist,' said August with a wry smile, handing Tom a real dead nettle together with a bundle of wax and wire and card. 'See if you can copy that. And remember, be very frugal with the wax, otherwise it will end up as a ghastly mess. Good luck.'

Tom retreated to his room, not relishing this daunting prospect one little bit. All afternoon he battled away with the wire and the card, bending it first one way, then twisting it back another. When he had finally got one almost right he began to run it through the molten wax to create the tiny bristles as August had instructed, but that's when his nettle started to go horribly wrong. The hot wax made the card buckle and droop and after his fifth attempt Tom was forced to admit defeat. No matter how hard he tried his drooping grey and brown stumps looked more like melted candles than any dead nettle, and Tom knew they would never match up to August's exacting standards. He lay down on his bed and waited with dread for nightfall, wondering quite how he was going to explain his mess.

But as it turned out, Tom was relieved to find that he never had to. When the dinner gong struck that evening Tom crept downstairs and sheepishly entering the dining room he was surprised to find that he was alone. August was still busy in his workshop, so Tom gratefully wolfed down his food as quickly as he could then slunk off to the library, where he spent a happy few hours playing billiards with Tove, the new serving girl, who had taken Noah's place in the kitchen. Tove beat him so many times that at around eleven o'clock he eventually had to admit defeat at that too, and quietly crept back upstairs and into bed. And still August was nowhere to be seen.

'Aaahhhhh!'

The scream invaded Tom's dream. The wolves that were chasing him were closing in and his sledge was bouncing across the snow towards the precipice . . . whump, whump, whump—

Crash!

There was a great clatter of cutlery and china and Tom sat bolt upright in bed. It was early morning, and there were no wolves here, and that sound was not a dream, it came from out on the landing. Rubbing his eyes, Tom shuffled out of bed and over to the door of his bedroom and peered out. There on the other side of the landing Sir Henry's nurse lay in a twisted heap at the entrance to his room, and the tray of bowls she had been carrying lay smashed at the bottom of the stairs. That's odd, thought

Tom groggily, she must have fainted. Oh. Pushing the tangled heap of blond hair out of his eyes Tom wandered around to where the poor woman lay, and found that she was still breathing. That was good. But why had she fainted? Stepping over her large body into Sir Henry's room, Tom squinted into the bright light and at first sight found that everything looked completely normal. The curtains were open, the daylight was flooding in, the medicines were laid out on the dressing table, the bed was made . . .

Tom blinked, and then he looked again: the bed was made, *but there was no one in it.* Sir Henry had gone. Tom was jolted wide awake now.

'Mr August!'

There was no reply; maybe he was still asleep . . . or . . . perhaps he was already up. Quickly Tom ran down the stairs, picking his way through the broken crockery, and sprinted across the hall into the breakfast room.

'Mr August!' he called. 'Mr August, Sir Henry's—'

'Good morning Tom.'

Sir Henry was sitting at the table in his pyjamas and dressing gown. His beard was trimmed and his hair was brushed, and he had a long line of boiled eggs set out before him like soldiers.

'I really am most extraordinarily peckish,' he said, slicing the top off one and crunching into a piece of toast. 'Won't you join me?'

Tom stood open-mouthed at the doorway. He couldn't say a word.

'No? Suit yourself then.'

'But . . . but . . . but you're . . . OK?' mumbled Tom. 'You're—'

'OK?' he snorted. 'Absolutely OK! Tip-top! Just wildly hungry.

I can't think what you fellows have been feeding me, but I feel as if I have been eating nothing but disgusting, cabbagy soup for months!'

Tom sat down. He wanted to smile and laugh and shout all at the same time, as there was Sir Henry, thinner and a bit crazier, but back to his old self once more.

'But how . . . I don't understand how you woke up. I mean—'

'Oh, I think you *do* understand Tom,' winked Sir Henry, tucking into his third egg. 'You know very well how I woke up. August told me everything.'

'August *told* you everything?'

That seemed very unlikely.

'Near enough everything. But I'm afraid that he has left us.'

Sir Henry pushed a small envelope across to where Tom sat and he recognized the spidery hand immediately. He pulled out the letter inside and began to read:

'My dear Henry,' it said,

'By the time you read this I will be on board the packet bound for Holland, and from there I shall be embarking on a very long journey that may take me several years, or perhaps even the rest of my life, I don't know yet. The reason for my departure is simple. Modern medicine had no answers to your condition, my friend, so as a last resort I used some of my own. You may wonder what this is, but all I am willing to tell you is that I used this same preparation to revive the great tiger, which had such disastrous consequences for us all. That was an act of madness which will haunt me for ever, and that is why I felt I could not stay. Tom can vouch

for this, as he has seen for himself what my potion can do. Please convey my good wishes to him, as he is, I'm sure you will agree, a most remarkable young man.
I remain your humble friend,
Yours ever
August.'

Tom finished reading, and put down the letter in stunned silence. He glanced across at Sir Henry, who had finished his final egg and was drinking his tea thoughtfully.

'August has some kind of magic potion, eh?' he said.

Tom nodded.

'I should have guessed as much. He always was too dashed clever for his own good. Curious thing is, I felt nothing at all, except when I woke up I found this on my pillow.' Reaching into his pocket Sir Henry pulled out August's small violet handkerchief. 'August must have dropped it or something. Odd smelling thing. I don't suppose it means anything to you?'

Tom smiled and shook his head; so that's how August did it.

'Thought not,' said Sir Henry, folding the handkerchief neatly back into his pocket and taking another sip of his tea. 'Tell me something, Tom. If August could revive the tiger, and then me, why the devil couldn't he do the same thing to Mina?'

Tom took a deep breath and stared at the table uncomfortably; how could he present the events of that terrible night as they actually happened?

'I know that he wanted to, he really *did* want to,' he said quietly, remembering August feverishly splashing about in the river on his hands and knees. 'I think he found he just didn't have enough of his potion left.'

'Hmm,' growled Sir Henry, staring out of the window at the leaden winter sky. 'That was a shame, but there it is. I'm sorry he felt he had to go. He didn't have to, of course. I'd have forgiven him.'

They sat together in awkward silence for a moment. Suddenly Tom also felt rather sad and empty that August had just run away without ever saying goodbye. In some strange way it was just like when his father, Sam Scatterhorn, had gone, and then, as now, Tom could not help but wonder if it was all his fault. Then it began to dawn on him that without August, he no longer had a place in this world either.

'So Tom, what will *you* do now?' asked Sir Henry politely. He could obviously tell what Tom was thinking.

'After all . . . you're his apprentice, are you not?'

'I am . . . was, I mean,' replied Tom awkwardly.

'Of course, you're very welcome to stay as long as you like. That is, if you want to, though I can't pretend life in this old place will be very interesting without him.'

'No.'

Sir Henry paused a moment, fixing Tom with his quick eye. He seemed to be weighing something up in his mind.

'I tell you what,' he said suddenly, 'I've just had a rather brilliant idea. How about if you became my protégé instead?'

Tom was taken aback. 'What, do you mean as a . . . hunter?'

'Hunter, explorer, adventurer, something like that. I could teach you how to live in swamps, track animals across the African plains, survive in the Arctic wastes, climb mountains, that sort of thing. How does that sound?' he said, arching his eyebrows. 'You've obviously got a taste for it.'

For a moment Tom was lost for words; what an offer that was! Suddenly he imagined no more school, no more struggling and scraping to get by, just years of wild adventures to the furthest corners of the earth. And there could be no better guide to the animal kingdom than Sir Henry, of that he was certain.

'Interested?' winked Sir Henry as he got up. 'Well, you mull it over, old bean. August was my best friend you know, and now that he's bolted I can't help feeling a little bit responsible for you. Plus there's something about you, Tom, that reminds me of myself when I was your age.'

He grinned down at the small boy with his tangle of blond hair and fierce, dark eyes.

'Stubborn as a mule, lean as a whippet, and hungry as a hawk!' laughed Sir Henry. 'By the way Tom, what's your full name? August never did tell me. Tom what?'

'Tom Scatte—' and he stopped himself, just in time, and blushed awkwardly. 'Tom Scatt. With a k. That's all.'

'Really?'

Sir Henry fixed him with a keen eye.

'*Odd* name, Tom Skatt—eh?'

'That's right.'

'You don't think we could be related?'

Tom looked up at his great-great-great-uncle and smiled.

'I don't think so.'

'No,' grinned Sir Henry, 'no, of course not.'

Later, Tom wandered up to August's workshop to think more about Sir Henry's proposal. What if he did decide to stay in this world, what then? He was sorely tempted, not least because as Sir Henry's protégé he might have a chance to be good at it. Tom reached across the messy workbench and picked up the extraordinary bunch of violets that August had presented to Queen Victoria all those years ago. He couldn't even begin to make something like this, even after all August's patient instruction. And there in the corner stood the grey heron and the eel, locked for ever in mortal combat. Tom felt humbled just to look at it. August Catcher was a genius in a way that he could never be, and he didn't even understand much about those chemical preparations that August spent many long hours experimenting with, either. It was always a dash of this, a splash of that; Tom was sure he hadn't ever seen a measuring jar, let alone a recipe. Walking over to the shelf where the long-eared owls stood, he drew back the black velvet curtain that concealed August's small gunmetal cabinet of secrets, and behind it he found nothing more than a blank wall. August must have taken the cabinet with him, along with all the other chemicals, for there were only a handful of half-empty bottles dotted around the shelves. So, Tom thought to himself as he closed the curtain once more, August really *had* gone for good. Perhaps he should take up Sir Henry's offer after all . . .

Just as Tom sat pondering his decision he heard the crunch of gravel outside and there was a sharp rap at the door.

'And what's your name, girl?' said a familiar high-pitched voice.

Tom peered out of the large oval window, and recognized the wiry shape of Dr Shadrack standing in front of a small black carriage in the snow.

'Tove, sir.'

'Tove? What sort of a name is that?'

'It's Finnish, sir.'

'Finnish? *Finnish*? Well, Finnish Tove, be so good as to remind your master that I had an appointment today to see him.'

Tove remained on the doorstep, anxiously stepping from one foot to the other.

'I'm sorry, but Mr August's not here, sir.'

'Not here? Do you mean he has forgotten?'

'I don't very well know, sir.'

'Well for heaven's sake where is he? I have a very important colleague of mine here to see him.'

'He's gone, sir.'

'Gone? Gone where, Tove?'

'I don't know, sir.'

'You don't know much, do you, Finnish Tove?'

'No, sir. But . . . but Sir Henry's here.'

'I am aware of that. I visited him only yesterday. Now would you kindly—'

'No, sir. I mean he's got up.'

Dr Shadrack was stunned. '*What* did you say?'

'That's right, sir. He's had ten eggs for breakfast, sir.'

'Ten eggs for breakfast?' spluttered Dr Shadrack.

'Has he indeed?' said another deep and rumbling voice that Tom knew well, and out of the small black carriage stepped the tall menacing figure of Don Gervase. Tom instinctively shrank back from the window. Don Gervase . . . how could he possibly know Dr Shadrack? But standing there together in the snow, they looked strangely similar, as if one was a smaller version of the other.

'So,' boomed Don Gervase as he squinted down at Tove, 'Sir Henry has miraculously recovered, and August Catcher has vanished into thin air. Is *that* what you're saying, girl?'

Tove shrank back before this enormous, frightening looking man who had appeared before her.

'Yes, sir . . . I mean, no, sir.'

'Well, little . . . Tove, be so good as to tell Sir Henry that Don Gervase is here to see him. I am an old acquaintance of his and I should like to be the first to congratulate him on his recovery.'

'Very good, sir.' And in a blink the relieved Tove had scampered inside.

No sooner had Tove disappeared from view than Tom heard a scratching on the roof outside.

'Up to the window,' said a low soft voice, 'it's usually open.'

There was a grunt and another set of footsteps began to climb up the ladder on the roof. Tom's heart began to beat faster; who could that be? Not August, he was not coming back—that was someone trying to break in. Tom boldly stood his ground, then on second thoughts decided against it. Running down the length of the workshop he just glimpsed a thin, bony face appear at the skylight above him. It was Dr Skink!

'Can you see him?' whispered the soft voice out on the roof.

'I'm zorry miss, I can't zee anything,' hissed Dr Skink as he squinted down into the room.

'Well if you can't *zee* anything,' repeated the soft voice insistently, 'go *inzide zen*.'

At once Tom recognized that soft voice: that was Lotus—Lotus Askary. Suddenly Tom realized what was going on: of course! It was a classic housebreaker's trick. Don Gervase and Shadrack keep the owner talking at the front while Lotus and Skink break in the back. They must have known August had gone; they probably saw him on the boat, and, as he suspected, the strange looking Skink and Shadrack weren't doctors at all: they were thieves too, or spies, or something like it, working for Don Gervase.

These thoughts flashed through Tom's mind in a second as he slipped out onto the dark landing. They were going to search the workshop, that much was clear, but they didn't know *he* was still there. He must escape, back to the museum, back to his own time . . . But then a terrible thought hit Tom so hard that he stopped dead on the stairs. The travelling trunk. *August's* travelling trunk . . . what if he had taken it with him?

Tom realized that he hadn't been into the small wooden room since August had left. If it had gone there would be no way back and he would be stuck here for ever. Don't think about it, he told himself harshly, he won't have taken it. It *will* be there. It *must* be.

Tom's heart was thumping in his temples as he crept down to the landing and began to work his way around towards the corridor. He was almost halfway across when there was a loud clatter of footsteps below.

'Don Gervase Askary, gosh . . . erm . . . what an unexpected pleasure.'

Peering over the banisters Tom watched as the huge figure of Don Gervase loomed forward and wrung Sir Henry's hand.

'Why, Sir Henry!' he beamed. 'I am so glad to see you are on your feet again.'

'Indeed. It's really marvellous,' replied Sir Henry, rather stunned at the sight of his visitors, 'only this morning, in fact.'

'How truly remarkable,' sneered Dr Shadrack.

'Yes it is rather,' Sir Henry went on. 'As you probably heard, I had a bit of a tussle with the tiger and received a monumental bash on the head for my trouble,' and he laughed politely.

'So my good friend Dr Shadrack tells me,' smiled Don Gervase. 'I'm so happy. And August is not at home?'

'No, no, I'm afraid he's not.'

'That *is* too bad,' Don Gervase continued, 'he must have forgotten. You see, I was to visit his workshop today by prior arrangement.'

Sir Henry was a little nonplussed.

'Oh gosh. Well, erm—'

'It was arranged last week. When you were *asleep*,' he added pointedly.

'Right. Well, I'm sorry old chap, there's really no point hanging about as I expect he's going to be gone a while.'

'A while?'

'Yes,' blustered Sir Henry, 'probably *quite* a while, I suspect.'

'That is a shame.' Don Gervase looked mildly irritated. 'So, there's no chance of my having a look around without him?'

'Erm . . . ' Sir Henry thought about this for a moment, then smiled at his strange-looking guests. 'Sorry old chap. All sorts of chemicals up there, I expect, and we wouldn't want an accident.'

'Ah. Chemicals, of course. Ho-hum.'

Don Gervase twisted his long fingers into a knot; he seemed very disappointed. Then Dr Shadrack stood on tiptoe and whispered something in the tall man's ear.

'But of course!' he smiled. 'What about that boy of his, Tom is it? I don't suppose *he* has gone away with his master?'

'Tom Skatt?' cried Sir Henry. 'Why no, Tom's still here. Yes, I suppose he could show you around.'

'Could he?' grinned Don Gervase wolfishly. 'Well, that would be capital.'

'Of course, if it's by prior arrangement.'

'Oh it is,' said Don Gervase quickly, 'prior arrangement.'

'Well then, I can see no harm in that. I'll go and find him for you. Tom!'

And the next moment Tom heard Sir Henry's footsteps marching up the stairs.

'Tom!' shouted Sir Henry once more. 'He's up here somewhere.'

But Tom did not answer, he was already closing the door to the small wooden room behind him and feeling his way forward into the darkness. He knew that August's trunk was in the far corner, and working his way along the wall towards it he knelt down and felt something hard and cold and metallic; was that it? Yes . . . but wait; Tom's fingers felt another identical trunk next to it, and another beyond that: there were travelling trunks everywhere . . .

'Tom!' shouted Don Gervase, who had obviously decided to join in the search.

Tom cursed himself, why hadn't he thought of this earlier? Idiot! It was a box room—of course it would be full of boxes! But he *had* to choose one, and choose quickly. The last thing he wanted was to be interrogated by Don Gervase, not now . . . Fumbling his way back to the trunk in the far corner Tom forced open the lid and slithered inside. There he lay, trembling in the pitch-blackness, and his fingers closed around the rags beneath him, but they felt different somehow. Desperately Tom began to worm his way this way and that, but it was so long since he had done this he had almost forgotten how. It *definitely* felt too solid, nothing was happening; this must be the wrong trunk. August had taken it. He must get out and try another . . .

'Tom *Scatterhorn*?'

The door creaked open and Tom knew that Don Gervase was standing in the room. By now his heart was beating a crazy rhythm against his chest, and he prayed that there were a hundred identical trunks in the room and Don Gervase would be forced to open them all.

'Are you hiding in here?'

Then, quite suddenly, Tom's groping fingers brushed against a ridge of horsehair beneath him; was that it? Yes! Gripping it tightly Tom forced himself down and the very next second he fell away into the darkness, whizzing up, or down, he couldn't tell, until a great rushing of air filled his ears and the rags smothered him.

Bump.

Opening his eyes, Tom found himself buried at the bottom of the wicker trunk once more. He closed them again, breathing a huge sigh of relief. He had made it back to his own time, to the museum; he was home. Well, almost.

Tom slipped out of the cupboard and up the backstairs to his bedroom like a sleepwalker. He barely noticed the cold, or the damp, or anything at all in fact. He felt that he had had enough adventures to last an entire lifetime. Kicking off his shoes he flopped down wearily onto his bed, and grabbing all the blankets around him he rolled himself up into an enormous ball.

Barely had he come to a rest before he was drifting away once more, this time into a deep and dreamless sleep.

Tom had been so tired that he hadn't noticed that his bedroom window was once again wide open, and he had never even looked towards the end of his bed. If he had he would have been surprised, for there, perched in the shadows, was a dark shape that he might have recognized. The huge eagle watched as Tom began to sleep, then settled itself on its perch and cast a wary eye out of the window, towards Catcher Hall.

CHAPTER 18

The Big Question

Tom woke up the next morning to find Uncle Jos bending over him with a steaming cup of tea.

'Morning, Rip Van Winkle,' he said with a twinkle in his eye, 'feeling better now?'

Tom opened his eyes and stared groggily around the room. Was he really still there? Just for a moment he wasn't sure.

'Oh, hi.'

'I can see why you didn't bother taking your clothes off,' said Jos picking his way through the books and boxes towards the open window. 'No wonder it's so perishing cold in here. I can't understand why the dratted thing won't stay shut.' Shoving his considerable weight against it he wedged the frame hard.

'That's better,' he wheezed. 'Now there's bacon and eggs on the go in the galley so look lively, lad. Melba and I are out Christmas shopping after breakfast so you'll have the run of the place to yourself.'

'Christmas shopping?'

'That's right, lad, don't tell me you had forgotten? *Two* shopping days left till Christmas, as they keep reminding us. I think it's all hands to the pumps!' And with a cheery laugh he clattered back down the stairs.

Tom sat up in bed rather confused and sipped his hot tea. Christmas . . . did that mean it was still . . . looking over at the clock beside his bed he saw that it was the twenty-third of December. When had he last been back in his own time? When the tiger chased him down the stairs, so that must have been the twenty-second of December—*only last night*. But that felt like a lifetime ago now. Rubbing his eyes Tom pulled on a sweatshirt and shuffled over to the door, and he was just on the point of going downstairs when he noticed that he was wearing a cheesecloth shirt, a pair of brown tweed britches with braces, and some long white socks. These clothes wouldn't do here: how complicated Tom's life had become. Quickly slipping them off he pulled on his T-shirt and jeans and hid the evidence inside his duffel bag.

'Morning Tom,' said Melba briskly as Tom opened the door of the kitchen. She was not in the least surprised to see him.

'What's new with you, this merry morning?'

'Not much,' mumbled Tom, just about managing a smile.

He sat down in a daze, and Melba set a plate of bacon and eggs before him and continued to bustle about the kitchen.

'Thanks.'

Tom began to eat distractedly. This was all the same, it was almost as if he had never been away. *Had* he been away?

'The annual Christmas shopping trip,' announced Jos grandly, pulling up a chair and sitting on it the wrong way round, 'is a day of almost mythical importance in the Scatterhorn calendar. Any ideas what you'd like, Tom?'

Tom struggled to think. It seemed so long since he had thought about toys or games or computers or football teams or in fact anything else normal boys might think about. But then something did come to mind.

'Can you get chemicals these days?'

'Chemicals?' repeated Jos, scratching his nose. 'What sort of chemicals, lad?'

Tom thought for a minute.

'I don't know . . . erm . . . boracric acid, bichloride of mercury, maybe a bit of arsenical soap. That sort of thing.'

Both Melba and Jos stopped what they were doing and stared at him, utterly astonished.

'Now what on earth do you want with that lot?' asked Melba.

'I do hope, lad, you are not intending to do yourself in,' rasped Uncle Jos, shaking his head gravely. 'Things may be bad, but they're not *that* bad.'

'Oh no,' replied Tom quickly. 'No, no, it's just that I had an idea about . . . err . . . teaching myself some chemistry; try a few things out . . . like August Catcher, that's all.'

'Well,' said Melba taking a deep breath, 'there are *children's* chemistry sets about; I've seen one at Catchpole's, Jos. Do you think that would do?'

'Oh, I'm sure that would be brilliant,' smiled Tom as charmingly as he could, 'if it's not too expensive, that is.'

'I doubt that very much,' muttered Jos, furrowing his brow.

Melba was still staring at Tom curiously. What an extraordinary thing for an eleven-year-old boy to want for Christmas; perhaps the poor lad was on drugs. And then of course his parents were *so* odd; perhaps they were all on drugs. Maybe she should call the police.

Tom's strange request fairly silenced the conversation, and after breakfast he gratefully slipped back upstairs to his bedroom. Jos and Melba obviously thought he was weird, and now Tom was beginning to wonder if he hadn't gone a little mad himself. Arsenical soap! What was he thinking of? Cursing himself, Tom threw his old duffel bag onto the bed and pulled out the britches, the cheesecloth shirt, and the long white socks and examined them more closely. These rough old clothes felt comfortingly familiar; they were his—he knew it. They were as real as the ice fair, the museum opening, even the catastrophic tiger hunt; it had all happened, and he was a part of it. And yet . . . here he was now, back in this draughty old icebox of a room, and this was real too. How was it possible to live in two places at the same time, almost like two different people? Tom stared down at the cheesecloth shirt, and suddenly he had a good idea, and like all good ideas, he immediately wondered why he hadn't thought of it before. The tiger hunt, of course! Perhaps he could find some record of it somewhere, or maybe that scrap of newspaper from the *Times of India* describing his amazing adventure; that would surely prove that he really had been in the past. Where could he find something like that?

Then Tom had his second good idea. Slipping out of the back door, he ran out across the frosty grass to the overgrown storeroom at the end of the garden and found the door still wedged open just as he and Uncle Jos had left it. Brushing past the cobwebs, Tom picked his way through the piles of old tennis rackets and flags towards the winking shrew still standing poised on the shelf at the end. Beneath it were several tea chests crammed full of documents, files, newspaper cuttings, all sorts of bits and pieces that Jos's father had thrown out long ago. This must be the best place to start.

Carefully Tom began to rummage about, rubbing the thick coating of dust off each folder with his sleeve and squinting at the closely printed text. Here there were ledgers, old bills, and spare keys to cupboards that had long since disappeared. In amongst all the bundles of crumbling papers were a few old photographs, and these were much more interesting. There was Mrs Spong and another woman, posing rather stiffly beside the dodo, and Tom could not help noticing that all three looked remarkably similar. Then came August, looking very serious as he led the gorilla down the street on a trolley, on its way to being installed in the museum, followed by two men with enormous moustaches bearing the anaconda on their shoulders like a log. Finally there was Sir Henry, riding the mammoth up the steps with a large grin on his face. All of this was great fun, and had Tom not been so preoccupied with finding the evidence he needed he would have happily spent hours leafing through this strange collection. He was just about to put all the photographs and cuttings back in the chest when he noticed a slim green scrapbook lying right at the bottom, on the front of which someone had written in faint, spidery letters the word 'India'. Could that be it?

Excitedly Tom pulled the scrapbook out of the tea chest and blew the dust off the cover. This might be what he was looking for, but as soon as he opened it Tom's heart sank; every yellowing page was empty, as if someone had bought it long ago but never got around to mounting anything inside. There was no newspaper cutting here. Disappointed, Tom tossed the scrapbook back into the tea chest and he was about to start rummaging through the next one when he noticed a photograph lying face down on the floor, which must have been wedged inside the back page of the scrapbook.

Picking it up, Tom turned the picture over and squinted down at the grainy brown image. In an instant he recognized it: there was Pulany, August, Mina and Sir Henry standing solemnly in a line, there was the pilot with the two small Indian children to one side, and stretched out on the ground before them, with its head propped up as if it were asleep, was the enormous Bengal tiger. And at the far left-hand corner was a boy in a bush hat and shorts, smiling.

Was that *him*?

Tom swallowed hard and peered closer. The face was dark, half hidden in the deep shadow of the hat, but beneath the photograph was a list of names: 'T.S.' it read, under the smiling boy. It *was* him! It said so, it must be—this was the proof. Tom stared down at the picture and he couldn't help smiling at the picture of himself. So he wasn't crazy after all, he hadn't dreamt it all up. There he was, in the picture; it was real, and so was he.

Feeling a lot more sure of himself now, Tom put the photograph to one side and reached into the next chest, pulling out a large framed photograph of what looked like the opening night of the museum. Rubbing away the dust, he examined the sea of faces looking up at the camera. A great many people were out of focus as they moved about, and squinting through the dancers Tom blinked as he suddenly came face to face with Lotus. And there, a few rows in front of her was Don Gervase in his long black coat and velvet collar, exactly as Tom remembered him. To his left, hiding behind a pillar, was the blurred head of another small figure; that blur was *him*, Tom felt sure of it, that was exactly where he had been hiding. So now there were two photographs, two bits of evidence that proved it had not been a dream, or anything remotely like a dream. He had been in India, he had been in the museum too, and so had Don Gervase, and Lotus. They had all been there . . .

'Looking for something?'

Tom jumped. Glancing up he saw the round silhouette of Uncle Jos standing staring at him in the doorway.

'Chemicals perhaps?'

'No, no,' said Tom quickly, feeling the colour rise in his cheeks, 'just a few old photos.'

'I see,' said Jos, raising one thick eyebrow, 'and what's that one you've found? Looks interesting.'

Jos pointed to the picture of the tiger hunt.

'It's . . . err . . . actually I'm not sure what it is.'

Before Tom had time to think of anything to say Uncle Jos had shambled over and picked it up. Now I've had it, thought Tom, he's certain to recognize me and I'll have to explain everything.

'Well blow me down if that's not our tiger,' he wheezed. 'I've never seen that one before.'

Pushing his glasses up onto the bald dome of his head Jos pressed his eye right up to the photograph.

'There's August, and Sir Henry . . . and—'

'And Tom Scatterhorn,' Tom was waiting for him to say; but for some reason he didn't.

'*Mina Quilt?*' rasped Jos in disbelief. 'But surely the tiger's . . . *dead*. I thought the tiger killed Mina Quilt.'

Jos handed back the photograph to Tom looking very confused.

'Well, now I'm flummoxed. That story must have got it all wrong.'

And with a tatty old handkerchief Uncle Jos began to clean his glasses.

'Curiouser and curiouser,' he mumbled to himself. 'And there's a blurry lad in there looks like a bit like you, Tom. I 'spect that's what caught your eye, was it?'

'Erm . . . yeah,' Tom laughed awkwardly, staring at the grainy image of himself in the bush hat. 'Maybe.'

'Some flunkey I reckon. We'll never know who half these characters are. He might be the one who made up all that blow about the *shaitan* for all we know. What a load of cobblers *that* was. Eh?'

Tom said nothing. He was just relieved that Sir Henry had lent him his bush hat for the photograph and he was almost unrecognizable beneath it.

'Now let's see who we can find in this one.'

Jos was peering at a large photograph of the opening of the museum.

'Aha. I spy with my little eye August and Mina, right in the middle.'

Tom leant over his shoulder and sure enough, at the end of Uncle Jos's stubby finger was Mina beaming up at the camera. August stood behind her but he seemed preoccupied with something on Mina's shoulder, as if he was inspecting her dress. Whatever it was had obviously captured his attention, for he was entirely in focus.

'Hagfish in a houseboat,' muttered Jos to himself. 'I'd recognize *that* blur anywhere. Look, Tom.'

'Who's that?' said Tom as innocently as he could, knowing full well who Uncle Jos had found.

'See here?' he rasped, pointing at the blurred image of Don Gervase and Lotus standing amongst the dancers. 'That must be one of old spit-and-catch-it's Peruvian mob. Looks just like him, don't it? And, if I'm not mistaken . . . look at that! There's a little Miss Fancypants as well.' Uncle Jos pressed his eye closer to study the grainy image of Lotus. 'Uncanny. Well, I stand corrected there, lad. I was never sure about all that distant cousins stuff, but there's them relations right next to August. I suppose it must be true.'

Jos shook his head and placed the photograph back in the box. Tom wondered what happy accident had made the image of his fellow time travellers Don Gervase and Lotus blurred as well, so that even Uncle Jos couldn't quite recognize them. Or maybe he did, but he just didn't believe it. And it *was* just an accident, wasn't it? And then Tom thought of something else.

'Do you have any pictures of Sir Henry?' he asked.

'Lordy, there's loads,' replied Jos, 'loads and loads.'

Reaching up to the top shelf Jos brought down a handful of small black frames.

'Strange thing about pictures of Sir Henry is that he always looks the same. Never ever changes. Here, see for yourself.'

Wiping away the grease he set them out like a deck of cards across the dresser.

'Sir Henry in India, Sir Henry in Africa, Sir Henry in Tibet, Sir Henry in Russia, Sir Henry in Alaska, Sir Henry in Borneo . . .

once the museum had opened he travelled all over; barely stopped in thirty years.'

Tom scanned down the list of names and places hungrily. So these were the adventures he might have shared if he had taken up Sir Henry's offer; and what adventures they might have been . . . Jos was right, in every photograph Sir Henry looked more or less the same: apart from a change of hat or jacket, there was that same handsome, rugged face and clear, piercing eyes, never appearing to get any older. The only unusual element to these otherwise entirely conventional portraits was the large brooch that Sir Henry always wore on his waistcoat beneath his jacket, which seemed to be shaped like a beetle. Even though the photographs were all in black and white Tom noticed that the egg-shaped stone which formed the beetle's body was pale, and it seemed almost to glow from within. Tom's mind began to whirr, could that be . . . it couldn't, could it?

'What is that brooch?' he asked innocently, pointing at the strange looking object.

Jos squinted forward.

'I have no idea, Tom; some strange affectation no doubt. As he got older Sir Henry became interested in all sorts of curious things: parallel worlds, time travel, life after death, and all that jazz. Probably the badge of some secret society he belonged to. Became quite an eccentric, you know.'

'Did you ever meet him?'

'Sir Henry? Yes indeed I did. Must have been about five years old, I suppose,' said Jos cocking his head to one side. 'A kindly, reclusive man he was, very nice to me. I always remember his skin.'

'Why?'

'Well, he was old, he must have been in his seventies by then, but there were no lines on his face. Not one.'

'That's strange.'

'Yes it was. Timeless almost. A bit spooky, to tell you the truth.'

'And what happened to him in the end?'

'I wish I knew, Tom. He certainly left Dragonport years ago, gave the museum to my grandfather to look after, who was a distant cousin of his. Then one day, must have been in the 1950s, I suppose, Sir Henry just walked out of his house and never came back. Disappeared. Never to be seen again. The story goes that he went to find his old friend August Catcher who had written to him saying he was in dire trouble. Got caught up in a massive earthquake, or volcano was it? Somewhere in the old Soviet Union, one of them Central Asian places I think, part of the old communist bloc. I can't remember the details now. Cock and bull story anyway, so my father always said.' Jos coughed loudly, putting in yet another of his theatrical pauses. '*He* always believed that Sir Henry had set off in search of revenge.'

'Revenge,' repeated Tom, 'for what?'

'Oh, something that August had done. They may have been best friends, but a Catcher always shows his true colours in the end.' Jos grimaced, and glanced in the direction of Catcher Hall. 'Like them that's up there now. First they're all matey, "nice to meet you at last" and all that baloney, then before you know it you're walking the plank.'

Tom said nothing. He had forgotten about Don Gervase's

ultimatum. Jos had two days left to decide whether to sell him the museum and he was still in a pickle about it.

'The truth is, Tom,' wheezed Uncle Jos, 'even if he *had* set off for Kyrgyzstan or Turkmenistan or some such crazy place, that was a dangerous undertaking back then. They weren't exactly accessible, plus them Soviets didn't take kindly to any Westerners snooping about. And he was an old man remember. I wouldn't be at all surprised if he had been rounded up as a spy somewhere, then—' Jos inhaled loudly, 'quietly done away with. Pushed off a cliff, something like that. It happened, you know.'

'And the sapphire?'

'Ah yes.' Jos's eyes twinkled beneath his enormous bushy eyebrows. 'The *sapphire*. I'd forgotten about that. Well, no one ever saw it, did they? I wonder if it ever existed; and if it did, I imagine he would have taken it with him. Wouldn't you?'

Later, when Jos and Melba had gone out shopping, Tom wandered into the museum and gazed down at the large model of Dragonport. It was early afternoon, but already the museum was beginning to descend into darkness and he could barely make out the miniature houses and streets spread out beneath him. Tom's mind was buzzing with ideas, possibilities; though he had no doubt that he had been to the past, to a place somehow like the model below, there were still some fundamental questions racing around in his mind. *How* had he got there? What *was* that basket? And, perhaps most importantly of all, why did no one else but him think it was unusual? It was almost as if he had become two different people, both called Tom, who just happened to look the same, and now his life had become some strange fantasy that was unfolding in two places at the same time; both in the past, *and* in the present as well . . .

Tom looked around at the faded tatty animals solemnly peering out of their cabinets. Perhaps *they* knew the answer; after all, they must be curious to know how Tom, that eleven-year-old boy they had first met as August Catcher's assistant, could suddenly reappear, unchanged, over a hundred years later? Perhaps it was time to ask *them* what was really going on, time to ask some big questions.

'Hello?'

His voice echoed away into the dark corners. There was silence.

'Hello,' he said again.

There was a scratching sound behind him.

'Actually . . . '

Tom turned round to find the mammoth's trunk waving close to his ear.

'Actually—'

'Sssh!' hissed the wall. It was the anaconda.

'*Actually,*' the low booming whisper continued, 'there is a house rule here, Tom, that we don't talk during hours of daylight.'

'Oh. Sorry.' Tom stared guiltily down at the stone floor.

'But,' continued the mammoth, 'since the museum *is* closed and it's dark as a mole's armpit at two o'clock in the afternoon, I for one can't see why this shouldn't be an exception. After all,' he said out loud, 'what are rules for except to be broken?'

'Amen to that,' echoed the gorilla from his tree.

Tom looked up at the mammoth's great bulk and saw his small black eyes winking.

'All right,' hissed the anaconda disapprovingly, 'but if someone comes in, on your head be it.'

'Fine, old boy,' boomed the mammoth, shaking out his legs stiffly. 'Now, Tom, how may we be of assistance?'

Tom wondered where the best place was to begin . . . there was so much. Might as well come straight out with it.

'Can you remember seeing me before?'

The mammoth chuckled. 'Can we remember seeing you before? Oh yes,' he boomed, 'we know *exactly* who you are, Tom.'

'I don't mean like yesterday,' Tom continued, 'or last week even, I mean a long time ago, like at the opening of the museum, a hundred years ago.'

'That's right, I remember you there,' smiled the gorilla, 'what a party!'

This was good; at last he seemed to be getting somewhere.

'OK,' said Tom slowly gathering his thoughts, 'so if I *was* there then, and I *am* here now, why aren't I any older? Don't you think that's strange?'

'Why *would* you get any older,' squawked the dodo. 'Do I look older to you?'

Tom peered hesitantly across at the tatty turkey-sized bird. 'Well, not *that* much. But I'm not like you, am I? I'm alive.'

'And we are not?' asked the proboscis monkey, casually letting himself out of his cabinet. He began to saunter around the museum, sliding open the back of each case in turn.

'You've certainly been here as long as I have, boyo,' puffed the dodo, shaking her feathers and stepping down onto the floor, 'and *I* am extinct you know.'

Tom was struggling to understand.

'But . . . but how can I have been? I mean, I'm only *eleven*, my parents are in Mongolia, I've come here from school. I had never even met Uncle Jos before now.'

'Just as you say,' said the gorilla, unconvinced. 'You're still Mr Catcher's assistant.'

'Yes, I am. I mean I *was* . . . then, but I . . . I'm not from the past! I got there by accident. I'm . . . I'm—' Tom could feel his voice rising; *how* could he make them understand? Perhaps he'd better tell them the whole story, maybe that was the only way.

'All right,' he said, taking a deep breath, 'supposing, just supposing I told you *why* you have seen me before.'

He looked around and found that he now had the attention of the entire museum. They all sat either inside their cases or on top of them, waiting patiently for him to continue.

'Go on,' boomed the mammoth.

Tom pointed to the cupboard.

'In that cupboard under the stairs there is a wicker basket which has a false bottom.'

The dodo craned her neck around to look at the cupboard.

'False bottom?' she squawked. 'Meaning what, exactly?'

'Ha-ha! I know what it is,' declared the gorilla. 'Don't tell me, it's one of those trick baskets, like magicians use to make people disappear.'

'But it's *not* a trick,' Tom continued, 'because if you lie down inside it you fall out of the bottom and fly through the air then find yourself somewhere else. Inside a metal travelling trunk.'

'A metal travelling trunk?' repeated the proboscis monkey. 'So there's a basket and a trunk, with a nothing in between?'

'That's right,' replied Tom uncertainly.

'Is one on top of the other?' asked the mammoth.

'No. No, it can't be, because the trunk is in a room inside Catcher Hall about a hundred years ago. It's just like that model over there.'

Tom pointed to the large snowbound model of Dragonport in the corner.

'And that's how I got into the past. I fell out of the basket by accident. And then I became August Catcher's assistant, and so I was there at the opening of the museum. That's the reason.'

There, he had said it now. This news was greeted with a dumbfounded silence, as all the animals looked from the cupboard to the model, and back again.

'Excuse me,' squeaked the anteater, 'I seem to be missing something. Did you say there's a tunnel?'

'No. There isn't.'

The dodo looked at him quizzically.

'And do you mean to say that you really *believe* that?'

'Yes. I do.'

'And you're not havin' a jolly jape?'

'No I'm not.'

'Why then Tom,' she snapped, 'I'm afraid you've entirely lost your wits. How *disappointing*.'

'What an extraordinary idea,' boomed the mammoth.

Tom was exasperated. He looked around the museum helplessly.

'So . . . so you don't believe me?'

'Of course not!' trilled the aardvark. 'Flapdoodle.'

'Piffle and poppycock!' shouted the pangolin.

'All right!' shouted Tom loudly. 'I'll show you then!'

Angrily he marched towards the cupboard and threw open the door. 'Who wants to come with me?'

'Come with you where exactly?' boomed the mammoth.

'Back there!' shouted Tom, pointing wildly across the hall, his blood boiling. 'Into the model, the past, whatever!'

Why couldn't they understand!

'I say, steady on, old boy,' said the mammoth, 'keep your hair on.'

'The poor lad's touched,' whispered the anteater.

'He's been here far too long,' agreed the sturgeon. 'I've heard puffer fish have a similar problem, they think they can shrink too.'

'But Tom old boy,' said the gorilla, peering down at the model and scratching his head doubtfully, 'even if we *believed* you, don't you think we're a little—well, large?'

'Not all of us,' said the anteater helpfully. 'What about a mouse, or possibly a shrew—'

'But you can't just take *a* shrew,' declared the proboscis monkey. 'It's all for one, one for all with that lot, and there are just so many of them.'

'But not as many as the multitudes that walked the earth on judgement day!' squeaked a tiny voice.

'See what I mean?' sighed the monkey.

Tom looked up to where a long line of small rodents sat on the edge of a drawer.

'Did you not see the mice in their millions, lining up at the gates? Did you not hear the trumpets sound?' called the preacher shrew, raising a bony claw to the ceiling.

'That's right! Indeed we did!' echoed the mice and shrews together.

'Many were called!'

'But few were chosen!'

'Brothers and sisters,' squeaked the preacher shrew. 'If man, mammoth or marsupial needs our help, then we shall gladly offer it. We stand or fall as one.'

'Hallelujah!'

The mice and shrews all punched the air together, and their squeak rang out around the hall. The anteater smiled kindly.

'You see, Tom? Plenty of volunteers.'

'But you don't have to be *small* necessarily,' said Tom, regretting that he had just opened up a vast subject of debate. 'It's not actually inside *that* model, just—'

'Something with a bit more bite then?' suggested the porcupine keenly. 'Now the stoat, he's a narrow chap, nasty teeth too.'

'What about a tree frog? They're poisonous and there's bound to be water.'

'Very fine swimmers frogs,' agreed the mammoth, nodding his vast head, 'if aquatics are involved I always plump for a frog.'

'But he said something about flying; should he take a bird?'

'Hummingbirds are tiny—'

'Nothing to say for themselves,' the porcupine cut in, 'woolly-headed. Tell me have you *ever* had an intelligent conversation with a hummingbird?'

Suddenly a hum of voices filled the museum as the merits of every single small mammal, bird, reptile, and fish were loudly debated, and Tom could see that he was getting nowhere at all.

'Perhaps *I* can be of assistance,' drawled a gravelly voice from somewhere up in the rafters.

Immediately the conversation died away and the eyes of every animal turned to face the ceiling.

'After all, we had a little to-do back there, didn't we, Tom?'

Looking up to the balcony Tom saw a familiar silhouette perching there. It was the great eagle, and Tom had never felt so pleased to see it.

CHAPTER 19

A Bird Explains

'Oh Lord,' said the mammoth under his breath, 'the jolly swagman's back. Hold steady, chaps.'

The arctic rabbit let out a terrified squeak and cowered behind the brown bear's leg.

'Sharp claws, sharp beak, no brain,' sniffed the dodo, carefully side-stepping back up onto her podium.

'Bird brain,' corrected the porcupine, 'and straight from the billabong.'

The eagle ignored these insults and swooped down from the rafters, landing with a clatter on the smooth stone floor.

'Now take it easy, fellas, there's really no need to get so narky. I ain't come in here to raz you up,' it growled. '*Yet*.'

And the great bird turned towards Tom and fixed him with its angry yellow eye.

'I just want a word with young Tom here, in private.'

Tom stared back at the huge eagle defiantly. He remembered that it had a habit of making him do things he did not necessarily want to do.

'Outside,' it added.

'Why?'

'Just need to parley a while,' said the bird casually, casting around in the gloom at all the stuffed animals, 'away from the country club.'

Tom must have seemed unconvinced, as the bird leant forward and whispered conspiratorially, 'I think it's high time you were let in on a few matters of . . . travel arrangements.' The bird nodded at the model. 'If you get my drift.'

Tom thought for a moment. The last thing he wanted to do was set off on yet another adventure. But something told him that he should trust this bird, however frightening it might appear. After all, it seemed to be the only animal in this museum that had any idea what he was talking about, and it had saved his life, hadn't it?

'You promise nothing's going to happen?'

'Scouts' honour, mate,' breezed the eagle, 'just climb aboard and we'll take a little tootle.'

'Climb aboard? You mean *fly* somewhere?'

'Flyin' goes with the territory—if you're a bird. And besides, I've never got to grips with this walkin' lark.'

Tom looked uncertainly at the enormous eagle as its great talons slipped on the smooth stone floor.

'You promise we're not going far?'

'Yes yes yes! Now quit yer wibblin' and *git on*.'

Tom took a deep breath, what choice did he have?

'OK.'

'Be very careful, old boy,' whispered the mammoth. 'It's as mad as a hatter, uncouth as a—'

'Mind your language, yer mouldy hayrick!' snapped the great raptor.

Gingerly Tom stepped up behind the creature and wrapped both his arms around its wide neck.

'Like this?' he said nervously. There was not much else to hold on to.

'That'll do for starters,' rasped the bird. 'Now swing your leg over me back and for Pete's sake don't let go.'

Tom did as he was asked, then with a few beats of its vast wings, the huge raptor jolted forward and flew up towards the skylight. Moments later it had nudged its way through the broken window and taken off once more, soaring out over the rain-soaked rooftops. Gripping tightly around the bird's neck, Tom leant forward to see the grey town spinning below him. The Christmas lights were on and the pavements were teaming with small figures laden down with bags of shopping, hunched against the winter rain. A few children stopped and pointed up in amazement at the great bird as it flew overhead, but no one else seemed to notice.

'Bloody awful weather I'm afraid,' remarked the eagle gruffly. 'Let's see if we can't get clear of it. Hold on back there.'

Suddenly the great eagle started to climb sharply through the low clouds, and Tom felt his arms begin to take his own weight as they climbed higher and higher, flying almost vertically and the wind began to rush in his ears. At last there was a dazzling burst of light, and they emerged through the top of the cloud bank into an entirely different landscape. Endless hills of pink clouds stretched out before them, edged with gold against a brilliant blue sky. The eagle levelled off its climb and began to fly in a long, steady rhythm.

'I thought you said we were not going far!' shouted Tom above the rushing wind.

'We're not!' the eagle replied. 'Look up ahead.'

Shielding his eyes from the sun, Tom saw a radio mast with a flashing red light on top of it, poking up through the sea of clouds like a periscope not half a mile distant.

'Not a bad spot for a chat now is it?'

A minute later they were there. Tom was relieved to find that what looked so spindly from a distance was in fact like a large metal climbing frame close up, and quite wide enough to sit on. Once the eagle had landed, Tom swung his legs down through the metal struts and holding on tightly he swivelled round to face the setting sun. The eagle was right—this was quite a spot; he felt as if he were on top of the world.

'That's better,' muttered the eagle, settling down opposite him. 'I prefer to stay up high if that's all right by you. Like to be incognito, if you know what I mean.'

Now that they had come to rest Tom was able to take a better look at the enormous bird. It was certainly unlike any eagle he had ever seen, and in the low golden light it appeared rather magnificent. Its feathers were large and wide and so black that they seemed almost purple, with flecks of white at their tips, and its belly was speckled with spots like a leopard. Its huge head was a dusty grey colour, with piercing yellow eyes and a long white beak that gave it a permanently angry expression. Around the base of its neck was a curious blue silky ruff and its vast orange talons were the size of rakes. This bird looked powerful, fast, and somehow not from any part of the world that Tom knew.

'I suppose you're wondering what kind of creature I am, are you Tom?'

Tom nodded; he had never seen any large eagle up close, but he was quite sure they did not look anything like this.

'So, you're a—'

'Smorgasbord, mate. Mongrel, if you will. Ostrich, owl, golden eagle, cassowary, condor, shoebill, lammergeier . . . you name it. All the best bits stuck together. And that's why the fellas down below don't like me.'

'Why not?'

'Because I'm not bonafide. Not a creature that ever lived, nor could have. So I'm not *worthy* to be in their museum. Not that I'd want to be stuck in that gloomy hole anyway,' snapped the great bird. 'And I ain't got the temperament for hangin' round.'

'So August . . . *made* you?'

'He did indeed. In one of his crazier moments, I expect. Flight of fancy I am. And it's remarkable when you think about it. I mean look at me—everything works! Old August certainly knew how to put things together, didn't he?'

Tom stared at the extraordinary creature. It was incredible to think that this was cobbled together from many different birds and yet was so, well, *real*.

'So why are you so interested in me?'

'Well, Tom Scatterhorn, you are a fellow traveller, we're similar you and I. There aren't many birds like me, and there aren't many people like you.'

Tom did not understand.

'What do you mean fellow traveller? I'm not like you.'

'Oh yes you are, mate. I believe that story about that little basket of yours, because I travel too. Only I use different routes.'

The bird fixed him with its angry yellow eye and nodded. 'That's right, mate.'

'How?'

The great creature shook its feathers and looked out towards the setting sun.

'Hirundo!' it called. 'Budibudi!'

A small speck appeared out of the clouds and flew towards them at lightning speed. Arcing high over the radio mast it dived down and began flying in tight circles around them. As the tiny blue shape flashed past Tom could make out that it was a swallow. The great bird inclined its head and began to call out gently in a strange language Tom had never heard before, and the swallow began to answer back.

'This is my pilot, Tom,' said the eagle quietly, 'see? We understand each other.'

The eagle carried on communicating with the swallow, which came to a sudden halt on a metal strut above them.

'Now you may be wonderin' where on earth I learned to talk to this little fella. Well, I'll let you into a little secret,' rasped the bird. 'When August Catcher brought me into this world he gave me an accidental advantage over our friends down below. I am privileged enough to speak the language of birds. *Real* birds, you understand, not dummies. It's all locked up in here.' The bird raised one huge talon and tapped its odd-shaped head. '*Descriptive Dictionary of the Aboriginal Languages of Western Australia*, 1891. That's right. In there was an ancient dialect, once known to humans, now lost for ever.'

Tom was amazed, and yet he could believe it. He had seen

August fill the brain cavities of his specimens with newspapers or any old books he could find.

'And seein' as I was never entirely welcome in that place, and being of a wanderin' frame of mind, I began to talk to these little chaps on my walkabouts,' the great bird continued, 'and that's how I discovered there are ways to go backwards. Or forwards, if you like.'

'Go backwards and forwards . . . do you mean, through *time*?'

'If you like, yeah.'

The sun had dipped below the pink clouds and the sky all around was turning from rose to purple. Tom's mind was spinning giddily, he was struggling to take it all in.

'So birds can travel through time?'

'No no, mate,' growled the eagle, 'not *all* of them. A very special few, who know the right places. It's all about atmospherics, magnetics, and all sorts of stuff you folks know nothin' about.'

'What sort of places?' asked Tom.

'Well, let's see now.' The great bird thought for a moment, staring down at the sea of pink clouds lapping around the radio mast below them. 'The gap between a thunder clap and a lightning strike, could find one in there, or sometimes you spot one reflecting off the rim of a rainbow, or sliding down the wall of a twister. You have to fine tune your angles, approach speed, what have you.'

Tom stared at the enormous sleek bird in amazement; it was so matter-of-fact that it seemed to be telling the truth.

'So, you can see these places?'

'Not *see* them exactly. You sort of get a *feel* for where they might be after a while. I know it might sound like a load of blow but it's true.'

'So you've really been to the future?'

'Yes, kiddo.'

'So what's it like?'

'Oh perfect, mate,' replied the eagle sarcastically. 'Absolute paradise. Just dandy.'

'And the past—'

'You know I have been *there*. Just like you have, kiddo.'

Tom stared towards the pink clouds edged with gold on the horizon, trying to make sense of it all. It was one thing for a bird to use some ancient knowledge to find some kind of gateway between worlds in the air, but he had fallen through a basket in a cupboard. It had just happened. That couldn't be the same thing, could it?

'I just don't understand how I got there, that's all. It's like the model—'

'Think of the model as a doorway, Tom,' interrupted the great bird. 'It's like a way in. An entrance. A portal. Once you're there, then that world opens up right before you and you're in the thick of it. Now I ain't no philosophizer but the way I sees it, time isn't a flat line, it can't be. It's more like . . . millions of pieces of paper, layers and layers, wrapped around each other into one great big ball. Today, tomorrow, a hundred years ago, last week, every day that has ever been and every day that ever will be is all there, right next to each other. They all exist, at the same time, but—you just can't see 'em. And in amongst all these layers, in certain *very* special places you find these crinkles and crankles, bends if you will, where one world *connects* with another. And that's where I reckon you fell through. Could be like a hole, tunnel, ladder, maybe there are as many nooks and crannies on the earth as there are in the air, Tom, I dunno. And maybe you folks used to know about them a long, long time ago. Maybe. But sure as eggs is eggs you've forgotten now, just like you've forgotten about everything else.' The eagle shook its feathers and cast an angry glance at the sunset. 'Na, only us birds remember this stuff now. And y'know . . . the other lot.'

Tom said nothing; he thought he understood what the great eagle was saying, just about. He must have just been very lucky, or unlucky, depending on which way you looked at it, to find that hole in the basket. And maybe the eagle was right, maybe there *were* lots of these places, and this happened to people all the time. Maybe . . . He stared down at the sea of pink clouds below his feet, and felt the great bird's angry yellow eyes burning into him.

'Yep mate, you've *definitely* been in the past,' it muttered, scrutinizing him hard, 'and I'm bound to say that ain't the only place you're goin' to, neither.'

'What do you mean?'

The great eagle cleared its throat and glanced around, as if expecting to be overheard. Suddenly it seemed very serious indeed. The swallow above them began chattering noisily.

'Well, it's a delicate subject, Tom, and not one easy to put into words. But seein' as I'm lookin' out for yer, an' bein' a sort of messenger for these blokes, there is something important you should know. It's just—'

The eagle broke off as the swallow darted from its perch and flitted around them, twittering louder than ever.

'I *know*, just be patient, I'm getting to it,' barked the eagle crossly, and let out a strange ululating response.

'What's he talking about?' asked Tom, glancing up at the agitated little bird.

'The thing is,' the eagle continued, ignoring the question, 'you have a very important part to play in future events, Tom Scatterhorn. Perhaps one day you'll even be the lynchpin.'

Tom stared at the eagle blankly, and its hard yellow eyes met his. He had no idea what the great bird was talking about. What did it mean 'the lynchpin'? The lynchpin of what? He didn't want to be the lynchpin of anything.

'But just because . . . just because I fell through a basket into the past doesn't mean anything, does it? It was an accident,' protested Tom.

'I don't doubt it.'

'It could have happened to anyone.'

'Indeed it could, mate. But here's the rub. It didn't.'

'Well, so what,' Tom continued bravely, but feeling less and less certain every moment. 'I'm still like everyone else, aren't I?'

'Maybe you were once,' replied the great bird enigmatically. 'Before.'

Tom felt the eagle's sharp eyes studying his face intently and he turned away. He wasn't sure he wanted to hear any more of this.

'So, so what are you saying? That it wasn't just . . . luck?'

'Ah. Luck. See, I ain't a great believer in luck,' replied the eagle. 'When you travel through time like I do you can't help but see patterns in things. Reasons. Origins. Accidents don't ever come into it. Call that coincidence, fate, even destiny if you like. But make no mistake about it, you have a destiny now, kiddo.'

The eagle broke off and stared out at the setting sun. 'Ah yes. And who knows, perhaps . . . perhaps *that's* why they want to kill you.'

'They?'

'I don't know who they are precisely. But I think *you* do, kiddo,' replied the bird, shaking its great head. 'Don't tell me you've forgotten the last time we met?'

'No.'

'Good,' replied the eagle fiercely, 'you'd do well to remember that.'

Reluctantly Tom's mind spun back to the night of the ball in August's workshop. It was like recalling the details of a long forgotten nightmare; the knife flashing past his head, the exploding glass and the man in the steel mask, his huge leather hands tightening around his neck . . . his chocolate breath. With a shiver Tom saw the great bird slamming into the man's shoulders, and its scaly talons ripping away the steel mask . . .

'So . . . that was . . . who I think it was?'

'I believe so,' muttered the bird darkly.

Tom's heart quickened, and he gripped the cold steel strut more tightly. He knew exactly what the eagle was about to say but somehow he had managed to bury the events of that evening in August's workshop at the very back of his mind. He just didn't want any of it to be true.

'The Mexican with the machete,' rasped the bird finally, 'Don Gervase Askary's man. And hell did he scream like a pig.'

'But why kill me?' shouted Tom breathlessly. 'I don't *know* anything, I haven't *done* anything!'

'I know kiddo, I know,' growled the eagle. 'Your guess is as good as mine. But—' The eagle stopped short, then fixed Tom with its hard yellow eye.

'You should appreciate that these folks is dead serious. *Dead* serious. I've seen more than enough to know that. And I can tell you they ain't going to stop. Ever. So, if I were you I'd be very, very careful. Because we're all counting on you, mate. Much more than you know.'

The great eagle let out a long call to the swallow above, who had been listening in silence, then shook out its black tail feathers and turned away.

'Here endeth the first lesson, kiddo. I've said my piece, make of it what you will. Now climb aboard.'

It was dark by the time they reached Dragonport. Flying down in a series of ever decreasing circles, the eagle landed precisely on the roof of Tom's bedroom. Turning around, it picked up Tom with its beak and very carefully set him down on the window ledge so that he was able to hold onto the frame.

'Thanks.'

'No problem.'

'No, I mean thanks for . . . ' Tom wanted to say for saving my life, but somehow he couldn't.

'Everything.'

The great bird shook its head.

'I'm lookin' out for ya, Tom. I'll do whatever I can—*if* I can. But you look after yerself,' it said with a friendly nod, 'and promise not to go shootin' yer mouth off about our little chat.'

'Don't worry, I shan't.'

'Glad to hear it,' replied the eagle, 'because believe you me, there's one or two people down here who'd dearly love to know all about it.'

And with that the enormous creature let out a strange cry and clattered noisily down the roof. The tiny swallow appeared out of nowhere and together they soared up above the town towards the river.

Tom watched until the dark specks disappeared into the clouds, then he turned and wearily climbed back through the open window into his empty room. He really wasn't sure whether he should feel relieved or concerned by everything he had just discovered. In one way, it was comforting that the huge eagle was protecting him somehow, but when his mind turned to Don Gervase and Lotus Tom felt a shudder run up his spine like a cold wind. What was it that Don Gervase had said to Lotus at the ice fair all those months ago? 'Travellers are not tolerated, whoever they are.' Was that what he had meant by not tolerated? Death?

Tom flopped down onto his bed and stared angrily at the low sloping ceiling, his eyes pricking with tears. Somewhere there was a part of him that did not want to be involved in any of this; he almost wished he had never even gone into that cupboard under the stairs. It would be so much easier just to be plain Tom Scatterhorn again, the one with the strange dad, who lived in the scruffiest house in Middlesuch Close, and spent his holidays in a rusty old camper van.

'You have a destiny now, mate . . . '

What did that mean? You have a destiny—surely everyone had a destiny . . .

Just then he heard the sound of footsteps outside.

'They're very steep, dear, so do be careful,' said Melba's voice on the stairs, 'and I apologize in advance for the mess—Lord knows how his mother manages at home—and just to warn you, it's perishing cold as well, which for some reason he makes worse by leaving the windows wide open all hours of the day and night.'

The door creaked and there stood Melba in an overcoat and a scarf.

'Tom!' she cried, munching on a square of chocolate. 'I'm so glad you're here. I have a surprise visitor for you.'

Out from behind Melba stepped a girl in a white woollen coat.

'Hello Tom.'

Tom gasped; he couldn't help it. Lotus stared at him, her great green eyes narrowing like a cat's, and a rich smell of chocolate and cinnamon wafted into the room.

'I wondered if we would meet again,' she said, smiling sweetly.

'H-h-hi.'

Tom tried to look as uninterested as he could, but inside his heart was racing. What was she doing here—did she recognize him? He wasn't sure; he certainly recognized her. She was dressed in almost exactly the same clothes as the last time they had met, but instead of skates she now wore a pair of tightly-laced, shiny black boots.

'Tom, this is Lotus Askary, do you remember?'

Melba pulled Plankton out of her large pocket and gave the rat a small square of chocolate. His little pink eyes bulged and he began to nibble greedily.

'Yeah. Yeah I do.'

'Lotus has come to make herself useful. Get to know the ropes a bit, see how we run the place, that sort of thing, before the sale.'

'The sale?' Tom was not quite sure that he had heard correctly. 'What sale?'

'The museum, dear. Tush! What a memory you have! Surely you have not forgotten yesterday's little performance?'

Melba winked at him knowingly, and Tom had no idea what she was talking about. Yesterday seemed like a very long time ago.

'Well, your uncle has been blowing hot and cold like an old boiler, but thankfully Don Gervase has at last persuaded him to *see sense*. We've been up at Catcher Hall only just now and everything has been agreed. On Christmas Eve, that's the date, isn't it, dear?'

'It is,' replied Lotus winningly. 'I can't tell you how excited I am.'

'Me too,' Melba tittered.

'What a Christmas present!'

'Yes Tom, that's when Don Gervase Askary will become the proud owner of the Scatterhorn Museum. Isn't it absolutely marvellous?'

CHAPTER 20

Into the Web

It took a few minutes for the announcement of the sale of the museum to sink in. Tom trudged gloomily around the cabinets behind Melba and Lotus, wondering how Jos had decided to give in to Don Gervase so easily; it seemed so out of character. In two days the museum would be sold, and it would all be over. He shuddered to think of what would happen to him then.

'Seems to spend every moment he can in here,' Melba was saying, glancing back over her shoulder in Tom's direction. 'I should think you must have explored almost every nook and cranny by now, haven't you Tom?'

Tom mumbled noncommittally.

'I bet you've found all sorts of surprises,' smiled Lotus. 'What a brilliant place to get lost in.'

'Don't you doubt it, my dear,' Melba continued, pulling Plankton out of her pocket and slipping another square of chocolate into his grabbing pink claws. 'He's been rootling around in all the cupboards, under the stairs—even in the go-down at the end of the garden.'

'Is that so?'

Lotus was trying hard to conceal her curiosity.

'Oh yes, fascinated by all the stories around this old place, and the art of taxidermy.' Melba lowered her voice and whispered in Lotus's ear, 'He even asked for a chemistry set for Christmas.'

Lotus's eyes widened. 'Did he?'

'Fancies doing a bit of restoration himself.'

Lotus turned to Tom and he could feel her eyes probing him.

'I should *so* like to find out what you've been up to,' she said enthusiastically, 'I bet you're an expert by now.'

Tom shrugged and pretended to stare hard at the proboscis monkey.

'I really don't know much,' he said flatly, 'just a beginner, I'm afraid.'

That was true, unfortunately. August had rarely bothered to explain how he made anything, particularly his potion, but Lotus was still staring at him, clearly not sure whether to believe him or not.

'Your relation August Catcher was a *very* clever man,' said Melba, giving Plankton an affectionate squeeze as he gobbled up the last of the chocolate, 'but I am sure you know that already.'

'People said so; though of course, growing up in Peru, we didn't hear much about him. In fact we only discovered this museum existed by accident.'

'You did?' Melba seemed mildly shocked. 'Gosh! Well, that must have been quite a surprise.'

'Oh it was. But sometimes when you're looking for something very particular you have to expect the unexpected, and Sir Henry Scatterhorn and August Catcher were quite a mysterious pair, don't you think?' she said, flashing another smile.

'Indeed, my dear,' replied Melba, not quite sure what Lotus was talking about. 'Never mind, I'm sure Tom will show you the ropes. He knows where everything is around here almost better than I do. Don't you Tom?'

Tom smiled thinly.

'I do hope so,' beamed Lotus, 'I can't wait.'

Tom trailed sullenly up the stairs after them knowing that he couldn't wait either: this game of cat and mouse with Lotus and Don Gervase had gone on long enough. Were they just a gang of sophisticated jewel thieves, who somehow had found a way to travel back in time? Ever since his conversation with the extraordinary eagle this afternoon he could barely believe that explanation any more. Could the sapphire *really* account for everything that had happened so far? It was immensely valuable, certainly, but Tom had a deep, gnawing suspicion that the great bird was right. There *was* something else at work here, a larger, darker force that Tom could not fully understand. And it was hanging over him and the museum like a great black claw, just waiting to strike.

Tom watched Lotus as she strode on ahead of him in the half-light, her long black hair twisted into a tight plait that gleamed like a snake. *Why* did they want to kill him? Tom felt numb just thinking about it, but he was determined that he would not be chased for ever. He was not going to wake up in the middle of the night to find some strange assassin with a machete looming over him, no: attack was the best form of defence, as his father always said. To discover once and for all what the Askarys were really looking for, to find out what they really wanted, *he* would have to take the initiative. He would have to go up to Catcher

Hall and find the answer himself, before the museum was sold and it was too late. Which meant tonight.

'Melbe-tee-na,' sang Jos in a woozy kind of voice as he opened the door. 'Melbetina Melbetina Melbe-tee-na.'

There was no answer. Jos had spent all evening in the pub, and Melba had gone to bed hours ago.

'Melbetina? Hagfish,' he muttered to himself, and fumbling his way across the unlit corridor he began to whistle a tuneless ditty as he trudged slowly up the stairs.

Tom lay in bed, fully clothed, listening. As soon as the bedroom door slammed shut he turned to his watch and began to count off the minutes in his head. He was excited and a little nervous about this night's work, and by the time he reached seven minutes all was silent. Good. Hopefully Jos was so drunk that he had fallen straight asleep. Slipping over to the window Tom pulled on his gloves and stared out over the rooftops. The rain that had been lashing down all day was now falling as snow, and great flurries swirled in wild patterns around the orange streetlights. What's a little blizzard? thought Tom, and smiling grimly he pulled his hat low over his ears, knowing that there was no turning back now. He had started on this crazy adventure the moment he first fell through the wicker basket, perhaps even the moment he first stepped into the Scatterhorn Museum. The time had come to finish it.

Carefully opening the window, Tom climbed up onto the ledge and turning round, he stretched out his feet until they caught hold of the drainpipe in the corner. Pushing at it a little,

Tom decided it was strong enough to take his weight, and in one quick move he swung first one hand then another across to the pipe. Seconds later he was slithering down until he landed with a thump in the backyard. The pipe felt so cold that it burnt. Rubbing his stinging hands on his trousers, Tom ran across to the end of the garden and used the old storeroom to lever himself up onto the crumbling wall. The snow was falling thickly now, and wiping the heavy flakes away from his eyes Tom was just about to slip down onto the pavement when he felt the back of his neck begin to tingle, as if he was being watched. Glancing back at the museum, he could just make out the great, sad face of the gorilla pressed against the glass. He raised one huge hairy hand and opened the window a fraction.

'Good luck,' he whispered.

'Oh. Thanks.'

Tom waved back, smiling grimly.

'Fortune favours the brave, old boy.'

Fortune favours the brave. Tucking his chin inside his fleece, Tom slithered off the wall and set off across the town. It was a ghostly journey, as Dragonport seemed almost abandoned in the snow, the buildings nothing more than grey shadows in the sea of swirling snowflakes. Except for a few girls shivering outside a cashpoint machine, and a minicab, Tom reached the bottom of Catcher Hill without seeing anyone at all. He was quite happy about that; as a burglar he did not want too many witnesses. Striking out up the steep hill, he passed the rows of snug terraced houses huddling together in the darkness, and through each window Christmas trees twinkled with lights and presents. It was like catching glimpses of another world, a place full of warmth and families and happy, smiling faces—just like an advert on TV. Tom gritted his teeth and ploughed on, doing his best to ignore it; that was normal life; that was the kind of place he had lived in many years ago. He was different now. He had to be.

But Tom wasn't that different; despite the bitter wind that was beginning to make his cheeks ache he found himself suddenly missing his parents more than anything. Where were they now? In his mind's eye he saw his father in his snowbound tent on the edge of some vast forest, his eye pressed to his microscope, oblivious to the rest of the world, while his mother picked her way across some lonely mountain pass, calling out his name. And here he was, out on this wild night about to break into someone's house. The Scatterhorns truly were scattered across the face of the earth, and there was nothing whatever he could do about it, except go on. The great bird was right, he had a destiny now, and this was it.

Reaching the top of the hill, Tom crossed the road and slipped silently into the drive of Catcher Hall, ready to jump into the laurels at the first sight of the Bentley, or Zeus the dog, or anyone else patrolling the grounds on this bitter winter's night. There was no one, and soon Tom found himself staring across at the great bulk of the Hall, silhouetted against the pale orange sky. Skirting around through the yew trees, Tom reached the low terrace wall in front of the study and, raising his head just above the parapet, peered in through the gaps in the shutters. He could just make out the flickering blue reflections of computer screens in the glass cabinets, and somewhere there was the distant sound of a piano. Wiping the snowflakes away from his eyes

Tom expected to see either Lotus or Don Gervase walk past any moment, but after five long minutes there was still no movement within. Perhaps they were out; maybe he should try to open the window. No, that was far too dangerous. Best stick to the original plan, and use August's secret entrance.

Slithering over the low parapet, Tom crept forward to the corner, and searching around for the old iron drainpipe he was relieved to find it was still there, now half-hidden beneath a large bush. Grabbing hold of the branches as tightly as he could, Tom carefully hoisted himself up onto the wall. Slowly he began to work his way up, feeling through the tangle of branches for the cold metal pipe and pressing his toes into the same footholds in the stone that he had the last time he was here, over a hundred years ago. It was hard work, and hot too, and by the time he reached the second floor Tom was panting steam and beads of sweat itched uncomfortably under his hat. With one last heave Tom swung his body up over the battlements and flopped down gratefully on the wide lead gutter to catch his breath. Wow—that was quite a climb; it had better be easier on the way down. His heart racing, Tom peered up at the roof to see that the narrow skylight that gave into August's workshop was still there. That was a relief, but it looked a long way up, and it took a moment for Tom to realize why: the short wooden ladder that had run up towards it had gone, it must have rotted away. Tom cursed himself angrily; how could he have made such a simple mistake? The roof was far too steep to climb up without the ladder and it was covered in snow; it would be like trying to climb up an ice wall. He would just have to go back down again and try to find another way. No. Not now that he had made it this far; there must be another way up. Think, Tom.

Think.

Squinting up through the blizzard once more, Tom noticed that above the skylight there was a broad chimney looming up into the sky. Something seemed to be strapped to the side of it—a flat piece of metal. Could that be a lightning conductor? Lightning conductors run down to the ground, reasoned Tom, they have to. Perhaps . . . running his hand under the snow hopefully his cold fingers bumped against something. Scraping the snow away he found a wide string of copper, sitting proud above the roof tiles like a rope. Clearing away the snow above it, Tom found that every few feet or so, large flat brackets secured the copper rod to the roof. Tom breathed a deep sigh of relief, now he could go on. All he had to do was to climb up the lightning conductor until he was above the skylight, step across onto it and pray that the window was open. And if it wasn't, what then? Tom glanced down giddily. In all probability he would slide back down the roof, bounce off the battlements like a ball and fall three floors onto the terrace below. Tom shook his head at the madness of it all. Well done, Tom; good plan! This was so simple. Had he gone completely crazy? Maybe he had. Somehow, ever since he had come to stay with Uncle Jos, Tom had discovered a reckless side of his nature, and one day he felt sure it was going to land him in big trouble. But not tonight, tonight he would be OK.

He *had* to be.

Tom gritted his teeth and got going. Five minutes later he had managed to shimmy his way up the slippery copper lightning conductor, and now he found himself balanced precariously on the rim of the skylight. Despite the bitter night wind tugging at him Tom's eyes were prickling with sweat. He daren't look down now, it was far too terrifying; he seemed to be miles up in the air clinging to the edge of a precipice. One slip on the snow-covered roof and he was gone. Holding on to the rim as tightly as he could, Tom unfastened the catch that held it and stamped with all his weight on the iron frame. The rusting hinge squealed then jolted down an inch, then another, then it stopped, appearing to catch on something. Again he stamped, and again and again, willing it to give.

'Please,' Tom whispered to the skylight, 'open up . . . '

But the frame just refused to move any further, as if something on the inside was preventing it. Tom's fingers were so cold now that they hurt; he knew he couldn't hold on much longer. It was such a long way down . . .

'Open up, you pig!' he yelled, and he swore loudly into the blizzard. In desperation Tom raised both feet and began to bounce wildly on the glass itself. If he cut himself he didn't care, he just had to get off that roof . . . Suddenly there was a muffled crunch and Tom dropped like stone.

Thump!

Tom hit the dark floor of the workshop so hard that the air was punched out of his lungs. Broken glass from the skylight tinkled down all around him.

For a long time Tom lay completely still, his face pressed against the floor. His head was swimming, and for a moment he wondered if he was paralysed. Opening one eye he saw his hand before him, shaking uncontrollably. Only now that he was safely inside was he prepared to admit quite how dangerous that had been. He was scared out of his wits. Tom closed his eyes again, and breathed in the cold, mouldy air of the workshop, which still had the unmistakable scent of animal upon it. That was a wild, crazy stunt and somehow he had got away with it. Maybe he wouldn't be so lucky next time.

Maybe . . .

The animal smell was strangely comforting, but it slowly began to dawn on Tom that there was no reason to feel safe here at all. Without August, Catcher Hall was a dangerous place to him now. He had entered the spiders' web.

Pulling himself up off the filthy floor, Tom switched on his small silver torch and peered around him. The workshop was in chaos. Shelves had been ripped off the walls, cupboards lay smashed on the floor and there were wires and rags scattered everywhere. In one corner the cabinet labelled 'Curiosities' lay on its back with the remains of the four-legged duckling lying in pieces beside it. It was almost as if a rampaging wild animal had ripped the place apart.

So, what was the plan now? Tom wasn't sure. If Don Gervase had been looking for something up here he had been very careless, as the destruction was complete. On the other hand, the workshop might have been smashed up by anyone in the last hundred years, it didn't prove anything. He had to find out more. Taking a deep breath Tom tiptoed over to the door and slipped out into the dark stairwell. There was a vague banging of distant pipes but other than that the house was deathly quiet. Which way? Downstairs, into the study? No, thought Tom quickly, not yet; he did not want to enter the heart of the web just yet. Much better to stay upstairs. Just then there was the sound of quick footsteps on the stone floor of the hall beneath him, and leaning forward, Tom caught a glimpse of Lotus's white fur coat at the doorway.

'How long will it take?' called Don Gervase from the study.

'An hour at the most.'

'Make sure you stick to that.'

Lotus did not reply, but the front door slammed and she was gone.

Good, thought Tom, that was one less person to worry about. Now, concentrate. To the left was the long dark corridor, which Tom remembered led to the small wooden room where he had first arrived in the past. To the right there was another corridor that ran along the east side of the house. This led to August's bedroom, but Tom had only dim memories of what lay beyond that, except that it was a much older part of the house that was rarely if ever open. Tom looked quickly from one to the other, and decided upon the wooden room. Perhaps the trunk was still there, perhaps Don Gervase and Lotus had found it too. That would at least explain something.

Darting across the landing, Tom crept down the corridor he knew, careful to stay on the centre of the threadbare carpet to muffle his footsteps as best he could. On reaching the door he turned the small ebony handle softly, but when it opened he was completely unprepared for what he found: the small room full of boxes he was expecting had now been turned into a bathroom, with a wide, floral print wallpaper and a shaggy white carpet. In the corner where the trunk had once stood there was now a cast-iron bath. Closing the door softly, Tom retraced his steps to the landing, his mind whirring; however they had found their way into the model, the past, it was *definitely* not through that route. They must have found another way . . . Reaching the top of the stairs Tom stopped and strained his ears for any sound; and once more he could hear nothing. The silence meant that Don Gervase must still be in the study downstairs.

What next? The other corridor: perhaps he could find some clue down there, perhaps the old wing was no longer locked. Feeling a lot braver now, Tom flitted across the dark landing and ran down the narrow winding corridor past August's bedroom to the door at the far end. Cautiously he tried the handle and it gave, whereupon he found himself standing in a long low-lit picture gallery that he had never entered before. Stretching the length of one wall was a long line of portraits of grim-faced Catchers, dressed in suits of armour and wigs. Opposite, beneath a series of tall windows, there was a procession of pike, salmon and trout all caught and mounted by August. Tom began to edge his way along, his breath forming little puffs of mist in the musty air, and gazed up at one stern Catcher after another. He had not gone more than a few paces when he heard a low mumbling sound . . .

'Hhmmm-ummm-ummm.'

Tom froze; every muscle in his body tensed.

'Grummm . . . Mummm-ummm-umm-umm-ble.'

There it was again—it seemed to be coming from the wall. Shining his torch directly at the pike Tom saw the faintest movement of its lips. Was that a trick of the light? Then there was another sound from further up the gallery, from the trout. Mumbling sounds . . . like monks chanting . . . Tom suddenly realized what it was. It was the fish; they were singing! Tom smiled to himself and switched off his torch. So August must have used his potion here too. Slowly he crept down the gallery, listening to the dismal droning that came from inside each case.

'Glorious will be the last of days,' murmured the pike.

'In point of fact, glorious they shall be,' corrected the eel.

'When your race's run and the trumpet sounds,' added the trout. 'And Canon Mumble does his rounds.'

'Sending some to the sea and some to the fire.'

'To burn for ever upon the pyre.'

'Burn for ever,' they droned, 'burn for ever, burn for ever on the fires of hell.'

'Be you fish or beast or fowl or priest.'

'You're all going to burn upon the fires of hell.'

Tom stifled a giggle; so this is what August had done with Canon Mumble's little book of sermons for judgement day! He had used it to stuff their heads. If only he could see them now—this would have made him laugh. Tom was so caught up in the strange fishes' song that he barely heard the footsteps before it was too late.

Click-clack! Click-clack! Click-clack!

It sounded like ice picks hammering on stone, getting louder with every step . . .

Click-clack! Click-clack!

Tom looked around him frantically, where could he hide? Halfway down the gallery one of the windows was set back into an alcove, beside which hung a heavy pair of embroidered curtains. That was the place. Tom raced forward and dived behind the thick material, pressing back into the shadows just in time to see the tall thin figure of Don Gervase sweeping down the gallery towards him, dressed in a long black coat. Don Gervase seemed far too interested in the small piece of paper he was carrying to notice the bulging curtain, and marching straight past Tom he continued down the corridor to the end.

'Well, there it is,' he growled impatiently.

Folding up the paper he jabbed it into his pocket, whereupon he flung open the cupboard door in front of him. Bending down he stepped inside, and the door slammed shut behind him.

Tom stayed precisely where he was, not daring to move a muscle. Surely Don Gervase was about to reappear at any moment. He waited, straining his eyes and ears for any sign of movement, but none came. Slowly the seconds turned into minutes, and still the enormous man did not reappear. Perhaps it was not a cupboard at all, thought Tom, but the door to another part of the house to which he had never been, new servants' quarters perhaps. Maybe that's where Don Gervase and Lotus were living now.

After several long minutes of waiting, Tom could contain his curiosity no longer. Stepping out from behind his curtain he tiptoed towards the row of cupboards and stood before them. Tom counted nine doors in front of him, and they all looked identical. So which one was it? Somewhere in the middle, he thought. Tom reached forward and carefully grasped a handle. Even though it was very dark and cold, his hand was sweating; supposing Don Gervase suddenly came out, what then? Supposing he slept in this cupboard or something crazy like that? Too late: Tom had opened the door.

Inside there was nothing more than mops and brushes. Tom

swallowed hard; he must have chosen the wrong one. Hesitantly he tried the cupboards on either side, but they too looked exactly the same, nothing but mops and brushes. This couldn't be right, surely Don Gervase had not simply *disappeared,* had he? That was impossible. Closing the doors, Tom peered again inside the first cupboard. Beyond all the paraphernalia he could just make out the dark grey wood of the back wall; it certainly looked solid enough. Then Tom remembered how Don Gervase had closed the door behind him directly after he had stepped inside. Perhaps *that* was it, some sort of trick mechanism, whereby you had to close the door at the front before you could open the door at the back? Maybe. This was Catcher Hall after all, and August was full of surprises. This would be yet another.

'OK,' breathed Tom softly, 'I can do this.'

Wiping the sweat off his hands he stepped carefully into the cupboard and closed the door behind him. Nothing happened. Tom stood in complete darkness, listening to his heart racing. What should he do now? Find the other door. Stretching his arms out in front of him, Tom groped forward until his fingers brushed against the rough wood of the back wall. Slowly his fingers traced down, until they bumped against a small metal ring, which felt as if it might be some sort of handle. Holding it lightly Tom twisted the ring a quarter turn. It gave.

'Yes!' Tom's heart leapt. This *must* be it.

Without a further thought Tom turned the ring and pushed. There was a creaking sound, then a small wooden door no bigger than Tom swung open. It was rather like an old-fashioned door within a door, like Tom had once seen in a castle. Beyond it was a long dark room that at first sight appeared to be some sort of storeroom. If it was it was certainly a very odd one, as it seemed to be full of fishing equipment and large wooden barrels. Walking over to one of them, Tom lifted the lid a fraction, whereupon he was hit by a stink of rancid fish so awful that he had to cover his mouth to stop himself retching. Holding his nose, Tom shone his torch down into the murky water. There, floating just beneath the surface, five large yellow spheres the size of footballs nudged against each other. What were those things? At first Tom thought they might be some kind of giant egg, or an obscure deep sea jellyfish, but the smell was so repellent Tom had to close the lid before he was sick. Perhaps they were some kind of bait.

Doing his best to ignore the rotting stink all around, Tom threaded his way through the tangle of glass buoys and nets towards a large barn door at the end. With every step he became more and more convinced that he was now in some kind of fisherman's storehouse, which somehow was connected to Catcher Hall. How could that be, unless it was a whole new building at the back . . . Maybe it isn't, thought Tom, hearing the screech of seagulls and the long drone of a foghorn in the distance; maybe he was no longer in Catcher Hall at all. The great barn door was locked, but to the left was another rough wooden door, beside which hung long lines of black swallowtail coats. There must have been hundreds of them, and picking one up Tom studied it curiously. It had two neatly tailored pockets on either side and a line of shiny black buttons all the way down the front. This did not look as if it could belong to any fisherman, and what's more, Tom was sure that he had seen coats like these somewhere before . . .

Outside the foghorn boomed once more. Opening the door a crack, Tom was surprised to find himself at the top of a flight of rickety wooden steps that led down into a narrow snow-covered alley between two buildings. He was in a warehouse somewhere, close to the sea. Was this the model of Dragonport? Was he back in the past? A cold, cutting wind sent flurries of snow swirling down the alley and a crackle of fireworks burst overhead. Somewhere in the distance Tom heard the music of a barrel organ and voices laughing. Maybe it was . . . Feeling braver now, Tom clambered down the snowy steps and made his way down the alley towards the sound, and he had almost reached an archway at the end when he smelt the familiar, rich charcoal smoke of the chestnut sellers.

'Look where you're goin', lad!'

Tom scrambled up onto the narrow pavement just as a horse and sledge whipped past him, bells clanging angrily. Catching his breath, Tom turned the corner and there, spread out before him, was the frozen river, busy with skaters at the ice fair.

So he was right. For him the way back was through the wicker basket in the museum; for Don Gervase and Lotus, it was a cupboard in Catcher Hall: two different ways of arriving back into the model. So the eagle was right, there *were* other nooks and crannies on the earth where one world met another. But why at Catcher Hall? Surely it could not be an accident; they must be connected, somehow. Tom stood in the doorway for a moment, trying to puzzle it out, and he was just on the point of stepping out of the shadow of the arch onto the waterfront when he had an instinctive feeling that he shouldn't. Someone—or something—was watching him.

Glancing across the street Tom noticed two small men dressed in black fur coats standing under a lamppost, stamping their feet to keep warm. They appeared to be waiting for someone, and even though they were almost completely obscured by their fur coats, there was something familiar about these two gentlemen. But before Tom could think what it was a third man in a long black cape strode across the street to join them. It was Don Gervase, and the moment he arrived the two small men cowered slightly and bowed their heads as he began firing questions at them impatiently. Tom could not hear a word they said, yet it was quite clear from their nervous behaviour that Don Gervase was the master and they were his minions who had made some sort of mistake. Eventually one of the little men pointed sheepishly in the direction of the town, whereupon Don Gervase threw up his hands in exasperation and marched off down the street with the two small men scampering behind at his heels.

Tom's first thought was that he should follow them and find out where they were going, but then a much, much better idea came to mind: as long as Don Gervase was here in the past, *he knew where he was*. This was a perfect opportunity to search the study of Catcher Hall without being found out. But he must leave now, before Lotus returned.

Darting back into the alley, Tom retraced his steps up the wooden staircase and threaded his way back through the stinking barrels until he reached the far end of the warehouse. The small door opened easily before him and, stepping quickly into the dark space beyond, he pulled it shut behind him and felt forward with both hands. At last his fingers reached the inside handle of the cupboard. Turning it, Tom found himself back in the picture gallery of Catcher Hall once more. This was so easy! No scrabbling about trying to find an opening under the rags, no flying through the air, hoping he would land in the right place. Stealing back down the dark corridors, Tom soon reached the top of the stairs, where he paused to listen again for any sign that Lotus might have come back before him. There was nothing; the house was as quiet and muffled as it had been the moment he had left it. He must be alone. There was still time.

Creeping down the stairs, Tom crossed the empty hall and let himself into the study. Everything in here was much the same as Tom remembered it from his days as August's apprentice: the dark oak panels still lined the walls and either side of the black marble fireplace stood two tall bookcases crammed full of ancient leather-bound volumes. What was different was the mess. Spread out across every flat surface were hundreds of bits of paper covered with scribbles and equations, and stretching out across the great Persian rug were piles and piles of newspapers. Tom walked over to the nearest heap and began to read. '*Sir Henry Scatterhorn's mysterious disappearance*' read the headline, from the *Dragonport Mercury* dated 12 May 1953. Placing it back on the pile Tom leafed down a few more layers. '*Lecture to the Dragonport Scientific Society on the principles of stuffing birds, presented by August Catcher*', '*Sir Henry finds Spix's Macaw*', '*Mammoth in need of repair*'. The list went on and on; it seemed that every newspaper report ever written about August, Sir Henry, or the Scatterhorn Museum had been cut out and collected in this room. Tom was very puzzled: why would they bother doing all this research if they were about to buy the museum anyway? What might the papers contain that the museum itself did not?

Whatever they were looking for they were obviously not going to leave any stone unturned.

Picking his way through the newspapers to the trestle table in the centre of the room, Tom found a pair of computer screens wired up to some kind of sensor device that was buzzing quietly. Tom had never seen anything like it, but it looked battered and very well-travelled; perhaps it was some piece of high-tec military equipment. As his eye travelled down the table Tom recognized more familiar objects. There was the kookaburra, (so that burglar on the wire *had* been Lotus after all) its head now removed from its body and sliced in half like an apple. Beyond the remains of the bird were bits and pieces of August's heron and the eel, expertly dissected into sections and neatly displayed. At the far end Tom found some small heaps of brilliant red feathers that must have once belonged to the bee hummingbird, and beside them stood the small round ball of cotton wool that August had used to stuff the tiny creature. Tom stared at the remains, recalling that magical moment when the small flame-headed bird staggered drunkenly back to life in the palm of August's hand: now here it lay, laid out like some exotic dish for a mad Roman emperor. A spark of anger began to dance in Tom's mind: if it was the sapphire they were after, why bother to dissect a hummingbird? The creature was barely five centimetres tall, and they must know that the sapphire must be twice as large as that. No: it was definitely something else they were looking for, there could be no question about that now, and by the look of things they hadn't found it yet.

Tom was on the point of tiptoeing back to the door when his eye caught a pile of newspapers resting on a low leather footstool beside the fire. They were a slightly different colour to all the rest, and there was something peculiar about them: they seemed to be printed on some kind of plastic. Drawing closer, Tom pulled one out of the pile and felt along the strange waxy surface that was almost wet to touch.

'*MERICAN FERI SASTER L8-EST*' read the headline, '*NYNE TWENI TOWSAN FURD DRUYND*'. Beneath these strange words was a photograph of what must have been a ferry, but it looked more like an enormous bar of soap, lying on its side in a choppy sea. The picture itself was oddly three-dimensional, rather like a hologram, and as Tom looked at it the waves seemed to shimmer and somehow he was sure he could hear the sound of people shouting for help. The story of the disaster was written in a kind of English that Tom could not quite understand, but neither the words, the picture, nor even the material they were printed on were the strangest things about this newspaper: it was the date. This newspaper was not from the past, nor was it from the present, either. It was from the *future*: nine hundred and seventy years in the future in fact.

Tom smiled to himself; it must be a misprint—how was *that* possible? Bending down, Tom examined the similar coloured papers underneath; they too were printed on the same, wax-like paper, written in the same dialect, from exactly the same year. It couldn't have been a misprint; how could hundreds of different papers all share the same date? There were just too many of them. Tom stood up and stared down at the pile of greenish newspapers, utterly perplexed. How on earth had Don Gervase and Lotus managed to get hold of newspapers from the future?

Unless . . . an idea started forming in Tom's mind that he hardly dared to believe . . . unless *they*—

At that moment the front door slammed.

'Dad? Dad, I'm back.'

Tom heard Lotus's soft footsteps pad across the hallway outside.

'Dad, where are you?'

Tom just had time to slither under the leather footstool before the door opened.

'Hello?'

Lotus was standing in the doorway carrying a small rucksack. She sounded extremely irritated.

'By the way, I've got it.'

CHAPTER 21

A Moment Later

Tom Scatterhorn lay absolutely still, trying to ignore the blood drumming in his ears in a crazy rhythm. From where he was hiding, pressed below the leather footstool, he could see nothing more than Lotus's black boots stamping fresh snow into the Persian carpet. What was she doing? Craning his neck round the other way Tom turned back towards the fireplace, and from there he was just able to see the tall overmantel mirror reflecting the entire room. There was Lotus, wearing a tight black catsuit zipped right up to the neck, brushing the snow off her white fur coat and hanging it neatly behind the door. Pulling off the hood she shook out her long black hair, then she picked up a small blue rucksack and tossed it down on the trestle table. There was a muffled squeak and the rucksack moved a little, as if there were something alive inside it trying to get out.

'Don't you fret, you revolting little beast,' she hissed. 'Your time is about to come.'

Lotus looked crossly at her index finger on which there was a dark trace of blood.

'Devil.'

Putting the cut finger in her mouth she sucked it hard. Tom was wondering what it was in the sack that had bitten her when he heard the familiar click-clack of footsteps echoing down the stairs and across the hall. The door flew open, and in marched Don Gervase carrying a wooden box full of bottles.

'Those fools can't be trusted to find anything at all!' he boomed irritably. 'Even a jellyfish would have shown more gumption.'

Lotus murmured something, then flopped down sulkily in a chair and watched as Don Gervase began to set the dusty old bottles in a long line across the table.

'I thought we'd already checked these ones before.'

'Unfortunately not, my dear. Tiresome as it may seem to you.'

Tom immediately recognized this collection from the windowsill in August's workshop. Don Gervase must have broken back into Catcher Hall in the past to get them. All the labels had gone, and most of them were almost empty; obviously August had decided they were not important enough to take away with him the night he left. When he had finished, Don Gervase picked up the wooden box and was about to drop it on the ground when he noticed something rolling about in the bottom.

'Wait a minute.' Stretching a bony hand into the box Don Gervase picked up a small dusty blue bottle, its stopper still intact.

'Hmmmm.'

Don Gervase held it up to the light and pressed one large milky eye against the dark blue glass: was there anything there? The moment Tom saw the bottle he felt all the blood drain out of his face: it was one of the bottles containing August's potion. Why hadn't he taken it? Surely he couldn't have been so absent-minded as to leave one of his precious bottles behind?

'Well that one can be discounted immediately,' growled Don Gervase, seeing that the inside of the bottle was completely dry and there was nothing more than a layer of purplish residue at the bottom. With a grunt he flung it carelessly into the waste-paper basket. Tom heard a dull 'clink' behind him, and craning round he just made out the small blue shape lying intact on some old newspapers at the bottom of the basket. The glass stopper was nowhere to be seen.

'Now my dear, to business, *if* you don't mind.'

Impatiently Don Gervase opened a drawer of the desk and brought out a clear glass bottle with a skull and crossbones marked on it.

'I'll be very glad if this doesn't work,' said Lotus huffily, examining her cut finger once more.

'Now now, Lotus, a little bite won't kill you,' sneered Don Gervase. 'If it's vicious then crush its legs or poke its eyes out, as I have told you countless times.'

Reaching into his pocket he produced a pair of shiny leather gloves and threw them at her. Lotus pulled the gloves on in stony silence.

'Quite ready now?'

Lotus said nothing.

'Good.'

Bending forward Don Gervase carefully unscrewed the top of the poison bottle with his long bony fingers. Quickly he tipped it three times into a handkerchief, and then he nodded across to

Lotus, who plunged her gloved hand violently into the rucksack. The bag erupted with piercing shrieks and squeals but Lotus ignored them all, chasing around with her hand until she finally caught the terrified creature.

'Got you, you little fiend,' she hissed, and squeezing hard she brought the small thrashing thing out into the room.

'Ugh.'

Don Gervase stared with revulsion at the ball of white fur with pink eyes twisting wildly in Lotus's gloved hand. It was Plankton.

Tom had never liked that rat, but seeing its predicament now even he felt a little sorry for it. Plankton's pink eyes bulged in terror, then he sank his teeth into Lotus's leather glove in a desperate bid to escape. But it was too late for that now: in one swift move Don Gervase clamped the poisoned handkerchief over the rat's face and pressed it down hard. Plankton struggled blindly, his feet paddling in the air, but soon his movements became feebler, and then with a final splutter he lay absolutely still in Lotus's hands.

'*Excellente*.'

Don Gervase screwed the top back on to the poison bottle with a smirk, then switched on the computer and the sensor device lying on the table next to it. The machine hissed and whirred to life.

'Dead you are, rat,' whispered Lotus, her voice full of venom, 'dead as a dodo.'

Don Gervase picked up the sensor and slowly passed it over the length of Plankton's lifeless body. There was a brief crackle of static but the machine registered nothing more.

'You appear to be right, my dear,' he grunted.

Lotus stared at Plankton's pink staring eyes and contorted mouth in disgust.

'Can't we just . . . leave it like that?'

'You know full well why we can't, Lotus, or are you learning nothing whatsoever? Fresh kill is best and even these dregs might prove useful.' He snapped his fingers briskly. 'Swabs, if you please.'

Lotus sighed wearily and drew up a chair opposite Don Gervase. Reaching down the table she picked up a pile of thin wires and a ball of white cotton wool lying next to them. Tearing off a pinch of wool, she expertly twizzled it around the end of the wire with her fingers.

'Thank you,' he said, taking the swab. 'Now let's hope we are in luck. *Numero uno*.'

Picking up the first bottle in the line Don Gervase removed the cork, then slid the wire down inside so that the cotton wool was soaked in the clear liquid at the bottom. Retrieving it, he carefully brushed the damp swab around the mouth of Plankton, and, when he was satisfied, he picked up the sensor and slowly passed it over the lifeless body of the rat. The machine hummed, and there was a brief, almost inaudible crackle of static, then nothing more.

'Humph,' growled Don Gervase, clearly frustrated.

Wiping the traces of liquid off the rat's nose he repeated the same process for the next bottle in the line. The sensor showed exactly the same reaction from this one, and the next one after that. Don Gervase repeated the process again and again, working his way down the line of bottles, growing steadily angrier by the second.

'I hope your wish is not about to come true, my dear,' he murmured, discarding yet another swab. 'Time is no longer on our side.'

With each new failure Don Gervase's eyes seemed to bulge as if he was physically boiling inside, but still Plankton lay absolutely dead, with a fixed expression of mad terror on his face. Lotus said nothing, she merely scribbled down the size and shape of the bottle and marked a cross next to it in her notebook, then twizzling up one more stick she handed it over. Lotus had seen this many, many times before and was thoroughly bored with it. Failure was to be expected.

By now the air in the study was heavy with the sickly smell of chemicals, but neither Don Gervase nor Lotus seemed to notice. Trying very hard to contain himself, Don Gervase reached across and picked up the last bottle in the line.

'I think,' he said slowly, 'that if *this* does not succeed, my patience will have finally run dry.'

His eyes glittered with silent fury as he puzzled over the remains of the label.

'Goat?'

'Essence of goat perhaps?' suggested Lotus, sarcastically. 'Maybe August Catcher wanted his stuffed goat to seem more goatish, so he boiled one up, then added a sprig of rosemary, two sliced sheep's eyes, a spoonful of bird's brains, wombat's nose—'

'Very amusing, Lotus,' interrupted Don Gervase. '*What* a sense of humour you have.'

Lotus smiled at her own little joke as she twizzled up the last swab and passed it across. Goatby's Fluid, thought Tom; that contained strychnine, didn't it? He watched as Don Gervase dabbed the poison around Plankton's mouth, knowing that if anything was certainly *not* going to revive the rat, this was it. The sensor crackled quietly, then went dead. Predictably, it had registered absolutely nothing at all.

'*CAA-RRRAMMM-BAA!*'

Don Gervase suddenly leapt to his feet and hurled the lifeless body of Plankton into the wastepaper basket. His skin had turned from yellow to beetroot, and his eyes were blazing red.

'This is . . . is . . . is . . . ' Words failed him.

'A complete waste of time?' suggested Lotus with a bored expression. 'So then why don't we just wait till the museum is ours, then rip it apart.'

'*Exacto!*' spat Don Gervase. 'So we shall, piece by piece! But even *then* we may not find it in time!' He began pacing about the room in short quick strides. 'Do you not realize, Lotus, that the Contagion is barely hours away? Millions upon millions will be gathering, in every single place, and *what* am I supposed to tell them? What do I tell the Chamber? That yes, after a lifetime of searching, through every century, to every corner of the planet—I, Don Gervase Askary, *have* at last discovered the source, in *Dragonport*—the most unlikely of places, inside the very museum that *hundreds* of our agents had already inspected! But unfortunately, no, Your Graces, I cannot provide a drop of it, nothing, not even one tiny little atom. And worse still, I have to admit that August Catcher himself has escaped—*escapado*—from me. FROM ME?!'

Don Gervase kicked the wall so hard that his toe made a hole in it, and his fingers twisted around each other like snakes.

'This should have been my moment,' he hissed, '*my momento.*

But no, instead, I am humiliated. Surrounded by fools and half-wits!'

Lotus yawned; she was well acquainted with Don Gervase's wild outbursts.

'You could still interrogate the boy before we kill him,' she suggested with studied nonchalance. 'If he's one of them he will certainly know something.'

'*Exacto*, Lotus! How I might have done! I might even have sliced him into small pieces and examined every speck in his body, had *you* not let him go!' Don Gervase was shrieking now, and he was on the brink of losing control. 'Or have you forgotten that?'

'I wasn't sure—'

'You weren't sure! There will be a price to pay for this failure, Lotus, a very high price indeed.'

Don Gervase stared at her, his forehead bulging. Suddenly his voice turned dark with menace.

'*Someone* will have to take responsibility for this. There will be a reckoning and it will not be pleasant. May I remind you that there are creatures out there whose existence you could barely dream of.'

'Like what?' snorted Lotus, pretending not to care.

'Prototypes, crossbreeds, perversions. Odd-balls.' Don Gervase's eyes widened. 'I *know*, Lotus, I have encountered them myself. I am familiar with all their tricks.' His small tongue flickered over his lips and his eyes narrowed to slits. 'But *you*, my dear . . . you are not.'

Lotus shot a glance up at Don Gervase looming over her like a giant bat. For the first time Tom could see a glint of fear in her eyes.

'What are you saying, Dad?' she blurted out. 'That it is my fault? That *I* have to take the blame for *your* failure?'

'Someone has to,' reasoned Don Gervase, 'and let's forget this "Dad" business, shall we? It really is very sentimental.'

Lotus scowled at him stubbornly, biting her lip.

'So—*what* do you want me to do?'

'Bring me Tom Scatterhorn,' growled Don Gervase, his voice no louder than a whisper, 'it is time we made sure of him for good.'

No sooner had Don Gervase said these words than Tom heard a faint scraping sound behind him. Turning his head round towards the wastepaper basket he saw Plankton's white body lying on top of the newspapers.

Sccrrrch . . . scrrrch . . . scrrrch . . .

There it was again. Tom wondered if he was imagining it, as the sound was barely audible under the crackle of the logs in the grate. Then, quite suddenly, one of Plankton's pink eyes blinked. Tom gasped. Then the pink eye blinked again, twice. The next second he sat up and looked straight at Tom, making him almost cry out in astonishment. Plankton was alive! But . . . it must be the blue bottle; there was no liquid left, but—*that didn't matter.* There was that purplish residue crystallized on the bottom . . . somehow it must still be producing that heavy smell of hyacinths and floor polish . . .

Neither Lotus nor Don Gervase had noticed what was happening in the wastepaper basket, which was just as well, as Plankton was now standing up on his hind legs sniffing the sickly cocktail of chemicals in the air.

'Plankton,' whispered Tom as quietly as he could, 'come here, here boy.'

He beckoned frantically to the rat standing on the edge of the basket staring at him. At first Plankton seemed to recognize Tom, though he also seemed to be wondering what on earth he was doing lying flat under the footstool.

'Here, boy, *over here . . .*'

If he could only coax Plankton out of the basket towards him, then he could grab the wretched rat and stuff him into his pocket until this was all over. The last thing Tom wanted was for Lotus or Don Gervase to discover he had come back to life. Plankton however was a single-minded rat who had never done anything anyone had asked of him, and he was in no mind to start now. Wrinkling up his nose defiantly, he hopped over the edge of the basket and scurried away across the carpet.

'Come back,' pleaded Tom. 'Plankton!'

He watched helplessly as the white rat dodged in and out of the piles of newspapers towards the door.

This is it, thought Tom, they'll see him now for sure. But when he turned back to face the mirror Tom realized there was the slimmest chance that they wouldn't. There was Lotus slumped in a chair beside the fire, listening in stubborn silence as Don Gervase paced up and down beside the bookcases. By now he had quite recovered his composure, and he was delivering a lecture in his deepest monotone.

'It is, I grant you, quite inconceivable that the boy travels by accident,' droned Don Gervase, his long fingers clasping and unclasping behind his back. 'Obviously he has been sent by someone—or something—to find the elixir before we do. His father we can rule out immediately. He was approached in the standard way, letters from the Movement, flattery, cajolery, the promise of great secrets, all the usual flimflam. *And* he was watched: but what did he find? Nothing, he knows *niente*. Just like all the rest, a rank amateur of no consequence. And those nitwits he was travelling with likewise—mere scavengers, buffoons riding their luck. But that revolting bird puzzles me: I have had dealings with such creatures before and they are extraordinarily irritating. Why does it protect him? Surely not because that fool Jos Scatterhorn tells it to, or his ridiculous wife, Snelba, Zelba—what *is* her name?'

Lotus did not reply; in fact, she was no longer listening to a word he said. Out of the corner of her eye she had spotted something white threading its way quietly behind the piles of newspaper towards the door, and ever so slowly she swivelled around to face it. On reaching the last pile Plankton suddenly broke cover and made a dash for the corner, and he was just about to crawl underneath the door when he cast one last look back into the room. At that very moment his beady pink eyes met Lotus's, and for a split second they were both too astonished to react.

'Of course the timing *must* be significant,' rumbled Don Gervase to the bookcase. 'The boy must *surely* know that the Contagion only happens once every two thousand—well, very nearly every two thousand—'

Suddenly there was a wild squeal and Plankton scrambled under the door just as Lotus sprang out of her chair and raced after him. Turning round, Don Gervase was surprised to find himself completely alone.

'Lotus?' he snapped angrily. 'Lotus! Come back here this minute!'

There was a screeching sound from out in the corridor, followed by the clatter of a tennis racket hitting the stone floor.

'What is going on now?' he growled, and marched out into the hall.

Listening to the commotion outside, Tom realized that this was his one and only chance. He had no idea who Don Gervase or Lotus were or what part they had already played in his life. They may have been from the future, they may have been from the past, but one thing was certain—they would stop at nothing to find August's potion. They would destroy the museum, and they were preparing to kill him. They must not have it. He must steal it to protect himself.

Sliding out from his hiding place Tom knelt before the wastepaper basket and rummaging frantically amongst the newspapers he fished out the small blue bottle and the glass stopper. Holding it up to his nose he recognized that smell instantly: hyacinths and floor polish—it was still there, as strong as ever. Jamming the stopper back into the top of the bottle, Tom just had time to slip it into his pocket before he heard the sound of angry footsteps approaching.

'This is *impossible*!' roared Don Gervase.

Without a moment's thought Tom dived behind the easy-chair next to the fire as the door flung open.

'Utterly completely *impossible*!'

Don Gervase entered the room like a man possessed, and in short quick steps strode over to the wastepaper basket where he began inspecting the newspapers for clues. There were no signs of chemicals, the papers were not even damp. How could the rat have been revived?

'I simply refuse to believe it,' he growled thickly. 'Empty it was, dry as dust.'

But where was that empty blue bottle? Don Gervase turned the wastepaper basket upside down and shook it hard, sending papers tumbling out all over the floor on top of all the others. It was not *there*. Flying into a fury once more, Don Gervase whirled the basket above his head and flung it hard across the room at the bookcase.

BANG!

The glass above Tom's head exploded, and he cowered as shards of glass showered the floor.

'NO RAT, NO BOTTLE, NO POTION!'

Don Gervase was screeching now, utterly out of control. He seemed ready to rip this whole room apart. Lunging forward he dug his fingernails deep into the leather of the desk in a desperate effort to stay calm.

'But how?' he spluttered unsteadily. 'How, how, how?'

Then a thought suddenly occurred to him and his great milky eyes narrowed. Maybe he had been right after all, maybe the bottle *was* empty, and the rat *was* dead. So that meant the rat had been revived by something else, *inside* the bottle . . . something he couldn't see . . . what could that be? Don Gervase's small tongue darted over his broken black teeth.

'Of course,' he hissed suddenly, and his huge eyes widened at the revelation. 'Yesss!'

It was becoming clear to him now. It was not a liquid that he was looking for at all, it was something colourless and invisible—a gas! A gas that had been trapped inside that empty blue bottle, a gas so concentrated that even the merest whiff of it was still powerful enough to revive the rat! And *that* was why he couldn't find it, because *he* couldn't smell it. In fact, Don Gervase could smell precisely nothing at all, which is why August Catcher's secret had eluded him for all this time.

'Well, well, well.'

Don Gervase sniggered to himself: what a fool he had been, *he* of all people; such an elementary mistake. The olfactory sense might have saved him a good deal of trouble. To think of all the places he'd been, all the chaos he'd brought, in pursuit of something so simple as a *smell* . . . dear oh dear. But where was that bottle? Don Gervase began to walk around the room, kicking the piles of papers in all directions. It couldn't have just got lost, it was far too conspicuous for that . . . small blue bottles containing the secret of life didn't just disappear . . . Don Gervase paused a moment, and a flicker of red flame danced in his eyes. Someone who knew its value must have stolen it, someone very, very close at hand. A time traveller, an enemy, an *assassin*. Tom Scatterhorn—who else.

Don Gervase glowered about him murderously, and shaking a small steel knife out of his inner sleeve deftly flicked it open. Tom shrank back when he saw the blade: it was dull and bluish, and spiked like the sting of a scorpion.

'Now, where's a good hiding place?' Don Gervase whispered to himself, tottering towards the fireplace, twirling the blade in his powerful hand. 'Over here perhaps?'

Tom's heart was hammering in his temples, and he was trying hard not to breathe. From beneath his chair he saw two very small, slightly pointed feet in black boots advance straight towards him.

'It would be better for you if you showed yourself,' whispered Don Gervase silkily. Those boots came closer and closer, stopping directly in front of his chair. Tom felt a tingling shiver of fear down his spine as the air all around him seemed to grow colder, and he could almost smell Don Gervase looming over him.

'Come out, little mouse, come out, come out, wherever you are . . .'

There was a pause and Don Gervase coughed. Then the boots squeaked noisily and spun around abruptly on their heels, turning to face the room once more.

'I do *know* you're here,' he continued. 'Who else would want that bottle? And what a shame it would be if you had to suffer the same fate as . . . your parents. That would be *most* regrettable, don't you think, Tom?' Don Gervase's eyes flickered from side to side, watching for the slightest movement. 'Almost careless.'

Tom had no idea whether this threat was true or not, he didn't care. Jumping up onto all fours he launched himself at the back of the chair, pushing into it so hard that it tipped up onto its front legs and slammed into the back of Don Gervase's knees, sending him crashing forward onto the carpet. The very next second Tom vaulted over the sprawling black shape and raced out of the door.

'Lotus!' roared Don Gervase as he scrabbled to his feet. 'The boy's got it! He's escaping!'

Tom sprinted up the stairs two at a time, and reaching the top he glanced back to see Lotus walking out of the dining room with Plankton writhing in her hands. The instant she saw him her mouth fell open in astonishment.

'Tom? Where—'

'Don't just stand there, girl!' screamed Don Gervase as he clattered across the hall, angrily snatching the rat and flinging him away into the darkness. 'Kill him! Kill Tom Scatterhorn!'

CHAPTER 22

Through Time and Out

Tom dared not look behind him. He tore down the dark corridors running faster than he ever thought possible, the carpet blurring beneath his feet. Where was he going? Back: back to the only place he could get lost in the crowd. Fighting for breath Tom slammed around the corner and into the long picture gallery, urging his legs on to the end. The row of cupboards, which one was it? Somewhere in the middle . . . try them all . . . there's time. But there wasn't. The sharp click-clack was growing louder and louder as Tom flung open one door after another, only to find more mops and brushes, they all seemed identical. Which one . . . which one . . . which . . .

'Aha!' boomed a voice from the end of the corridor.

Tom whipped round to find Don Gervase and Lotus half-running, half-trotting towards him with short quick steps, and Don Gervase held that small steel knife in his hand. Tom tried hard to control his panic; he was so frightened now he wanted to be sick.

Don't look back, you idiot.

But he was paralysed in front of the cupboards: which one was it? If he made the wrong choice he was dead for certain. His mind boiled with indecision; opening them all had only made it more difficult. Too bad: too late.

Tom jumped into the nearest cupboard and closed the door behind him. His heart was hammering in his head so loudly he could barely think, but he forced himself through the mops and brushes to the back wall and felt down for the small metal ring. There it was—thank God. He had been right, now go . . . Tom had only half opened the door when he knew instinctively that he had made the wrong decision.

Beyond the door was a dark space, but it was not the fishermen's warehouse he remembered. He must have chosen the wrong cupboard, as this was the inside of a tiny wooden hut, and it was so hot and wet inside that it was difficult to breathe. Where was *this* place?

Tom stumbled across to the rough wooden door, gasping for air, and pushing it open he was hit by a wall of jungle noise. The sweet smell of decay was unbearable. Covering his nose to stop himself retching, Tom looked about him and to his astonishment found that he was standing in a clearing in a rainforest. Giant trees with huge snaking roots towered overhead, and the floor was littered with stinking yellow fruit, blooming green and purple with mould. There was something terrible about this rancid, rotting place, something so frightening and dangerous that even though he was pouring with sweat a cold shiver crept up Tom's spine. Something bad had happened here, he knew it, and when he looked up at the tree canopy he began to realize what it was. All around him pieces of shining metal and wisps of material were suspended in the branches, just like litter . . .

At that moment a jabbering gang of parrots chased each other across the clearing, and spinning round to watch them pass Tom noticed the remains of an aircraft's fuselage hanging directly behind him. Just above that was a blue seat, suspended in mid-air like a child's swing. Screwing up his eyes Tom saw a small black thing lolling inside it. The thing was wearing jeans, and it might once have had a face, but now that was little more than a dried-up husk. It looked as if something had been eating it . . . suddenly Tom's head began to spin.

The air crash . . . the jungle . . . a wave of nausea broke over him and falling to his knees upon the damp spongy earth Tom was violently sick.

So this was where Don Gervase and Lotus had come from . . . the air crash in the dark heart of the Amazon, which they alone survived. It was true. But they hadn't followed the raindrops at all, they had just stepped through this door . . . *into* Catcher Hall . . . The poisoned jungle swam all around him as Tom gulped for breath . . . who *were* these people? How did they know about these places? And how could he just follow them?

Feeling faint, Tom forced himself to his feet and clung onto the side of the small hut. There were more blue seats in the trees all around him, but Tom did not even want to look at the hideous figures strapped inside. All he wanted to do now was escape from this stinking nightmare. Stumbling back into the dark hut he slammed the door shut behind him and as he did so he caught sight of two red eyes glinting in the corner. There was a low angry hiss: a snake. In an instant the nightmare behind him was forgotten and every muscle in Tom's body tensed.

A snake.

Bursting through the door had probably woken it up. This was its home. How big was it? This was the rainforest—it could be massive. Tree python, anaconda, cobra. Tom peered hard into the darkness around the door. Keep calm, he told himself, snakes don't attack humans unless they are provoked, and he didn't want to provoke anything; all he wanted to do now was to return to that cupboard.

Please, Mr Snake, let me through that door.

Taking a deep breath Tom took a step forward and there was another angry hiss. Tom stopped dead. Perhaps it was a mother guarding her brood, perhaps it was a whole nest of snakes, maybe the hut was alive with them. Looking up into the hot darkness above him Tom instantly recoiled. It was. Angry red eyes glared at him from every corner, their bodies writhing and tangling, seemingly joined together like some horrible creeping coiling plant whose tentacles danced before him, ready to strike.

'Let me out!' he shouted into the heaving mass of eyes and bodies.

There was no reply.

'Right that's it,' he said firmly. 'Kill me if you want, I don't care!'

Ducking down low Tom sprinted under the slithering knot to the back wall and wrenched the door open. Stepping through into the cupboard he slammed the door hard shut behind him, and stood there in the total darkness, trembling uncontrollably. Where had he been? Through a gateway in time to hell. To hell—and back. Closing his eyes Tom felt hot tears begin to stream down his cheeks and he wept. He never wanted to go through that door again as long as he lived.

Pulling himself together, Tom recognized that his ordeal was far from over. Where were Don Gervase and Lotus? Why had they not followed him through this cupboard into the jungle? They must have assumed he would have escaped into the model and they had taken that route. Or were they still waiting for him, just outside the door? Tom pressed his ear to the door and listened. There was no sound out there; the house was absolutely silent. Not even the creak of Don Gervase's boots. Perhaps he should risk it.

Opening the cupboard door a fraction Tom peered out into the long picture gallery. It was empty; perhaps they had gone after all. If he could just tiptoe to the end and reach the stairs then at least he had a chance. He had to try: he couldn't stay here. Stepping silently out of the broom cupboard, Tom closed the door behind him and listened.

'I was beginning to wonder when you'd come back,' said a velvet voice.

The heavy embroidered curtains twitched once then a shadow slipped out between them. It was Lotus. She moved into the moonlight and stared at him curiously.

'You see, in the dark, it is very easy to make mistakes. I just wanted to make sure.'

She began to walk unhurriedly towards him, like a cat, and Tom instinctively took a step backwards. What was she going to do? There was something very cold and deliberate in her look, and Tom's fingers felt nervously for the nearest cupboard behind him.

'In case you're thinking of bolting, I'd better warn you that there are plenty of people waiting for you on the other side of that door.'

So *this* was the right cupboard. Thank you Lotus. Tom's fingers silently closed around the handle.

'They are not very nice.'

'You're not so very wonderful yourself.'

'I'm sorry that you feel that way Tom,' she said silkily, 'I thought we were friends.'

'Who are you and what do you want?' Tom blurted out.

'I might ask you the same thing,' she replied, slowly walking ever closer, 'though I see you have discovered our little secret. Not that it matters. You won't be keeping it for much longer.'

Her eyes narrowed cruelly and Tom did not reply. However he got inside the cupboard he would have to be very quick as Lotus was beginning to flex her fingers like a gymnast about to perform a stunt. Whatever crazy leaping karate kick she was about to execute would hit him in the next few seconds . . . somehow he had to stall her. And then he remembered how gullible she was.

'Yeah, but I wasn't really surprised, you know,' he said quickly, with as much nonchalance as he could manage. 'I never really *believed* that story about how it took you months and months to escape from the jungle.'

Lotus seemed somewhat taken aback. 'Oh? Why not?'

'Just the way you said it,' Tom continued, feeling bolder now. 'Didn't make sense, following water out of the rainforest. Because in the equatorial rainforest, water doesn't flow downhill; it flows *uphill*. Gravity works differently there, because of the equator.'

Lotus stopped walking for a moment. She was genuinely puzzled.

'Are you sure?'

'Definitely. Sir Henry told me. I'm surprised you never found that out. Remember it for next time, it'll sound a lot more convincing.'

'Oh.' Lotus seemed very confused. 'But—'

But Tom had gone. Quickly closing the cupboard door behind him he felt for the metal ring, and a moment later he had dived back into the cold dark warehouse and slithered into the black core of the nearest coil of ropes he could find.

'Did you see him?' screeched a whining voice.

'To zer left, I zink.'

'No, to the right, definitely right. Into the ropes.'

'Okey-dokey. Cover me vile I take a shot. On zer count of three: vun, two—'

Suddenly the door was flung open.

'Where is he?'

Lotus slammed the door angrily behind her, incensed that Tom had tricked her yet again.

'I thought Don Gervase specifically told you to net this door!'

'That's correct, miss, he did, but—'

'Well?'

'Ve zought, zeeing as we had zer shotguns, zey ver de best vay to bag him.'

'Shotguns?' she exploded. 'Shotguns! Supposing you idiots missed? Do you have any idea what's in these barrels?'

There was an embarrassed silence as Lotus strode up to the nearest barrel and ripped off the lid. Two small black shapes bearing weapons stood up from their hiding places and peered down into the dark water.

'Oh my good God,' whispered one, clearly terrified.

The other stood speechless, gazing at the soft white orbs floating there.

'Are zoze . . . are zey . . . ? No vay,' he stammered, 'no vay, no vay!'

'Precisely, you twits,' snapped Lotus angrily, 'need I say more?'

The effect on the two dark shapes was electrifying, they seemed to have been drilled to the spot.

'Now,' hissed Lotus, carefully enunciating every word so that they understood, 'he's in here somewhere. *Take a net and flush him out.*'

'Yes, miss.'

'For sure, Miss Lotus.'

The two black shapes moved back uncertainly and unhooked a net from the wall. Tom had no idea what they were talking about, but obviously those weird soft eggs in the barrels were so valuable that if he stuck as close to them as he could, they would never dare shoot him. It was his only chance. He had to take it.

Come on, Tom.

Slithering out of his hole on all fours Tom crept forward, edging his way around one barrel and then crawling on towards the next. There seemed to be far more of them in the warehouse than the last time he was here, and the stench of rotting fish oozing from their sticky sides was almost overpowering.

Ignore it. Smell won't kill you. Just get to the door.

Tom held his breath and kept going. Nothing could compare with that hell-hole he had just come from.

A minute later Tom had managed to crawl his way from one end of the warehouse to the other until he had reached the very last barrel. By now he was absolutely filthy, and his elbows and knees were rubbed raw. Never mind, he had made it this far, and they hadn't found him yet. Wiping the sweat away from his eyes Tom peered around the barrel at the rough wooden door that led down into the alley—what next? If there were people up here there were bound to be more guarding down below. Straining his ears Tom could just make out the shouts of men and seagulls outside. Could that be Don Gervase? Maybe, and it sounded as if there were others too: should he risk it? Tom thought of those long bony fingers twirling that dull, blueish blade and he shuddered.

No. There had to be another way out, a trapdoor perhaps, all warehouses had trapdoors, didn't they? Tom glanced nervously around him and in the corner he noticed three floorboards shorter than the rest. Could that be . . . ? Waiting until he heard Lotus and the two men moving across to the next row of barrels Tom crawled on his belly over to them and found that he was right, it was a trapdoor; at one edge were two long rusty hinges. Sliding back the bolt as silently as he could, Tom tugged at the heavy iron ring and found that it gave a little, but it was far too heavy for him to lift lying down. The only way to do this was to stand up, and as soon as he did that they would see him, surely. Tom stared at the iron ring, his heart hammering. What choice did he have? None. Sooner or later they were going to find him anyway.

Fortune favours the brave.

Springing to his feet Tom bent over the heavy trapdoor and yanked at it with all his might. The hinges protested, then gave way with a noisy shriek—and he was spotted.

'Zere he is! Zere he is! Zere, by zer door!'

Tom didn't dare look back. Lowering himself quickly through the trapdoor he clung on to the rim by his fingertips and glanced at a pile of fishing nets beneath him. How far was that? Four metres, five even, but the footsteps were clattering in his ears and there was nothing for it. Tom let go, and in an instant the dark green nets came rushing up towards him and swallowed him up. There was silence.

'Don't vorry, miss, he von't get far,' barked a voice from high above.

Tom opened his eyes to see two thin, ratty faces leering down at him through the trapdoor. It was Shadrack and Skink. Shadrack grinned hideously, and ran a finger across his stringy neck.

'Bye bye, Tom Scatterhorn,' he spat, and disappeared.

Tom's heart was pounding in his temples now, he must escape, but how—where to?

Think, Tom, think fast.

Scrabbling up out of the nets he glanced over towards the open doorway where a gang of burly stevedores in black oilskins were unloading barrels from a sledge. One by one they were carefully rolling them down a gangplank and into the warehouse. Could he give himself up to them, explain that he was about to be killed, and hope that they would protect him? Tom squinted at the heavy sweating faces of the men glistening in the lantern light . . . no, some sixth sense told him that they couldn't be trusted, and those barrels looked exactly the same as the ones on the floor above. But supposing . . .

Tom had no time to finish his train of thought: suddenly his head was yanked backwards violently, and he was dragged back off the pile of nets behind a wooden crate. Tom lashed out with all his might, kicking hard into the shins behind him and in desperation sank his teeth into the hand clasped over his mouth. There was a grunt and at once the grip was released, and Tom spun round, ready to fight or run for his life.

His attacker was not a stevedore; nor was it Shadrack, or Skink, or even Lotus Askary. It was a hungry-faced boy not much bigger than himself, dressed in ragged clothes tied together with bits of string, and a woollen cap. Tom recognized him instantly. It was Abel.

'Did you have to do that!' he whispered savagely. Abel thrust his bitten hand between his legs and rubbed it hard.

'I'm sorry . . . I thought—'

'Ssssh,' hissed Abel putting a finger to his lips, 'it ain't safe in here at all.'

Glancing nervously towards the open doorway he saw Shadrack and Skink appear in the alley and start remonstrating with the men. One of them pointed a boathook in their direction.

'What are you doing here?' whispered Tom.

'Stealin', same as yous,' said Abel quietly, still rubbing his sore hand.

Looking up he saw a gang of stevedores now making their way towards the pile of nets. One of them was carrying an axe.

'Look's like they've got a bead on you. Follow me quick.'

With that Abel ducked down and scurried back through the tangle of barrels and boxes towards the dark end of the warehouse.

'All the best mice have their own holes,' he grimaced as they arrived in the corner, and pulling back a loose timber Abel disappeared out into the snow. Tom followed through after him and soon they were running through a maze of narrow alleys and wooden walkways that seemed to connect all the warehouses together.

'Where are we going?' asked Tom breathlessly as they came to a small plank bridge. Abel looked down carefully before scampering across into the shadow of the next building.

'You'll see soon enough. Come on.'

Tom followed, and together they crept down the edge of a large brick maltings until they reached a tiny shack, barely bigger than a dog kennel, perched on the edge of the ice. Abel glanced quickly in either direction, then he beckoned Tom inside.

'It's safe in here,' he whispered.

Tom still did not understand why there was such secrecy but he went along with it. Inside the shack there were a couple of wooden boxes and a rough woollen blanket rolled up on the floor: nothing else. Abel looked carefully out of the window before closing the door behind him.

'So Tom Scatterhorn, you's a warehouse rat like me now. I didn't see that one comin'.'

'I'm not a thief exactly,' replied Tom, remembering the small blue bottle still pressed hard in his pocket. 'I'm—'

'Well what the hell you doin' in Askary's warehouse, then?' Abel spat savagely into the dirt. What indeed? It was easier to lie.

'OK, yes I am.'

'Well, I'd be careful if I was yous. Them men they's got there is no better than dogs. They'll kill you now if they catch yer.'

'I know,' said Tom grimly; that was definitely true. 'What were you doing in there?'

'Findin' stuff to sell,' he replied belligerently. 'What else can I do now I'm on me tod?'

Tom looked around him: so this tiny hut was Abel's home. He had nothing more than a blanket.

'What about your mum?'

A shadow passed across Abel's face and he punched his fist violently into the palm of his hand.

'Mum's gone,' he said bitterly, 'taken wi' all the others for the new 'sylum. Somethin' for all 'em doctors to study, no doubt.' He cracked his fist into his hand again. 'She's never come back.'

Tom did not understand. 'Doctors? What doctors?'

'En't you seen 'em? They're all over Dragonport. Invaded the bloomin' place. Askary's got 'em 'ere for a conference or somethin' up there at the 'sylum.' Abel spat in the direction of Catcher Hill. 'Boatloads of 'em keeps arrivin'—look.' He nodded over his shoulder at the river.

Tom stood up next to Abel and squinted out through the small greasy window towards the ice fair. Out on the ice a dark mass of skaters moved in unison around the ice palace. There were children with toboggans, marzipan sellers, and couples skating arm in arm, but as he looked closer Tom saw that Abel was right: almost every other skater was a small, bony-faced man, wearing a wide-brimmed hat lined with fur and a long black coat, just like Skink and Shadrack. Tom looked across to the waterfront and he saw more doctors, walking up and down the stalls in pairs, idling in front of shop windows and swarming through the streets from the docks. Everywhere he looked there were more of them, there must have been tens of thousands gathering.

Tom shrank back from the window; he was shaken to the core. Was *this* what Don Gervase was talking about, the Contagion, or something like that? Was this all some part of a great plan? Perhaps it was . . . Tom felt a cold knot of fear tighten in his stomach as he began to realize that somehow he must be part of that great plan too; and now that Don Gervase knew he had the bottle, he was almost certainly at the very heart of it. Unconsciously Tom's hand drifted up to the small shape nestling in his pocket: it was still there. At this moment, it was the only thing that might keep him alive. Tom swallowed hard.

'Abel, you have to help me escape.'

'I do?' said Abel sarcastically. 'Sure, where do you want to go? Australia, Africa, America, take your pick. As you can see I'm mister moneybags.'

'Please,' pleaded Tom, with real desperation in his voice, 'I mean it. If I don't, then I am dead.'

Abel's eyes narrowed. Glancing across into Tom's face he saw that his fear was real enough. He spat roughly on the floor.

'Escape? Like how?'

Tom tried to think . . . how could he escape from that great multitude? Staring out across the river he saw a dark line of trees about a mile distant, and in the middle of them there was the twinkle of lights.

'What are those lights over there?'

'River pilot's cottage,' snorted Abel, 'Burdo Yarker.'

Burdo Yarker . . . the name was familiar. A tiny memory flickered in Tom's mind.

'Did he have an ear trumpet?' he asked, trying to remember the ancient old man in the blue velvet coat who had arrived for the opening of the museum.

'That's the boy. Deaf as a post.'

'Didn't he used to take eggs out of nests and put them in his mouth?'

Abel looked at him curiously. 'Well he *might* a' done; he was certainly daft enough. A good friend of August Catcher, I recall.'

Tom's heart leapt. Burdo Yarker, a friend of August's, he would help him, surely.

'Do you think the ice would be thick enough to skate across there?'

'Mebbe,' replied Abel with a shrug.

'Do you have any skates?'

'Mebbe so.'

'Could I borrow them?'

Abel contemplated the dark mass of men swarming over the ice. A resigned expression flickered in his eyes.

'Please, Abel?'

'They're Noah's,' he muttered quietly, 'all I got left of him. But he liked yous, Tom, so I don't see why not.'

Turning round, Abel reached behind the boxes that did for his bed and pulled out a small hessian bag. Inside was a brand new pair of leather skates, polished and in perfect condition.

'Bought these with that sovereign Mr August gave us, remember?'

'I do.'

Abel stroked the dull red leather fondly, and wiped the shining steel blades with his cuff.

'He were dead fast in these wern'ee?'

'He was.'

The two boys looked down at the skates in silence for a moment, each lost in their own memories of Noah.

'Well, you's about his size so they should just about fit,' said Abel at last, and he thrust the skates roughly into Tom's arms.

'You best get 'em on an' get goin'. They're sure to find this place soon enough.'

Spitting harshly on the floor, Abel turned back to the window once more and stood guard. Tom could see that his eyes had filled with tears.

Five minutes later they had left the hut and were standing further up the frozen river close to a small jetty. Tom had Noah's skates laced up as tightly as he could manage, and his own shoes tucked into the pockets of his fleece. Abel looked down at the skates admiringly.

'How's they feelin'—all right?'

'Fine.'

'Good. An' how's *you* feelin'?'

Tom smiled bravely, struggling to hide his nerves. There before him the ice was swarming with doctors, making their slow leisurely circles round the ice palace. Supposing they recognized him? What then? Shivering slightly in the wind, he pulled his woollen hat down low over his ears and took a long deep breath.

'If I was yous I'd go round with 'em till the edge of the stalls, then dead straight,' whispered Abel, pointing at the tiny lights twinkling on the far shore, 'that's where the ice is thickest. And don't whatever you do catch any of 'em in the eye. They're all in league together.'

Tom grunted, and at that moment there was a crack of splitting wood behind them. The two boys spun round to see an enormous stevedore in black oilskins smashing down the door of Abel's miserable dog kennel with an axe. When it was done, the bony-faced doctor standing beside him marched inside.

'See what I mean?' said Abel ruefully. 'They're on to both of us now. An' once they've started they never stop. Ever. Best be off meself.' Turning back to Tom he gave him the briefest of nods.

'Bye now, mate. Good luck.'

'Bye.'

Tom watched as Abel's spare frame loped away towards the dark warren of buildings.

'And thanks.'

Abel turned to give him a quick thumbs up sign, then glancing quickly in either direction he slipped between two warehouses and was gone. Right, thought Tom. Just go dead straight.

Starting out in a slow rhythm, Tom found that the long blades of Noah's skates cut hard into the ice and soon he was making good speed. In no time at all he was amongst the chattering crowd of doctors and, keeping his eyes well down, he slowed to listen to the gabble of conversation all around him.

'They say he's actually found it.'

'Yes, that's what I'd heard.'

'Then they'll certainly announce it—'

'From Mongolia to Canada—'

'Everywhere, on every continent—'

'He'll be elected this time for sure—'

'Which will mark the dawn—'

'Of a new world order—'

And so it went on, hundreds of identical voices finishing each other's sentences and talking to each other at the same time. Was that Don Gervase they were talking about, and was 'it' August's potion? Tom didn't know and at this moment he didn't care; the small blue bottle was still in his pocket, and that was all that mattered. All he had to do was to take it across the ice to safety.

Breaking away from the crowd, Tom skated away through the last of the stalls and struck out across moonlit ice beyond. Urging himself on, Tom began to take longer and longer strokes until the glittering ice started to blur dizzily beneath him. Ahead of him the twinkling lights of the cottage were gradually growing ever nearer.

Keep straight. That's where the ice is thickest.

His legs were burning now, and gulping in the cold night air Tom glanced over to his left where he could just make out the ghostly wicker barriers around the hole that had swallowed up Noah. That was halfway.

Keep going. Dead straight.

Bending forward Tom lengthened his strides and his skates began to hiss. Swish . . . swash . . . swish . . . swash . . . this was great, he was going to make it; all he had to do was keep that rhythm going. Ten strokes later Tom looked up again, but this time something ahead of him had changed: the lights of the cottage had disappeared, and in their place there was an inky blue mist that seemed to be rolling over the ice towards him. A sea mist, thought Tom as he panted hard, a har, as his mum used to say.

But wait . . . the trees above the mist on the far side seemed to be moving too, like antlers silhouetted against the sky. What was happening out there? Tom broke off his rhythm and skidded abruptly to a halt. Catching his breath, he squinted up into the dark cloud of blue mist that was swirling ahead of him. Something was not right . . . it was almost as if the whole far shore of the river had started to move.

And then he heard it. Drumming. Hooves, drumming on the ice like thunder. And they seemed to be getting louder; getting closer. Tom's blood froze: out of the mist something dark was coming towards him fast, and the ice all around him was starting to swell and rumble and shake like an earthquake. Seconds later a large sledge emerged out of the blue mist, pulled by a pair of wild-eyed black horses. Standing above them, cracking a huge whip, was the unmistakable figure of Don Gervase, his domed head glittering like steel in the moonlight. Beside him stood Lotus, her long black hair billowing behind her, holding some sort of crossbow under her arm. They were coming straight at him, and they both looked completely insane.

CHAPTER 23

One Blue Bottle

So this was how it would end.

Blindly Tom turned back, and the distant lights of the stalls began to swim before his eyes. They were so, so far away. Somehow he forced himself to start skating once more, but he had no speed, his legs felt sluggish and cold, as if he had been running a race and just as he was about to cross the finishing line it had suddenly disappeared out of sight. He lunged on mechanically, like a robot, knowing in his heart that this was not a race he could ever hope to win; that terrifying sledge was galloping closer with every second, there was no way he could outskate it now. Don Gervase had been right all along: he had got involved in something far bigger than he had ever dreamed of. Hot tears of frustration welled up inside him as the rumbling hooves grew louder and louder. He hadn't asked to be any part of this, but if they wanted to kill him, fine: let them, he'd had enough. It was over, and all Tom wanted to do now was to curl up in a ball and cry. But somehow an angry little flame kept blazing deep inside him, refusing to let him stop . . .

Thonk!

Something silver flashed past Tom's ear, and instinctively he dodged left.

What was that . . . ?

Then came another, fizzing past his other shoulder and whanging off the ice ahead of him. Lotus's arrows! The next shot would certainly find its mark. Instinctively Tom hunched up his shoulders and he screwed up his eyes . . . it must come now, surely. This was the end. His neck burned, waiting for that arrow . . . go on, fire it . . . just fire it! Fire the crossbow, you stupid girl . . .

Then, quite suddenly, a great rush of air whooshed overhead.

'Tom!' shouted a familiar voice.

Looking up Tom glimpsed the huge dark shadow of the eagle wheeling ahead of him in the moonlight.

'Grab the rope, mate! I ain't comin' down any lower!'

The rope? What rope? There! Bumping along the ice just ahead of him was a thick hemp rope! The other end trailed upwards into the sky and fastened around the bird's neck. Suddenly a tiny spark of hope leapt in Tom's heart. He had a chance.

'Quick!' shouted the eagle. 'We ain't got all day!'

Ignoring the thundering hooves roaring behind him, Tom sprinted after the trailing rope with every ounce of strength he had left. Swish swash . . . swish . . . swash . . . swish . . . swash . . . closer . . . closer . . . almost there . . .

'Come on!' shouted the bird, glancing back nervously at the sledge.

Three more strokes, two more . . .

Come on, Tom!

His lungs were bursting but he was almost level with it. Almost . . . he could hear the harnesses jangling, the wild-eyed horses snorting . . . the ice shook . . . one more . . . just one—suddenly he lunged at the rope and grabbed hold with both hands. The sledge seemed to be almost on top of him and the next second he lurched forward with a terrific jolt. Tom staggered dangerously but somehow managed to stay on his feet as he shot away across the ice. Another arrow slammed past his shoulder but Tom ignored it and leaning back like a water skier behind a speedboat he began to accelerate, faster and faster and faster, till the wall of wind screamed in his ears and his skates fizzed.

Hold on Tom, for God's sake. Hold on . . .

'Tom!' shouted the great bird. 'Ready to fly?'

Tom gripped tighter, ignoring the pain in his fingers, and he barely had time to reply before he felt the bird start to rise . . . but at that moment a dart of silver flashed past Tom's head and sliced clean through the rope ahead of him. Only three strands remained . . .

'Don't!' screamed Tom desperately, staring in horror at the slender twisting strands just beyond his reach. 'It's cut! The rope! It's cut!'

The bird glanced down at the almost severed rope and cursed loudly.

'All right!' it hollered. 'Just . . . do what you can, mate! Hold on!'

The great bird dropped lower and began to accelerate hard. The speed was truly terrifying now—Tom had never been as fast as this in his life. Showers of moonlit ice crystals cascaded from the back of his blades and he rocketed across the moonlit river. Somehow the three small strands were holding . . .

Please don't break now . . . don't break . . .

Shooting a glance over his shoulder he saw Don Gervase grimace and crack his whip hard across the horses' flanks urging them on ever faster, but Tom was pulling away.

'Look out down there!' shouted the eagle, and the very next moment Tom felt himself lurch crazily to the right and he was in amongst the stalls of the ice fair. Oh no! This was madness! Terrified bony-faced men flashed past him as he weaved desperately in and out of the stalls, barely struggling to stay on his feet.

'Stop that boy this instant!' roared Don Gervase.

Screams of panic erupted all around as the sledge thundered headlong into the ice fair after him, scattering skating couples, stallholders and doctors in all directions.

'Kill him!' shrieked Lotus.

But no one dared stand in Tom's way for fear of being mown down by the galloping sledge. Suddenly the ice palace loomed up out of the darkness.

'Go left!' shouted the great bird. 'Left!'

Tom saw it too late, and veering wildly to the right he smashed into a tall man holding a large grey wolfhound on a leash. In a moment the rope had slipped from his grasp and he was knocked head-over-heels onto his back, spinning helplessly across the ice as the momentum carried him forward. Grasping desperately for the rope still just trailing ahead of him, Tom's fingers closed instead around the leash of the dog.

'There he is!' screeched a doctor, watching Tom spinning out of control. 'Stop that boy this instant!'

'And then kill him!'

'Yes, that's what they said!'

'Stop him then kill him!'

'Stop him then kill him! Stop him then kill him!'

Tom lay helpless on the ice as the dark mass of chanting men raced after him and closed in all around.

'No . . . please . . . please,' whispered Tom, 'don't.'

A cold pair of hands grabbed at his skates as a great beating of wings thundered overhead.

'The leash Tom, do not let go, whatever you do!'

The very next second Tom's shoulders were almost wrenched from their sockets as the wolfhound took off, pulling Tom's feet clean out of his skates and dragging him headfirst on his back through the crowd. Tom felt thin white hands tearing at him as he sped away through a chaos of skates and hands and faces, knocked out of the way by the powerful grey dog. Don Gervase could not believe it; his face was purple with anger.

'Clear out of my way!' he roared, and hauling the sledge around the ice palace he cracked the whip hard across the horses' flanks and set off in hot pursuit. Tom squinted up at the stalls spinning giddily past his head and there was the eagle banking in behind him. Thundering down inches above the ice the bird muttered something into the wolfhound's ear in an ancient language that Tom could not understand.

'Don't go back to Catcher Hall!' called the eagle as it wheeled up high above the wharves. 'Hide in the museum! He'll take you there!'

Whatever the eagle had said only forced the hound to gallop even faster, and they were rapidly approaching the old bridge just below the Scatterhorn Museum. Very soon the ice would run out and somehow he would have to let go of the leash, but it was so tightly wound around Tom's wrist there was no way he could force it loose. Hide in the museum, the last refuge: if only he could.

The old bridge was almost upon them when suddenly a dull 'thonk' split the air just above Tom's head and in an instant he was spinning free, careering past the wolfhound which lay crumpled on the ice with a steel arrow quivering in its neck.

'Now we have him!' came a high shout.

Glancing back, Tom saw Lotus grinning manically next to Don Gervase as he brought the steaming horses skidding to a halt. The next shot would be her last. Ratcheting up the bow, she placed a delicate steel arrow in the groove and brought the crossbow to her shoulder. Levelling the sights she took aim as Tom scrambled desperately up the small slope and onto the bridge.

'Shall I?'

Lotus's lips had parted and her face was flushed with excitement. She would not miss this time.

'Yes?'

'Wait!' commanded Don Gervase. His eyes narrowed as Tom staggered up the steps of the museum.

'But he's going to get away!'

Tom threw himself at the door, frantically trying to force it open. Don Gervase watched him struggle and the ghost of a smile flickered across his lips.

'Oh no he's not,' he muttered, and a wolfish grin split his face, 'on the contrary, he's—'

Lotus was not listening any more.

'Too late, Tom,' she whispered, and her finger began to squeeze the trigger. 'Goodbye.'

'I said NO!'

With one sweep of his bony hand Don Gervase smashed the crossbow clean out of her shoulder and it clattered harmlessly down onto the ice. Lotus stared up at him in disbelief, her huge eyes blazing with fury.

'Why did you do that!' she screamed petulantly. 'Why why why! It's so unfair, you never let me kill any of them!'

'Temper, young Lotus! Really,' he snorted, jumping down onto the snow.

'You said—'

'I have changed my mind,' he interrupted, glancing up at Tom as he finally managed to force the museum door open just wide enough to fall inside. 'That boy is extraordinarily devious, so I need to make *absolutely* sure. And in there, where that ridiculous bird cannot possibly help him, I will make sure—believe me.'

Lotus shot him a sulky look but Don Gervase ignored it.

'You'll get *another* chance, I guarantee it. Just carry out everything as I instructed, and we shall meet on the other side. Shortly.'

Lotus was still far too angry to speak. She rubbed her bruised shoulder and stared crossly at the horses' backs.

'I shall take that as yes. Good. Thank you, Lotus. Now leave this wretched Tom Scatterhorn to me.'

And turning on his heel he scurried up the hill.

The inside of the museum was as cold and dark as Tom remembered it. Even though he was back in the past, and the animals were almost new, there was a musty smell of old rags hanging in the air. What next? Tom was so tired he felt he could barely stand up. Spots danced before his eyes as he staggered into the main hall. Where to hide?

Scratching his head desperately, he turned to face the shaggy brown mass of the mammoth. That was the place, high up there on its back. If only he could get there . . .

'Looking for something?' enquired a low, booming voice that sounded as if it came from a long way away but was in fact very close. Tom was startled; then he remembered that he shouldn't be. His throat was so dry he could barely speak.

'A lift?' he croaked. 'Please?'

The beady eyes twinkled down at him. 'Why of course, old boy,' boomed the mammoth, 'nothing ventured nothing gained and all that.'

In one quick move the hairy trunk curled around Tom's waist and picked him clean off the ground, setting him down gently on the thick carpet of fur. And at that moment the door banged open.

'Well, well, well.'

Don Gervase stalked into the hall, his heels scratching on the flagstones.

'Where better place to hide than in the Scatterhorn Museum?'

Reaching the centre of the room he spun around like a dancer, his eyes darting over each case in turn.

'I should like a word with you, Tom Scatterhorn, wherever you are.' His bark echoed away into the ringing silence. 'NOW!'

There was still no sound.

'Fine,' said Don Gervase, proceeding to take off his leather gloves finger by finger. 'No doubt you can hear every word I am saying. This game of cat and mouse has gone on so long as to become almost tedious, so I shan't waste my time trying to flush you out again.'

Folding his gloves neatly into his pocket he began pacing about the hall in short mechanical steps.

'As maybe you are aware,' he droned, 'tomorrow, back in *your* time, of course, I formally take possession of the Scatterhorn Museum. When that happens, everything in this museum will belong to me, and I shall be able to do exactly what I want with it. Now, *what* I want is really very simple. After that rat's miraculous recovery *I know precisely what it is*, and, after your little adventure in my study, no doubt you do too. Which incidentally,' he added, 'I haven't quite forgiven you for yet.' Don Gervase glowered menacingly into the gloom. 'But I might be persuaded.'

Seeing that there was still no sign of movement, Don Gervase stopped his pacing and drew a long slim cigar out of his breast pocket.

'So I am presented with a choice,' he went on, eyeing the dodo. 'Either I can stick to my original plan and rip every bird and beast in this place apart, limb from limb, until eventually I find what I am looking for . . . ' Don Gervase paused to strike a match on the pillar, and puffed hard until the end of his cigar burned red hot, 'or not, as the case may be. But you may rest assured that whatever life these creatures have now, it will cease entirely by the time I have finished with them.'

The tall thin man held the lighted match between his fingers, watching it burn.

'What a curious thing fire is,' he murmured, passing his long bony hand back and forth through the flame without flinching, 'so useful to some and yet so destructive to others.'

With a puff he blew the match out and casually threw his arm around the dodo's neck.

'Aaaaah!'

The dodo let out a piercing scream and began thrashing about wildly in Don Gervase's hand, but the harder she struggled the tighter his long bony fingers held her in a vice-like grip. Slowly but surely his lit cigar began to burn a hole in the back of her head.

'Please!' she shrieked desperately. 'No, please don't, don't! DON'T!'

Tom couldn't stand it any longer. Leaping to his feet on the back of the mammoth he looked down at Don Gervase gripping the frantic dodo by the neck.

'NO!' he shouted angrily. 'STOP IT!'

'So there you are,' sneered Don Gervase, 'I wondered when you would show your face.'

The dodo was writhing in agony as white smoke began to pour out of the back of her head.

'Stop doing that!'

'But why?' replied Don Gervase casually, holding the thrashing bird down. 'Why delay the inevitable? There is just so little time for so much pain.'

The dodo was screaming even louder now, and Tom's blood was boiling.

'All right!' he shouted. 'Put it out and I'll come down!'

'Just as you wish,' smiled Don Gervase, releasing the bird at once and cuffing it hard around the head. The dodo collapsed onto the floor and began sobbing violently.

'Oh do shut up, you appalling creature,' he snarled, kicking it viciously with his toe. The dodo groaned and continued to whimper quietly to itself, rubbing its singed feathers on the floor.

Tom slithered down the mammoth's trunk and jumped to the ground, feeling so angry that he was ready to launch himself straight at Don Gervase's chest, forgetting that he was a skinny eleven-year-old boy and Don Gervase was an immensely tall, fully grown man. Somehow he managed to control his temper, and took up a position across the hall with his back to the door. All Tom's tiredness was forgotten now, and he stood tensed and quivering with rage, waiting for Don Gervase to make the first move. But the tall bony man did not look the least bit interested in fighting; he merely leant against a pillar, puffing on his thin cigar.

'That's better,' he said casually, 'I prefer to have our little chat tête-a-tête as they say.'

Tom grunted savagely. This was obviously yet another act.

'You have something of mine, I believe,' said Don Gervase slowly, 'a bottle. A small, blue bottle.'

Tom did not move a muscle, but he knew from the bulge in his pocket that it was still there.

'Why do you want it?' he said thickly.

'So you *do* still have it.' Don Gervase exhaled luxuriously. 'Well that *is* good, as that bottle contains something I have been searching for, for a very, very long time.'

Tom peered at Don Gervase uneasily. In the half-light the crease down the centre of his forehead seemed to pulse as he fixed him with his milky yellow eyes.

'You see, Tom,' Don Gervase went on, his voice dropping down to a dangerous growl, 'though we have met before, in your present, I am not who you think I am. I am an *employee*. Isn't that extraordinary? Highly prized and talented as I am, but nevertheless, *a worker*; working for a higher purpose. And my job is to find certain things, shall we say, that are very useful . . . *elsewhere*, shall we say. In the *future*, shall we say, which is why your little bottle is very important to me, and to us, and indeed, to them. My . . . people.'

'Your people?' Tom stared at him angrily. 'What, those ridiculous men dressed as doctors out there?'

'Correct. Some of them are here, and there are many, many more elsewhere.'

'What do they care about it?'

'They probably don't care about it very much at all,' explained Don Gervase, puffing greedily on his cigar, 'because they are not like you and, to some extent, me. They do not enjoy the luxury of a long adult life to expand their minds and civilize themselves. They are basically *earthy* types. Juvenile, delinquent if you like; but it's not their fault. They spend so long, *so long*, growing up, believe me, that by the time they . . . they . . . ' Don Gervase paused a moment as he searched for the right word, '*mature*, shall we say, there simply isn't time to teach them all that there is to know beyond basic skills. Such as how to imitate their brothers and sisters, how to hold a knife and fork, eat with their mouth closed, use the toilet, that sort of thing.'

'And kill people?'

'Indeed, that too: but killing *is* a basic skill, don't you think? It rarely requires much intellect, just brute force. Which is why,' his mouth curved into a mean smile, 'even *you* managed to evade them. Even *you* were much too clever for them. Most of this rabble are from the lower orders, half-wits if the truth were known. But they *will* find you and kill you in the end. There are simply too many of them.'

Tom did not doubt it. He shifted uneasily from one foot to the other as Don Gervase blew a thin plume of smoke out into the moonlight, then stared at him so hard Tom felt as if he was looking right through his skull into his brain.

'Of course, I could always call them off, *if* I wanted to,' Don Gervase continued in his reasonable tone. 'You see, Tom, keeping that bottle harms no one but yourself. We both know that I will get what I want sooner or later, and it just so happens that sooner would suit me better. So, that's why I am prepared to make you a deal.' Don Gervase's eyes narrowed to little more than slits, and they held Tom like a magnet. 'Supposing I said to you that I *would* be prepared to call off my people. And not only that, I would also give you this entire museum, in return for that little bottle in your pocket. How does that sound?'

This really was the very last thing Tom was expecting, and it took a second or two for him to conceal his surprise. His first instinct was to suspect that this was one more trick, and somewhere deep inside him a voice was telling him not to hand over the bottle; and yet . . .

'Why should I trust you?' asked Tom uncertainly.

'You have good reason not to,' replied Don Gervase smoothly, 'I am not quite sure that I would even trust myself. So you will just have to take me at my word. Time is of the essence, Tom, and at this moment, that little blue bottle is all I want. When you give it to me, I promise that you will never see either me or those doctors ever again.'

Tom hesitated: how could he believe a single word Don Gervase was saying? Reason said he couldn't. Whatever promises he made might be entirely worthless, but standing here in the cold moonlight, what choice did he really have? The moment he stepped outside that door those legions of thin, bony-faced doctors would chase him once more, and Don Gervase was right, they would kill him in the end: there *were* simply too many of them. Even if by some miracle he did manage to escape—what then? Don Gervase would buy the museum and destroy it. Now he knew what he was looking for, and he was bound to find enough traces of hyacinths and floor polish somewhere amongst all those animals to serve whatever vile purpose he had in mind. Glancing around into the shadowy cases Tom realized that they were all staring at him: the gorilla, the mammoth, the anaconda, the proboscis monkey, the pangolin, the antelope . . . even the tiger. Should they all be sacrificed because of his stubborn nature? Tom was faltering now, and Don Gervase could see it; the ghost of a smile flickered across his lips as the orange glow of his cigar cast a cruel shadow across his face. He knew that he had so nearly caught his fish . . .

Swallowing hard, Tom reached into his pocket and took out the small blue bottle of August's potion, turning it over in the palm of his hand. What *was* the point of keeping it? After all, it was just a small, empty bottle. Until this moment, it had kept him alive. Now, if he held on to it, it was going to kill him. Don Gervase's eyes glittered as he watched the bottle revolve in Tom's hand. So close now . . . so close . . . come on little fishy . . .

Tom's heart was beating so fast he could hardly think. Desperately he racked his brains, trying to find something, anything he could possibly use to make Don Gervase keep his word, because at this moment, believing Don Gervase was all that he had left.

'Tell me if my parents are all right,' he blurted out.

Don Gervase looked so surprised that he might have burst out laughing. 'What?' he spluttered.

'Tell me that or I will drop it!' said Tom fiercely, and suddenly held out the bottle by its slender neck above the stone floor. 'TELL ME NOW!'

'No, no, don-don-don't do that!' stammered Don Gervase, his eyes bulging. 'But how can I *possibly* know where they are?'

'You told me once that they were in great danger, and then you said they might die, you must know!'

Don Gervase recognized from the harsh tone in Tom's voice that he was deadly serious. Opening his fingers Tom began to let the bottle slip down.

'All right! All right! They're OK, I promise,' growled Don Gervase, his eyes fixed on the small blue bottle pinched between Tom's fingers.

'How do I know that you're not lying?'

'I'm not! I'm not lying! Why on earth would I be?'

'Good,' said Tom pushing his advantage, 'because if you *are* lying, the eagle will know about it.'

'The eagle?'

'Yes, that revolting bird as you call him. And all the others like him. We're in league together.'

Tom was bluffing wildly now, but for some reason Don Gervase was not aware of it. Little beads of sweat began to glitter on his brow.

'All in league together, eh?' he snarled sarcastically.

'That's right. Every single one of us.'

'Hmm.' Don Gervase muttered to himself, his fingers twisting around each other like eels. 'I always suspected as much.'

'And we'll be watching you, wherever you are, make no mistake.'

Don Gervase's hand flew up to his chest and he began to scratch viciously, and Tom was both pleased and rather shocked that this empty threat had somehow hit its mark. For the very first time, for whatever reason, Don Gervase appeared to be taking him seriously—if *only* he knew why! Would this threat force Don Gervase to keep his word? He had no idea, but he had pushed it as far as he dared already, and at this moment it was the best he could do. After all, Don Gervase still held all the cards.

'That's fine,' he said huskily, pulling himself together, 'I have absolutely no problem with that; none whatsoever, it's a deal. Now, hand it over, boy.'

'OK, I will,' said Tom boldly. 'Catch!'

In one move he threw the small blue bottle across the hall to Don Gervase, who was so surprised that he fumbled and juggled and almost dropped it.

'Thank you, Tom,' he sneered breathlessly, cradling the bottle to his chest. 'Thank you very much indeed. You really have no idea what pleasure this gives me.'

Recovering his composure, Don Gervase carefully held the empty blue bottle up to the moonlight.

'At last,' he murmured, 'at long, long last, the elixir has been found; *I* have found it.' Don Gervase was panting a little, and his forehead was sweating and bulging in a most curious way.

'You're a brave boy, Tom, most resourceful for one so young. It's a shame, as I had hoped that one day perhaps you could become—' A bead of sweat ran down the tip of his nose onto his upper lip, and his thin tongue darted out to lick it off. 'But alas, no; just like everyone else in the end, so . . . sentimental. Why *is* that, I wonder?'

Tom shrugged his shoulders, he had no idea what Don Gervase was talking about. He was behaving so strangely that Tom wondered if he might have finally gone mad.

'Still, there it is.'

Don Gervase slipped the bottle into his breast pocket and patted it fondly. Taking out his matches he paused to relight his cigar. Tom watched him nervously.

'So . . . so you're going to keep your promise then?'

Don Gervase puffed on the match and watched the flame grow higher and higher.

'Promises; parents; sweet, furry creatures that talk, honestly Tom—it's tragic.' He smiled at Tom hideously and blew a thick cloud of smoke out of his nose. 'No wonder you're almost extinct.'

And with that Don Gervase flicked the burning match at the mammoth.

CHAPTER 24

FUTURE IMPERFECT

For a moment, time stood still. The eyes of every animal in the museum watched as the tiny dart of fire spun through the darkness and landed halfway up the mammoth's flank.

'No,' gasped Tom as the match smouldered tantalizingly, then a long strand of shaggy coat glowed red and burst into flame. A moment later there was a terrible hissing rush as the mammoth flared up like a mountain of straw.

'Fire!' screeched the parrot. 'Fire down below!'

The museum erupted with shrieks and roars and howls as the animals clamoured in their cases.

'Holy baloney!' whistled the proboscis monkey scrabbling out of his case. 'Don't panic, don't panic!' In an instant he was swinging around the museum opening every cabinet with his fingers and toes. One after another every creature that could leapt to the ground and raced towards the mammoth, frantically stamping and patting at the flames with their hooves and paws. In a moment Tom ripped off his jacket and he was beside them, beating down the flames in a frenzy, and out of the corner of his eye he spotted Don Gervase slinking quietly up the stairs with a gruesome smirk on his face. Where was he going? There was no time to worry about that at this moment; the fire was quickly taking hold.

'Sorry to be a bore, old chap,' boomed the mammoth to the gorilla as the flames licked around his legs, 'you couldn't possibly bring us one of the firebuckets by the door, could you? Feeling a little warm.'

'Of course,' panted the gorilla, lolloping over to the door and staggering back with two buckets of water in his hand.

'Thanks old boy.'

Sucking a bucket dry with its trunk the mammoth blasted the water at his back.

'Quite remarkable how flammable one really is,' he muttered, emptying the second bucket in the same fashion.

By now every bird that could was swooping through the smoke, momentarily landing on the mammoth's burning back and pressing their wings on the flames for as long as they dared before taking off again. But the rapid beating of their wings only seemed to make matters worse, and the museum was rapidly filling with acrid black smoke.

'Somehow I don't think this is working,' sighed the mammoth, flailing this way and that with his trunk, 'becoming rather painful, in fact.'

'Never give up, brother mammoth!' came a squeak from below. 'Rise up above the fires of Gilgamesh!'

At the base of one huge flaming foot a legion of mice were beating the flames with tiny dead leaves in a blurry rhythm, all chanting together.

'Slowly but surely!'

'Our hands are small!'

'Slowly but surely!'

'And our sticks may be little!'

'But with a slice of luck!'

'And lashings of pluck!'

'Panic not! We'll have you out of this pickle!'

'That's the spirit, lads,' squeaked the preacher mouse staring up at the towering inferno above him. 'It may take time, but—'

'There is no time!' shouted the anteater. 'Look!'

Suddenly an enormous fireball burst out around the mammoth's middle, and with a shriek the animals scattered before the ferocious heat.

'Is it serious?' boomed the mammoth above the flames.

The gorilla stared in horror as the crackling flames licked higher towards the ceiling.

'I think it might be, old chap.'

'Oh what can we do!' screamed the dodo, staring helplessly at her friend who now looked more like a blazing haystack.

'Only water will put it out!' panted the arctic rabbit. 'And we've run out.'

'What about the river?' shouted Tom.

'The river?' boomed the mammoth. 'Did you say there's a *river*?'

'Of course! Just out there,' Tom pointed to the door, 'at the bottom of the road!'

'A river at the bottom of the road?' repeated the mammoth. 'Well why the blazes didn't anyone tell me before?'

'I thought—'

'STAND BACK!' he thundered. 'STAND CLEAR, EVERYONE!'

Seconds later the flaming mammoth turned round and charged at the door.

'Are you sure you wouldn't like me to open . . . '

The gorilla didn't have time to finish what he was saying, as the next moment there was a fearful splintering of wood as the mammoth smashed out of the museum and skidded down the steps into the snowbound street.

'Obviously not,' said the gorilla, a trifle miffed.

'MAKE WAY!' boomed the flaming beast as it scrambled to its feet. 'MAKE WAY FOR THE MAMMOTH!'

With an ear-shattering trumpet the mammoth dashed headlong down the busy street, parting everything before it like a wave. Dogs barked, horses bolted, and people stared open-mouthed as the fireball the size of a house rumbled past.

'A good take off is vital,' panted the mammoth, gaining speed with every step, 'legs straight, arms out, head down and . . . '

The mammoth leapt off the side of the bridge in a racing dive, and at that very second, glanced down to see the expanse of ice stretched beneath it.

'Fiddlesticks!'

There was the most colossal crash, followed by a deep reverberating groan as the flaming mammoth plunged headfirst through the ice and into the freezing water. Every skater at the ice fair came to a sudden halt and stared in wonder at the enormous jagged hole, swirling with bubbles.

'What was *that*?' sniffed Dr Shadrack, standing in front of the ice palace.

'A bonfire on legs?' suggested Dr Skink.

'A giant dog, more like,' said a third.

Then the water inside the hole began to boil, and with a great whoosh the singed mammoth broached the surface, steam billowing off his back.

'Hooray!' he cheered, shooting a triumphant fountain of water high into the air, showering the onlookers all around. 'I have always wanted to do that!' Shaking his massive blackened head the smoking beast began to splash around merrily amongst the slabs of broken ice.

'A svimming . . . *mammoth*?' whispered Dr Skink, unable to believe his eyes. 'I have heard of zuch zings in Ziberia, but—'

'A swimming mammoth . . . it's a swimming mammoth, a swimming mammoth they said . . . '

The rumour began to sweep through the crowds of doctors, and slowly they edged back towards the ice palace in terror.

Booom . . .

A long low sound rang out like thunder across the ice fair, and in an instant every single person stood still and silent.

'What was *that*?'

Dr Shadrack looked nervously at the ice beneath him, to where the sound had come from.

B-b-boooom . . .

A second hollow groan rang out, which this time seemed to carry directly from the mammoth's hole straight across to the centre of the river, to the spot where Noah had fallen.

Boom . . . b-boom . . . boom . . . b-boom . . .

More and more started coming, one tumbling directly after another, spreading out across the ice fair.

'It's startin' a gew!' gasped a marzipan seller with lanterns round his hat, staring at the zigzag crack that had just opened up beneath his feet. 'The beast must a' weakened it and—'

'Me dad's coconut shy!' shouted one young boy, pointing across to the edge of the fair, where a stall and its owner had broken away on an ice floe.

'I'm floatin'!' wailed the man, desperately waving his arms as he began to drift downstream. 'Help!'

'ABANDON THE ICE!' shouted a policeman. 'EVERYONE TO THE SHORE! THE ICE IS BREAKING UP!'

'Abandon zer ice,' repeated Dr Skink, 'everyone to zer shore?'

The words spread like wildfire amongst the thousands of doctors standing in a great herd around the ice palace. Moving as if one body they all dashed towards the waterfront at exactly the same time, but at that very moment the ice groaned under their combined weight and there was a fearful snap; suddenly the large slab on which they stood tipped violently then broke away, sending dozens of black-coated doctors tumbling off the rim.

'Help! Help!' they screeched, splashing desperately in the dark swirling water. 'We can't swim!'

'We can't swim?' murmured the rest. 'We can't swim? . . . We can't swim!'

The air was filled with terrified screams as the doctors ignored those already in the water and swarmed back up over the ice palace, climbing on top of each other and struggling to hold on.

'Don't just stand zere!' yelled Dr Skink to the stevedores watching helplessly on the shore. 'Rescue us, you idiots!'

'Yes, rescue us, you idiots!' shrieked Dr Shadrack.

'Rescue us!' they all shouted together.

But there was nothing that anyone could do to help them, as everywhere the ice was starting to break up. Terrified skaters leapt from floe to floe to the safety of dry land, while men scrambled to salvage what they could as one by one the stalls broke away on tiny islands or slipped beneath the icy water.

'I have to say this is *the* most tremendous fun,' murmured the mammoth to himself, quietly swimming through the channels opening up in the ice to pick up abandoned dogs and hens and small children with his trunk; and placing them on his back he ferried them all ashore.

'There you are, young lady,' he gurgled to one bedraggled young girl, setting her down gently on the river bank, 'now run home, jump straight into a hot bath and don't tell a soul who rescued you.'

'Is yous . . . yous a . . . a . . . *nelephant* lifeguard then?' she stammered, staring in amazement at the vast shaggy creature.

'Something like that,' he boomed, setting off into the frozen waters once more.

'You're very good at swimming!' she called out, and the mammoth bubbled with pride.

'So nice to feel one has a purpose in life for once,' he mumbled to himself, 'makes one almost wish one was not extinct after all.'

Tom stood in the smashed doorway of the Scatterhorn Museum, scarcely able to believe what was happening. It seemed incredible that the mammoth's plunge could have set off such a catastrophic chain of events.

'Actually, he's not so bad for a big fella, is he?' said a sing-song voice next to him. Tom looked down and there was the dodo, now with a large burnt patch at the back of her head, watching the mammoth with an admiring look in her eye.

'He was so full of chat I was never sure whether he could really cut the mustard or not.'

'Oh yes, he can cut it all right,' added the gorilla behind her, and Tom noticed that he was smiling too. 'One hell of a good effort, don't you think?'

They stood watching as a jolly-boat set off in pursuit of the doctors on their floating island, now rapidly disappearing into the darkness.

'What I don't understand is why they want to go and build a fair on the ice in the first place,' hissed the anaconda. 'What's wrong with the ground, I ask you?'

'Well, obviously they didn't imagine some mammoth would come barging in and smash it up,' said the pangolin, peering out through the gorilla's legs.

'He wouldn't 'ave done it if some *pyromaniac nincompoop* hadn't set fire to him first!' squawked the dodo with feeling. Nudging Tom's knee sharply she glanced up at the windows on the first floor. ''E's still 'ere, y'know, *the pyro,*' she whispered nervously, 'up there.'

In all the chaos Tom had almost forgotten what had been the cause of it all, and following her eyes up to the first floor windows he recognized the unmistakable profile of Don Gervase, staring out at the river with a mixture of astonishment and fury.

'He's not very happy, I should say,' murmured the gorilla. 'Serves him jolly well right too. Probably hoped to give you the museum then torch the place, now that he's got his precious bottle.'

At that moment Don Gervase seemed to be aware that he was being discussed, for he swivelled his great head round and scowled at the odd collection of animals clustered around the small boy in the doorway.

'Oh,' whimpered the dodo, cowering behind Tom's legs. The anaconda turned her head to the wall and the pangolin shrank back into his armour, even the gorilla avoided his eye. Only Tom met Don Gervase's withering stare directly, and the very sight of his huge ugly head sparked a flame of fury that began to burn him up inside. Whatever promises he'd made to Tom counted for nothing now. The gorilla was right; Don Gervase had just failed to destroy the mammoth, but that wouldn't stop him, he probably *was* just about to set fire to everything else. He must not be allowed to do it. Unconsciously Tom clenched his fists tight and somehow Don Gervase sensed this defiance, for the next moment he slunk back from the window.

'Get after him, Tom, hound him out before he tries any more of his tricks,' hissed the anaconda, but Tom was already racing back into the hall. Seeing Don Gervase's long shadow disappearing into the bird gallery he leapt up the stairs two at a time till he reached the dark landing. Straining his ears for any sound Tom noticed that the tiger's alcove was empty.

Click-clack click-clack click-clack . . .

Don Gervase's short quick footsteps echoed somewhere near the back of the museum. Where? Tom sprinted straight through the bird gallery and out the far side into a long dark corridor lined with engravings of crocodiles and snakes. Which way had he gone? At one end, a narrow stone staircase led back down to the ground floor, and at the other there was a small black door set into the wall. Catching his breath Tom stared at the door curiously; he had never noticed it before and he was sure that it did not exist in his own time; perhaps it led to some sort of annex that no longer existed. Turning round he waited in the centre of the corridor and listened again. Suddenly a door slammed somewhere below him.

Click-clack, click-clack, click-clack . . .

There he was, Don Gervase was coming back! It sounded as if he was trotting up the stairs. Tom darted back into the bird gallery just as the sound changed and Don Gervase stepped onto the carpet in the corridor. Those quick footsteps were coming straight towards him . . . this was his moment: what should he do, hide, fight, what? Tom closed his eyes, he did not know; something, *anything* . . .

Suddenly Don Gervase's footsteps stopped abruptly. There was silence. He must have stopped dead in the middle of the corridor. A knot of cold fear began to tighten in Tom's stomach; what was he doing now, was he setting fire to something else? But the corridor was empty . . . Tom pressed his face to the wall and peeped around the corner a fraction. There was Don Gervase standing motionless, only his fingers twitching impatiently. Tom could see that his cold yellow eyes were fixed on something at the far end of the corridor and there was a look of pure evil on his face. Holding his breath, Tom very slowly withdrew, and turning round he peered in the same direction. The small black door was exactly as he had seen it moments ago, only now a large shadow was crouching before it.

'Rrrrrrrrrrr.'

The low, familiar growl rumbled down the long corridor and seemed to pass right through Tom and out the other side. He fought the urge to run, to escape as fast as he could, but he knew instinctively that it was not him the tiger was after; it was Don Gervase. Tom's mind was racing; what was going to happen now? It was like a gunfight. The tiger was watching Don Gervase intently, as if sizing up her prey, but the tall man did not move an inch: only his fingers continued to twitch. Then with the smallest flick of his wrist Tom saw his palm open and the small steel blade slipped down.

'Don't think you're going to get away with this,' the tiger growled.

'Oh, but I am. Do you really think you're going to stop me? You, a mere—'

'I wouldn't underestimate me, if I were you,' she went on, her voice dripping with menace, 'others have made that mistake.'

'Come on then,' he whispered, and his thin mouth curled up like a sickle. 'Pussycat.'

The huge cat's flame-coloured eyes flashed angrily and drawing back her black lips she let out a terrifying snarl, revealing her massive front teeth. She began to stalk forward, her tail thrashing from side to side. Don Gervase was not in the least bit intimidated; he stood imperiously in the centre of the corridor, leering at the great tiger as it came closer and closer . . .

'Here, puss puss,' he goaded, 'my, *what* a big cat you are.'

Tom's heart was galloping now; why is he not afraid—why doesn't he run? That tiny knife won't save him. The tiger drew level with Tom and dropping down to her belly she flattened her ears. Again she spat viciously and Don Gervase did nothing more than sneer back, then with one swift move he threw his small steel knife onto the floor.

'You see, puss puss,' he grinned wolfishly, opening wide his hands, 'I am now completely unarmed.'

Tom heart was in his throat; perhaps Don Gervase *had* gone crazy. Doesn't he know what this creature can do? Glancing down he saw the tiger's back legs padding on the carpet, preparing to spring. Don Gervase sensed it too, and his head began to bulge in anticipation.

'Hssssss!' he spat, needling the tiger once more. 'Hsss! Hsss!'

The tiger's tail thrashed violently from side to side . . . any second now . . . any second Don Gervase would be ripped apart surely. Tom covered his face with his hands, he could barely bring himself to watch, but there was still something so odd about Don Gervase's behaviour . . . he was grinning insanely, and his whole head seemed to be pulsating, boiling inside, almost growing larger every second, and his chest had started to swell . . . the tiger readied herself to spring and he seemed to be struggling to stay upright on his tiny feet . . . something was happening inside him . . . Don Gervase was losing control . . .

Suddenly there was an angry roar and a flash of orange and red, and the great Bengal tiger ripped through the air like a thunderbolt. In that very instant, Don Gervase's long arms became two enormous shining pincers and four extra limbs appeared to shoot out of his chest. In one quick move the pincers scythed upwards and caught the flying tiger in mid-air, slamming it to the floor like a doll. Picking it up between his huge pincers he shook it furiously, then hurled the great cat down the corridor with such force that it smashed lifelessly against the wall. Tom remained rooted to the spot, frozen in silent terror. Everywhere Don Gervase's skin was starting to burst open, his bulging forehead was splitting in half and glistening chocolate brown plates swelled up underneath. Two huge blueish eyes broke the surface of the skin where his cheeks had been and forced their way through. All over his body his skin and his clothes were ripping away, stretching and curling back to reveal the smoothly polished surface of an enormous armoured beetle. Tom felt himself start to retch, he wanted to be sick but he was just too frightened. The Don Gervase that he knew was now hanging in empty tatters, slithering off the back of the monstrous shining carapace. Then the gigantic beetle stepped out of Don Gervase's small black boots and ran a massive barbed claw over its head, sloughing off the last remnants of skin.

'What a relief,' it said, carefully turning over the empty rags to poke about in the jacket pocket. '*Excellente,*' whispered the creature, gently extracting the small blue bottle, 'they will not be disappointed after all.'

Carefully stowing the bottle away somewhere behind its head, the beetle's dead eyes turned back towards the empty corridor and, seeing no one, it dropped down onto six legs and scuttled past Tom's hiding place towards the small black door. Casting one last backward look at the museum, the gigantic creature turned the handle with its pincer and squeezed through into the dark space beyond, slamming the door hard shut behind. It was gone.

For a few seconds Tom crouched in silence, too stunned to move. What he had just witnessed was so strange and disturbing that it belonged in the worst kind of nightmare, the kind you wake up from and dread going back to sleep. In fact, he wasn't at all sure that it wasn't a nightmare. Dragging himself shakily to his feet, Tom edged out into the corridor and stared down to where the great Bengal tiger lay at one end, snapped in half like a broken toy. That looked real enough. And there on the carpet before him lay the empty shell of Don Gervase, ripped and deflated like a popped balloon. Plucking up all his courage, Tom approached the skin and poked it with the tip of his toe; there was no doubt at all that it was real too. Tom felt his head start to spin; this was all so weird, so completely unbelievable . . .

Steadying his nerves, Tom sank to his knees and forced himself to inspect the skin of Don Gervase. The details were all there, it was definitely him. Reaching out, his fingers brushed against what had been the face. It felt warm and rubbery, and slightly sticky to touch . . . Tom swallowed hard. Did that mean that he had been some kind of giant beetle all along, on a mission to find August's elixir? It seemed so: he must be. Perhaps he was a hybrid from the future—perhaps all of them were: Skink, Shadrack, the legions of doctors, the stevedores, even those strange museum inspectors, *and* the men in the car in Middlesuch Close; maybe every single one of them was some monstrous insect. And so was Lotus too. Tom shook his head blankly, struggling to take it in. It was almost beyond comprehension. So had they eaten people or infected them, got *inside* them somehow? Maybe they had. Maybe Don Gervase and Lotus had even been real people once, before . . . and what's more, they knew how to travel from one world to another. But how? How could they do that?

'*Only the birds know now. And, y'know . . . the other lot.*' The words of the great eagle floated up out of Tom's memory. So was this what it had meant by the *other lot*? The insects? *Was* it? Tom stared down at the evidence, the skin and clothes of the tall man lying in ribbons on the carpet before him. It seemed so. It must be.

So where had he—it—gone now? Tom glanced up at the small black door at the end of the corridor. What was beyond that door; was that another place, in another time? Getting up slowly Tom took a step closer and listened. The door seemed to rattle slightly on its hinges, and though he might have imagined it, he was sure he could hear the distant rumble of thunder and the wind blowing through a forest. Wherever it was, he felt sure it was not part of the world he was in now.

Was that . . . the *future*, perhaps? Tom took another step closer, straining his ears for any sound . . . that was definitely the sound of wind in the trees, he could even hear the branches bending and the leaves rustling, and there was a low rushing noise underneath it . . . was that a river too? A forest, with a river running beside it . . . a jumble of images raced through Tom's mind and suddenly a wild longing gripped him: supposing that wasn't the future after all, supposing that was a door to a forest on the other side of the world, *in his own time*. Supposing that was Mongolia, or somewhere like it . . . Tom's heart quickened; perhaps that was where his father was, where his mother had gone to look for him, maybe that was how Don Gervase knew so much about them. Supposing he wasn't bluffing, and they *were* both in great danger . . . surrounded by beetles, about to be attacked by them . . .

Tom stared hard at the small black door, listening to the wind rushing beyond it: all he had to do was to go through. He could find them and tell them about everything, and he must warn them about Don Gervase, Lotus, and everyone else, he must . . .

Reaching forward Tom's hand gingerly grasped the small ebony handle. It felt warm; it seemed to be willing him to turn it. Just one small twist was all it took. He could see his parents clearly now, sitting on the edge of a great forest, just on the other side of that door, only seconds away, even at this very moment . . . But then Tom hesitated. What if he couldn't find them? The forest might be a vast, hostile place; what if he got lost and never found his way back to this door? Did he really want to be trapped in the same world as Don Gervase, that . . . creature? He might be one of thousands—millions even, and Tom might find himself in the middle of a Contagion, whatever that was. Then he would be alone, absolutely alone, in a truly terrifying world.

Suddenly Tom felt a great weakness sweep over him; he could not do it. Whatever the chances, he did not have any strength left. His hand dropped limply to his side and hot tears began to prick in his eyes. For the first time in a long, long while Tom felt like exactly what he was: a thin, tired, and rather lonely eleven-year-old boy.

'A very wise decision,' said a gravelly voice behind him, 'and a brave one too.'

Biting his lip fiercely, Tom turned round and peered down to the far end of the corridor, where the silhouette of the great eagle perched uneasily on the body of the tiger.

'Only a fool would go through that door,' it continued kindly, 'and you ain't no fool, are you, Tom?'

Tom tried to force a smile but he couldn't. 'No,' he said quietly, 'no, I'm not.'

'Good,' replied the bird, hopping off the tiger and walking unsteadily towards him, 'then you won't object to my next suggestion, which is more of an order, in fact.'

'What's that?'

'To take you home, kiddo. What's done here is finished now, it's over.'

'It's over?'

The eagle nodded.

'But what about Don Gervase, he's got the bottle of August's potion and—'

'Don't let that concern you now,' interrupted the great bird, 'you can't change it, no one can. You did the best you could do—nobody could have asked for more. So let me take you home.'

Home . . . the word sounded so sweet that Tom found himself grinning. Right now there was nothing he wanted more in the world.

'Do you really mean it?'

'It would be an honour,' rasped the eagle, and turning its great head it let out a long ululating call. Seconds later the tiny blue shape of the swallow darted into the corridor and perched on a picture frame, twittering noisily.

'We're ready, mate, if you are. Now hop on board and make yerself comfortable.'

The huge bird leant forward awkwardly, and in a moment Tom had hauled himself up onto its back.

'Are yer on?'

Tom nodded and threw his arms tightly around the eagle's neck, feeling the warm soft feathers of the eagle's back envelop him.

'OK then. Here goes.'

With three mighty beats of the eagle's wings they were airborne, flying low down the corridor, banking hard into the bird gallery and gliding out over the main hall.

'Hang on back there,' it rasped, and following the swallow into a steep dive the huge bird swooped down through the smashed front door and shot out into the cold night air. Soon they were climbing fast towards the stars.

'If I were you, Tom,' cried the great bird above the rushing wind as they sped higher and higher, 'I'd get a bit of kip as this is going to be a long flight.'

But Tom did not hear a word the eagle said; he was already fast asleep.

CHAPTER 25

D-DAY

Tom opened his eyes groggily, and found himself staring at a familiar sight. There above him was the low, sloping ceiling of his tiny attic room behind the museum, and he knew at once that the eagle had kept its promise. He was back; in his own time, in his own bed, just as the great bird had told him he would be. Thank you bird, and your intrepid swallow guide, thank you very much. Tom yawned lazily, watching his breath forming little clouds of steam in the air. Only then did he realize how cold it was. Sitting up, Tom saw that the window was wide open *yet* again, and an icy wind was whistling in off the river. With a resigned shiver Tom gathered all the blankets around him and hopping across to the window he slammed it hard shut.

'Now please, *please,* just stay like that.'

Tom made a silent promise to himself that if he ever saw the eagle again, the first thing he would do would be to teach it how to close a window. Surely it couldn't be *that* difficult, even for a giant bird.

Scratching his mop of untidy blond hair, Tom was surprised to find bits of burnt mammoth hair stuck in it, and when he twisted his neck his shoulders felt sore. Stretching his arms out painfully, he realized that he still had all his clothes on, and what's more, they smelt as if they had been in a bonfire. In fact, he was even more of a mess than usual, and glancing in the mirror Tom was shocked to see that his face was caked in soot. Of course, it would be. It was all coming back now, the whole wild adventure.

Washing away the grime as best he could, Tom rubbed the filth off his clothes with a towel then set off down the back stairs, and with as innocent a look as he could manage he opened the kitchen door to find it empty. That was strange, maybe Jos and Melba had gone out, but it was only eight o'clock in the morning. The calendar above the sink read December 24, Christmas Eve, which Jos had marked with a big red circle, and Melba had decorated with a couple of balloons around the side. There must be something significant about this date, thought Tom, idly picking up a piece of toast, was it someone's birthday? *Then* he remembered: today was the day Uncle Jos was going to sign over the museum to Don Gervase.

'D-Day,' Tom whispered to himself; this was a very significant day indeed. There was a distant sound of a vacuum cleaner in the museum. That's where they were; Jos and Melba must be clearing up the chaos left over from last night. The mammoth probably left debris everywhere . . . *wait a minute.* That hadn't happened last night; that was in the past.

Come on Tom, wake up.

But Tom was still muddled enough to want to make absolutely sure. Shuffling quickly down the corridor to the big oak door that connected to the museum, he pushed it open and immediately his nose was stung by a strong smell of burning hair; mammoth hair. But . . . but that was impossible, it couldn't be, could it? A jumble of confused images blurred through Tom's mind and his shuffle broke into a run. The smell was getting stronger and stronger . . .

'Morning Tom!' shouted Melba as Tom ran breathlessly into the hall. She was manoeuvring an ancient looking polishing machine around the great hairy feet of the mammoth, who was standing in exactly the same position as he had done for the last hundred years.

'Sorry about the stink!' bellowed Jos cheerfully above the noise. 'This old girl tends to get very hot and I'm afraid that we might have given our shaggy friend here a bit of a singeing.'

He gave the mammoth a friendly pat on the trunk and Tom breathed a huge sigh of relief; it was OK, it was all OK. Looking around he saw the tatty, faded animals peering out of the gloom, just as they always did. They were all here, every single one of them. Though on reflection the mammoth's flanks *were* a slightly different colour to the rest of him, and the feathers on the back of the dodo's head *weren't* precisely the same as those at the front. But then they'd always been like that; it's just that Tom hadn't noticed it before.

'Anyway, what's a few little scorch marks here and there,' said Jos, winking at him beneath his bushy eyebrows, 'it's not going to be *our* problem for much longer, is it? Come on lad, give us a hand with this lot.'

In the centre of the main hall Jos had set out a long table and Tom helped him arrange two lines of chairs either side of it; one each for Don Gervase, Lotus, and his team of lawyers, and on the other a chair for Jos, Melba, and Tom. It all looked very formal and serious, as if they were about to sign a treaty of surrender; which in a funny way, they were.

'Catchers finally buying the Scatterhorns out, eh?' wheezed Jos to himself. 'My father will be turning in his grave. Still, there's no choice in the matter, it's got to go.'

Tom said nothing, but at the back of his mind he wondered whether they really would see Don Gervase today.

When they had finished, Tom wandered over to the model of Dragonport and turning on the lights he took a good long look at it once more. At first glance everything seemed exactly the same: the snowbound streets were still busy with miniature horse-drawn sledges and the pavements were packed with people; but on closer inspection, Tom saw that things had most definitely changed. Out on the frozen river the stalls of the ice fair were still there, but minute cracks now crisscrossed the surface like a web. Over on the far side, where Burdo Yarker's cottage stood, the snow had been disturbed by insect tracks marching out of the woods towards the town, and tracing these tracks across the wide expanse of river Tom found that they disappeared inside one of the warehouses on the waterfront. All around the entrance to this low wooden building the snow seemed to have been smoothed down, as if something large had been rolled in and out; barrels maybe, or perhaps something rounder—like a ball. At once those strange white spheres came back to Tom's mind; were they responsible for these marks, were they some kind of beetle egg?

Walking around the model to the far side, Tom stared down at the miniature Scatterhorn Museum and discovered that that had changed too: the front door had been broken open, and there was something like a scorch mark on it as if it had been burnt by a match. At the back, on the level of the first floor, there was a small black hole no wider than a pencil, which seemed to have been bored out through the wall. Beneath it there was another corresponding hole, tunnelling into the wooden base of the model itself. Could that be where Don Gervase had gone? Tom stood for many minutes revolving the possibilities over and over in his mind: what was it that the great eagle had said? The model was just a gateway, a portal into the past, that's all. But something *else* seemed to have happened here: it was almost as if traces of his own adventures had left their mark on the model itself, and surely that couldn't just be a coincidence. Could it?

'That's a curious little excavation, isn't it?' said Uncle Jos, shambling up beside him and peering down at the small black hole behind the museum. 'What's made that, do you think, woodworm?'

Tom shrugged his shoulders. 'It looks too big for that. Maybe a beetle.'

'A beetle?' wheezed Jos, raising both of his eyebrows. 'Lordy Lord, let's hope not, or we may have ourselves an *infestation*. Believe me, that's the very last thing you want in a place like this. Best come away now Tom,' he said, patting him on the shoulder and glancing hurriedly at the foyer, 'whatever's got in there we don't want to draw their attention to it. The vultures will be here any minute.'

And as if on cue, there was a distant rap of a gloved hand on the door.

'Speak of the devil.'

Jos nervously brushed the crumbs of toast off his cardigan and did his best to flatten down the tufts of his hair.

'This is it, lad, this is it. D-Day.'

Drawing back the bolts Jos forced the great creaking door open, but instead of the lean looming figure of Don Gervase he had expected, there on the steps stood a tired, grey-faced man with large glasses, carrying a briefcase. Behind him was a long-nosed woman who looked very much like an anteater, also carrying a briefcase.

'Mastodon and Flippitt,' announced the man, presenting a gloved hand for Uncle Jos to shake limply, 'lawyers acting on behalf of Askary.'

'Lawyers, excellent,' repeated Jos, momentarily confused. 'So . . . er . . . Mr Askary is not with you?'

'Does it look like it?' said the woman sternly. She must have been Flippitt.

'Well no, no—it doesn't.'

Jos paused for a moment.

'Unless, of course, he's hiding in your bag, Mr Mastodon.'

'What?'

'Oh, I know he's in there somewhere. Come out, Don Gervase, coast is clear!'

Mastodon and Flippitt exchanged glances then peered up at Uncle Jos as if he was quite mad.

'Right. OK. No,' wheezed Uncle Jos, pushing his glasses rather awkwardly back up his nose, 'please,' and spinning round he led the way into the main hall. 'That one went down like a depth charge,' he wheezed, winking at Tom as he passed. 'Can't help myself with these people.'

Mastodon and Flippitt followed him into the gloom in single file, taking their places at the table without a word. Jos, Melba and Tom sat down formally on the other side and watched as the two lawyers opened their briefcases and began to pore over a thick document that Tom presumed was the contract of sale.

'Looks like you've done all right out of this one, Mr Scatterhorn,' said Mastodon after a minute, bending forward to read the small print. 'Mr Askary must *really* like all this junk.'

'This "junk", as you call it, has been in our family for over a hundred years,' replied Jos, smarting a little at the word 'junk', 'and that comes at a price.'

'So I can see,' Mastodon continued, 'and once you've sold the family silver what are you going to do with all the loot; sit on some tropical island and get sozzled I expect?'

'Actually we've found a cottage at the end of Flood Street that will suit us down to the ground,' replied Melba briskly. 'It has a roof that doesn't leak, central heating, hot water, and nothing whatsoever to mend, polish, or buff.' She shot a glance at Jos, who was still eyeing the floor crossly. 'In fact it is absolutely perfect.'

'Really?'

'Indeed it is,' added Jos, folding his arms across his chest, 'and seeing as we also have a boat, when we get bored we might just take off round the world to that tropical island *and* get sozzled as well. Every day, if we feel like it.'

Mr Mastodon peered over his spectacles and smiled thinly.

'Lucky you.'

They've certainly kept this very quiet, thought Tom. For all Jos's bluster about never selling the museum he had obviously realized that he might be an awful lot better off without it; he was probably even secretly looking forward to disappearing over the horizon on his beloved *Sugarmouse*, leaving the museum and all its problems behind for ever. So *this* is what Melba had meant, when she said she had finally persuaded Jos to see sense. But was Don Gervase *really* going to turn up? Tom shifted uncomfortably in his seat, watching the lawyers scratching away with their pens. Was it possible that Mastodon and Flippitt were also . . . no, Tom decided, definitely not. They seemed too real somehow. Slowly the minutes passed, and after half an hour there was still no sign of Don Gervase. Melba was starting to get anxious.

'Excuse me, Mr Mustderdo . . . Mosderdi . . . Misdodo—'

'Mastodon,' corrected Mr Mastodon. 'M-A-S-T-O-D-O-N, as in ancient beast. Like ice-age Tony here,' he said with a short laugh, indicating the great shaggy mammoth looming above him. There was a distant cough and the mammoth blinked; no one had ever called him 'ice-age Tony' before.

'Mastodon and Flippitt.'

'Well, Mr Mastodon, Mrs Flippitt, I—'

'Muzz Flippitt,' corrected the woman without looking up from her papers.

'Just so,' continued Melba as carefully as she could. 'I don't suppose you know what time your client Mr Askary will be coming? We were told nine o'clock.'

'Likewise,' replied Mastodon, 'and we charge an hourly rate.'

'Double on Christmas Eve,' chipped in Flippitt, smiling coldly, 'that usually gets them out of bed.'

'Have either of you . . . er . . . actually spoken to Mr Askary today?' asked Tom in a small voice.

Mastodon put down his pen abruptly, and peered at him over the top of his half-moon glasses. 'I'm sorry, I didn't quite catch your name. You are?'

'Tom Scatterhorn.'

Mastodon paused, not quite sure whether to bother explaining himself to a child.

'No, Tom Scatterhorn, as a matter of fact we have not. We are his lawyers not his keepers, and no doubt he is a very busy man. Whether he chooses to arrive early or late is entirely his business.'

'We have done this before, you know,' added Ms Flippitt under her breath.

Tom shrugged his shoulders and said nothing; he had his own ideas about what was going on, but he had no intention of sharing them with Mastodon and Flippitt. He settled back into his chair and waited.

One hour went by. The stony-faced lawyers continued to scratch on their contracts and neither said a word. Another hour passed. Melba had now fallen asleep and was snoring softly while Jos began pacing about, scratching his head and muttering oaths to himself. That trip round the world aboard *Sugarmouse* was getting further away by the minute . . . Finally, the clock struck twelve and Jos could contain himself no longer.

'Bilge rats and behemoths!' he exploded. 'The lizard-faced landlubber is *three hours* late! I might have expected as much from a Catcher!'

Mastodon looked up wearily from his books. It seemed that even he was finally beginning to lose patience.

'Perhaps you should pay him a visit,' he said coolly.

'Perhaps I will, sir,' thundered Jos, 'and seeing as he is your client—*you* shall come with me! Tom, show Mr Mastodon to the car, if you please!'

By now Jos's face had turned the colour of an orange, and he looked so wild and furious that Mr Mastodon had no choice but to agree.

'This is *most* irregular,' hissed Ms Flippitt between her teeth, but she wasn't about to cross Uncle Jos either. After all, an expedition to Catcher Hall was only going to take more time, and more time *always* meant more money for Mastodon and Flippitt.

Cramming themselves into Jos Scatterhorn's battered red Mini, the three of them set off across town at breakneck speed, Uncle Jos revving hard and sliding through the slush like a rally driver.

'You need all the power you can get in weather like this,' he grimaced above the whine of the engine. Mr Mastodon's grey face was rapidly turning a pale shade of green as they bounced up the hill and swung into the drive of Catcher Hall, narrowly missing the laurel bushes and skidding to a halt at the front door.

'Now!' bellowed Jos. 'Where is Don Gervase Askary?'

Marching up to the bell he rang it as loudly as he could. Tom climbed out of the back seat, feeling a little queasy himself, and looking up he saw that the house was absolutely dark. The windows were shuttered, the lights were off, and even Don Gervase's Bentley was no longer parked in the drive.

'Is he not there?' enquired Mr Mastodon weakly, wiping the sweat off his face with a handkerchief and looking decidedly ill.

'No answer,' wheezed Jos furiously. 'I'll bet you he's done a runner.' Marching around the side of the house he squinted in through the ballroom windows. 'He has as well!' he exploded. 'And he's taken his clobber with him, look!'

Tom approached the study window and peering in through the closed shutters he saw that Jos was right; all the newspapers had gone, so had the computers, the sensor apparatus—even the books. In every other room it was the same story, it was empty, and there was nothing but a few sticks of furniture left. It was as if Don Gervase, Lotus, their Peruvian housekeeper, and perhaps even Zeus the angry dog, had all simply disappeared into thin air: or returned to the future.

'So, what do you make of that, Mr Mastodon?' demanded Jos as he stomped back to the car.

'It's unusual, certainly,' admitted Mastodon, whose face had by now returned from green to its usual grey, 'though I'm sure there's a perfectly rational explanation. Perhaps he's gone out to lunch or something like that.'

'Out to lunch?' spluttered Jos as he started the engine once more. '*Out to lunch?*'

'Yes, I mean he's probably just forgotten,' Mastodon continued smoothly, 'after all, what's one little museum to a man of his means? He's probably bought ten museums already. To *you*, of course, it's your entire life, and if the sale falls through it's nothing less than an unmitigated disaster. No fancy little cottage in Flood Street, no trips to tropical islands; but to him, the Scatterhorn Museum is a trinket, it's a mere bauble! A Christmas bauble, heh heh!'

Mastodon began snorting at his own little joke.

'Hagfish,' muttered Uncle Jos under his breath. This lawyer was starting to give him the hump.

'But rest assured, sale or no sale, he'll have to pay what's owed to Mastodon and Flippitt,' Mastodon went on blithely. 'Oh yes, fees are fees. I mean, it's not as if he's just *vanished*, is it?'

They reached the end of the drive and skidded to a halt opposite a long line of rubbish bags neatly piled up awaiting collection.

'Isn't it?' growled Jos, eyeing the bags that looked very much as if someone had cleared the entire contents of the house and left it for good. But Mr Mastodon did not appear to hear him; the smile had withered from his face and he was staring in open-mouthed horror across to the other side of the road.

'What in heaven's name is . . . *that*?' he said in a hoarse whisper.

Jos followed his gaze and there, leaning up against a tree on the far side of the road, was what appeared to be a life-size model of Lotus. It was wearing a black cat suit and boots, but the legs and arms had been completely ripped and shredded, though the face remained intact. It seemed to be made of some sort of leathery yellow plastic, and there was a knowing smile on its lips.

'It's like her . . . her—' Mastodon was lost for words.

'Skin?' suggested Tom helpfully from the back seat.

'Impossible,' replied Mastodon quickly, 'what a suggestion. How disgusting; quite revolting in fact.'

'We agree about something then,' growled Uncle Jos, staring hard at the extraordinary object. 'Catchers can be very, very, *odd* people. Sometimes, the less you know the better.'

When they arrived back at the museum Melba was at the door to meet them in a state of confusion.

'I think there may be some bad news,' she began as Mr

Mastodon brushed past her to find Ms Flippitt pacing up and down, roaring loudly to herself in the gloom.

'What the devil's the matter with her?' whispered Jos.

'She's just received a letter from her office. I think it's about Don Gervase—'

'Scarpered has he?'

Melba blinked. 'How did you know?'

'The house is all closed up. Nothing there; he's gone,' said Jos, clicking his fingers, 'just like that.'

'Oh no.'

'Mr Mastodon, there is a problem,' announced Ms Flippitt, marching towards him brandishing a piece of paper.

'Indeed? I expected as much,' he replied evenly, carefully removing his coat. 'Not to worry, Ms Flippitt, your many hours of hard work are not in vain. Invoices have to be paid, Don Gervase Askary knows that as well as the next man.'

'He *does*?' Ms Flippitt could barely contain herself. 'Then read that!' she howled, thrusting the piece of paper into his hand. 'Read it out loud!'

Mr Mastodon was quite taken aback; he had never seen Ms Flippitt so angry, this really was a most unattractive side of her character. Her little outburst would be remembered, make no mistake about it. Nevertheless he *would*, on this occasion, bow to her wishes and do as she asked. Slowly putting on his glasses, he cleared his throat and began:

'Dear Mastodon and Flippitt,
No doubt you will be reading this in the Scatterhorn Museum. What a marvellous place that is! So full of

the unexpected! And what a shame I shall not be buying it after all. Due to unforeseen circumstances I have decided to leave the country—with immediate effect—and return to my estate in Peru, by way of Central Asia—'

'A likely story!' snorted Ms Flippitt. 'Who ever returns to Peru via Central Asia?'

'I have no intention of ever coming to England again,' continued Mastodon, *'and I will be leaving no forwarding address so do not hope to contact me, or expect to be paid, because you won't, and there is absolutely nothing you can do about it.'*

'What?' spluttered Mr Mastodon. Even he was struggling to believe this now. Clearing his throat he carried on.

'If young Tom Scatterhorn is standing beside as you read this, please pass on my warmest regards, and I am sure that in time he might prove a very worthy custodian of Sir Henry's legacy—just so long as he does not let his imagination run away with him. The last thing I would want would be for him to step out of time, sorry, I mean line (my English is not so good) and come to any harm.
Apologies, and toodle-pip, as you say,
Don Gervase Askary
24th December.'

There was silence for a moment. Mr Mastodon seemed truly stunned. Carefully he took off his glasses and, folding up the letter, slipped it neatly into his pocket.

'Custodian of Sir Henry's legacy, come to any harm, what's that pillock on about?' growled Uncle Jos, who was now exceedingly puzzled. 'Does it mean anything to you, lad?'

'Nothing,' replied Tom, trying to look as innocent as possible, 'perhaps . . . erm . . . he's just gone bonkers.'

But Tom knew full well that this was some kind of warning; about what, he could not tell.

'It appears you were quite correct, Mr Scatterhorn,' said Mastodon, his voice turning cold and brutal, 'our client has, as you put it, "done a runner". However, since he owes us thousands of pounds in fees—'

'Tens of thousands, Mr Mastodon—'

'Precisely, Ms Flippitt, precisely. He cannot hope to succeed. No one plays fast and loose with Mastodon and Flippitt and gets away with it.'

'Indeed,' grunted Ms Flippitt, wringing her fingers at the prospect of revenge, 'no one.'

'We must telephone the police this instant,' said Mastodon abruptly, 'there must be checks on all ferries, roadblocks on all roads, armed guards at all airports; radio, television, we need pictures of him on every front page—' he announced in a shrill voice. 'Ms Flippitt, were you intending to take Christmas off?'

'Not any more,' she smirked, 'Christmas is cancelled.'

'Well done,' he trilled, and turned to Jos, Melba and Tom with a triumphant gleam in his eye. 'We shall find this Don Gervase

Askary, make no mistake about it. Even if it means going to hell—and back!'

With that the two grey-faced lawyers looked positively excited as they tidied up their papers.

'Good day to you all,' barked Ms Flippitt, closing her briefcase with a loud snap, and turning on her heel she marched rapidly towards the door.

'Merry Christmas,' said Jos with a wave, but there was no reply. The door slammed and silence reigned once more.

'Dear oh dear,' wheezed Jos, stifling a chuckle.

'Do you really think they'll find him?' asked Melba.

'Not a chance. That Don Gervase Askary is as slippery as an eel. Not that it makes one jot of difference to us.'

'What do you mean?' asked Tom.

'Now we're back where we started. We'll just have to sell the museum to someone else,' replied Jos, scratching his head. 'It's still got to go, Tom, we can't escape the fact. What's the point in keeping this old place if we can't even afford to open it?'

Tom knew that Jos was right; he had just tried to forget the hard truths about life in the real world. Uncle Jos was frowning hard at the floor, his eyes screwed up like bullets beneath his long bushy eyebrows. He looked very much like a grumpy gnome.

'But at least we've cleaned her up for Christmas,' said Melba soothingly. 'All we need to do now is find that wretched rat.'

'Humph.'

'Well, have *you* got any better ideas?'

Uncle Jos knew that he hadn't; and he wasn't very good at staying cross for long.

'Come on then, my old Tusker,' smiled Melba, playfully ruffling the tufts of hair that sprouted like clumps of weeds on Jos's bald head, 'you were right. Don Gervase *was* a bad apple from the start, but so what? Something else will turn up—it usually does.'

And Aunt Melba was right, something did turn up; two things in fact. The first was Plankton, the pink-eyed rat. After a long search Tom finally discovered him dozing underneath the model of Dragonport. He seemed very pleased with himself.

'Goodness me,' cooed Melba as she pulled him out, 'you look as if you have swallowed a balloon, Plankton; what on earth have you been feasting on down there?' Shining his small silver torch inside the hole Plankton had made in the base, Tom's heart leapt when he saw a small mountain of black insect skins glinting in the darkness.

'Beetles!' he said excitedly. 'Loads of them!'

'Well done, Plankton,' smiled Melba, planting a kiss on his wriggly pink nose. 'We don't want any nasty little beetles in here, do we? What a good boy you are.' Tom couldn't help grinning either; at last that rat had done something right—he must have eaten hundreds of them. *They* wouldn't be coming back in a hurry.

I wonder, thought Tom to himself, if he ate a particularly large brown one with claws, carrying a small blue bottle?

But that—unfortunately—would have been too much to hope for.

The second something turned up right at the end of the day, when there was a knock at the museum door. Uncle Jos opened it to find the red-faced young postman standing out on the snowy steps.

'There yer go, Mr Scatterhorn,' he said, thrusting a large pile of letters into Jos's arms.

'Bills?' exclaimed Jos, looking down at all the brown envelopes. 'Is that all you've got for me on Christmas Eve, lad?'

'There's a few cards in there an' all,' replied the postman cheerily, 'an somethin' for a "Mr T. Scatterhorn". Is this the right address for him?'

'It is.'

'Hang on then.'

Dipping back into his van, the postman pulled out a letter and a cardboard box plastered with airmail stickers and exotic coloured stamps.

'Them's *got* to be presents, en't they?' he said, handing them over. Jos studied the stamps carefully and realized that both the letter and the parcel were sent from the same country.

'Looks like they've come a good distance an' all.'

'I think you may be right there,' said Jos, smiling down at the letter, 'and I know they're going to make someone very happy. Thank you, lad.'

'No trouble, Mr Scatterhorn. That's me round done now, finished. Merry Christmas to you, sir.'

'And to you too,' said Jos, waving as the van sped away, 'and to you too.'

With a knowing grin Uncle Jos tucked the box and the letter under his arm and, trotting up the steps, he bolted the great museum door shut behind him. He had already decided that he would keep this unexpected delivery as a surprise for Tom in the morning. After all, a little delay never hurt anyone, did it?

CHAPTER 26

Genghis Khan

'This one is for you.'

Tom looked down at the long rectangular present, already wondering how he was going to conceal the inevitable disappointment of unwrapping it, as he had a very good idea what was inside.

'I hope it's what you wanted,' winked Jos.

Now he knew exactly.

It was Christmas Day, and they were sitting in the fuggy little living room with a good fire hissing in the grate. Uncle Jos was already wearing his present: another knitted cardigan from Melba, which he had somehow managed to button over the top of his other two. Melba was also wearing her present, a large orange hat with a wide floppy brim, and now they both sat watching Tom expectantly with bright, eager eyes.

'Go on then!' she said.

Best not delay any longer. With as much enthusiasm as he could muster, Tom tore open the paper and found himself looking down at a long blue box. On the cover was a photograph of two beaming children in lab coats and plastic spectacles, holding a test tube and a pair of tweezers. '*Catchpole's Chemistry For Beginners*', it said, '*Suitable for children aged 9 to 90*'.

'Wow. Thanks, that's brilliant,' said Tom, trying to sound as grateful as he could.

Melba looked down at the picture of the two grinning children. 'It *is* what you asked for,' she said apologetically.

Melba was right; it was what he had asked for, but just not quite what he had in mind.

'Well, isn't this marvellous,' wheezed Jos cheerily. 'I do like it when everyone gets what they want. Great stuff.'

There was a moment of silence as Tom looked down guiltily at the chemistry set. This really wasn't what he wanted at all.

'Jos?' Melba dug him hard in the ribs and nodded meaningfully at Tom.

'What?' he said, raising his eyebrows.

'Go *on*. Put the poor boy out of his misery.'

Jos stared at her blankly, in another of his theatrical pauses.

'Oh yes! Yes I almost forgot, silly me.'

With some ceremony Jos pulled out the letter and the cardboard box from under his chair.

'These came for you last night in the post, Tom,' he said, placing them in Tom's lap.

Tom stared down at the letter and the box, and at first he was so surprised that he didn't know what they were. Both were addressed to 'Mr T. Scatterhorn', written in different hands, and both were familiar. On the stamps were colourful pictures of horses and eagles.

'Bamboozled?' chortled Jos. 'I confess I was a little.'

Tom smiled and looked down at the letter and the box; which

should he open first? The letter. Carefully Tom tore down the edge of the envelope, his fingers shaking with excitement. Gingerly his hand reached inside and pulling out the thin pages he instantly recognized the handwriting: it was from his dad! Breathlessly Tom turned the letter over to find that on the reverse the writing changed to a different hand—it was from Mum. She must have found him.

'Your parents?' asked Jos, his beady eyes twinkling.

Tom barely nodded, he was too excited to speak.

'I thought so.'

'What do they say, dear?' asked Melba smiling.

Trying to keep calm, Tom turned back to the top of the page and began to read out loud.

'Dearest Tom,

I really hope this letter reaches you. I am writing from the Tosontsengel valley where I am resting up for a bit. I had a little accident yesterday but I'm OK now, I think. You wouldn't believe what's going on, Tom, it's incredible—a little terrifying in fact—things are changing so, so fast. But I can't tell you the whole story now in case someone else reads this. You see, I might not be the only one looking for the 'you know what'. Do you remember that odd letter I got from the International Movement for the Protection and Advancement of Insects all those years ago? Well, it's a long story, but everything is beginning to make sense now . . .'

'So your dad's out there looking for the "you know what"?' repeated Jos. 'And what is "*the you know what*"?'

'It's . . . er . . . something to do with insects, beetles,' said Tom quickly, 'and it's top secret. Government stuff.'

'Oh. Right. Beetles, eh,' repeated Jos, 'government stuff.'

'Yep.'

'If you say so.'

Jos raised his eyebrows and looked across at Melba knowingly; it was as he had always suspected, Sam Scatterhorn was quite crazy.

'And what does your mum say?' asked Melba politely.

Tom turned the letter over.

'Darling Tom,' he read,

'As you can see I found him, and not a moment too soon. He's got a shaggy blond beard and he's thin as a rake—he looks just like a caveman, you wouldn't recognize him! I've been thinking about you so much, Tom darling, really missing you, and Dad has too, though you know he finds it hard to say anything like that, let alone write it down. We've both been wondering what you make of old Jos and Melba, they're a funny old pair, aren't they? I hope they're feeding you properly, and they've got the heating fixed in that room of yours. I'm afraid I forgot to tell you about that. Uncle Jos will swear it's warmer than Mongolia but believe me, it isn't! We slept in there once about ten years ago and nearly died of cold . . .'

Tom's voice trailed away and suddenly he felt rather embarrassed. Looking up he found Uncle Jos staring at the floor.

'Ah well, your mum's got a point there.' He smiled ruefully. 'I didn't realize the damn thing's been bust *that* long. Never mind, you haven't had too bad a time, have you lad? Maybe the quarters aren't any great shakes but your auntie here's a demon in the galley.'

'She is,' replied Tom, smiling at them both. Whatever else had happened, Aunt Melba and Uncle Jos had tried to look after him as best they could, and he was truly grateful to them for that. But it didn't stop him missing his parents.

'Shall I go on?'

'You keep it to yourself, dear,' said Melba kindly, patting him on the shoulder, 'after all it is addressed to you, not us.'

Tom read on down, greedily devouring his mother's descriptions of the long bumpy bus rides and the dusty little towns, until he had almost reached the bottom of the page.

Now Tom, wrote his mother, *I have been saving the most interesting news till last. It's about how I found Dad in the first place. I had been told by the authorities that he was in jail in a town miles from anywhere, but when I got there I discovered he'd been let out the day before. So I asked around and apparently he'd just gone up into the forest with some people, so I took a bus up to the nearest village and waited for them to come back. Dad had got himself mixed up with a very bad lot, gangsters stealing beetles apparently. Anyway, it's totally illegal out here and his bunch had some sort of terrible accident. He won't tell me much about it, except that he really shouldn't be alive at all. Anyway, I didn't know any of this, and after two days waiting in the village I was buying some vegetables at the market when a pair of elderly gentlemen arrived on horseback. They turned out to be English, which was strange enough, so we got talking, and they told me they had some shack higher up the valley on the edge of the forest, and that they had been coming here for years, studying the beetles. So I said 'Oh, my husband's here to do that,' and when I said his name they both fell about laughing. Dad was staying with them at that very moment! I was flabbergasted. But Tom, that is not the strangest part. You will never believe what their names are . . .*

Tom's heart began to gallop; he could barely bring himself to turn over the page.

August Catcher and Sir Henry Scatterhorn!

Tom felt as if he had just been hit by an express train. His hands struggled to hold the letter still.

And they are convinced they have met you before. Is that true, Tom? I can't see how. Anyway, they were quite insistent, and when I told them where you were they suddenly got very excited and desperately wanted to send you a Christmas present, so I gave them the address of the museum. Funny old sticks, real characters, the pair of them. August seems to have quite taken Dad under his wing; he wants him to stay out here with him, but Dad won't tell me why. You know how secretive Dad is, he'll never tell you anything. But I just can't for the life of me think how they met you . . .

Tom's heart was beating so fast now that he could barely breathe.

'Are you sure you're all right, dear?' asked Melba, suddenly concerned as Tom looked paler than ever. 'Is there a problem?'

'No, no everything's fine, fine,' he stammered, 'it's just . . . '

Tom looked down at the cardboard box and at once recognized that handwriting: it was August's long, spiky hand. Pulling his penknife from his pocket he nervously flipped it open and slit along the sides with the blade, then lifting up the lid Tom delved around inside until his fingers closed around a package carefully wrapped up in newspaper and string. What was this? It felt like a figure. Cutting the string away Tom unravelled the layers of dirty newspapers until there in the middle of it all he found a small, gaudily painted china warrior, his sword raised high above his head. '*Genghis Khan*', read the label on the base. Melba craned forward and stared with surprise at the hideous little character.

'Is that from them too, dear?' she asked politely. 'A most original present.'

'Genghis Khan, eh?' wheezed Jos with a rasping chuckle. 'He's the man, isn't he?'

Tom could not understand it at all; why on earth had they sent him this? Attached to Genghis's back was a small envelope and Tom immediately ripped it open.

My dear Tom, read August's spidery writing,

You're alive! What a remarkable turn up for the books! It all makes perfect sense now, how you appeared and disappeared at random. We always thought there was something very ***unusual*** *about you, Tom, and Sir Henry was convinced that humans might be able to 'travel': he* *swears he'd seen geese do something similar during a thunderstorm in Alaska. I confess I was always a little sceptical—until now. Well, as you can see, we are still here and in pretty good shape too, considering we're both now knocking on 150 years of age. And it may surprise you to know that we have now become rather interested in coleoptera. It all began at a volcano about sixty years ago. I won't bore you with the details, but ever since then Sir Henry and I have been keeping a weather eye on the insect kingdom, and beetles in particular. They really are quite remarkably devious, almost evolving before your very eyes into something far worse than before, and some are now virtually indestructible. Thank goodness that the one thing that continues to hold them back is their lifecycle. Even the larger ones, who spend almost fifty years as grubs, munching their way through dead trees growing fatter and fatter until they are almost the size of pumpkins, only manage to live for a few months at the most.*

Lord knows what would happen if they ever got their pincers on my little invention and discovered how to make it. They are so strong and there are so many of them that one day they might very well take over the earth. Now there's a thought for you!

Never mind, we're confident we can stay one step ahead. Why, only three weeks ago we found a certain Mr Sam Scatterhorn almost up to his neck in them! Luckily Sir Henry got him out in the nick of time. Very nice to meet your old dad at last, though not quite in the circumstances we would have wished. Strong as an ox and stubborn as a mule, he's going to make a very good member of our society. One day we'll tell you all about that.

Now, a little bird tells us you've been having a spot of bother, one way or another, at the dear old Scatterhorn Museum, so Sir Henry thought the great Genghis Khan might be just the chap to cheer you up for Christmas. Lovely looking, isn't he? They've got statues to him all over the place out here, sort of a national hero.

Very best wishes,
August & Henry.

Slowly Tom put the letter down, utterly crestfallen. What terrible thing had he done? The excitement of hearing from his parents again had instantly evaporated as he realized the enormous consequences of his actions. He'd given away August's potion to Don Gervase, and now he knew exactly why the beetles wanted it so much. They didn't live very long. They couldn't.

Lord knows what would happen if they ever got their pincers on my little invention and discovered how to make it . . . one day they might very well take over the earth . . .

Well, they had it now, and there was nothing Tom could ever do to change that. His one feeble hope was that the bottle was so small and the potion so complex that they would never work out how to make it. After all, no one else ever had. But that was hardly any consolation to Tom right now.

'Bad news?' asked Jos, looking puzzled.

'Kind of,' replied Tom, avoiding his eye. He felt as if the world was caving in all around him; he'd never felt like so much of a failure in his whole life. He'd failed his dad, his mum, August and Sir Henry, perhaps even the entire human race. Now the terrifying beetles from the future possessed the secret to immortality and it was all his fault, no one else's. Guiltily he looked down at the badly painted warrior in his hand; how could Genghis Khan possibly cheer him up now? Idly he flipped the letter over to find more writing on the back.

PS, it read, '*Do come out and see us in the school holidays if you can, and if Genghis does not amuse, smash him, then buy yourself something that you really want.*

Tom stared at Genghis Khan and felt every nerve in his body begin to tingle. His frustration was boiling up into anger, anger at nobody else but himself. Smash him, smash him . . . *smash him* . . . OK, I will. Suddenly Tom leapt to his feet.

'AAAAAAHHH!' he shouted, and hurled Genghis Khan at the wall.

CRASH!

A thousand small pieces of china flew across the room, showering Jos and Melba where they sat.

'Oh dear,' whispered Melba, peering out nervously from

beneath her large orange hat. Jos was too stunned to even speak; he just gaped up at the wall, his mouth hanging open in astonishment. Tom stood trembling in the centre of the room, his cheeks on fire. Now what must they think of him? He was angry and embarrassed at his sudden outburst but he couldn't help himself, something somewhere had to give. Smash him, the note said, so he had done it, and he had to admit it made him feel an awful lot better. Swallowing hard, Tom glanced down at the debris scattered all over the floor.

'Sorry,' he mumbled awkwardly, 'I'd better get a dustpan and—' Then his words trailed away and he noticed a small brown object lying in the corner beside the fire. That hadn't been there before. Kneeling down Tom picked up what appeared to be a dull, pebble-shaped hessian bag, not much bigger than a plum, that had become worn and frayed from many years of travel. Through the rough stitching he could just make out an object hidden inside.

'Was that inside Genghis?' asked Melba, looking curiously at the bag. 'What do you think it can be, Tom?'

Tom had no idea what to think. Taking out his knife he prised the stitching open around one side far enough to make a gap, then squeezing the bag gently, he felt a smooth, cold object slip out into the palm of his hand. It was a stone, as round as the world, coloured the deepest, clearest blue he had ever seen. The firelight danced and leapt across its surface.

'Is that a . . . a . . . sapphire?' Melba gasped, staring at the stone in wonder.

'Surely not *the* s-s-sapphire?' stammered Jos. 'Not . . . the great sapphire of Champawander?'

Tom gazed down into its blue depths and he smiled. He knew that it was.

Later, when Jos and Melba had gone to bed, Tom sat down in his room and began to write a letter himself.

Dear August and Sir Henry, he began,
I cannot think of anything to say except thank you. Thank you for giving me the greatest present of my life. I have already decided what I am going to do with it. I am going to sell the sapphire, and use the money to repair the museum and all your animals, so that the Scatterhorn Museum can open once more. Uncle Jos has promised to give me a hand, and he said he even wants me to take it over one day.

Please thank my dad for his letter, and look after him as he is a bit crazy sometimes, and tell my mum I can't wait to see her when she gets home.

I would really like to come and visit you in Mongolia, as there is so much I want to explain that I can't write here, but there is one very important thing you should know. If you ever meet Don Gervase Askary again, or his daughter Lotus, please be very, very careful, as they now have a small blue bottle that belongs to you.

Best wishes,
Tom

When he had finished, Tom folded the letter up carefully and then addressed the envelope to:

Mr A. Catcher and Sir H. Scatterhorn,
The Tosontsengel Valley,
Outer Mongolia,
The Present.

Opening the window, Tom stood the small envelope up on the ledge and gazed hopefully across the rooftops at the moonlit sky. Would the great eagle ever find his letter? There was always a chance . . . and anyway, Tom could do nothing more until the next school holidays, and he had plenty to think about until then. After all, how many other children were given the world's second largest sapphire for Christmas? Leaving the envelope standing out on the windowsill, Tom pulled the stiff frame shut and with a smile he threw himself onto the bed. That was one question to which he already knew the answer.

EPILOGUE

FROM THE DRAGONPORT MERCURY.

SCATTERHORN MUSEUM REOPENS!

There was great excitement last night as the extraordinary Scatterhorn Museum reopened its doors to visitors again, almost exactly a year to the day after they might have shut for good. Its new owner, Tom Scatterhorn, aged just twelve, has spent a year completely restoring this famous landmark that had fallen into a very bad state of repair. 'The Scatterhorn Museum used to be one of the coldest, darkest, and frankly spookiest places on earth,' recalled Leonard 'Leaky' Logan, Dragonport's new mayor, 'but now the animals look so friendly and real they might walk out of their cases at any moment!'

Mayor Logan's enthusiasm was also shared by Mr Jos

Scatterhorn of Flood Street, the previous owner, who made sure that he and his wife Melba returned from their round-the-world cruise in time to attend last night's ceremony. 'It's absolutely terrific what that lad's done here,' he said. 'To be honest I'm totally flummoxed, I didn't think it was possible to bring this moth-eaten old collection back to life.' According to one source, the painstaking task of cleaning and restuffing the thousands of animals was given to an old Mongolian craftsman, whose secret techniques revived not only the specimen collection, but also the famous model of Dragonport, that had been suffering from a decade-long infestation by insects.

So having put this famous old museum back on the map, what next for Tom Scatterhorn? 'Next school holidays I will be visiting Central Asia with my dad,' he told the *Dragonport Mercury* last night. 'We want to visit a couple of old friends and my dad is going to collect some rare beetles. He thinks that as one in every four animals on earth is a beetle and they have been around for two hundred million years, we should have a few in the Scatterhorn Museum. I don't mind, so long as we can keep them under control. Maybe we'll have to build a brand new wing to house them all!'

With a determined young boy like that at the helm, the future of the Scatterhorn Museum certainly looks in good hands. We shall watch this space with interest . . .